Dear Reader,

With ▒▒▒▒ desserts and darling doggies, Duets has a doub▒▒ ▒se of delights for your reading pleasure!

Wedd▒▒ ▒ mean one thing to caterer Delilah James: wedd▒▒ cake, something she is far too intimate with, ▒ ▒east as evidenced by the inches on her hips. ▒▒ch Tanner, the hero of Kimberly Raye's *How ▒▒eet It Is,* however, finds every inch of her absolu▒▒ly delectable. In *Second-Chance Groom* by Euge▒ ▒a Riley, the bride-to-be never gets a chance to cut i▒▒ her wedding cake as she runs off with the best man! But he's not the marrying kind.... Both of these deli▒▒ous stories are found in Duets #11.

Duets #12 meanwhile goes to the animals! In Sandra Paul's *Head Over Heels,* Prudence Mc▒▒ure, dre▒▒▒▒ a cat at a Halloween party, casts her feline sp▒▒ ▒▒▒ ▒▒▒▒▒▒ ▒▒▒▒▒▒▒ Nicholas ▒▒▒ ▒▒ but what hap▒▒▒
mate▒▒ ▒▒▒▒ ▒▒ ▒▒▒▒ ▒ans' love

Enj▒▒

M▒▒
Ser▒

"Please, please don't let it be Nicholas."

Prudence knew her prayer was unanswered when she glanced over to see a man's tall, broad figure framed by the screen door. Her stomach dropped, then twisted with nervousness.

She retreated a couple of steps backward in her kitchen as Nick walked in. His knowing eyes only met hers for the barest second, but even that was long enough to send a wave of heat flowing up her body to burn in her cheeks. He was going to cause trouble—she just knew it.

"I've come to return something," Nicholas said as his gaze burned into her.

Her throat tightened as he stepped closer.

Pulling a piece of black lace from his pocket, he laid it on the table. "Here are your panties. You left them on my ceiling fan."

For more, turn to page 9

Puppy Love

The money was his!

David could hardly wait to celebrate. But the lawyer had insisted there was *something else* that belonged to David.

Well, whatever that *something* else was it was kicking Mr. Trenton's tail big-time. "Don't you bite me, you little demon," he heard the lawyer yelp. Then Mr. Trenton's tone changed. "There now, that's better. No one's going to hurt— Ouch! Why you little—"

David eyed the closed door. But before he could get away, the lawyer entered. He wasn't alone. Or unscathed.

Inside the small carrier the lawyer carried, the whirling little critter suddenly stilled...and glared at David with beady eyes. Then it lunged at the securely locked door. David jumped back. "Is that a badger, Mr. Trenton?"

"No, it is a dog. A very spoiled and nasty-tempered little dog, to be sure. But—and you have no idea how greatly it pleases me to say this—*it is now your very spoiled and nasty-tempered little dog, Mr. Sullivan.*"

For more, turn to page 197

HARLEQUIN DUETS

ISBN 0-373-44078-2

HEAD OVER HEELS
Copyright © 1999 by Sandra Novy Chvostal

PUPPY LOVE
Copyright © 1999 by Cheryl Anne Porter

This edition published by arrangement with Harlequin Books S.A.

® and TM are trademarks of the publisher. Trademarks indicated with
® are registered in the United States Patent and Trademark Office, the
Canadian Trade Marks Office and in other countries.

Visit us at www.romance.net

Printed in U.S.A.

SANDRA PAUL

Head Over Heels

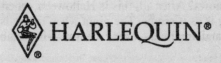

TORONTO • NEW YORK • LONDON
AMSTERDAM • PARIS • SYDNEY • HAMBURG
STOCKHOLM • ATHENS • TOKYO • MILAN • MADRID
PRAGUE • WARSAW • BUDAPEST • AUCKLAND

Dear Reader,

Halloween...ah, the memories. My husband and I were friends in high school and I remember the year that I bought him an ape mask. At the time I gave him the gift, he was baby-sitting his younger sister and brother and promptly put it on to scare the wits out of his unsuspecting siblings. I can still remember their bugged-out eyes and white little faces. Halloween... ya gotta love it.

And who can resist the allure of trick-or-treating? In my family it was a tradition to get a pillowcase (king-size was the best) and go from house to house until you had enough candy for one heck of a dentist's bill.

But even the simple joys of gluttony and terrifying small children pale beside the true delight of Halloween: the chance, the opportunity—why, almost the obligation—to become someone different for a night. That's what happens in my book. Who is that cynical, determined man in the corner? Surely not Nicholas, the impulsive youth our heroine used to know. And that sexy witch luring him closer with passion-filled eyes? That can't be our reserved Prudence...can it?

Who knows? After all, this is Halloween, when nothing is as it seems. The night when magic is in the air and anything—even true love—is possible.

Boo!

Sandra Paul

For my creative and imaginative sister-in-law,
Jay Chvostal Riess,
who loves Halloween more than anyone I know.

And thanks to Barbara Benedict, Angie Ray and
Maureen Child for their wise and pithy critiques.

1

THE LITTLE WITCH had disappeared again.

Nicholas Ware propped his shoulder against the fireplace mantel and scanned the crowd gathered in the living room of the rambling Victorian house. She wasn't among the goblins and ghosts gyrating on the dance floor, or huddled around the steaming punch bowl with Frankenstein and his friends. Nor was she necking in any of the dark corners of the big room with Count Dracula or his cronies.

Still, Nick knew she hadn't left the party. Not this early. Not only would she consider deserting her aunt Hepzibah's annual pre-Halloween bash a shocking lapse of manners, but that annoying sixth sense he'd developed upon first meeting Prudence Anne McClure told him she was nearby. Brewing mischief.

He left his vantage point, circling the room as the niggling unease pricked him again. Once he would have questioned the feeling. Hell, at the age of twenty-two he'd scoffed at it and shaken the dust of Cauldron, Oregon, from his feet. But he'd learned a lot in the past seven years. Four months back in town with Prudence—with *Ms. McClure,* as she'd primly informed him he now preferred to be called—had taught him even more.

He stalked slowly through the crowd searching for a glimpse of her tousled brown curls or black dress.

When he'd first caught sight of Pru earlier in the evening, he'd chuckled at the huge peaked hat and hooked nose she was wearing. But then she'd turned and the chuckle had died in his throat. A long slit ran up the side of her witch's outfit, the clinging material parting wickedly to reveal her slim white leg to midthigh.

Oh, yeah. Tonight Prudence was definitely dressed for trouble.

He glanced around again. She wasn't in the room. Hollow-eyed spooks and preening black cats—construction-paper samples of Prudence's handiwork dangling from the ceiling—seemed to urge him to a door leading to the back rooms.

Little Bo Peep with female wolf in her eyes way-laid him in the hall.

"Love your disguise, Nick." Shifting her long hooked staff to her other arm, the redhead ran a finger down the sleeve of his gray suit jacket. "Imagine, someone like *you* posing as a staid businessman."

"I am a staid businessman, Rhonda."

"Oh, pooh, I don't believe it. What exactly do you do?"

"I go in when my company buys out a new business. Start the evaluation and the hiring-and-firing process."

Her brown eyes gleamed with excitement. "Kind of a hatchet man, huh? It sounds exciting."

All too often it was damned unpleasant. He glanced down at her fingers as they trailed back up his arm. "Have you seen Prudence?"

He stepped away and her hand dropped. Her red lips curved into a pout. "Ah, yes, she's working as your secretary, isn't she? Although why you need a secretary when you're only here temporarily, I can't understand.''

''Can't you?'' he drawled.

''No.'' She paused to allow a Scarecrow and a Tin Man to pass before adding, ''Unless the rumors running rampant that you're planning to relocate your business to Cauldron are true.'' She batted her false eyelashes at him, her expression inviting him to confide.

Nick resisted the unspoken invitation. ''Aren't rumors always running rampant in Cauldron?''

''Well, yes. But not many that involve money.'' She waited. When he didn't reply, she stepped closer, widening her eyes. ''C'mon, Nick. Everyone's dying to know what you're up to. Give me a hint of why you're lingering in Cauldron so long.''

''And have it plastered all over *The Crier*?''

''I'll keep it off the record, I promise.''

He looked down into her hopeful face. Did she really think he believed that? Rhonda gloried in her role of Cauldron star reporter too much to resist printing a good story.

Tiring of the game, he said firmly, ''I wanted to spend time with my dad. After he died, I decided to stay on awhile to wind up his affairs. Now, have you seen Prudence?''

''No,'' she said sulkily. She gestured vaguely down the hallway. ''She's probably in the kitchen helping her aunt get ready for the bewitching hour.'' She stressed the last two words, rolling her eyes as she added, ''Someone should really tell dear old Hepzibah that kissing at midnight is a New Year's Eve, not a Halloween, tradition.''

When Nick didn't respond, Rhonda slanted him a

considering glance from beneath lowered lids. "Although maybe the custom has some merit. I'm sure Prudence has big hopes it will loosen up Edmund."

About to move on, Nicholas paused. "Edmund?"

Rhonda nodded. "Eddie Swain. He decided 'Edmund' sounded more appropriate for someone running for mayor. If he's here, then you can bet Prudence will be nearby."

Nick's eyebrows rose. "Why is that?"

Rhonda looked surprised. "Didn't you know? They're becoming quite the steady couple. They've been keeping their relationship hush-hush, of course. Waiting for his mother's approval, no doubt." She added with faint bitterness, "Eddie won't do anything without his mama's say-so."

"And Isabella doesn't like Prudence?"

Rhonda shot him a disbelieving glance. "Are you kidding? When Prudence has no money and a crazy aunt to boot?"

"Heppy's not crazy."

"She's not all there, either. Trying to cast spells!" Rhonda gave an unladylike snort.

Nick shrugged, returning to the point that concerned him more. "So why doesn't Ed's mother break them up?"

Rhonda grimaced. "Probably because Prudence has become so darn popular in this town—a regular little Pollyanna, in fact." She gave the wooden floor a discontented thump with her staff. "Being seen with her is bound to help Ed's campaign. Heaven knows he won't win any popularity contests on his own. He hasn't changed much from high school."

Nick stared down at Rhonda thoughtfully, studying the resentful look on her face. Becoming aware of his gaze, she looked up and forced a smile. "But let's get back to more important issues, like you… and me." Her finger went on the move again, roving along his biceps and across his chest as she breathed, "Will I see you at midnight?"

Nick caught her hand as it edged beneath his lapel. "Probably."

She moved closer, apparently willing to forgo waiting, but Nick released her hand and sidestepped, managing to escape. The vague feeling was driving him harder now, joined by growing anger as he headed down the hall. So Pru yearned for the town's fair-haired boy, did she? She'd certainly kept that little tidbit a secret from him. Not that he expected to receive her confidences. These days, Prudence worked damn hard at maintaining as much distance between them as possible.

So far he'd let her, amused by the wariness in her smoky gray eyes. But not tonight. Tonight was *his* and he wanted her within reach. Something was up; change was in the air. Like the nip of a cold breeze he could *feel* it with an unnamed but ancient instinct that kept him on the prowl.

Instinct drove him onward and the same damn instinct stopped him at the kitchen door. There he paused with his palm pressed against the paneled wood, his eyes narrowing as he heard the words, "Love potion…"

"…WOULD BE NICE, don't you think so, dear?"

"Mmm?" Prudence missed her aunt's question, distracted by a shivery feeling at the back of her neck. Instinctively she reached up beneath her hair, her fingers brushing the elastic at her nape. Catching hold of the band, she drew her half-mask off and dropped the hooked nose on the counter next to her hat.

She turned back to the old-fashioned stove and picked up a wooden ladle to slowly stir the golden liquid bubbling in a black pot. Steam rose, dewing her cheeks with fragrant mist and crinkling the fine hairs at her temples into tiny curls. Filled with the rich, spicy scents of pumpkin pies and apples, the air in the big kitchen felt warm and thick. She stared down at the liquid, watching it swirl round and round. Her eyelids drooped heavily.

"I'm so glad you agree with my idea," Hepzibah said.

Pru blinked, her aunt's voice dispersing the slight drowsiness stealing over her. Patting a faint yawn, she said apologetically, "I'm sorry, Aunt Heppy, I must have missed something. What were you saying?"

"I was telling you," Hepzibah repeated patiently, "about my idea to make a love potion."

Prudence's head jerked up, her sleepiness replaced by alarm. She glanced at her aunt, who was busily rolling crisp red apples in melted caramel. Hepzibah met her gaze, adding serenely, "I found a new recipe in the book."

Prudence's heart sank. To think she'd actually been thrilled to discover the ancient leather-bound tome in the attic of the old bookstore Hepzibah owned. With its handcrafted binding and gilt lettering, Pru had been sure the book was a collector's item and had expected her aunt to make quite a profit on the find. What she hadn't expected was that Heppy would become obsessed with the volume and convinced she must have hidden powers she'd simply never noticed before. ''Although I *have* always loved Halloween,'' Heppy had pointed out triumphantly to her niece. ''Surely that should have told us something!''

Privately Pru thought the only thing it told them was that Hepzibah enjoyed costume parties. Now she said warningly, ''I thought you agreed to leave that book alone.''

Her aunt's blue eyes widened in surprise. ''No, I didn't, dear. I said I'd be careful.''

Pru's alarm increased. She didn't buy Heppy's innocent look, not for a second. With her round dimpled face, double chin and white hair bundled into a bun on the top of her head, her aunt might look like a fairy-godmother escapee from a Disney film, but anyone who came within reach of Hepzibah's wand was only asking for trouble.

Abandoning diplomacy, Prudence said firmly, ''But you aren't careful. You are not—I repeat, *not*—going to try one more spell out of that book.''

''But, dear—''

''You almost killed off the Millers with the fumes from that concoction you made to scare away mice.''

''But it worked!'' Aunt Heppy declared indignantly. ''The mice went away!''

''Yes, and so did the Millers. They had to rent a motel room in Grant's Pass for two weeks until the stench cleared from their house.''

''A slight miscalculation.''

''And what about that wart tonic?''

''That worked, too!''

Prudence put her hands on her hips. ''How can you say that? You humiliated one of Cauldron's most respected matriarchs. Old Sally Watson ended up with more pimples on her chin than a hormonal teenager.''

''But she didn't have a wart on her!''

''She didn't have a wart on her before she drank it, either.''

''That's true,'' Heppy admitted, her indignation fading a bit. ''I don't know how Sally got hold of that tonic. I intended it for Michael O'Sullivan. Everyone knows Michael is covered in warts.''

Everyone also knew about Heppy's mistake. Rhonda Burrows had taken great delight in relating the incident in the gossip column she wrote for the town newspaper. As a result, several of Cauldron's leading citizens were up in arms over Hepzibah's antics, most notably Sally Watson and Edmund's mother. Before Edmund calmed her down, Mrs. Swain had even threatened to call Social Services if anything else occurred, coldly claiming Heppy was becoming a ''danger to society.''

Well, Prudence wasn't about to let that happen. ''Concocting potions is dangerous, Aunt Hepzibah. What if the wrong person takes one again and becomes seriously ill?''

Heppy's face brightened. ''Don't worry, dear. This time I plan to use Aunt Barbara's lucky antique glass.'' Abandoning her apples for a moment, Hepzibah rose on tiptoe to reach into a cavernous oak cabinet. ''No one can mistake this glass for another.''

Prudence glanced at the goblet Heppy was holding aloft. She couldn't argue with that. No one *could* mistake the glass for another. There wasn't one like it in the whole town; possibly the whole state. Made of opalescent green crystal, the goblet featured a snake—which had always reminded Prudence irresistibly of a grinning green worm—wrapped around the stem.

Aunt Barbara had been inordinately fond of snakes.

Looking away from the glass, Prudence met Heppy's gaze. Ignoring the hopeful expression on her aunt's face, she said distinctly, "No love potions."

"But you already told me I could," Hepzibah said reproachfully. "You told me I could give one to Eddie."

Prudence's eyes widened in horror. "Aunt! I did not agree to give Edmund anything of the kind."

"Yes, you did, dear."

"No, I did not."

"Yes, you did. Oh, my goodness, I'm out of nuts."

Hepzibah jumped down off her stool, and hitched up her skirt. Like Prudence, the older woman was dressed as a witch—the McClure women always dressed as witches at Heppy's Halloween party. Aunt Heppy claimed the practice started in honor of their ancestors, persecuted as witches in that long ago Salem on the eastern seaboard. Prudence suspected the custom really began in honor of an old McClure maxim: waste not, want not. Why make new costumes when these were available?

Both dresses were styled the same, but Hepzibah's outfit contained a good deal more material, necessary to cover her short plump figure. A yard or so of the excess dragged behind her on the old oak floor as she crossed the room to the pantry.

She disappeared inside, the remainder of her skirt trailing her like one of Aunt Barbara's snakes as Prudence repeated loudly, "I did not tell you to give Edmund a love potion."

Heppy popped out again, a bag of walnuts clutched in her hand. She headed for her apples. "Don't you remember, dear? Less than ten minutes ago you said you were getting impatient for him."

Pru drew a deep breath. "To *arrive*, Aunt. I said I was getting impatient for Edmund to arrive at the party."

"Oh." Hepzibah looked surprised. "You didn't mean you're getting impatient for him personally? To make love to you?"

Prudence's cheeks grew hot. Her late father had been such a stern moralistic man. Where on earth had his sister Heppy gotten such a liberal attitude about sex? "No, of course not," Pru said. "I didn't mean that at all."

"So you don't want to make love with him?"

"No—I mean, yes. I mean, don't worry about it."

"I *do* worry about it, dear. You aren't getting any younger you know. Thirty is right around the corner."

"It's four years away! Twenty-six is hardly over the hill."

"It's not all that young, either. Besides, you've known the boy for over nine years. Why are you waiting?"

Because I'm not ready yet, Prudence wanted to reply. Which was stupid. She was twenty-six years old, for goodness' sake, and yet she was more hung up about sex than her maiden aunt. Like Aunt Heppy had said, she'd known Edmund since she was sixteen. True, she hadn't liked him then, but what did one know at that age? Now, she…she *cared* about him. He was steady, reliable. A perfect family man. Why, look how devoted he was to his mother. More importantly, Edmund planned to remain in Cauldron the rest of his life. He'd even talked about buying a house in the center of town, close enough to her aunt that Prudence could watch over her.

She stirred slowly, frowning a little. So what was she waiting for? After all, as Edmund had pointed out time and time again, how could they be sure they were compatible until they made love? It was definitely time to take what he termed "the next logical step" in their relationship. Then maybe she could put the past behind her…and this panicky *hunted* feeling that had been haunting her for the past few weeks might finally go away.

Prudence drew a deep breath. "As a matter of fact, I've decided that it might be time for Edmund and me to…become more intimate." Her nape tingled again. Pru rubbed it absently as she added, "I'm telling him so tonight."

Heppy clapped her hands together, ignoring the nuts that flew around the room at the gesture. "How thrilling! How excited you must be."

"Er…yes," Prudence said rather doubtfully. She added more firmly, "So you can see a love potion is completely unnecessary."

"Of course, dear. You're absolutely right. Eddie doesn't need a potion at all."

Prudence's relief evaporated in midsigh as her aunt continued thoughtfully, "I'll give it to dear Nicholas instead."

Prudence's pulse gave a startled leap. "Nicholas? Nicholas Ware?" She stared at her aunt in disapproving surprise. "Why on earth would you give *him* a love potion?"

Absorbed with arranging her apples on a blue-speckled platter, Heppy said absently, "He's lonely, dear. Even as a teenager he never seemed to fit in. Now that he's come home, I think he needs someone."

Prudence barely restrained herself from snorting in disbelief. Nicholas lonely? Heppy's tender heart was definitely leading her astray this time. No one was more independent and self-sufficient than Nicholas Ware. He might be a loner, but he certainly didn't have any trouble attracting women.

"Exactly who are you planning on fixing him up with?" Pru asked, a sarcastic edge in her voice. "Rhonda? Because if so, you don't need to bother. Rhonda's had her eye on him since he came back to town."

"Oh, no, dear. He and Rhonda wouldn't make a good couple at all. Actually I had someone much more suitable in mind for Nicholas. But that's changed now of course."

"Oh? How come?" Prudence asked, her curiosity piqued. "Who were you considering?"

"Why, you, dear."

Prudence gasped. "*Me?* Why on earth would you try to fix Nicholas up with me?"

"Well, your relationship with Eddie didn't seem to be progressing...*right* somehow. And you and Nicholas have become so close..."

"No, we haven't," Prudence said, revolted. "We aren't close at all."

"But you used to be, dear. When you first came

to Cauldron to live with me, you two were inseparable.''

''Hardly inseparable, and that was years ago.''

''But you were engaged...''

''For all of a week.''

''And so much in love.''

''We were simply infatuated.'' Pru turned back to
the stove, adding lightly, ''If he had loved me, he
certainly never would have left so abruptly.''

''He was young...and impulsive.''

''Nicholas was never impulsive. He always knew
precisely what he was doing and what he wanted.''
Pru lifted the brimming ladle, then let the liquid spill
back into the pot in a glittering, golden fall.

''He seemed to want *you*.''

Prudence remained stubbornly silent.

Her aunt added coaxingly, ''Don't you think he's
gotten handsome now that he's older?''

''Not at all.''

''Perhaps you're right, dear,'' Heppy said agree-
ably. ''Handsome isn't quite the right word. Compelling is much better.''

''And overbearing is even more so.'' Prudence
stirred the pot harder.

''But he's so masculine...''

''So arrogant.''

''And big and strong.''

''And used to getting his own way.'' Prudence
wrinkled her small nose disdainfully. ''How could
you ever think I'd still be interested in him?''

''But, dear, since he's come back, you talk about
him all the time. Much more, in fact, than you talk
about Eddie.''

Aghast, Prudence whirled around, amber liquid

from the ladle dripping on the floor as she declared, "I do not!"

"Oh, but you do, dear. You say 'Nicholas says this' and 'Nicholas says that,' and 'Do you know what *that man* had the gall to do today?' Why, you talk about him constantly."

"I *complain* about him constantly. That's not the same at all. And so would you if you were his secretary." Pru plopped the ladle back into the pot. "The man has the chauvinistic attitude of a feudal lord."

"Do you really think so?" Heppy said wistfully. "He always seems so polite and charming to me."

Prudence scowled. "Charming—of course he's charming. He's too smart not to be charming when it's to his benefit. Which brings us to the question of why he's still here now that his father's gone. To relocate his business here, perhaps?"

Heppy brightened. "Do you really think so?"

Pru considered the matter for a moment, then shook her head. "No. He's too hungry for power to settle in a small town like this. He probably just enjoys stringing everyone along. Making them wonder—especially the women." Her eyes narrowing, she stirred fiercely. "Nick's intelligent enough to know a little honey can go a long way toward greasing the wheels."

Heppy looked confused. "Honey? Grease wheels? I don't think that would work, dear. Honey is quite sticky, you know."

"I don't mean honey exactly. I mean...oh, you know what I mean. He charms everyone in sight—Susan, Christine, Dorrie Jean. The man is a born gigolo.'' She thumped the ladle against the side of the pot.

The pucker on Heppy's wide brow deepened. ''But aren't gigolos poor? Nicholas seems to be quite wealthy now.''

''He's wealthy all right. And accustomed to getting his own way no matter what methods he has to use.'' Prudence stirred faster and faster. ''Those intent looks of his—that little gleam of amusement in his eyes. The way he smiles as if he knows exactly what you're thinking. But he doesn't. If he did, he'd know I think he's a—''

''Dear—''

''Complete and total—''

''*Dear!*''

Unheeding of her aunt's urgent tone, Pru paused, absently rubbing her nape as she savored exactly the right epithet to describe the infuriating Nicholas Ware. ''A complete and total bas—''

''Good evening, ladies,'' drawled the complete and total bastard from behind her.

2

PRUDENCE WHIRLED AROUND. Nicholas was standing in the doorway.

A faint shock ran through her—the same tiny jolt she experienced every time she saw him unexpectedly. He must have just returned from Los Angeles because he hadn't changed into the jeans and casual shirts he usually wore—much less attempted any kind of costume—but wore a gray suit that emphasized the darkness of his hair and the breadth of his shoulders. He was even wearing a tie, she noted absently. Black silk with some kind of tiny silver design scattered all over it.

Her gaze lifted to his face. The hard angles were set in his usual unrevealing expression, but any hopes she harbored that he hadn't heard what she'd said about him were immediately dispelled by the mocking expression in his golden-brown eyes.

The panicky flutter in her stomach increased, and Prudence's hands curled into fists. Okay, maybe she shouldn't have been talking about him, but *he* shouldn't have been skulking about eavesdropping.

She lifted her chin and Nick's eyes narrowed, the mocking expression hardening briefly into something more menacing. Power implicit in every line of his solid body, he leaned negligently against the jamb.

The shivery feeling at Prudence's nape skittered down her spine.

"Hello, Nicholas," Hepzibah chirped, breaking the charged silence. "I'm so glad you made it to the party."

His lids lowered, and when he looked up again, the menacing expression had disappeared, replaced by a softer look as he glanced at Heppy. "You know I wouldn't miss it, Hepzibah."

Prudence made a slight scoffing sound.

He swung back to face her. "Did you say something, Ms. McClure?" he asked, raising a dark brow.

She met his gaze innocently. "No, nothing at all."

His eyes narrowed again, but before he could pursue the subject, Heppy said hastily, "Well, it's nice that you managed to come and catch up with old friends. Like Rhonda. And Christine. Have you seen them yet?"

He nodded and Heppy launched into an interrogation on the women—all the women—who'd spoken with him since he'd returned to Cauldron.

Prudence wrinkled her nose. There certainly were a lot of them, but of course, there would be. Single women outnumbered the single men in Cauldron two to one, and none of the town's bachelors were as...as not *bad-looking* as Nicholas.

Because he certainly wasn't good-looking, she maintained, stealing a glance at him to confirm the issue as he patiently listened to Heppy's recital of each woman's virtues. Oh, when he'd been younger he'd been appealing, she admitted grudgingly. Always mature for his age certainly, but softer-looking. More adaptable, with the pliant and yielding strength of youth.

But the past seven years had changed him. There was nothing yielding about Nick now. Pru's gaze traced the bump high on the bridge of his nose, the prominent bones of his cheeks and jaw. His face was almost hawkish. With his dark hair and skin he looked like he must have Native American or Latin blood in his ancestry, but if he did, no one had ever admitted it. Nicholas's father, William, had shown her the family tree once. A long line of proper English names stemming from the *Mayflower* had marched rigidly down the page.

"Dorrie Jean is a very nice girl," Heppy was saying. "If only she wasn't so shy…"

Nicholas would scare Dorrie Jean to death, Pru thought, unconsciously grimacing. Dorrie needed someone gentler. Calmer. Nick could be so…intense at times.

He glanced over suddenly, catching sight of her expression. A mocking light flared in his eyes. Prudence hastily looked away but was aware of his slow scrutiny. Oh, he was aggravating! As if she cared how many woman hankered after him. She refused to give him the satisfaction of looking his way again.

Nick strolled over and annexed a stool a few feet away. Propping one hip on it, he idly listened to Heppy chatter while he studied Prudence, who was determinedly keeping her back to him. She'd suddenly become oh-so-busy at the stove, staring down into the liquid with an absorption worthy of Shakespeare's Cassandra. The steam in the kitchen had caused her curls to tighten and twist, and they cascaded down around her face and shoulders with a riotous abandon at odds with the rigid stiffness of her stance as she continued to ignore him.

The thin black silk of her dress revealed the delicate thrust of her shoulder blades, the slight sway of her trim bottom as she industriously stirred the contents of the big black pot. He'd thought her gown was solid black; now, in the bright light of the kitchen, he could see a pattern of dark gray whorls stamped into the silk, curving up from the hem and giving the illusion of smoke rising around her feet.

Other than that peekaboo slit, the dress itself wasn't especially revealing. The sleeves were long, the V-neckline discreet. But the silk clung to her slight curves possessively, while its dark color emphasized the delicate whiteness of her slim throat, the enticing smoothness of the upper curve of her breasts.

Her face was half turned away, and his gaze rested consideringly on her rosy cheek and impudent nose. That rather snub nose was tilted at an imperious angle, her pink dab of a mouth pursed in disapproval. She had a kittenish sort of face—wide across the temples, tapering to a small rounded chin—and like a mischievous kitten she occasionally needed someone to pick her up by the scruff of the neck and carry her out of harm's way. Or give her a good shake.

In his opinion, she certainly deserved a shaking. She'd been figuratively hissing and scratching at him ever since he'd returned. He'd hired her as his temporary secretary hoping to lull her suspicions, to lure her quietly back into his arms. Unfortunately it was clear from what he'd overheard a few moments ago that her defenses were well up, while the secretarial work he needed done was just about exhausted.

His jaw tightened. She intended to become intimate with Edmund Swain, did she? *He didn't think so.*

He hadn't lingered for months in this seething little pot of a town—full of gossiping busybodies—just to watch her get involved with another man. That particular event was *not* going to happen.

As if he'd voiced the decision, Pru glanced up sharply, the red in her cheeks deepening and her eyes sparkling dangerously. Partly to annoy her, partly out of curiosity, he walked over to see what she was stirring.

She shot him a wary glance as he neared, her hair tumbling in rebellious curls as she quickly turned away again. One stray tendril clung to her damp flushed cheek, and Nick casually smoothed it back as he paused beside her.

Pru flinched, stepping closer to the stove. He followed. Uncomfortable at having him so near, she moved again, until the cool porcelain pressed into her belly. Wet heat from the steaming pot dampened her cheeks and bodice. Dry heat from his body seared her back and bottom through her dress as he leaned over her shoulder.

He took a deep breath. "Mmm, that smells good—cinnamon and spice." His warm breath brushed her nape as he added in a lower tone, "Just like you." He surveyed her mouth from beneath heavy lids, adding, "I can't wait for a taste."

She stiffened. "Well, you're not going to get one!"

His eyes gleamed. "Not even a sip?"

Prudence's mouth tightened, but Heppy sighed. "Poor boy. Let him have a sip, dear."

"It's not ready yet," Pru said just to be contrary.

Annoyed at his baiting, she hunched her shoulders, wishing he would move away. "Shouldn't you rejoin the party?"

"Prudence!" Aunt Heppy exclaimed in dismay at her rudeness.

But Nick smiled slightly and stepped back to lean against the table. Folding his arms across his chest, he said plaintively, "How can I enjoy myself when I'm so thirsty? There's nothing left to drink out there. Henry VIII finished up the last of the punch."

"I'll bring some out in a moment," Prudence said in a broad hint for him to leave.

He didn't move. "Good idea. Especially since more people have arrived."

"They have?" Prudence bit her lip. Why on earth couldn't he have mentioned that in the first place? Edmund must be here. She felt a sinking sensation and an odd reluctance to meet Nicholas's gaze. Shaking off the feeling, she firmly gathered her resolve. Trying to sound casual, she asked, "Like who?"

Nicholas thought for a moment. "Well, Mindy came in—Jackie and Colleen were with her, I think. And Susan, Lou—"

"Did you see any *men?*" Prudence interrupted him, gritting her teeth. "Like Edmund, for example?"

"Edmund?" Nicholas looked puzzled. "I don't think... Wait, do you mean Eddie Swain, the wimpy little guy who was always worried about getting his clothes dirty as a kid? He may have been in the last group. Is he dressed as Mary, Queen of Scots?"

Prudence clenched her teeth. "No, he is not," she said in exasperation, and set down her ladle, resisting the temptation to bop Nicholas on the head with it.

Wimpy! Edmund wasn't wimpy! He was...elegantly slender.

Turning a cold shoulder to Nicholas, she said to her aunt, "I'd better go out and greet everyone."

"You do that, dear," Hepzibah said.

"Yes," Nick seconded silkily, "you do that."

Feeling oddly uneasy under his gaze, Prudence jammed her peaked hat on her head and stalked across the kitchen.

Nick watched her progress without moving, but Hepzibah, observing him from her stool, could almost feel the tension crackling in the air. Or was that due to the approaching thunderstorm? No, she was sure it was due to Nicholas. Something in his stance as his gaze followed her niece's slim figure gave the impression he was about to pounce.

She was pondering that theory when the door closed behind Prudence, and Nicholas suddenly seemed to relax. Strolling over to the stove, he picked up the ladle Pru had abandoned and idly began stirring the pot.

"Hepzibah..." he began slowly.

"Yes, Nicholas?"

"I hear you've become something of an expert on witchcraft."

Heppy tried to look becomingly modest. Obviously her fame was spreading. "Not quite an expert—it takes years to achieve that status. But I have been studying the subject extensively. I found a very interesting book on the topic."

Nicholas looked suitably impressed, so she continued, "It has all kinds of spells—lucky charms, recipes for curing warts and gout, love potions—"

"Love potions?" He lifted a dark brow.

Heppy beamed. "My favorite of the whole bunch."

"I'll bet they are," Nicholas murmured, stirring slowly. "I suppose the ingredients are rather unusual. Eye of newt and all that."

Heppy laughed. "Goodness, no. You've been watching too many movies. I would never use eye of newt—newts are quite hard to catch for one thing, even if I could find one. Besides, aren't they some kind of lizard? And aren't lizards related to snakes? Aunt Barbara, may her soul rest in peace, would never forgive me if I hurt a snake."

"That's true." Nicholas kept stirring. "So what ingredients *do* you use in a love potion?"

"Well, some are very big on human hair," Heppy confided. "But I don't add that, either. Have you ever gotten a hair in your mouth? Such an unpleasant sensation."

Nicholas's lips twitched. "So I take it you don't follow the exact recipes from the book?"

"Oh, goodness no. Those recipes are so old—why, some haven't changed for hundreds of years. I'm updating them."

"Isn't that difficult?"

"Not at all. Whenever the book calls for something I don't like, I simply substitute my own ingredients."

"How ingenious. What ingredients?"

"This and that," Heppy said vaguely. "In my latest one, I started with apples—the fruit of love, you know. I mashed them up to make cider."

Nicholas stared down at the liquid bubbling in the pot. "I see. Then what?"

"Sugar—to sweeten the apples—and just a teaspoon of aromatic bitters. Then a small orange studded with cloves—so good for bad breath. A pint of cranberry juice for color. Cinnamon and allspice—they prevent flatulence, you know, which is definitely *not* conducive to romance. Finally I let everything stew for a few hours, removed the orange and cloves and added my final secret ingredient.''

''Which is?''

''Rum.''

''Rum?'' Nicholas frowned. ''How much rum?''

''Oh, I don't know. A gallon or so.''

Nicholas's head jerked up and he stared at Heppy in amazement. *''A whole gallon?''*

''I like rum,'' Aunt Heppy said defensively. ''A gallon might seem like a lot to some people—Prudence would probably think so, but then she doesn't drink spirits. Her father was terribly against them, you know. In fact,'' she added thoughtfully, ''my brother was against just about everything.''

''I hope,'' Nick said dryly, ''that you would never give any of this potion to a minor.''

''Definitely not!'' Hepzibah pursed her mouth in indignation. ''Such things are not for children, and should only be used in the direst circumstances. Why, the only reason I even considered creating such a thing is because Pru has been so restless lately. I just wanted to help her.''

Nicholas remained silent for a moment, then asked gently, ''It's not always wise—don't you agree, Heppy?—to meddle in people's lives.''

''But what if they need help? If they're making a big mistake? I don't think she loves him, Nicholas—''

She broke off as Prudence burst back into the

room, her peaked hat tilting precariously. "Edmund hasn't arrived. I don't know why you thought he had…"

Prudence paused, her gaze flitting from Hepzibah's guilty expression to Nicholas's unrevealing one. They were up to something—that was obvious. Nicholas and Hepzibah had always shared a special affinity. Was he encouraging her aunt in one of her crazy schemes?

Her lips tightened. He'd better not be. Mrs. Swain—not to mention Sally Watson—had a lot of influence in Cauldron and neither were the type to make idle threats.

Prudence's eyes narrowed on the suspected culprit. Nicholas gazed blandly back.

Pru clenched her fists. She wanted him out—out of the kitchen and away from her troublesome aunt. Striding across the room, she snatched up the snake glass—the closest one to hand. Taking the dipper away from him, she lifted it and filled the glass to the rim. "You want a drink? Here you go." She thrust it into his hand and gave him an encouraging push toward the door. "Now you'd better get back to the party—a good chance to mix and mingle, you know. Go talk to a few people you haven't seen in a while."

Nick allowed her to herd him to the door, but before she could urge him through the portal, he paused to look down at her. "You will be joining me soon, won't you, Ms. McClure?"

Fuming, Prudence glared up at him. The words were posed as a question but she was more than familiar with the tone of command in his voice. He'd never used it before he'd left Cauldron, but during his absence, he seemed to have honed it to a fine art. In the three months she'd worked for him, Prudence had heard it more times than she cared to count.

"This is a party, you know," she said mutinously. "I'm not at work now."

He stared down at her, his eyes glinting. "Somehow, when we discussed your salary, I seem to remember our agreement included the provision that you be available *whenever* I might need you. If you'd like to renegotiate, I suppose we could..."

"Fine, fine, fine." Drat the man. He knew she wanted that extra money to build her savings. Aunt Heppy's bookstore provided a living for Prudence and her aunt, but not much more. Pru was determined to build a nest egg so Aunt Heppy would be secure in her old—her *older*—age even if it meant putting up with Nicholas and his bossy ways.

He watched her now with a false solicitousness that made her long to hit him in his white teeth. "I'll be right there!" she snapped and with a satisfied nod, he finally left. Resisting the urge to slam the door behind his broad back, Prudence turned to her aunt. "Now I want your word that you'll forget all about this love-potion business."

"All right, dear. If you insist."

Prudence eyed her suspiciously. Heppy was making this too easy. "You won't try to give it to Edmund?"

"No, dear. I won't."

"And I certainly hope you aren't still considering Nicholas after seeing how infuriating he can be."

"I don't think he's infuriating. He's a kind, considerate young man. Just a trifle high-spirited."

Prudence drew a deep breath, summoning patience. "High-spirited or not, promise me you won't give him a potion."

"I've said I won't, dear. It would be a waste."

Prudence relaxed a little. "Because you've finally realized he's incapable of loving anyone?"

"No, dear." Hepzibah smiled seraphically. "Because *you* already gave him one."

3

NICHOLAS'S EYES NARROWED in satisfaction a few seconds later as Prudence appeared in the living-room doorway. He wasn't surprised when her gaze immediately sought him out. It hadn't taken more than one small sip to assure him he had Heppy's love potion, and judging from Prudence's hurried entrance, she had realized it, too.

He casually lifted the brew to the light to examine the liquid depths, pretending not to notice as her eyes flickered from his face to settle on the light green glass in his hand. Even from this distance he could see the panic in her expression. She plunged into the sea of dancers, working her way toward him.

It was curiously satisfying to have her chase him for a change, Nick decided. He moved across the room to make it harder for her. With the determination of a spawning trout swimming upstream she came after him, battling her way through the crowd. Ah, yes. She'd definitely taken the bait.

And this time he planned to reel her in.

Seven years ago, furious at her unreasonable demands, he'd let her escape, certain he could get along quite well without her. And he had, for the most part. Not having a serious relationship with a woman meant he could devote all his attention to his career. But at the oddest times—like during a boring business meeting or sitting across a candlelit table from a beautiful woman—thoughts of Prudence would drift into his mind and he'd find himself thinking how she used to smile or frown. He'd remember the silkiness of her hair, the sweet curve of her cheek. And no other woman—no matter how beautiful, how sensuous—had ever quite measured up to those haunting memories.

His mouth tightened grimly. Prudence plagued him, no doubt, because they'd never consummated their relationship. Unfinished business had a way of nagging at a man; he should have taken her to bed when they'd been engaged and discovered she was no different from any other woman. But instead, he'd been young and foolish enough to put her on a pedestal.

Well, he was older and wiser now, and so was she. She said she was ready for an affair and she'd get one. But not with Edmund Swain.

"I see you found her," Rhonda said, following his gaze as she sashayed up beside him. "Oh, and there's Eddie."

Nicholas nodded, glancing across the room to where a blond man was gesturing wildly, trying to attract Prudence's attention above the pounding music and conversational din.

"Just look at him, making a fool of himself. I don't know what he sees in her," Rhonda said almost beneath her breath.

Nick glanced at Pru again. Another woman probably wouldn't understand her allure. It wasn't Prudence's looks so much that caught a man's eyes, but rather the way she moved, like a small, sinuous cat, keeping just out of reach of the man trailing her.

"Doesn't she see Eddie?" Rhonda asked, a faintly annoyed note in her voice. "He's practically chasing her."

Prudence *didn't* see Edmund. Her entire focus was on Nick's tall dark figure standing by the fireplace. It wasn't until Edmund clutched her elbow, yanking her to a halt, that she even realized he had finally arrived.

"Prudence, surely you're not going to rush away without even saying hello," he said, his tone gently chiding. "I found your compact in my car and I wanted to return it."

"Oh, ah...thank you, Edmund if you'd just hang on to it for me, I need to— Oh!" She broke off, trying to hide her surprise and dismay at the sight of the woman standing behind him. "Hello, Mrs. Swain," she said, forcing a smile. "How nice to see you. I didn't know you intended to come to the party."

"I didn't intend to." Mrs. Swain's lip lifted in a pained expression that Pru recognized as her attempt at a smile. "But I thought it would be polite to stop by and show my support of your aunt's little...get-together. Even though I must say—" she stared disdainfully around the room "—that some of these costumes are rather vulgar."

Prudence's smile froze into a grimace at the response, but she reminded herself not to take Mrs. Swain's remark personally. Isabella Swain was as well-known in Cauldron for her blunt manner of speaking as she was for her cold demeanor. Edmund had inherited his pale blue eyes from his mother, but while his were big—even a tiny bit protuberant— Mrs. Swain's were pressed deeply into the strong bones of her face, contributing to her austere expression. Along with that was the fact that the woman rarely smiled. No laugh—or worry lines, either, for that matter—marred the perfection of her patrician face. In fact, Mrs. Swain's skin was so masklike that Prudence had once succumbed to the temptation of asking Heppy if she thought the woman had had plastic surgery.

"Issie?" Heppy had asked. Heppy always referred to Mrs. Swain as Issie rather than Isabella—primarily, Pru suspected, because it enraged the woman to be reminded that she and Heppy had once attended school together. "She's always had that same cold expression," Hepzibah had said, "even as a girl. It's bred into the Swains' souls."

"Not Edmund's," Prudence had said swiftly. Edmund smiled almost constantly. A slightly rueful smile that modestly acknowledged his superiority, yet humbly apologized for it.

He was smiling that smile now as he explained, "Mother graciously decided to accompany me at the last minute. We'd driven into Medford for dinner and time slipped away before we knew it. I realized that if I was going to make the party at all, we'd better head right here. Do you forgive me?" he asked cajolingly, gazing down into her eyes.

Uncomfortable under his mother's frozen gaze, Prudence said, "Of course I do. Oh, you're not wearing your costume!" she added, suddenly noticing his shirt and tie.

Edmund's smile turned wry. "No, I'm afraid I left it at home."

"A fortunate circumstance in my opinion. It was

a ridiculous getup,'' Mrs. Swain declared. ''Imagine, my son posing as a cartoon character!''

Prudence's cheeks heated with embarrassed anger. Every now and then her creative urges seemed to build up and she'd find herself undertaking projects that—if they didn't satisfy all her artistic cravings—at least calmed them for a while. Like making Edmund's Batman costume. Why, she had spent six hours sewing the cape alone. And although his legs had looked a little thin in the tights, she'd thought the cape and mask had made him seem dashing—even rather dangerous.

Her face must have reflected her feelings because Edmund squeezed her hand, turning his reproachful gaze on his mother. ''Prudence made that outfit, Mother.''

''Did she?'' Mrs. Swain glanced around the room. ''Well, I see we're not the only ones not in costume. Isn't that Nicholas Ware over there?''

Prudence stiffened. Nicholas! How could she have forgotten about the love potion! ''You'll have to excuse me,'' she said, trying to pull away from Edmund's hold on her hand. ''I was looking for Nicholas. I need to talk to him a moment.''

Edmund's grip tightened. ''We'll come with you,'' he decided, not releasing her. ''I haven't had a chance to speak to old Nick since he came back to town. No doubt he'll want to contribute to my campaign. I'd better speak to him before Daza gets the chance,'' he added, his gaze sharpening as he noticed his opponent in the mayor's race, Timothy Daza, across the room.

Prudence had no choice but to let the Swains accompany her as she worked her way through the crowd again toward Nicholas. Every couple of steps someone stopped her to say hello or congratulate her on the party, and Edmund took full advantage of these interruptions, pausing to shake hands or slap the person on the back, while his mother made a few sedate remarks. Prudence replied randomly to the comments directed her way, chafing at the delays.

Couldn't they hurry? What if Nicholas took a drink? She doubted it would make him fall in love— the thought of Nicholas really in love was too much to believe. More likely it would simply poison him on the spot. She glanced over anxiously and kept her gaze fixed on him, watching him talk with Rhonda, who had backed him into a corner near the fireplace. Jackie came up to try to join them, but the deft maneuvering of Rhonda's hoop skirt prevented her approach, and the pretty blonde moved on.

Nothing subtle about Rhonda, Prudence reflected. But at least she was keeping Nick so busy talking that he hadn't yet been able to take a drink. Still, that wouldn't last forever. She had to reach him before her luck ran out.

"Excuse me, Edmund, but I'll meet you over there," she said, finally breaking in when his conversation with a local farmer—decked out as a nun— appeared as if it would run on awhile.

Mrs. Swain's eyebrows arched in disapproval while Edmund looked surprised. "What's the hurry?" he asked, faintly annoyed as the farmer-nun took the opportunity to make his escape. "Frank almost agreed to contribute a couple hundred to my campaign. Now Tim will probably snag him."

"I'm sorry, but I don't want to miss Nicholas."

"He's not going anywhere," Edmund said, but he followed her across the room.

Prudence reached Nicholas in a breathless rush—just as Rhonda started to lead him away. "Hello, Pru, Eddie," Rhonda said, fluttering her fingers at them as she strode past. "Mrs. Swain," she tacked on with a distinct lack of enthusiasm. "We're just on our way to dance. Oh, would you hold this?"

Whisking the glass from Nicholas, she thrust it into Edmund's hands and disappeared with Nicholas into the crowd.

Mrs. Swain stiffened. "How rude that woman is. My son is not a waiter!"

"He certainly isn't," Prudence agreed hastily, "Give it to me, Edmund."

"But I want to dance with you. Here, I'll just set it on the mantel."

He did so and pulled her toward the dancers without giving her a chance to protest. Automatically Pru followed, gazing back anxiously at the goblet. Should she go back and try to get it? No, Mrs. Swain had planted herself nearby. Prudence didn't see how she could pick the glass up without calling the woman's attention to it again. Perhaps it would be best to simply dance a little, then when they returned, she could grab the drink without anyone noticing.

Edmund stepped out onto the dance floor. Heppy had put on "The Monster Mash," and the crowd was going wild. Nearby, Rhonda lifted her skirt in an abandoned fashion, keeping pace with Nicholas. Prudence let the hard beat of the music wash over her, too, moving more sedately to the rhythm. The exercise helped soothe her anxiety. She smiled at Edmund, who danced with endearing awkwardness, his motions earnest and somewhat clumsy.

Next to him, Nicholas showed no awkwardness at all, his body moving with a powerful, masculine grace that caught every woman's gaze. Prudence stared at him in surprise. He never used to know how to dance like that. His suggestive movements caused Rhonda to lift her skirts ever higher in uninhibited response, rolling her shoulders in a wild movement that caused her plump breasts to jiggle and bounce.

Nicholas certainly seemed enthralled—as did all the men in the vicinity. Frank, the farmer-nun, almost tripped over his skirts in an effort to keep Rhonda in view, but Rhonda had eyes for no one but Nick. Prudence tilted up her nose, disgusted with the display. Thank goodness Edmund didn't behave like that— making a spectacle of himself. She glanced at him, catching a slightly contemptuous look on his face as he watched the other couple. For a second he looked oddly like his mother. To Prudence's relief, the music stopped and he smiled at her, looking like himself again. He pulled her into his arms with more haste than grace as a slower song began.

"Quite a show," he said next to her ear.

Prudence nodded and moved a bit closer, not wanting to pursue the subject. Edmund's arms tightened around her and he whispered, "You will dance with me, won't you, at the bewitching hour?"

The bewitching hour. A tiny shiver, half dread, half anticipation, tingled up Prudence's spine. "Of course," she managed.

"Are you sure?" Edmund held her away a little to look into her face. "Every year you disappear before the clock strikes. I can never find you."

Her heart seemed to beat more heavily. "I never knew you were looking," she said lightly. His eyes, fixed on hers, held a speculative gleam she'd never seen before—and wasn't sure she liked. Before she could analyze why it bothered her, his expression altered to his usual rueful smile, and he drew her closer, resting his head against her hair. "Well, I was. I've had my eye on you for years. So just be sure and stay close as the hour approaches, okay? Or you don't know who you might end up with."

Prudence nodded, knowing exactly what he meant. At the stroke of midnight Heppy would turn out the lights at the party, giving everyone exactly one minute to select their partners. Whomever you were with when the lights came back on was the person you were stuck with for the next hour. Not-so-brave citizens of Cauldron had been known to leave Heppy's parties early. Some strange combinations often emerged out of the darkness.

Of course, there were some strange combinations when the lights were on, too, Pru thought as Nick and Rhonda glided past. Wasn't he getting tired of the woman? Heaven knew Prudence had no reason to want to spare Nick, but she pitied him having to listen to the redhead's inane conversation.

Edmund murmured, "Isn't this nice, you and me together…"

"Hmm," Prudence replied absently, not really listening. Rhonda had wrapped herself so closely to Nick's broad frame that the poor man could hardly move—not that he looked bothered.

"You have to know I think I love you, darling, that I'm yearning to make love to you…"

"Uh-huh." Just look at the woman! Why, her hand was practically on his buttocks!

"Of course, Mother doesn't think the time is right for me to make a *public* commitment, but once I'm elected…"

"That will be nice." How could Rhonda act like that in public? Didn't she have any dignity? Any decency? And why didn't Nicholas move her hand? Did he enjoy putting on a show? Probably. Nothing ever bothered Nicholas. For a moment Prudence toyed with the thought of him—or better yet, Rhonda—covered with pimples from Heppy's potion, then resolutely banished the idea from her mind. She couldn't let Heppy get into any more trouble. She glowered at Mrs. Swain, still planted near the fireplace. *She had to get that glass.*

"Until then we can keep our relationship private. Just between the two of us…"

Edmund pulled her closer and Prudence stood on tiptoe, craning her neck to see over his narrow shoulders as Nick and Rhonda moved out of view. Were they heading back toward the fireplace? No, thank goodness. Maybe if she maneuvered Edmund to it right now… Oh, good Lord! Mrs. Swain was studying the goblet with intent interest.

Did she suspect…?

"Of course, it doesn't help matters that your crazy aunt—"

"My what?" Prudence's gaze snapped up to fix on Edmund's face. "What did you say?"

He paused, then said soothingly, "Nothing to upset you. It's just that mother's concerned that Hepzibah's becoming more, shall we say, eccentric?"

Prudence stopped dancing, pulling out of his arms.

"So what if she is eccentric? There's no law against that."

His smile looked a bit condescending. "Unless she's becoming a danger—"

"To society," Prudence finished savagely. "You and your mother make sweet little Aunt Heppy sound like public enemy number one. I don't want to hear any more of this."

She marched back toward the fireplace. Mrs. Swain was no longer looking at the glass but was watching their approach, her eyes narrowed. Prudence reached her at exactly the same moment that Nicholas joined the group with Rhonda's hand tucked in his arm. He glanced at Prudence inquiringly and she scowled back. Everything was going wrong tonight—and somehow it was all his fault.

"I'm sorry, darling," Edmund whispered from behind her. He slipped his arm around her waist but hastily lowered it when Mrs. Swain glanced his way.

Prudence edged closer to the fireplace as Mrs. Swain assumed the task of controlling the conversation. "I know that you're anxious to talk to my son about his plans for the town as mayor, Nicholas," Mrs. Swain said, stating the matter as if there could be no doubt.

Nicholas didn't respond, but Rhonda, clinging to his arm, stifled a giggle, and Prudence stopped her subtle maneuvering toward the goblet long enough to glare at her. Only Edmund and Mrs. Swain seemed unaffected by Nicholas's continued silence. Mrs. Swain's expression didn't change, while Edmund smiled with his easy charm, saying, "I think you might be surprised at what we've got going, Nick. Big plans are in the works to build employment opportunities in this town. We're losing our young people—they all want to go off to the big cities…''

Seeing he was well launched into his campaign spiel, Prudence seized the opportunity to inch toward the goblet again. She reached up to grab it, intending to throw the liquid into the fire. But just as her fingers closed around the stem, a strong hand grasped her wrist.

''I believe that's my drink,'' Nicholas drawled. Behind him, Edmund flushed slightly, obviously irritated at being interrupted, while Mrs. Swain frowned. Rhonda watched the byplay with pouty-faced annoyance.

''Is it?'' Prudence smiled brightly in Nicholas's direction. ''It doesn't look fresh. Let me get you another.''

''But Heppy made it especially for me,'' he said gently.

Mrs. Swain raised her eyebrows. ''If Hepzibah McClure made that drink, you would be very wise to get another,'' she said in decisive tones. ''Who's to say *what* that woman might decide to add. In fact—'' her gaze narrowed suspiciously on Prudence's tense face ''—is that the reason you're taking the drink, Prudence? Is there something wrong with it?''

Aware of everyone watching, Pru said, ''Not at all. The drink is fine.''

Rhonda, eyeing Nick's hold on her wrist with disfavor, said tartly, ''Then why don't you give it back to Nicholas?''

''Because I, well…because I'm very very thirsty and I wanted a sip.''

''So then take one,'' Rhonda snapped.

Everyone was watching expectantly. Prudence swallowed. She didn't want to drink the potion—she *really* didn't want to. A vision of Mrs. Watson's pimply chin flashed in her mind.

"I don't think you'd like this drink," Nick said. His hold on her wrist tightened and he lifted his other hand to remove the glass.

"There *is* something wrong with it," Mrs. Swain declared.

Pru sighed. What else could she do? "No, there is not," she stated. Breaking away from Nicholas, she took a deep breath, lifted the glass and downed the brew.

The room went black.

4

SHE'D BEEN BLINDED!

A small squeak of fright escaped Prudence. Strong arms wrapped around her, holding her securely against a broad hard chest.

"Pair up, everyone! It's midnight!" Aunt Heppy called out happily.

No, not blind, Prudence realized, sagging in relief. Her eccentric aunt had simply turned off the lights.

The bewitching hour had begun.

A chorus of shrieks and laughter filled the room, and Pru snuggled deeper into the comforting masculine warmth surrounding her. Her panic subsided, but her dizziness increased. An odd fuzziness clouded her brain. She drew a deep breath and her head swam, causing her to clutch at the man holding her. She swayed and his firm grip tightened, pressing her face against rough wool.

Inhaling a pleasant masculine scent, Pru's brow puckered. The bewitching hour—there was something she was supposed to do… Ah, yes! Find Edmund!

Pleased to have remembered, she smiled and lifted her head…just as hard warm lips lowered to lightly touch hers.

Nicholas.

Prudence stiffened. The room seemed to go still,

the laughter and shouting fading away while her senses leaped to startled alertness—the scent, the taste, the feel of him, all magnified in the dark. Her mouth throbbed where his had touched; even her fingertips seemed to tingle as she slid her hands uncertainly beneath his jacket and up over the smooth heated linen of his shirt to rest them on his broad shoulders.

She tried to push him away, but his grasp didn't loosen. Instead, he lifted her up on tiptoe to gather her closer. Her hands tightened and her breasts prickled with pleasurable pain as he rocked her slowly back and forth against him in a movement so subtle, yet so shocking, she opened her mouth to protest…and then forgot to as he kissed her again.

A rich spicy taste reminiscent of Christmas rum cake lingered on her tongue. The taste was on Nicholas's tongue, too, teasing and exciting her as his mouth pressed and drew and worked on hers until her lips felt puffy and almost unbearably sensitive. She moaned a little. He lifted his head. Soothingly he ran his tongue lightly over the swollen curves, then slipped between them to lure her into an enticing game of thrust and parry.

When he lifted his head again, she blindly followed the movement, trying to recapture his mouth, but the kiss went astray against his rough chin as he lowered her, and held her gently at arm's length.

The lights blazed back on. Prudence blinked and then blinked again. Her gaze locked with golden eyes staring down at her.

She swallowed. *Uh-oh.*

Hastily she lowered her gaze from Nick's compelling stare and focused on his tie, only a couple of inches from her nose. This close she could see that the apparently abstract pattern was actually tiny silver crescent moons, scattered on a black background. Hundreds of moons. Thousands of moons. Her eyes seemed to cross suddenly and all the moons coalesced into a big silver blur. Pru shut her eyes to escape the nauseating sight, laying her cheek against his shoulder again.

His breath brushed against her ear as he whispered, ''Are you all right?''

''I'm fine, just fine,'' she answered huskily.

She knew she needed to move out of his hold, to go find Edmund. And she would. In one little minute. As soon as everyone's excited chatter died down a bit. As soon as her legs quit threatening to turn into jelly. As soon as the moons on his tie stopped leaping about.

She opened one eye to check on their progress, but they were still jumping. And goodness, all the people in the room were jumping now, too! No, not jumping, she realized—dancing. Another pulsing, raucous song had come on.

Nicholas stepped away. Prudence stumbled, trying to follow, and he caught her hand in his, his heavy-lidded eyes watching her as he began moving easily to the beat. Still holding her hand, he swung slightly away and then back, his gaze challenging as he increased the intricacy of his movements, sexual intent symbolized in the sway of his shoulders and the thrust of his pelvis. He gave a slight tug on her hand, urging her to join him.

Prudence resisted. She had no intention of accepting his unspoken invitation; *she* wasn't an exhibitionist. And where on earth had he learned to dance like that, anyway? It made her blush just watching him.

Yet somehow she couldn't look away, either, and bit by bit the music began to pulse through her, pounding up from the floor, up through the thin soles of her shoes. In spite of herself, her feet started moving. She couldn't stop them. Her legs followed and then her hips—oh, my goodness, her hips were out of control!

Exhilaration rushed through her. She was dancing like she'd never danced before. Nicholas tugged at her hand again and this time she faced him, her movements instinctively altering to mimic and counter his. Without missing a beat, she took up his challenge, her hair flying, her hips undulating wildly, while the other dancers slowed and moved back, creating a small circle around them.

It wasn't until the music crashed to a halt that Prudence could finally stop. Breathless and excited, she collapsed into Nicholas's arms. A smattering of applause arose around them, then a slower tune started and the crowd broke up.

Somehow Prudence had landed with her nose squashed against Nicholas's tie, her eyes wide open. Now the moons were rolling up and down like waves on a dark sea. She glanced up at Nick to comment on the strange phenomenon and the words locked in her throat. Her hands flattened on his chest as she gazed up at him, her breath catching at the smoldering lazy hunger burning in the amber depths of his eyes. Something about those eyes was so familiar... Why, they were exactly the same golden color as Heppy's love potion!

Fascinated by her discovery, Prudence didn't even

notice when the lights dimmed again. Nicholas's lids drooped, half shielding his love-potion eyes, and she sighed as his arms tightened around her. He began swaying to the slow lazy beat and Pru swayed with him. Her head felt heavy—much too heavy to hold up any longer. She leaned it on his shoulder again while they turned in a slow circle.

Odd yet strangely familiar figures floated past. A cow danced by with hoofs locked around a sheeted ghost. Frank, the farmer-nun, had snagged Marilyn Monroe. He hummed along with the song as he twirled her around the room, both laughing whenever they tripped on Frank's robe.

Pru blinked, her head swimming even more. She felt like Dorothy in *The Wizard of Oz*, caught up in a swirling tornado. There were Tim and his very pregnant wife Kristie, dressed as Raggedy Ann and Andy—quite appropriate, Pru thought dreamily, since the Dazas never had much money. While Edmund was one of the richest people in town, the Dazas definitely represented the working class in the area. The couple had painted their mouths in big red smiles—not as beguiling as Edmund's smile, Pru decided. Edmund should have no trouble beating his opponent in the race for mayor.

Now the town's newlyweds, Les and Mary Douglas, danced into view. Their eyes were locked; they didn't even seem to see anyone else. Pru's throat tightened suddenly. She and Nick had been like that once—so much in love. Or so she'd thought.

The memory caused her heart to ache a little, and she pushed it away, soothing the hurt by burrowing deeper against him, comforted by the warm strength of his arms. She wouldn't think about that right now.

Tonight, she'd only think about happy things—like Aunt Heppy sitting in a corner, smiling gently across the room from amongst a pile of sleepy children.

And Edmund...why, there he was! Dancing nearby! He drifted past, a reproachful expression on his face and the stiff enraged figure of Rhonda in his arms. Dear, sweet, *safe* Edmund. *He'd* never hurt her. Prudence started to waggle her fingers at him, but Nicholas caught her hand, folding his fingers around her smaller ones and tucking them against his heart.

Prudence frowned. Nicholas certainly wasn't being very friendly. Then the thought evaporated into those wonderful foggy mists as more couples glided by. Frankenstein with Count Dracula. The big bad wolf and one of the three little pigs. How sweet. Everyone was paired off—like a Halloween Noah's ark.

Well, almost everyone.

Pru met the cold unblinking stare of Mrs. Swain, standing alone by the fireplace, and the sense of well-being that surrounded her evaporated a little. She shuddered, turning her face back into Nick's shoulder.

"Are you sure you're okay?" The words were a low growl by her ear. She nodded without looking up.

Not satisfied with her response, Nicholas kept swaying gently to the music, but stepped back a little to study her. When she wouldn't meet his gaze, he slipped his hand beneath her chin, forcing her face away from his chest and tilting her head back until he could see her eyes.

She gave a little mew of protest, but didn't resist his hand, gazing up at him beneath half-closed lids. Her eyes had a drowsy relaxed expression, but her color looked good, a faint flush of pink along her cheeks enhancing her smooth complexion.

He stared down at her, pondering whether or not to hustle her out and have Heppy put her to bed. She'd taken him by surprise, downing her aunt's concoction like that, but the only effect it seemed to have on her was an amorous one.

She smiled slowly, her smoky eyes full of shy invitation as she said huskily, "The lights are going to go off again soon…for the final kiss."

"Yeah, I know."

She blinked coyly up at him and a thick wayward curl of her hair slid down over her brow and eye. Unable to resist, Nick gently brushed it back, threading his fingers through the soft strands. She butted her head against his palm, like a kitten begging to be petted and his mouth twisted wryly. She was soused, all right. Prudence hadn't encouraged his touch once since he'd returned.

As further proof of her tipsy condition, she wrapped her arms tightly around him. "I like dancing with you." Her mouth caressed his neck as she breathed, "Do you remember the first time we danced together?"

He did. It had been at Heppy's party ten years ago. He'd heard days before about Hepzibah's newly orphaned niece who'd come to stay—nothing remained a secret for long in Cauldron—but the first time he'd actually seen Prudence had been at the party. She'd been all long legs and arms and her dress—similar to this one, minus the enticing slit up the side—had hung on her, making her look like a child dressed up in adult clothing.

But there had been nothing childlike about her ex-

pression. Her somber gaze had met his and awareness had flashed between them, a mutual recognition
he'd never felt before with anyone and had never felt
since.

Still, he hadn't planned to ask her to dance. He
hadn't been a good dancer in those days, and despite
that instant sense of familiarity, he'd also been all
too conscious of the three years' difference in their
ages. But then the lights had gone off for the bewitching hour, and somehow Pru had ended up in his
arms.

"I was surprised that you chose me," she admitted
now.

He rested his chin against her temple. "I know.
You looked so stunned when the lights came on."

"You were so sure of yourself."

"You were so scared."

"No, I wasn't." She shook her head and her soft
hair brushed against his mouth. "With everyone else
I was shy and awkward. But I felt…*right* with you
somehow." She paused and then added almost beneath her breath, "After you left Cauldron, I never
stayed for the midnight hour again."

He danced silently for a moment, not saying anything. He'd felt right with her, too. So right that when
she turned nineteen, he'd asked her to marry him and
she'd instantly accepted.

Only to break their engagement a week later.

He shifted restlessly, his jaw tightening at the
memory. Suddenly, holding her was as much pain as
pleasure. He meant to have her…but not when she
was in this condition. What he would do—the right
thing to do—was steer her back to her aunt and let
her sleep it off.

She whispered, "It looks like Heppy's going to turn off the lights again now."

He glanced over her head. Sure enough, Hepzibah was moving toward the switch. His hold loosened. He'd even taken a step in Heppy's direction when he suddenly caught sight of Edmund moving purposely toward them.

Prudence stiffened in his arms and Nick looked down at her again. She had noticed Swain, too. Her soft smile faded and a guilty look crossed her face.

How dare she look guilty about being in his arms! Abruptly incensed at her expression, Nick's arms instinctively tightened around her; she resisted, pushing gently against his chest.

It was that gesture that sealed her fate.

Maybe if she hadn't been so yielding before, maybe if the taste of her wasn't still on his mouth, he might have acted differently. But suddenly Nicholas knew he wasn't going to let her go tonight, after all. And most definitely not into the arms of another man.

He dropped a hard kiss on her swollen lips. She blinked, and he stole another, this one long and deep enough to make her expression melt into drowsy passion. "Come home with me," he whispered.

She barely nodded. It was answer enough. The lights went out. Turning, Nick swept her past Edmund and out the door.

5

OUTSIDE, THE NIPPY BREEZE attacked them, stinging Pru's cheeks and nose, tossing her hair in wild abandon, as Nicholas hustled her down the darkened main street toward his car, the only light provided by the old-fashioned streetlights and the full moon. The wind flirted with Pru's skirts as they hurried along, whipping them around her ankles. Struggling to hold down her dress, she drew back a little, gasping at the breathless cold and the quick pace he'd set. "It's freezing," she panted, "and I've forgotten my coat."

"We'll be there in a minute," Nick replied, but paused long enough to shrug out of his suit jacket. He dropped the garment around her shoulders, enfolding her in his warmth.

"But now you'll be cold," Pru protested, nonetheless clutching the lapels together gratefully. She suppressed a shiver, standing still while he carefully fastened the top button to hold it closed, his knuckles brushing her chin.

"I could use a little cooling down," he answered, and something in his eyes caused her pulse to quicken. Without another word he tucked her in his car.

His house was just a couple of blocks down the street, so the drive took less than a minute. But that was long enough for the growing tension emanating from Nick's big frame to communicate itself to Prudence. She sat beside him, pressing her hand against her stomach to try to still the frantic butterflies leaping about inside.

They hadn't calmed when his white frame house suddenly loomed before them. Nick came around to open her door. She stepped out. The sidewalk had the disconcerting habit of rising and falling like the deck of a ship, so Pru held on to his arm as they moved to the porch, then leaned against the railing while he unlocked the door.

Once inside, he led her into the living room and switched on a lamp. The bulb was dim, the light barely reaching the corners of the big room.

Pru swayed a little, glancing around in surprise at the sparse furnishings. "Where's the sofa? And chairs?"

"Gone. I sold them."

That seemed significant for some reason, and she frowned, trying to figure out why. But then Nick caught her hand, leading her down the hallway to his bedroom, and she forgot about his lack of furniture, aware only of the pounding of her heart.

Inside the bedroom he released her to stride over to the white curtains billowing at the far window. Prudence stopped just inside the door. The mists were filling her brain again and objects shifted in and out of focus—the bed, an old wooden chair—one minute appearing fuzzy, the next crystal clear. She watched Nicholas push the curtains aside. The storm had struck. The wind tousled his hair and rain spattered on his shoulders, molding his shirt to his broad frame as he forced down the sash.

He slammed it shut and turned to face her. The

fitful light from the window flickered across his face, unable to pierce the shadows slanting across his cheek and jaw, but revealing the hot gleam of his eyes.

Outside the wind shrieked and rain pattered protestingly. Lightning flashed, and Pru jumped as Nick's dark silhouette appeared and disappeared against one wall. Another bolt struck. The fine hairs on her arms and scalp rose, while the thunder and rain seemed to echo the beat of her heart.

A cold draft wafted over her skin. Prudence shivered, but her nipples puckered more from anticipation than the chill in the room. She waited—for what she didn't know—scared and excited, her breath coming in shallow pants as Nick stared silently at her from across the room.

Without taking his eyes off her, Nick slowly reached up to loosen his tie. Pru watched the movement of his lean hands, unable to move or look away. He pulled the tie off and dropped it, and Pru's gaze followed it as if mesmerized.

With an effort she finally glanced away. Her eyes lifted to his again. He was undoing his shirt buttons, his gaze still fixed on her as he completed the task and the shirt hung open, revealing the hard planes of his chest. Dropping his arms, he shrugged. To Pru's bemused gaze the cloth seemed to drift off him in slow motion to settle in a heap by his feet. He turned slightly, and the light from the window slid farther in, highlighting the straight breadth of his shoulder and running in a band along his flat hard stomach.

"Your turn," he said softly.

Her mouth felt dry. She swallowed, shyness and excitement battling inside her, making her tremble.

Hesitantly she reached up and clumsily undid the button holding his jacket closed across her breasts. Like the gentle caress of a man's hands, it slid down her shoulders and arms to the floor.

His eyes tracked the jacket's journey, then lifted to meet hers again. He placed his foot on a nearby chair and undid his shoe. He pulled it off and dropped it.

Balancing unsteadily on one leg, Pru slipped her shoe off and kicked it into a corner. His second shoe followed; her second followed his.

Nicholas pulled off his socks. He waited.

Pru bit her lip uncertainly. She wasn't wearing any stockings. It seemed imperative for some reason to continue to match him item for item, but she didn't have many clothes left and the fog in her brain was thickening, interfering with her thinking. Reaching up, her fumbling fingers struggled with the tiny hooks and eyes at the back of her dress, but she soon abandoned the task. There were dozens of them; it would take all night to get them undone. Struck by sudden inspiration, she tugged up her gown. She let the skirt drape over her thighs, preserving her modesty as she shimmied out of her underwear.

Her panties dropped gently on her bare feet. The gesture released the last of her inhibitions. She felt wicked, she felt free, she felt sexy in the way she only ever felt with Nicholas. Tonight was a wild night, filled with energy crackling across the sky and booming bursts of thunder. But the lightning had no more power than the heat building inside her, tingling along her veins and making her stomach muscles clench in spasms of excitement.

Stepping out of the black lace, she impulsively

grabbed the panties, tossing them as high as she could. They caught on the ceiling fan, dangling from a blade. Prudence laughed in delight. Riding a wave of exhilaration, she launched herself at Nicholas in what she intended to be a graceful leap, but ended up more as an awkward lunge.

Nicholas caught her, twisting to cushion her fall as they both fell back on the bed. She landed on top; she liked the position. They lay breast to chest, belly to belly, her legs sprawled along his. Her head swam as she bent down to nuzzle his cheek, his skin like sandpaper against the softness of her lips.

With a low groan he turned rolling her beneath him, sliding his fingers through her hair to hold her head still. Pru welcomed his weight, the warm solidness of his body on hers. She ran her hands along his smooth bare back. His skin felt cool there, slightly damp from the rain, but when he lowered his mouth to hers, his lips were hot, consuming her, stealing her breath until she felt dizzy again, unable to think.

Which was good; she didn't want to think. Perfectly willing to be carried away by desire, she ran her hands over the hard muscles of his arms. He broke the kiss and blindly she brushed her lips along his collarbone, kissing slowly along it to reach the warm smooth column of his neck.

She touched his skin delicately there with her tongue. He tasted slightly salty. She burrowed her face against him. His clean masculine scent mixed with the fresh crisp autumn air that clung to his hair and skin. She inhaled deeply and memories washed over her in the darkness—Nicholas smiling down at her, shadows slanting across his face as they strolled through the pine-scented woods, his golden-brown eyes dark and intense as they lay in the crushed grass, her head pillowed on his hard arm, his hand warm and possessive on the bare skin of her waist. Nicholas kissing her. Nicholas saying…

"I love—" Just in time, she bit the whispered words back. That was in the past—and she didn't want to remember the past. She kissed his shoulder again, welcoming the increasing cloudiness in her mind, waiting for him to touch her again, to lead her to that place where thought was no longer possible and only physical sensation remained.

But above her, Nick had grown still. A new harder tension tightened his frame. He slid off to lie next to her, his hand on her stomach and one muscular thigh thrown across hers to hold her in place as she tried to turn toward him. She abandoned the attempt; she couldn't move at all. Her arms, her head—everything felt too heavy to lift. A pleasant lassitude stole gently over her.

Dimly she realized Nick had raised himself on his bent elbow to gaze down at her. His hand lingered at her waist, stroking slowly, almost absently, over the soft material of her dress, leaving small ripples of pleasure on her skin in its wake. Her eyes drifted shut. "Who do you love?" he asked, his deep voice flowing into the night.

Disturbed by the question, Pru's brow puckered, then smoothed as the words melted away. She didn't want to think about love; she just wanted to enjoy the quivering, aching feelings drifting through her. She shifted languorously, running her hand down his side in an effort to distract him, reveling in the feel of his smooth skin beneath her fingers.

In response, his hand moved, tracing her hipbones and sliding across her tummy. Her muscles clenched in a pleasurable ache of anticipation, and she melted beneath his touch as he stroked back over her belly button and up her rib cage. Her breath caught in her throat as he firmly cupped her breast. Heat from his hand seared through her dress, warming her skin, penetrating all the way to her heart.

"Who do you love?" he asked again, his rough tone at odd variance with the light, luring stroke of his palm.

Floating on a soft sea of desire, Pru refused to respond. She moaned, arching involuntarily as his thumb brushed her puckered nipple, sending a shaft of pleasure coursing through her.

She struggled to open her eyes. Beneath her lashes she could see Nicholas looking down at her. His amber gaze burned through her, dark and intense.

"Who do you love?" he demanded once more.

Pru refused to answer; and in another moment she couldn't. He seemed to be wavering, drifting farther and farther way. Oblivion beckoned. Her lids fluttered down and she escaped into sleep.

SOMEWHERE WATER was running.

Prudence didn't want to open her eyes. She didn't want to lift her head. But the water was disturbing her dreams—nicely erotic dreams involving her and Nicholas and a big fluffy cloud. She tried to sink back into its depths but the water kept distracting her. Where *was* the sound coming from? The rain, she decided, snuggling her cheek more deeply into her pillow. The movement caused a small dart of pain in her head and she winced. No, not rain—it sounded too steady for that... Oh! The shower! She smiled, pleased to have solved the mystery. Heppy must be in the shower, whistling and now singing slightly off-key in a pleasant baritone—

That wasn't Heppy!

Pru bolted upright, then whimpered, cradling her aching head in both hands. Somehow the lightning that had filled the sky last night had settled in her skull and was now ricocheting from side to side in flashes of pain. She forced her eyes open and glanced around, then whimpered again. She was here, in Nicholas's house—in his *bed*, for heaven's sake!— while he bellowed merrily away in the shower.

What on earth had Heppy put in that potion?

Her mouth felt dry; bits of memories from the previous night passed through her mind in a confusing array. People had floated—no, *she* had floated. Nicholas had held her down—or had she held *him* down? Had he undressed? She wasn't sure. But he *had* kissed her and touched her...there and there and— oh, my goodness!—there!

She released her head to clench her fists. The jerk! How could he have taken advantage of her like that? It wasn't her fault she'd been a little...out of it. She'd only kissed him and stroked him and...well, jumped on top of him. She covered her face again as memories of her own actions seeped into her mind. Had she really sprawled on top of him, cuddled up to him like...like a cat in heat? Oh, what had she done? What had *they* done? At least they hadn't...or *had* they?

She groaned. Only one thing was clear: the need to get out of here before Nick finished his shower. She couldn't face him—she simply couldn't. Not yet.

Not in this condition. If she was lucky, she would never have to face him again in her entire life.

What she needed was a plan. She held her forehead, scrunching her eyes closed as she tried to concentrate. She opened them again. Okay, she had one; a good one. She'd sneak home—judging by the grayish light from the window it was still early, so no one would see her—and once there she'd clean up, change her clothes and then pretend the whole thing had never happened.

Anxious to put her brilliant plan into action, she tried to move her legs. Good Lord, he'd tied her ankles! Shoving the covers aside, Prudence glanced down. No, he hadn't. The skirt of her witch's outfit had simply wrapped around her feet. Stifling a moan at the pain the movement caused, she held her head with one hand and bent down to untangle the dress with the other.

She'd almost completed the task when Nicholas stopped singing. Her hands started shaking.

Just settle down, she told herself, struggling to loosen the material. *You'll get out of here in time, and even if you don't, there's no reason to be so upset. After all, we didn't* do *anything*—the memory of a warm palm cupping her breast flashed through her mind—*or at least we didn't do* everything. *My dress is still on. That's a good sign. Isn't it?*

The shower stopped. Prudence's pulse lurched in unreasonable panic and she leaped out of bed, stumbling over her skirt.

"Oh-dear. Oh-dear. Oh-dear-oh-dear-oh-dear." She couldn't seem to stop saying the two words, repeating them in a litany as she rushed around the room, hand pressed to her forehead, searching for her shoes. She found one in the corner. She slipped it on, hopping around as she looked for the mate. Somehow it had ended up under the bed. She grabbed it; the bathroom knob rattled. Holding her breath, she darted out the door and hobbled down the hall with the shoe clutched to her breast. She reached the front door just as the bathroom door opened. Heart pounding, she slipped outside and released her breath on a huge sigh of relief.

She had escaped; one hurdle was overcome. Now all she had to do was get out of here in case Nick decided to follow. Quickly she slipped on her remaining shoe and started walking briskly while trying to smooth her hair. She could tell from the feel of it beneath her fingers that it had frizzed, never mind the tangles. Thank heavens, it was barely light. No one would notice. Chances were slim she'd meet anyone, anyway—

"Oof!"

The breath rushed out of her as she ran smack into Jimmy Burrows delivering newspapers at the end of Nicholas's walk. She caught the boy's shoulders, preventing him from falling off his skateboard while barely managing to retain her own balance. Jimmy, however, wasn't fazed in the least by the collision.

"Hi, Prudence!" he sang out, his freckled face lighting up with a big smile.

Repressing a wince, Prudence let him go. Strange, she'd never noticed before what a shrill voice the little twelve-year-old had. "Hello, Jimmy," she replied, keeping her voice low in the hope he'd follow suit.

He didn't. His gaze had fastened on her head. He shifted the bag of newspapers on his shoulders, his brown eyes bugging out slightly as he exclaimed, "Jeez! Whadja do to your hair?"

"Nothing." She shot a look behind her, praying Nick hadn't heard anything. She started walking, hoping Jimmy would leave.

He didn't. In his own way Jimmy was as persistent as his older sister, Rhonda. He rode his board slowly along the sidewalk beside Pru, weaving from side to side, making her feel slightly seasick and causing her to have to sidestep whenever he swerved her way. "Yeah, y'did do something with your hair," he insisted. "It's all messed up and stickin' out, and it's got spiders—"

"Spiders!" She froze and Jimmy leaned closer to get a better view of her head.

"Nah, not spiders," he said, obviously disappointed. "Just a bit of black string. It *looked* like a spider, though. Sorta."

"Yes, well...I'd better get home to comb it better." She quickened her pace, but he stayed beside her, flinging a paper into the yard they passed without even bothering to aim. The newspaper landed neatly on the stoop.

A shock of straight red hair fell over his eyes as he stared at her, this time examining her dress. "So why are ya dressed like that? And why's your dress so wrinkled? Hey! Isn't that the witch dress ya wore to Miz McClure's party last night? I was there for a while till my sister made me leave. Didja sleep in it?" Without drawing a breath, he added, "My mom *never* lets me sleep in my clothes. And she or my sister makes sure I take a bath every night." His freckles bunched together as he screwed his face up in disgust, then spread out again as his expression lit up in sudden inspiration. "Hey! Maybe if I tell them *you* get to sleep in your clothes they'll—"

"I *don't* sleep in my clothes," Prudence interrupted, repressing a shudder at the thought of Rhonda's interpretation of that revelation.

She walked faster, glancing nervously over her shoulder. Jimmy stayed even. "Ya don't?" His freckles flocked together again in obvious disappointment. Another paper went winging away, landing on the doormat. "So why are ya dressed as a witch again? Hey! Are you on a scavenger hunt? I went on a scavenger hunt once, me and Tyler Decker—I don't talk to him anymore 'cause he stole my best baseball mitt, the one with the broken lacing that *he* said was his but I found first under the bleachers at the park—and we got lots of stuff. A clothespin, a needle, rubber bands—"

"I'm not on a scavenger hunt, Jimmy."

"—a pencil, a whistle—it was broke but it still counted even though Stephanie Roosen started crying and said it wasn't fair—cotton balls, a '94 penny, a red pen—"

"Jimmy—"

"—a broken spoon, a bookmark, a piece of bubble gum—it was all chewed up. Ty had stuck it under the bus bench and we scraped it off with the broken spoon. Miz Ruaz—she gave the party, ya know, for stupid Doreen—didn't want to touch it 'cause it had dog hair stuck all over it, but Ty thought if he chewed it up again—"

"*Jimmy!*"

He glanced up, innocently surprised at her loud tone. "Yeah?"

"I'm not on a scavenger hunt."

"Oh."

His face fell...then brightened. He opened his mouth again and desperately Prudence added, "In fact, the reason I'm dressed like this is to...is to let kids know there will be a party at Aunt Heppy's bookstore tomorrow for Halloween. A party just for kids."

"A party!" He jumped on his board, making it leap up and down off the curb. "Hey! Can I come?"

"Sure. At, ah...about ten o'clock." A vision of hordes of kids descending on the bookstore filled her mind, and she added in the faint hope of keeping things under control, "Just don't tell too many kids, okay?"

"I won't. I'll just tell Tyler. And Scott. And stupid Doreen—'cause she is kinda nice, ya know—and—"

"Tell whoever you want," Prudence said, caving in to the inevitable. "But I have to hurry now—I've got a lot of baking to do for the party."

"Ya mean cake and stuff? All *right!* Bye, Prudence! See you later!"

Heaving a sigh of relief, she watched him zip off, swooping over the sidewalk in graceful arcs. No doubt he'd tell the entire neighborhood. Well, no big deal. Aunt Heppy would be delighted. And now she could get home and—

"Pruuuu-dunce! Prudence McClure, is that you?"

Pru stifled a groan. Sally Watson, decked in a wide-brimmed straw hat and gardening gloves, had popped out from behind one of the rosebushes surrounding her picket-fenced house across the street. Imperiously waving her pruning shears, she beckoned Prudence over.

Reluctantly Prudence crossed the street. Ever since

the wart incident, the widow Watson had had a baleful gleam in her eyes whenever she met Prudence or her aunt. That look was definitely there now as she narrowly scanned Prudence's dress up and down.

Ignoring the rancor in her expression, Prudence said, "Hello, Mrs. Watson. How are you this morning?"

"I'm fine, or as fine as one can expect after the ordeal I went through last week," Mrs. Watson snapped, jowls jiggling as the shears opened and closed, firmly removing a faded red rose from a pristine bush. A few faint pink marks still remained on her fleshy chin, inexpertly covered by some kind of makeup.

Clearasil? Pru wondered. "We're very sorry about that," she apologized—for about the hundredth time—averting her gaze from the other woman's chin. "I promise you it will never happen again."

"Humph! It had better not! Bad enough I had to suffer, but to have the whole world told of my ordeal in the newspaper..." Her jaw clenched. Another wilting rose dropped to the ground. "Where are you going dressed like that?" The older woman demanded, her beady eyes narrowing on Prudence again. "Isn't that the dress you always wear to your aunt's party? Were you out all night—"

"Of *course* not," Prudence interrupted, widening her eyes in a show of surprise. Silently calling down blessings on Jimmy's red-haired head for the excuse, she said, "I'm dressed like this to advertise a kids' party we're having at the bookstore tomorrow."

"You're out advertising at this hour of the morning?" Mrs. Watson didn't look convinced. The shears snapped again, beheading a ragged yellow rose this time. "Personally I don't approve of parties. Nor children at parties, or parties at bookstores..."

Nor children or books, either, Prudence added mentally.

"And I definitely don't approve of all this fuss your aunt makes about Halloween."

Prudence didn't reply. Deprived of an argument, Mrs. Watson's thin mouth tightened while the shears sought another victim, annihilating a white rose that had the temerity to droop a little. "The way she imagines she's a witch, and all..." The shears bit viciously. "If there's any more incidents, Prudence..."

"There won't be." Not after last night!

The quick assurance failed to please Mrs. Watson, however. "There better not be. I hate to start trouble, but a person has to do what a person has to do— even if it hurts. And I'm not the only one in this town who feels that way. You'd better keep a close eye on your aunt."

Mrs. Watson smiled in grim resolve. The shears attacked again. A pink rose, delicately proud in its full-blooming perfection, toppled to the ground.

Prudence couldn't stand to hear anymore. The woman was starting to make her head pound again. "Good day, Mrs. Watson," she said briefly.

Worry and anger giving her energy, she almost ran the next two blocks to Heppy's house and hurried up the back walk. She opened the door to the kitchen. Her aunt had cleaned up the mess from last night— and created another one. Flour and sugar were strewn across the counters, and a couple of crisp red apples had fallen to the floor.

Aunt Heppy stood in the middle of the disorder,

pummeling a huge mound of dough. She glanced up, a smile lighting her face at the sight of her niece. "Hello, dear! I wondered when you'd get home. Did you have a nice time with Nicholas?"

"No," Prudence ground out as she strode past. She reached the doorway, turning abruptly as Heppy's occupation penetrated her absorption. She eyed the white mound Heppy was wrestling with, Mrs. Watson's warning springing to mind. "What are you making now?"

"Apple pies."

"*Plain* apple pies?"

"Aunt Barbara's recipe."

Prudence slumped against the doorjamb in relief. "Thank goodness." Aunt Barbara had been odd, but she had also been a very good cook. Pru watched Heppy struggle to roll out her dough. From the size of the pie crust she was making, Heppy would be busy awhile. She told her aunt, "You and I need to talk. Just let me change and I'll be right down."

"All right, dear!" Heppy agreed.

Prudence took a couple of steps towards the stairs, then froze at the sound of a light knock. She frantically signaled her aunt not to answer, but Heppy ignored her desperate waving and bustled over to the back door. "Hello, Edmund!" she chirped, opening it wide. "Come on in. I'm making some apple pies."

"Good morning, Hepzibah," Edmund said, stepping into the room. Glancing past her at Prudence, his polite smile froze and a look of horror crossed his face. He stiffened. "So it's true!"

A bewildered look crossed Heppy's face. "Of course it is. I just told you so."

Edmund spared her an impatient glance. "No, you

didn't. I got the news from Mrs. Watson.'' His rather full mouth tightened in disapproval. ''She called Mother just a while ago.''

''She did?'' Aunt Heppy looked surprised. ''But how did she know?''

''She saw your niece walking by her house this morning.''

''Oh.'' Aunt Heppy glanced at Prudence. ''How did you know I'd be making pies, dear? I don't think I ever mentioned it.'' A possible answer occurred to her and she clasped her hands together in excitement. ''Do you think you might be psychic?''

Prudence shook her head. ''No, of course not. I—''

''Oh, for God's sake, I'm not talking about pies!'' Edmund snapped, interrupting Prudence and swinging around to face Heppy. ''I'm talking about the fact that your niece was out so early, dressed so reprehensibly.''

''Oh, that.'' Losing interest in the conversation, Heppy returned to her kneading and rolling, while Edmund turned back to Prudence.

His pale blue eyes narrowed. ''How do you think I felt to hear my girlfriend was wandering the streets at that hour? Were you trying to make a fool of me?''

Prudence's heart sank. She'd never seen Edmund so upset. ''Of course not. I was just out for...for a little exercise.''

''Dressed like that?''

''We're giving a party for the kids tomorrow morning at the bookstore. I wore this as an advertisement.''

''Oh.'' The answer seemed to appease Edmund somewhat. The press of his lips relaxed a bit and the suspicious look in his eyes dimmed. He said stiffly, "I'm sorry if I misjudged you. But you did leave the party with Ware."

Prudence fought the tide of red rising in her cheeks. "Surely you didn't think—"

"No, of course not," he said hastily. "Mother merely thought—"

He broke off and Prudence drew a sigh of relief—she really didn't want to hear Mrs. Swain's opinion on the subject. Her sigh immediately turned into a silent gasp, however, as a firm authoritative knock sounded at the back door.

Her pulse leaped into overdrive. *Please, please, please don't let it be Nicholas,* she chanted silently, but knew her prayer was unanswered when she glanced over to see a man's tall broad figure through the screen. Her stomach dropped, then twisted with nervousness. The last thing she needed was Nicholas and Edmund in the same room together. Especially when her head was still pounding and she couldn't think straight.

Behind Edmund's back she gestured at Heppy to ignore the knocking, but her aunt had already started across the room. Prudence hurried to beat her, hoping against hope to send Nick on his way with a minimum of fuss—and without the chance to talk to Edmund.

The race was close, but Heppy won. She whirled in front of Prudence like a plump dervish and flung the door wide. "Hello, Nicholas!" Heppy said. "Come on in."

Pru retreated a couple of steps as he strolled over the threshold and glanced around. His knowing eyes met hers only for the barest second, but even that was long enough to send a wave of heat flowing up her body to burn in her cheeks. He was going to cause trouble—she just knew it! That wicked look was in his eyes.

Aware of Edmund's newly suspicious gaze darting between them, she fought to keep her expression serene and her voice calm as she said, "Hello, Nicholas. How are you this morning?"

He nodded at Edmund and smiled at Heppy. Then he turned back to Prudence and answered her question in a voice loud enough to make her wince. "I'm fine, just fine. Last night was a night to remember. So invigorating, so *stimulating*."

"You enjoyed Heppy's party, did you?" Prudence said hastily.

To her relief he followed her lead. "I certainly did." He looked at Heppy. "Your party was wonderful, Hepzibah."

Her aunt glowed at the compliment, launching into a recap of the evening. Prudence's pulse steadied a bit. Maybe they'd get through this okay. If she could keep Heppy talking—and Nicholas quiet—then maybe Edmund would never have to learn about last night. It seemed to be working so far. Edmund appeared to have relaxed somewhat listening to Heppy's innocuous remarks.

Sure enough, when a break occurred in Heppy's bubbling recital, Edmund's half-rueful smile was in place as he said, "Well, Ware, it's something of a surprise to see you out and about so early in the morning."

"Is it?" Nicholas replied, leaning back against the counter. He folded his arms across his chest. "I could say the same to you."

His voice held the hint of a challenge, and Prudence's pulse sped up again. "Would anyone like some coffee?" she asked brightly in an attempt to change the subject. "Nicholas? Edmund?"

Nick shook his head and Edmund replied, "No, thank you, darling." Then to Prudence's dismay, he turned back to Nicholas and resumed the conversation, saying a shade belligerently, "That's true—I'm definitely not a morning person, as Prudence here could tell you. I came by this morning on a special errand to return her compact."

He extracted a small heart-shaped box from his pocket and held it out to Prudence. When she grasped it, his fingers wrapped around hers to hold them in place. "Here you go, darling." His pale eyes held a possessive light as he added, "When we went out the other night, you left it in my car."

Murmuring her thanks, Prudence accepted the case without really looking at it, her entire attention focused on Nicholas. Her heart pounded in alarm. His expression hadn't changed, but something in his eyes had hardened as he stared down at the other man's hand still holding hers.

Nick's gaze lifted to meet hers again. Her throat tightened as he stepped forward. "What a coincidence," he drawled. "I've come to return something, too."

He pulled a piece of black lace from his pocket and set it on the table. "Here are your panties, Prudence. You left them on my ceiling fan."

6

EDMUND'S EYEBROWS snapped together. Flinging aside Pru's hand, he exclaimed, "So, Mother was right! You *did* have sex with him!"

"I did not!"

"Ha!" Edmund ejaculated. "Then what is *he* doing here waving your underwear around like some kind of trophy?"

"Hardly a trophy," Nicholas drawled before Prudence could answer. Picking up an apple, he polished it on his shirt. "Now if you'd said banner—"

"How true," Heppy agreed, giving her dough a thump. "Except you didn't really wave it. You merely set it down."

Ignoring these helpful comments, Edmund sank into a chair. Putting his elbows on the table, he cradled his head in his hands, groaning, "A sex scandal—five days before my election."

"Now, now, don't be so upset, Eddie," Heppy said soothingly, giving her dough another slap. "This might be a *good* thing. A sex scandal will make you seem more like a real politician."

He lifted his head, saying angrily, "I don't *want* to seem like a real politician. I mean... Oh, hell." His mouth twisted bitterly as he looked at Prudence. "How could you do this to me?"

Guilt caused her throat to tighten and tears to burn

behind her eyes. If only she could explain about Heppy's potion. But she couldn't betray her aunt. "I promise you Nicholas and I didn't sleep—make love," she said earnestly.

She swung around to face Nicholas, standing silently by the cupboards still rubbing a red apple against his shirt. "*Did* we, Nick?"

He lifted his eyebrows and gave the apple a final polish. "Didn't we?" His strong white teeth bit into the fruit.

Anger swept over Prudence so fiercely she felt like she might explode. "*You know we didn't.*"

"Oh, what does it matter if you did or didn't?" Edmund asked wearily. "Once it gets out that you left your underwear at his house, no one will believe you, anyway."

"I'm not so sure of that," Heppy said thoughtfully. "She does have a bad habit of leaving her belongings around. After all, she left her compact in your car. Maybe everyone will see this as just another incident like that."

Edmund stared at her. Before he could utter the blistering words Pru could sense were on the tip of his tongue, she said hastily, "No one needs to know I was with Nicholas."

"But everyone saw you leave the party with him, dear," Aunt Heppy reminded her. "I bet the whole town is talking about it."

"They are," Edmund said bitterly. "Mrs. Watson is proof of that."

"Surely not..." But Prudence knew it was the truth. Remembering the avid glint in Sally Watson's eyes, she sank into a chair next to Edmund, admitting, "The gossips are probably having a field day right now."

Edmund moaned in agreement. Nicholas took another bite of his apple.

Heppy hurried over to give Pru's shoulder a comforting pat, decorating the black silk with white flour handprints. "Don't be distressed, dear. I know exactly what to do in a situation like this."

Despite herself, a glimmer of hope shot through Prudence. "What?"

"We need to do a cover-up of course. And I think the first thing we should cover up are these panties in case someone else wanders in." Picking up a pot lid, Heppy plunked it over the offending garment.

Nicholas's eyes met Pru's. She saw his mouth quiver. *It's not funny,* she thought, and scowled at him in an effort to send the silent message his way.

Edmund was glaring at Heppy. "Oh, my God!" he burst out, veins bulging in his forehead. "What good does that do?"

"Well, the worst thing about the situation is that so many people know about it," Heppy pointed out. "It's much easier to let the cat out of the bag than it is to put it back in. Still, I could try whipping up a 'forgetfulness' spell—only I'm not sure I have enough St.-John's-wort to cover everyone. The spell is calculated by weight, you know," she added in an aside to Nick, "and I think I'd need a ton to take care of Sally Watson, let alone Issie Swain."

Edmund's pale face reddened. "Why, you—"

"Aunt Heppy—"

"Hepzibah's right," Nicholas said, his decisive tone cutting the other two off in midsentence.

"Are you calling my mother fat?" Edmund demanded.

"You *want* her to create a potion?" Prudence said at the same time, her eyes wide with horror.

Nick's golden eyes lit briefly with amusement. "No, of course not. I meant Heppy's correct in saying too many people know about the situation. I don't think we could successfully hide what happened—" his gaze flickered to the pot lid "— even if we did manage to destroy the evidence."

"I'm doomed," Edmund droned in sepulchral tones.

"Now, now, you're all taking too gloomy a view of the situation," Aunt Heppy said, bestowing a comforting floury pat on his blond head. "If you don't want me to cast a spell—"

"We don't," Prudence said firmly.

"—then there's only one other way to stop the gossip." Heppy paused to pick up her rolling pin, while the other three waited in varying degrees of anticipation for her to finish.

When she started rolling the dough without saying anything, Edmund could stand it no longer. "So how do we do it? How do we stop the gossip?" he demanded.

Heppy looked at him in surprise. "I would think the answer's obvious. Nicholas and Prudence will simply have to become engaged of course."

7

"No!" PRUDENCE SAID.

Her voice sounded louder than she'd intended. She could see the surprise on Edmund's and Heppy's faces. Nicholas's expression remained unrevealing.

"It would just be temporary, dear," Heppy said. "Only until after the election."

After the election? Prudence barely restrained herself from gasping in horror. The election was nearly a week away! Five days of pretending to be engaged to Nick, pretending to be in love with him? She shuddered. "Edmund and I could never agree to such a thing," she said definitely.

"I fail to see what good a temporary engagement would do, anyway," Edmund added.

Prudence sent him a grateful glance. She knew she could count on Edmund to squash this terrible idea.

Heppy, rolling pin raised, stared at him in faint surprise. "Why, Eddie, everyone knows that an old-fashioned engagement isn't nearly as enthralling to gossips as an illicit affair."

Prudence said, "But—"

"It's true, dear," Heppy insisted, interrupting Prudence's protest. Carefully rolling out her dough, she added, "People are always more interested in what you try to hide than in what you tell them."

"That's true," Edmund conceded thoughtfully.

Prudence looked at him uneasily, but Heppy beamed in approval. Laying down her pin, she picked up a knife and began cutting pie-sized circles, saying to her niece, "Believe me, your engagement to Nicholas would do wonders for Edmund's campaign."

"No, it wouldn't," Prudence said.

"Yes, it would, dear. People will feel sorry for him," Heppy explained, carefully laying her dough circles in her pans. "He'll gain a lot of sympathy votes. Then, right before the election, he can steal you back from Nicholas and everyone will be so impressed by such politician-like conduct—never mind his sexual prowess—that he'll get even more votes from those who favor a macho man."

Prudence rolled her eyes. "You have to be kidding…"

"No, wait!" Edmund said, an arrested expression on his face. "I think it's crazy enough to work." Turning to Prudence, he picked up her hand. "*I* believe you of course when you tell me nothing went on between you and Ware—"

Nicholas made a slight strangling sound. They both glanced his way. "Excuse me," Nick said blandly. "Something caught in my throat."

Prudence narrowed her eyes at him. The cad. He was enjoying this; he enjoyed watching her squirm. She smiled sweetly. "Let's hope you don't choke."

He grinned at her as if he knew she was hoping for the exact opposite, and she looked back at Edmund. Turning her palm upward, she clasped his hand, saying gently, "Go on."

"But you must see how other people might not be as understanding as I." Edmund trotted out his thoughtful look. "It's no secret Mrs. Watson is still angry with Hepzibah—"

Heppy dumped her apples onto the crusts. "Sally can kiss my—"

"And Prudence, by implication," he added hastily before Heppy could finish. He met Prudence's gaze again, his own rueful. "She'd be happy to cause you trouble, and that could only hurt me."

Prudence's heart sank. Surely he couldn't seriously want her to go along with this?

Edmund must have read her refusal on her face, because his hand tightened on hers. "Please, darling, you know how important this campaign is—not only to me, but to the people of our town. Do it for me, Prudence," he begged. "It's the only way to salvage the situation. I'm sure even Mother would agree."

"Edmund, you can't have considered—"

"Yes, I have. Thoroughly. And it will have another benefit, too." Glancing at Nicholas, who was watching from across the room, Edmund lowered his voice to an urgent whisper, "While posing as Ware's fiancée, you'll have a chance to work on him—convince him to contribute to my campaign—or to relocate one or another of his businesses here. Think of what that would do for the economy of this town."

Prudence stared at Edmund in speechless amazement. The same whirlwind that had caught her up at Heppy's party still appeared to be carrying her along, causing everyone around her to behave in bizarre and strange fashions. Heppy—of course Heppy always seemed to be caught up in a whirlwind—and now Edmund was, too.

Had he gone insane? Where on earth had he gotten

the crazy idea that she had any influence with Nicholas? She hadn't had any when she'd really been engaged to him, so he certainly wouldn't pay attention to her now. Besides, he didn't care a bit about this town.

She almost winced as Edmund's hand, slightly moist from tension, tightened even more. "Please, Prudence," he begged. "It's only for a few days."

Prudence looked at him helplessly. Heppy's plan was the worst she'd ever heard. Why couldn't Edmund see it? She didn't want to be engaged to Nicholas, not for a few days, a few hours, or even a few seconds—certainly not for nearly a whole week! And he wouldn't want to be engaged to her, either.

She paused, considering that thought. Maybe that was the way out of this mess. It was clear neither Edmund nor Heppy would easily accept her no as final, no matter how loudly she said it. But they wouldn't argue for long with Nicholas. No one did. And if he said no, then no one could blame her for not agreeing.

She glanced at him, seeing his eyes brimming with unholy amusement. Oh, yes, Nicholas was enjoying himself watching her try to come up with an excuse. Well, for once she was going to make *him* squirm.

"So what do you think, Nicholas?" she asked brightly. "Do you want to be engaged to me?"

"No, I do not," he said firmly.

Prudence gave him a narrow-eyed glare, unsure whether to be insulted or not. She decided not. At least he'd settled the matter. She started to breathe a sigh of relief, but sucked in more air instead, as he added, "The thought of having to kiss you and hug you and...do other sexual stuff to you to convince people we're in love leaves me stiff...with dread."

Prudence gritted her teeth. Oh, how he loved to taunt her! She unclenched her jaw to prompt, "So you refuse—"

"But on the other hand," he interrupted, "Swain's whole career as mayor—maybe state governor, maybe even president—is hanging in the balance. I'm forced to ask myself—is it fair of me to put my personal desires before the good of our country?"

"Definitely not," Edmund said, adding hopefully, "So you agree—?"

"Still, on the other hand—"

"You've used all your hands," Prudence said.

"We'll talk about last night another time," Nick responded smoothly.

Her face flamed with color. He smiled in grim satisfaction, adding, "What I want to discuss right now is a major issue that everyone here seems to have forgotten."

Prudence's cheeks still felt hot. "What's that?" she asked warily.

"This situation may have an adverse affect on me. My business dealings may be affected by all the gossip."

"Poor Nicholas is quite right," Heppy put in helpfully. "We've forgotten he's as much a victim in this situation as Edmund is."

Prudence stiffened. What about *her!*

"Thank you, Hepzibah," poor Nicholas said, his voice filled with throbbing gratitude. "I knew I could count on you to see my side in this. And I realize I must rise to the occasion and do the right thing."

Meeting Prudence's seething eyes, he primmed his

stern mouth in a way that looked incongruous with his boldly hewn features. With a die-away sigh worthy of the most martyred Victorian maiden, he said, "The only answer I can give is dismally clear. I'll have to become engaged to Prudence to save my reputation."

ENGAGED, WAS SHE? Throughout the rest of the day as she worked at Heppy's bookstore, every time Prudence thought of Nicholas's declaration the same seething anger and panic she'd felt at the time swept through her all over again.

That bastard! Why on earth had he agreed to Heppy's preposterous scheme? She didn't believe for a minute that ridiculous excuse he'd given. Nicholas Ware caring about his reputation? Ha! Hard to care about something you'd never had. Nicholas's mother had died when he was just a boy, but his father, William Ware, although a nice enough man, had always been a ne'er-do-well, a dreamer who let money slip through his fingers. Growing up, Nicholas had never had as much as the other kids in town, the lack of which hadn't affected his cocky self-confidence in the least. Even as a teenager he'd made it clear he didn't give a damn what anyone thought of him. He'd always preferred to travel his own path, to keep most people at a distance.

No, there had to be another reason he'd agreed to a temporary engagement. And Prudence suspected the real reason was to punish her for running out on him—and for *passing* out on him before they could finish what they'd started last night.

Standing behind a bookshelf, she pressed her hands to her cheeks as a wave of embarrassment washed through her. How could she have thrown herself at him like that? Where had her pride, her dignity, gone?

Dissolved in Aunt Heppy's love potion that was where, she thought bitterly. It was that dratted drink that had put such crazy love notions in her head, knocking her head over heels. She'd felt possessed, driven by a strange yearning desire, a fire that only Nicholas could quench.

Which in a way made an odd kind of sense. Nicholas was the only man she'd ever been intimate with, after all. True, they'd never actually made love, but they'd come close enough for her to know he'd definitely wanted to.

She'd never been sure what had held him back all those years ago. She'd certainly been infatuated enough to go along with anything he wanted. Maybe he hadn't desired her enough; maybe he'd been holding himself aloof from such an irreversible physical commitment.

Whatever the reason, last night proved he wasn't holding back any longer. How much more dangerous would he be now in his new temporary guise of fiancé? She thought about his comments on the "sexual stuff" he would have to pretend to do and gritted her teeth. If he so much as laid a finger on her, she'd make Heppy concoct a potion that would turn him back into the horny toad he really was!

In an effort to distract herself from her unsettling thoughts, she collected the sketchbook and a piece of vine charcoal that she stored under the counter near the cash register. Sketching usually soothed her. She was always faintly surprised at the charcoal images that emerged beneath her fingers. Characteristics she never consciously recognized somehow evolved between eye and hand, startling her—and all too often her subjects—with their clarity.

She dropped into a chair just outside the circle of youngsters collapsed on the rug in various poses of absorbed interest around her aunt. Most of the kids' parents were off preparing for tomorrow's Halloween festivities, as usual using Heppy and the bookstore as something of an informal baby-sitting service. Even Kristie Daza—looking worn-out from her pregnancy—had left little Tim there while she hurried off to help with her husband's campaign.

But Heppy didn't mind. She loved children. "I'm sure you've all heard the tale of Jack—the man who managed to trick the devil," she said now.

Although Heppy had related the story just last week, small heads shook in vigorous denial. A reluctant smile curved Prudence's lips. The younger children enjoyed the well-known stories almost as much as new ones. Her hand began moving across the paper, drawing one enraptured face after another as the comforting sound of her aunt's voice washed over her.

"...*And Jack tricked the devil into climbing up the tree to pick a big juicy apple...*"

An apple. Nicholas had certainly been a devil, polishing *his* apple like he had and agreeing to Heppy's suggestion. Oh, he could be so infuriating at times! Absently Prudence turned to a clean sheet.

"...*Then Jack carved a cross on the trunk of the tree so the devil couldn't get down. And he made him promise not to come for Jack for ten years...*"

Ten years—such a long time to a child. But already ten years had passed since the first time she'd seen Nicholas. She'd been young then—young enough to believe in love at first sight. A few quick strokes created the strong line of his jaw, the keen intensity of his eyes.

"...So Jack lived on, having a good old time..."

They'd had good times together, and she'd loved him with all her young foolish heart. She shaded in his thick hair. There'd been no logical reason for her feeling of contentment whenever she was with him— they fought all the time, he teased her constantly— but somehow he seemed to know things about her that no one else did. He knew when she was worried or scared, how to make her laugh—or cry. Around him life had always seemed more vivid. The day he'd given her his ring had been the happiest day in her life.

"...Then Jack died. St. Peter wouldn't let him in heaven, and the devil—who didn't like Jack— wouldn't let him into hell, either, but instead, threw a burning coal at him to keep him out..."

She'd thrown his ring back at him the day they'd broken up, tears burning behind her eyes.

"...Jack put the coal in the turnip he was eating, and thus the first jack-o'-lantern was created..."

He'd caught the ring and put it in his pocket without a word.

"...And Jack went off, doomed to wander the earth forevermore."

Less than an hour later Nick had left Cauldron.

Prudence paused, studying the determined line of his mouth. Such a terrible fate, to wander the earth. She'd traveled enough with her parents as part of her father's job as a doctor with the World Medical Corps to be sure of that. They'd gone from one poor country to another, her father and mother fighting disease and ignorance, while Prudence fought her own silent battle with overwhelming loneliness. They never stayed long enough in any one place for her to develop close friendships. How she'd longed for a safe place to stay, a place with traditions, filled with friendly people. Like Cauldron.

The charcoal skimmed across the page, shading in broad shoulders, a muscular chest. But Nicholas had never appreciated Cauldron. He'd been anxious to leave, to take on the world. Not having a permanent home didn't bother him. Being constantly on the move didn't bother him at all.

"I'm not going to stay in Cauldron," he'd told her only a week after he'd asked her to marry him. "There's nothing for me here. And if you love me, you'll come with me."

"If you love me, you'll stay," she'd countered. "We can live with Aunt Heppy until I finish my art degree, and then we can buy a house here—so I can be nearby in case she needs me."

Their simple discussion had escalated into an argument, then a full-blown war. Nicholas had refused to give in. And so had she.

Her hand faltered. She gazed at the image before her. He looked strong, independent. A man who needed no one.

Resolutely she turned the page. Well, that was fine. She didn't need him now, either. She had Edmund and Edmund needed her—to stand by his side, to help him succeed in his campaign. Edmund's face emerged on the pad before her—round high forehead, full soft lips. And once he was mayor, he'd need her even more to help decide what was best for

Cauldron and to mold his somewhat elitist attitude into one more attuned to the needs of the entire town—rich and poor.

He was obviously worried about his campaign. She hadn't realized how worried until this morning. Never had she seen Edmund—cool suave Edmund—so anxious. After Nicholas's irritating announcement, she'd thought about refusing to go along with the engagement, but seeing the pleading in Edmund's eyes, she'd been forced to agree. Dear Edmund, who was so sweet, so trusting. Thank God he'd believed that nothing had happened between her and Nicholas.

And nothing really had. But yet, she could *feel* a difference. She'd have sworn these past couple of months that Nicholas had no interest left in her at all, except as someone to do secretarial tasks now and again. But last night something had changed— as if he'd removed a mask hiding his real feelings. This morning there had been something in Nick's face—a certain possessive look—that made her stomach muscles clench in panic whenever she thought of it.

She turned to his picture again. Even on the paper he had that knowing look in his eyes—as if he knew exactly what she was thinking, and was laughing at her attempts to escape him.

Well, she'd done it before and she would do it again. She slammed the sketchbook shut.

Engaged, was she? Fine. Until the election, she'd simply stay out of her "fiancé's" way.

8

ONE OF THE GOOD THINGS about Cauldron—perhaps the only good thing about Cauldron, in Nicholas's opinion—was that it didn't provide too many places to hide, he thought as he strode down the block-long length of Main Street. Except, of course, for the woods surrounding the town where he used to escape as a kid.

He'd gone there often. He'd usually wanted to get away from people; physically being alone had, oddly enough, made him feel less lonely than being in a crowd. But Prudence, he knew, had never felt that way. She enjoyed people and considered the citizens of Cauldron almost an extended family.

The only one she'd be trying to escape was him.

Thus far, she'd been successful. After agreeing to the engagement yesterday morning, he hadn't lingered, preferring to talk to her without Edmund's—or Heppy's—distracting presences. She hadn't been home when he'd returned later that afternoon and had made herself scarce last night, also. Still, all things considered, things were going pretty much his way, thanks to Heppy's brilliant plan. As his fiancée, Prudence wouldn't have any excuses for staying out of his arms or resisting his caresses. He couldn't have improved the situation if he'd planned it himself. The only glitch in the system was that his new "fiancée" had disappeared.

But she couldn't escape him forever. Today was Halloween, so he knew exactly where to find her.

Sure enough, when he twisted the tarnished brass knob and stepped into The Loft, Heppy's cozy bookstore, he found Prudence and Heppy surrounded by people—kids actually, ten- to fourteen-year-olds from what he could tell. The younger ones were in costume, store-bought for the most part, and featuring the latest super heros. Faces flushed with excitement, they gathered around Heppy to bob for apples in the big plastic tub she had placed on the bare wooden floor in the middle of the children's reading section.

Heppy was obviously having as good a time as any of her young guests. She'd donned her witch dress again and added her tall black hat to the ensemble.

Her niece, on the other hand, wore a cat costume. The outfit consisted of a black sweater and stretch pants that outlined her long slim legs; she'd also pinned a pair of construction-paper ears in her thick curls, drawn whiskers on her cheeks and dabbed her nose black. A stuffed tail attached by three huge safety pins hung down over her trim bottom to complete the impromptu costume.

If that tail could twitch, it would, Nicholas knew, as she slanted him a glance from across the room and then deliberately looked away. She continued to ignore him, concentrating on her task of pinning back the little girls' hair before they gingerly lowered their faces to the water to try to catch apples with their teeth. Even when Heppy called out a greeting, causing several young faces to turn his way before cursorily dismissing him as too old to be of interest, Prudence still didn't glance up.

But Nick knew she was as conscious of him as he was of her. He could feel her awareness as if a small invisible current stretched between them, and he could see it in the slight stiffening of her shoulders and the way she rigidly refused to look in his direction.

He didn't press the issue. He was good at waiting, and Heppy's bookstore was a pleasant place to accomplish the task. It was one of the few places in town where he'd always felt welcome as a kid. The softened fall sunlight glistening through the broad plate-glass windows provided a pleasing contrast to the shadowy nooks and crannies created by the angles of the old oak shelves. The shelves were filled with books on all subjects, some enticingly faded with age, others crisply inviting in their bright paper jackets. Heppy had scattered overstuffed armchairs and end tables throughout the room to encourage browsing, making the place seem more like a library than a store.

Being Heppy, she'd also managed to bring nature indoors. Juniper and ash branches were arranged in crossed bunches across the door and windows. Orange and gold maple leaves protruded gaily from a cider-bottle vase on the counter by the cash register, while a graceful green vine explored the riser of the old staircase that led to the loft where the rarer books were kept.

The scent of apple pies filled the air and a slight smile curved Nicholas's lips. Fruit-smeared paper plates and crust crumbs on the reading tables and floor proved that Heppy had found a use for all those pies she'd been baking.

Settling into one of the overstuffed chairs, he carelessly threw his blue-jeaned leg over the arm and picked up a nearby magazine while he watched Prudence and Heppy operate. Heppy was clearly determined to draw the older kids into the games, even though they obviously considered themselves above such juvenile pursuits. They clustered in small groups, segregated by sex for the most part, their studied attempts to seem bored and unaware of each other almost funny to watch.

Their sophisticated efforts soon wore thin under Heppy's efforts. They managed to resist bobbing for apples, but agreed to blindman's buff, succumbing to the temptation of a legitimate reason to reach and grab for each other.

Nick knew how they felt; getting his hands on Prudence had been his primary objective ever since he'd emerged from his shower yesterday morning to discover she'd fled. He'd been angry to find her gone, and even angrier to find Edmund at her house so early in the morning. Exactly what did she find so attractive in such a pompous jerk?

He wanted some answers so he bided his time, and less than an hour later his patience was finally rewarded. Most of the kids were gone by then, dragged home by punctual parents to have lunch and rest awhile before the town's traditional Halloween activities: a fair, trick-or-treating and a bonfire on Spook's Hill. The few stragglers that remained had been coaxed into a group around Heppy, who read them a Halloween story laced with enough horror and comedy to keep even Jimmy Burrows quiet.

Prudence had taken on the task of tidying up the store, and she padded quietly about restoring furniture and books to their proper places. Nick waited until she disappeared up the winding staircase with an armful of books, her swaying tail beckoning irresistibly, and then followed, cornering her in the loft among the high shelves.

He saw her stiffen as he appeared. She turned away, presenting him with a slender shoulder and the aloof curve of her profile as he came up to stand beside her.

"Why did you sneak off like that?" he asked without preamble, keeping his voice low enough not to disturb Heppy's discourse, barely audible from the room below.

She took a book from the pile in her arms and shoved it into a place on a shelf. "I didn't sneak off. I need to put these books away."

"I'm talking about yesterday morning, when you snuck out of my bed." He watched in grim satisfaction as a tide of pink washed up her cheeks, marked with those ridiculous whiskers. "Surely you realize after what happened that we need to talk."

She glared at him angrily. "Talk? Apologize, you mean."

He considered that, then nodded, propping his shoulder against a bookcase and folding his arms. "Yeah, I guess you do owe me an apology."

Prudence's mouth fell open. She snapped it shut, her grip on the books whitening her knuckles. "Me!"

"Yes, you." He raised his eyebrows at her astounded expression. "Surely you don't imagine I owe *you* one?"

"Of course I do! *You're* the one who invited me to your house."

"But you're the one who chased after me in the first place. There I was," he said pensively, "enjoying myself with Rhonda at the party when you ran over to interrupt us."

"I did not! I only came over to...to join the group." Her whiskers twitched. Balancing the books on one arm, Prudence absently scratched her blackened nose, smudging it as she added defensively, "Edmund wanted to speak to you about contributing to his campaign."

"He definitely did that," Nick said dryly.

"Then the bewitching hour started—"

"And you snagged me."

"Oh!" Her breath escaped on an indignant huff. "It wasn't that way at all."

"Aw, come on. No one's around—you can admit the truth." Nick leaned closer, maliciously pleased when her thick lashes fluttered in alarm at the movement and she clutched the books protectively to her chest. He drawled, "You melted all over me like hot caramel on a candy apple."

Prudence gasped. Her smoky eyes flared, then narrowed to simmering slits. "I wasn't myself at that party," she said. "Believe me, you won't have to worry about my acting that way again."

"I know I won't, because Heppy—with your boyfriend's approval—came up with a scheme that ensures you're going to be all over me for at least the next week." He crowded a little closer. "What I want to know is why you agreed to the plan."

Her eyes fell. "Because I wanted to help Edmund. I lo—"

He made a sharp gesture with his hand and she broke off, her gaze darting up to meet his. Their eyes locked. "Try to convince me, Prudence," he invited softly, "that you love the guy. Especially after what happened between us two nights ago."

He could tell from her expression that she was tempted to complete the lie, but something in his face must have told her she'd be wasting her time. She looked away, sliding another book onto the shelf and saying angrily, "It's none of your business how I feel about Edmund. He's committed to helping the people in this community, and I'm committed to helping him."

"You should be committed—to a psychiatric hospital. Can't you see that Swain only cares about himself?"

She slammed in another book. "That's not true!"

"Isn't it? What do you call it when a man lets the woman he intends to marry pretend to be engaged to another guy to help his campaign?"

"Edmund knows he can trust me."

"Oh, yeah? Even after you left your panties in my house?"

More red crept up her cheeks. She shot him an angry glare. "I told you I wasn't myself that night. There were reasons I acted that way."

"So let's hear them."

Prudence opened her mouth—and then closed it again. The trouble was she *couldn't* explain—not without telling him about the potion and implicating Hepzibah. She didn't want to believe Nick would hurt her aunt, but he *was* very friendly with Rhonda. Rhonda had received a lot of flattering comments on her reporting of the other incidents involving

Heppy's "powers"; there wasn't a doubt in Prudence's mind that the redhead would greatly enjoy breaking the story about Heppy's latest contretemps. And wouldn't *that* set off Mrs. Watson and her vigilante group.

When she remained silent, Nick taunted softly, "Cat got your tongue?"

She stuck it out at him, but he only chuckled, his eyes darkening as he said huskily, "I wouldn't do that unless you plan to use it."

Hastily she withdrew her tongue and eyed him angrily. "The real question here is why are *you* doing this? To torment me? Are you trying to get revenge because I broke our engagement seven years ago?"

Faint amusement gleamed in his eyes. "That's a little melodramatic, don't you think?"

"No more so than that show you put on about your reputation. Since when do you care what people think?"

He shrugged. "Basically I don't," he admitted. "But I am a businessman. It's important that I maintain a certain image. Which is why I'm counting on you to restore my good name."

She stared at him silently for a moment in frustration, then turned, intending to brush past him. A long arm shot out in front of her, barring her progress, and she stopped short, almost bumping her nose on his bicep. Her nose twitched and she absently scratched it again. He smelled good. The clean spicy scent rising from his skin caused her to tingle with unbidden memories of being in his bed, and she shifted uneasily, anxious to get away.

"Excuse me," she said, stone-faced. "Heppy needs me."

With a sudden move she darted under his arm. Absurdly pleased at outmaneuvering him, she started to hurry away, only to be brought up short by a tug on the back of her pants.

Startled, she glanced over her shoulder. He had hold of her tail. Wrapping it around his fist, he jerked her backward so firmly that she fell against him.

A hard arm around her waist steadied her, but his warm breath against her cheek and neck caused her legs to weaken again as he said, "Heppy needs you and you go running. Edmund needs you and you do the same. Well, for the next few days or so—until this farce is finished—*my* needs come first. Get your stuff together. We're going to my house."

9

PRUDENCE STIFFENED, all her worst fears confirmed. "How dare you!" she said, pulling away from his grip.

He regarded her calmly, lifting his eyebrows in sardonic inquiry. "I beg your pardon?"

"And well you should," she fumed. "How dare you order me to your house to see to your needs."

The cynicism on his lean face deepened. He made a faint tsking sound with his tongue. "What a nasty little mind you have. The needs I'm referring to concern filing and sorting. You're still acting as my secretary, aren't you?"

"Oh. Yes, of course," Prudence said, feeling rather foolish. Irritated at herself for overreacting, she went downstairs to tell Heppy she was leaving.

"Have fun, dear," Heppy called out, looking up from the circle of children.

"I'm going there to *work*," Prudence said, feeling the need to stress the point as she gathered up her purse and sketchbook.

"Well, try to have fun, anyway. I always do."

That was certainly true. But Prudence didn't want to have fun with Nicholas. She hated having her emotions bouncing around like they'd been doing for the past two days. She'd been right to break her engagement all those years ago. What woman wanted to constantly live in turmoil? She wanted peace. She wanted to be back on that steady predictable path she'd been trodding with Edmund by her side.

Instead, Nicholas was by her side. He hadn't brought his car, so she walked stoically next to him through the town, clutching her sketchbook and hardly aware of the bright autumn day. She didn't want to think about him anymore. In fact, she was thinking so hard about not thinking about him that it took a moment for her to realize someone was calling her name.

"Pruuuuuu-dunce. Prudence McClure, is that you?"

Prudence looked up. Sally Watson was hailing them from her porch. Politely—if reluctantly—Prudence stopped by her gate, and Nicholas paused beside her.

"Hello, Mrs. Watson," Prudence said.

Nicholas merely nodded and Mrs. Watson curtly returned the gesture. On the step by her feet was a gopher trap and a box of snail bait. A can of red bug spray was clutched in her hand. Mrs. Watson was clearly prepared to eradicate all the pests in Cauldron.

Good. Maybe she'd get rid of Nicholas, too, Prudence thought grumpily, then realized the old lady was looking in her direction. Instinctively she stepped closer to Nicholas. He cast her a glance of amused understanding and put his arm around her waist, drawing her closer.

Mrs. Watson's eyes narrowed, but before she could comment on the gesture, a small black fly flitted within range, distracting her. With a surprisingly quick movement, she lifted her hand and zapped the bug, the can hissing viciously. The little insect dropped dead to the ground.

Mrs. Watson regarded it in grim satisfaction, then eyed Prudence up and down. "I see that you are in...costume again."

Startled, Prudence looked down. Until that moment, she'd forgotten she was still wearing her cat outfit. "Um, yes. We just had the children's party at the bookstore," she explained.

"Humph," Mrs. Watson replied. A line of tiny ants marching along her railing caught her eye. She lifted the can. "Personally, I don't approve of parties." *Hiss.* "Nor children at parties." *Hiss, hiss.* "Nor parties at bookstores."

Nor children, nor books, either, Prudence chanted silently as usual.

"And I definitely don't approve of all this fuss your aunt Hepzibah makes about Halloween." *Hiss! Hiss! Hiss!*

The old lady grimly surveyed the dripping railing and drowned ants, then looked at Prudence again. "Your aunt hasn't been making any more potions, has she?"

Prudence crossed her fingers behind her back. "Of course not."

"Good," said Mrs. Watson, but she didn't look pleased. She glanced around restlessly. Her eyes narrowed on a golden bee buzzing just beyond the porch.

The bee wavered closer, droning happily along above the roses, innocently unaware of impending doom. Mrs. Watson lifted her can. Prudence held her breath.

Nicholas made a sudden movement and Mrs. Watson glanced his way. She hurriedly looked back at the insect and sprayed, but the poison fell short. The bee buzzed on its way.

Prudence sighed in relief, but Mrs. Watson's beady eyes narrowed on Nick. She clutched her can more tightly. "Ah, Nicholas. Still hanging around, I see. I suppose you're out of a job. Like father, like son, they always say."

Nicholas didn't respond—his aloof expression didn't even change—but Prudence stiffened in outraged shock. *She* might be angry at Nicholas, but that didn't mean she'd allow anyone else to say mean things to him!

"No, he's not out of a job, Mrs. Watson," she said sharply. "Nicholas has a very important position with his firm, and we'll thank you to refrain from making any more rude remarks about his father—or my aunt, either, for that matter!"

"Well, I never!" Mrs. Watson said, her mouth thinning to an angry slit.

"Yes, you do. You make mean remarks all the time," Prudence said, and would have continued her lecture, except Nicholas's arm tightened around her. Obedient to the unspoken signal, she contented herself with saying frigidly, "Good day, Mrs. Watson," and they both turned away.

Nicholas slanted an amused glance at Prudence as they continued down the street. She'd always been quick to jump to his defense at the slightest provocation. She was so angry now she was walking stiff-legged, like an angry cat. The rather jolting stride gave an extra little bounce to her breasts and Nick narrowed his eyes, enjoying the sight and silently wishing her thin black sweater was just a tiny bit tighter.

Her slender shoulders were still tense. When she glanced up at him, her gray eyes were troubled.

Taking advantage of her softened mood, he tucked her a little closer to his side, until her breast rubbed against him.

She didn't notice, concern about his hurt feelings obviously uppermost on her mind. The sweet curve of her pink mouth drooped in sympathetic understanding. She gave him a small hug, saying, "I hope you aren't too angry at her."

"I'm not," he said sincerely. In fact, he sent a silent thank-you back in Mrs. Watson's direction. Wouldn't the old battle-ax be enraged to know that she'd just done him a giant favor by diverting Prudence's anger away from him?

"Mrs. Watson doesn't mean to be cruel, you know."

He thought of the glee with which the old lady had sprayed her bugs and arranged his face into somber agreement. He hugged Pru even closer, so her hip bumped companionably against his leg with each step. "Sure, she didn't."

"I always liked your dad."

For the briefest second Nick felt his chest tighten. He'd always known most of the town considered his chronically unemployed father a failure. The knowledge had made Nicholas all that more determined to succeed, to show them all.

Prudence and his dad, though, had always gotten along. Both had shared a love of Cauldron and been fascinated by the town's history. Neither had ever wanted to leave. Both had wanted Nicholas to stay.

Unconsciously he tightened his hold on the woman at his side. "My dad had a hard time holding a job, but he was a good man."

They walked on to his house without speaking. If the slight pucker of her brow was any indication, Prudence was still brooding over the incident. Nicholas, however, had a new problem to worry about.

He didn't have a bit of secretarial work for her to do. As she'd suspected and he'd denied, he'd only taken her away from the bookstore in an attempt to get her alone—to finish what they'd begun the other night.

Well, he'd learned a few things in the past seven years. He knew the best way to get your own way was to be persistent and never lose sight of your goal. Distracting your opponent wasn't a bad idea, either. He cast Prudence a considering glance. He'd simply have to come up with a job to keep her busy awhile, lull her suspicions. And *then* he'd pounce.

Thinking quickly, he unlocked his door and ushered her inside. "I'm afraid I brought you here under false pretenses," he said.

"Oh?" Prudence replied, wariness in her eyes. She stepped away from him.

Yeah, she was suspicious, all right. He nodded, trying to look innocent. He knew her weak spot. Anything to do with family or Cauldron. He headed for the study, saying, "Yes. It's not my business papers I need your help with, but my father's. He has a lot of genealogical-research information. I piled it all into some boxes, but beyond that, I'm not quite sure what to do with it all."

He could tell from the consternation that crossed her expressive face that Prudence was ashamed of

her suspicions. She said quickly, "I don't mind helping with your father's papers at all. I love that kind
of stuff."

She was as good as her word. With little crows of
delight she dived into the boxes, pulling out charts,
papers and pictures and dividing them into piles on
the beat-up desk.

He lounged in a ragged arm chair, watching her.
He didn't care about the old stuff at all; but he
couldn't help a reluctant smile at the sight of her
excitement.

"Look at this, Nicholas!" she exclaimed in awe.
"It's a picture of your great-grandmother."

She held up a faded gray photograph of a hatchet-
faced woman.

Nicholas frowned. "Are you sure that's not my
great-grand*father?*" he asked doubtfully.

"It's a woman. Your great-grandmother Ardith
Ware."

"Good Lord. Look at the beak on her."

"I've seen it before—on *you*," she said sweetly,
and turned away.

Nicholas stifled a grin. He doubted she'd look so
pleased with herself if she knew her own nose and
face were smudged almost completely black. She'd
forgotten the makeup she was wearing and kept absently rubbing her nose whenever the rising dust
from the old papers tickled it.

She set Great-grandmother Ardith aside and bent
over to pull out more photographs. He brooded on
how neatly her tail bisected the trim curves of her
bottom in the tight black pants as she rummaged in
the big box.

"And look at this!" she exclaimed, straightening

again. He looked at her vivid face, instead. One of her cat ears was on top of her head; the other dangled forlornly in the curls near her chin. "Here's your family tree! Why, did you know your great-great-aunt Mabel had thirteen children?"

"Great for her," he murmured.

"And your great-uncle Oscar was one of the founders of Cauldron?"

He stifled a yawn.

"And your great-grandfather Paul on your father's side named his children Paul, Paula, Paulette, Polly and Paulsen?" She plunged into another box.

Nick stood up and stretched. Time to get down to the real reason he'd brought her here. He strolled into the bathroom and emerged with a clean wet washcloth in his hand.

She was chortling over a paper she was reading. "Hey, your uncle Carl had a birthmark on his cheek that was the same shape as Texas."

"Don't you make fun of that birthmark. I have one just like it on my butt." He walked over to her.

"I won't ask you to prove that." She glanced up with her arms full of papers, her gaze fastening warily on the washcloth as he came closer. "What do you plan to do with that?"

"Clean you up. You've smeared your makeup all over."

She lifted her hand self-consciously to her cheek. "I can do it."

"I don't mind," he said casually. Before she could protest, he tilted her face up with a finger under her chin. "It won't take a minute."

He reached up and plucked off her cat ears, tucking them in his shirt pocket. With the cloth he slowly traced her snub nose, dabbed carefully along her soft cheeks, then ran the cool cloth under her delicate jaw, leaving her skin gleaming, pale and damp.

He smoothed it along her wide brow, pushing back her dark curls. He paused, fascinated by a tiny pulse beating beneath the delicate skin of her temple.

She fidgeted under his hold. Her long lashes flickered anxiously. "Did I get it up there, too?"

"Yes," he lied absently. He'd discovered another fluttering pulse at the side of her throat. He wanted to place his mouth there, to feel that small pulsating rhythm against his lips and tongue. He wanted to explore her silky body all over, discover other small pulses and tender places and kiss and caress them until she was moaning in his arms, carried away by the same consuming passion he felt whenever he was near her.

He wanted to carry her upstairs to his bed and finish what they'd begun two nights—no, *seven years* ago.

Throwing the cloth aside, he slid his fingers into her hair and held her head still.

Her eyes met his. Nervously she ran her tongue over her dry lips. Distracted by the movement, his gaze fastened on her mouth. He bent to complete the small task for her.

But before he could, she stepped out of his hold and backed toward the bathroom. "I better see that it's all washed off," she said breathlessly.

Reaching the safety of the bathroom, Prudence shut the door and leaned against it, fanning her heated cheeks with one agitated hand. She couldn't trust him for a second! The minute she lowered her guard, there he was—ready to pounce!

Realizing she was still clutching a bunch of photos and papers, she carefully set the pile down by the sink and threw cold water on her face. She looked in the mirror. Her cheeks still looked flushed, her wet lashes spiked around eyes that held an excited glitter.

Stop it! she scolded her reflection. *He's just playing with you. Like Mrs. Watson torturing a bug. Do you want to end up in his bed again?*

No, I don't, she assured herself firmly.

To reinforce the decision, she splashed more water on her face. Gathering up the papers, she marched out with her shoulders squared, braced to repulse any more of his advances.

But he no longer appeared interested in making advances. He was too busy looking at the sketches in her book.

"Hey!" Prudence said indignantly from the doorway.

He glanced up, then ignored her again as he continued to study the drawings as if he had every right to do so. "This one of Jimmy is very good. You should try to sell these."

"They aren't good enough," Prudence said, walking into the room and setting down the photos.

"I don't know. It seems to me you have the knack of catching a person's thoughts through their expression."

Despite hersefl, Prudence felt a small spark of pleasure shoot through her at his words. Drawing was her secret love, her passion, and it scared her how much it meant that he appreciated her work.

He flipped to another page, adding casually, "One of the ad firms we're associated with is always looking for artists. You might consider sending some of your stuff to them.''

''That's in Los Angeles, isn't it?''

When he nodded, she asked, ''But wouldn't I need to live nearby?''

He shook his head. ''I don't see why. You'd have to travel there at times, probably, but that's no big deal.''

Not to him obviously, but then Nicholas didn't have Aunt Heppy in his life to worry about. The only person he needed to be concerned about was himself.

When she didn't answer, he added slowly, ''You know, Pru, you only saw the worst of places when you were a kid. Don't you want to see some of the best? Like Rome? London? Paris?''

How had he guessed that she'd always yearned to see the Louvre, the Sistine Chapel? ''You've been to those places?''

''Lots of times. I often travel to other countries on business.''

Business. Of course, how could she have forgotten? Business was always his first priority.

''No,'' she said coldly, ''I don't want to leave Cauldron.''

For a fleeting second, his mouth twisted wryly, then his expression smoothed out again. He looked back down at the book. ''Of course you don't. And so your talent—not to mention your art degree—is wasted.''

An angry flush heated her cheeks and she stiffened. She opened her mouth to argue, but he raised a placating hand. ''Never mind, forget I said that. I didn't intend to start a fight. If you don't care to sell your work, that's your business. Still, you might at least help Swain with his campaign," he added, studying the portrait of the other man. "This picture isn't the most flattering, but maybe you could do one that he could use on his posters. It would be a much more original idea than the typical head shot he's using now. And who ever came up with that pitiful slogan? 'Edmund Swain, a big man for a small town.'"

No way was she going to tell Nicholas that Edmund had created the phrase. "Thanks for the suggestion," Prudence said frigidly. "But Edmund doesn't like my drawing style. He finds my work a bit too stark...and disturbing." She also wasn't going to tell Nicholas that she'd already tried doing publicity sketches of Edmund. Rather than the charming sweet man she knew him to be, on paper Edmund's eyes always looked crafty, his mouth weak.

Nicholas didn't comment, looking back down at the pad. He turned another page. Suddenly his eyebrows lifted, his eyes widening in surprise. "Now *this* is interesting."

Something in his tone made the hairs on Prudence's nape lift in apprehension. "What is it? What are you looking at?"

She walked slowly to his side. Looking over his shoulder at the paper, her eyes widened in horror. She gasped. Somehow, without thinking, she'd drawn him almost completely nude—like he'd been the other night. Shadows were slanting across his broad shoulders, the strong muscles of his chest were emphasized. She'd even added a flat, masculine nipple and an arrowing of hair that disappeared down— *way* down—into his unzipped pants.

Instinctively her hands flew up to her cover her burning cheeks. "I, uh, didn't realize...I wasn't paying attention...sometimes when my mind wanders..."

"It seems to me you were *definitely* paying attention. Were my pants really hanging that low?" He glanced back at the previous page. "And yet here's Edmund, complete with his little bow tie and all. I wonder what Freud would say about that."

She glanced up and met his gaze. Nick's eyes held that wicked twinkle that so enraged her. His white teeth gleamed in a mocking little smile.

Anger overcame her embarrassment. She grabbed hold of the sketchbook and gave it a tug. "Freud would say you're a nosy busybody, looking through my pictures without asking."

Nicholas tugged back. "Or maybe he'd say that when you aren't consciously thinking about—or denying them—your sexual feelings for me rise to the surface."

"Ha! Only a horny toad like you would interpret it that way. I'm an artist! I sketched nude models all the time when I was in school." She yanked harder.

Nicholas held on. "From memory?" he taunted. "Come on, do one now."

"Give me my book and I will!"

He refused to release it. He pulled the book closer, hauling her along with it until her face was only inches from his own. Their eyes locked and held in silent battle.

Neither blinked. Neither looked away.

Then Prudence licked her lips. Nick's gaze dropped to follow the movement, and with a whoop of triumph she whipped the book out of his slackened grip and skipped away.

Now *her* smile was mocking. She stood there, hugging the book to her chest, the slim tautness of her stance challenging him to come and get her. And Nicholas planned to do just that.

He took a menacing step toward her. She took a provoking step back.

He advanced.

She retreated.

He reached out—

A knock sounded at the door.

Both froze. The knock came again, louder this time. Then the door opened. "Yoohoo! Anyone here?" a feminine voice called. Footsteps clicked their way across the wooden floor to the den. "Oh, hello, Nick. Hello, Pru."

Nick sighed. "Hello, Rhonda."

10

WITHOUT WAITING for an invitation, the redhead strolled past him to perch elegantly on his father's old desk. Prudence had sunk into the armchair, and Rhonda pinned her there with her brown-eyed gaze. "Oh, so you *are* here. I just came by to verify the big news. Hepzibah said you're engaged."

"Yes."

A rather disgruntled expression flitted across Rhonda's face. She added in careless tones, "So where's the happy husband-to-be?"

"Right here," Nicholas said, his dark brows lifting in faint surprise.

Rhonda whirled around, shock widening her eyes. "You? But I thought Edmund..."

Nicholas shrugged. "You know what they say— if you snooze, you lose. Swain should have snatched her up while he still had the chance."

"Yes, it only took you seven years," Prudence couldn't resist pointing out.

He looked at her. "Actually it only took me two months from the time I decided I wanted you again before I had you in my bed."

Prudence's face flamed. Rhonda looked intrigued. She asked, "So are you planning on staying in Cauldron, Nicholas? I heard that you'd purchased some land on the south side of town."

Prudence straightened in her chair. He had? But why would he do that? She glanced at him. He didn't look pleased by Rhonda's question. His dark brows were drawn down over his eyes and his mouth was set in a stern line.

"No, I'm not planning on staying in Cauldron," he said. "And I prefer not to discuss anything else."

His tone was so forbidding that even Rhonda looked daunted for a minute. But ace reporter that she was, she quickly recovered her poise. "Then tell me, when did you two lovebirds realize you were still in love? And what about Edmund? Pretty cold, Prudence, to dump him like that."

Angry at the other woman's tone, Prudence opened her mouth to retort, but before she could, another knock sounded.

Raising his eyebrows in surprise, Nicholas went to open it. Edmund stood on the doorstep. "Come in, Swain," Nicholas said resignedly. "It's turning into quite a party."

He strolled back into the den with Edmund at his heels. Appropriating the arm of Prudence's chair, Nick sat down while Edmund hovered in the doorway. Glancing uncertainly at the two women, Edmund said, "Hello. I hope I'm not interrupting. I just stopped by to—"

"Eddie," Rhonda said, surging toward him, a sympathetic light in her eyes. "How *are* you?"

Edmund blinked. "I'm, er, fine."

Reaching him, Rhonda squeezed his arm—and then forgot to let it go. "How brave you are," she said warmly. Glancing at Prudence and Nick, she lowered her voice. "I know how it is when someone you trust proves unworthy."

Prudence stiffened. Unworthy? Her? She stepped toward Edmund, intending to stand next to him, but Nicholas's arm snuck around her waist, preventing her from moving. He was getting quite good at the gesture, she thought indignantly.

Nicholas said blandly, "Edmund completely understands about Prudence's and my...prior attachment. He's been a real brick throughout all this."

"Oh. Ah, yes." Stepping into his role, Edmund assumed a noble look. "A man has to step aside when he...uh, finds he's...uh, inadvertently blocking the path of true love."

"A brick in the path of true love," Nicholas murmured for Prudence's ears alone.

She glared at him while Rhonda squeezed Edmund's arm again. The redhead even pressed her bosom against it in admiration for his courage. "Oh, Edmund, why are you here?"

The noble look waned a bit. Edmund said, "Mother thought it might be a good idea if I went to the Faire..."

"To be seen mingling with the common man," Nicholas murmured beneath his breath. Prudence elbowed him in the ribs.

"To show that I'm in complete accordance with Pru's engagement and, perhaps, to do a little last-minute campaigning. However, I didn't want to go alone, and I wondered..."

Pausing uncertainly, he glanced at Prudence, but it was Rhonda who responded to the pleading expression on his face.

"I'll go with you, Eddie," she said.

He looked a bit nonplussed, but stammered, "Ah, well, that's great. But I thought perhaps Prudence..."

"Prudence is busy with me right now," Nick said definitely.

She eyed him rebelliously. "I want to go to the Faire. Why don't you wait here and I—"

"If you go, I go," Nick drawled, cutting Prudence off.

Annoyed at the determination in his tone, she opened her mouth to argue only to shut it again as Edmund said, his face lighting up, "That would be great! We'll all go. It will show the people of Cauldron that I support your engagement."

Ignoring the way Nicholas rolled his eyes, Prudence said grudgingly, "Okay, we'll all go."

"Good," Edmund said. Since the decision had been made, he was apparently eager to waste no time implementing it. "We better hurry. It will be dark soon and they'll be closing the booths down."

Edmund and Rhonda headed to the front door. Prudence started to follow when a tug on the back of her pants halted her in her tracks.

"You've forgotten your tail," Nick drawled.

"Oh, I—"

"I'll get it," he said calmly. Before she could protest he slid his long fingers down the back of her pants. Startled, she glanced over her shoulder and he met her eyes guilelessly. "Wouldn't want to accidentally prick you with one of these safety pins."

Prudence's eyes narrowed and she tried to turn. "Maybe I should—"

"Maybe you should just hold still. I've almost got them."

Rhonda and Edmund had paused by the door. Not wanting to draw their attention, Prudence clenched her fists and obediently stood still.

Rhonda shifted impatiently. "We'll meet you there," she finally decided, and went out the door. With an apologetic glance at Prudence, Edmund followed.

"Can't you hurry?" Prudence asked, trying to look over her shoulder.

"Stay still. They've gotten caught," Nicholas answered. She could feel him pulling at the pins, his fingers brushing the bare skin of her lower back. She wasn't quite sure, but it seemed to her he was reaching down farther than was at all necessary. And had he slipped his hand inside her silk panties? When he stroked the curve of her bare bottom, she was sure of it.

She turned to berate him, but he forestalled her by removing his hand and proffering the three pins. "Do you want to keep these?"

His tone was innocent, but his eyes held that devilish twinkle.

"No, thank you," Prudence said frostily, and ignoring his low chuckle, swept past him out the door. Going to the Faire suddenly seemed like the best idea she'd heard all day.

He wouldn't *dare* try anything in such a public place.

Would he?

SHE WANTED to kill him.

Usually Prudence loved the Faire. Like Heppy's pre-Halloween party, the Autumn Town Faire and the bonfire that followed it were annual traditions in Cauldron. Every Halloween, sawdust was scattered in the old maple grove located at the south end of town, and tents and booths were erected. Over the years the Faire had evolved into a fund-raising event for Cauldron High School and the bonfire served as a football rally. Sometimes rain canceled the events, but this year, even the weather was cooperating. Overhead, a frisky breeze herded fluffy, fleecy-white clouds across the clear blue sky, then swept down to rustle among the trees, fluttering the red, gold and orange maple leaves like tiny medieval banners. The sides of the white canvas booths heaved softly in the playful wind, disgorging a steady stream of sauntering teenagers and giggling children, who weaved among the adults sampling the wares at each booth.

Prudence usually reveled in the fun and excitement everyone was having. She usually enjoyed talking and laughing with neighbors and friends. But usually she attended the Faire alone—she wasn't attached by a steely arm around her waist to a man who seemed intent on glad-handing and backslapping every passerby in sight.

While Rhonda and Edmund trailed behind, Nicholas—the aloof, the non-joiner, the loner—treated everyone he met like a long-lost friend and raved on and on about Prudence's and his "renewed" engagement.

"Hello, Joe! How're the kids? Say, you've heard, haven't you?" *Big smile.* "Prudence and I are engaged again!"

"What could I do, Frank?" *Solemn look of concern.* "I knew my little cupcake was melting away, waiting for me to come back and do the right thing."

"What's that, Tim? When's the wedding? Prudence is thinking Thanksgiving, aren't you, muffin-face?" *Tender smile. Squeeze and wink.* "She's just so *thankful* I came back..."

Like she'd welcome back the plague, Prudence thought sourly. With all the talking he was doing, you'd think Nick, not Edmund, was the one who was running for office!

Edmund, of course, was gallantly doing his part, smiling bravely despite all the knowing looks cast his way. Managing to get him alone for a few seconds, she whispered, "Edmund, help me. I can't do this any longer."

Edmund looked surprised. "Why not?"

"Haven't you been watching? Haven't you noticed him pawing me?"

With a patronizing air that annoyed Prudence almost as much as all the "muffins," "cupcakes," and "cream puffs" Nicholas kept throwing around, Edmund replied, "He just has his arm around your waist. C'mon, it's only for a few more days."

More days of hell, Prudence thought, as a narrow-eyed Nicholas came up to end their tête-à-tête. Edmund, with Rhonda attached to his arm, wandered off, too busy spouting his campaign spiel to pay much attention to Prudence. Which left her completely at the devil's mercy.

She knew he was only calling her all those nauseating endearments in revenge for her insistence on attending the Faire. She also knew *Nick* knew they were grating on her like a fingernail scratching a chalkboard. All that talk of pastry was also making her hungry. With faint surprise, Prudence realized she hadn't eaten since breakfast.

In an effort to remedy the problem—and escape Nick's annoying presence—Pru slipped away over to the food booth, the high school's biggest money-maker, while Nicholas was deep in conversation with

Michael O'Sullivan. She stared down at the "souling bread" Heppy had donated to the booth. Her aunt's contribution was unmistakable. The loaves consisted of two long braided strips, and in remembrance of Aunt Barbara—whose recipe she used—Heppy always added currant eyes and a parsley tongue to each strip, so the loaves resembled two entwined snakes. Prudence thought how nice it would be to stuff one of the warm yeasty loaves in Nicholas's mouth. Maybe then he would stop talking.

"Oh, there you are, pumpkin puss. What are you looking at? Oh, hey, that's Heppy's bread, isn't it?" Nicholas said, coming up behind her and following her gaze. "Do you want some?" He reached for his wallet. "We can share it—"

"No," she said automatically. Not only did she enjoy saying no to him, she was afraid she wouldn't be able to resist the temptation to try to choke him with it. *Pumpkin puss, indeed.* "I'm in no mood for *snakes.*"

Then, noticing that Edmund and Rhonda had strolled up to join them, she added in a sweeter tone, "I'd rather have a piece of Heppy's pie."

The Cauldron High School cheerleader manning the booth cut a piece and handed it to Nicholas on a napkin—plates and forks were considered a frivolity at the Faire. As the teenager absently brushed a few crumbs from her orange and black uniform, Prudence noticed the emblem of the little brown animal on the front of the girl's sweater.

Nicholas must have notice the gopher, too, because he said, "Hmm. Maybe Heppy should make the bread in the shape of a gopher next year."

Prudence shook her head. "The latest rendering of

the school mascot looks more like a beaver than a gopher.''

She immediately wished she hadn't made the remark. The school mascot—the gopher—had been a source of heated debate in the town for years. Some clung to the animal for tradition's sake; others clamored for a more fearsome creature to inspire the school teams to victory.

Rhonda shared the latter opinion. She immediately snorted. ''I think so, too. It's too bad it isn't—even a beaver would be better than a gopher.''

Next to her Edmund stiffened. ''The gopher is a hardworking *noble* animal,'' he declared. ''Look at the way it burrows into the ground, creating hundreds of tunnels.''

Rhonda rolled her eyes. ''Come on, Eddie. The only reason you're defending the stupid thing is because your grandfather chose it as a mascot.''

Edmund stiffened even more. ''He suggested it, but the decision was made by the entire schoolboard.''

''And the entire schoolboard voted for it because he donated enough money to build a gym.''

''I don't appreciate you disparaging my grandfather. In fact, I think the motto he created, Gopher It, is actually quite clever.''

Rhonda made a scoffing sound. ''Even a mole would have been a better mascot. At least they're survivors. Half the time around here the gophers get flooded out because of the rain.''

Rhonda did have a point, Pru conceded, although she never would have said so in front of Edmund.

''You know,'' Nicholas whispered in her ear, ''I

never noticed before, but Swain sort of looks like a gopher.''

Prudence glared at him and opened her mouth to protest. But before she could, Nicholas nudged the piece of pie between her lips.

"Take a bite," he ordered. He'd obviously discovered he liked giving her orders as much as she liked telling him no.

She sent him a mutinous look, but obeyed and chewed slowly, savoring the sweet buttery taste of the fruit and crust. In spite of herself, Prudence felt a surge of pleasure as he fed her another bite. She'd really been hungry.

She was still chewing when Nick clamped his hand around her wrist and began towing her toward another booth. Trying to chew and walk, Prudence glanced at the sign hanging above it and tried to dig in her heels.

"Ooooh," Rhonda squealed from behind them. "The matchmaking booth. I want to try this, don't you, Prudence?"

Her mouth full of pie, Prudence tried to sputter a denial but started choking on a crumb. By the time she quit coughing—and Nick quit pounding her on the back—Janet Sanderson, who was sitting in front of the booth, had noticed them and looked up with a hopeful smile.

Usually Heppy presided over the divination, or matchmaking, booth, but this year she'd conceded the position to Janet. Janet and her husband, Virgil, were new in Cauldron, and although their children were all grown, Janet had accepted the job of Cauldron High PTA president when no one else stepped forward. "Since Janet has taken on the job of trying to civilize the teenagers in this town, she should at least have a little fun playing head gypsy,'' Heppy had said.

And Janet did appear to have thrown herself into the role. She wore a white off-the-shoulder peasant blouse and a bright pink-and-orange skirt. A huge fake emerald hung around her neck and a colorful bandana was tied turban-style around her curly brown hair. Gold rings dangled from her ears and circled every finger.

"Come closer," she intoned in a deepened voice as the four approached the table where she was sitting. "Call upon the spirits to help you discover your future husband—or wife," she added, glancing at the two men. Resuming her funereal tones, she went on, "Choose the method of prophecy you prefer—nuts, apple, seeds or bowl—to illuminate your future."

"Hi, Janet," Nicholas said, dragging Prudence up beside him. "How's business?"

"A little slow," the woman admitted in her normal voice, which held the hint of a Midwest accent. "Most of the high-school kids have been by already."

"Where's Virgil?"

"In the tent, covering the divining bowls." Janet studied their faces expectantly. "So what are you going to try?"

"Not the nuts," Rhonda said. "They take too long."

Prudence agreed. She didn't want to try anything. Besides, naming nuts after potential suitors—and placing them on a hot grate to see if they "burned with passion" or "popped," indicating unfaithful-

ness—had Freudian overtones that made her uncomfortable.

"What about the seed method?" Janet asked. "All
you have to do is name some seeds after men you
know, spit on them—the seeds that is, not the men—
and stick them on your face. The one that stays there
longest is the one you'll marry."

Prudence wrinkled her nose.

"Oh, yuck." Rhonda said.

"Ah, come on," Nicholas urged Prudence. "I'll
help you spit on them—the seeds, that is."

"No, thank you."

"I'll peel an apple," Rhonda decided.

"Fine. Apples it is," Janet said. "That will be a
dollar."

Edmund's jaw dropped. "A dollar?"

Rhonda elbowed him in the ribs and he shut his
mouth. "It's for the school, Eddie, our alma mater.
Give her the money."

He grumbled a little as he fished in his pocket and
Janet fixed her eyes on him disapprovingly. Then
Rhonda chose an apple from the bowl in front of
Janet and picked up a small paring knife. The process
was actually very simple. Any woman desiring to
discover her future husband pared her apple in a long
continuous peel which she then twirled over her head
and tossed behind her. The initial the peel formed on
the ground was supposedly that of her future husband.

Rhonda finished her peeling. "I'm done," she
said, setting down the knife. "What is it I'm supposed to say?"

Janet resumed her hollow monotone. "'I pare this
pippin round and round,/ My lover's name to appear

on the ground,/ I fling the coil over my head,/ So my lover's letter can be read.' ''

Obediently Rhonda repeated the chant, twirling the peel carefully three times over her head before releasing it. It landed a few feet behind her in the sawdust, and the four, along with Janet and couple of giggling little girls, crowded around to study the paring.

"I do believe it's a *w*," Prudence said with a sly glance at Nicholas.

"You're looking at it sideways. It's an *e*," he replied.

Edmund seemed disposed to argue. "I don't know how you can say—"

"Try…it…again," Janet intoned.

Reluctantly Edmund again set a dollar on the table.

"It's two dollars for the second try," Janet said brightly.

"What! But that's—"

"It's for the school, Eddie," Rhonda reminded him in a steely voice.

A sulky expression on his face, Edmund plunked down another dollar.

Rhonda peeled expertly, twirled and rhymed, and released her apple skin.

They crowded around. Edmund said tentatively, "A backwards *n?*"

"It's an *s*," Rhonda said.

Her tone brooked no argument. Picking up the peel as warily as if it were a snake, Edmund dropped it in a nearby trash can.

Rhonda attached herself once again to his arm. "Your turn," she said to Prudence.

"I don't want to try it."

"Why not?" Nicholas asked.

Because for the past seven years the peel had formed an *n,* Prudence thought. And wouldn't he be delighted to hear that. "I just don't want to."

"You're the one who insisted on coming to the Faire," Nick said. "The least you can do is join in."

"C'mon," Janet urged her. "It's fun."

Pru hesitated, but everyone was waiting expectantly. Unable to resist Janet's hopeful gaze—and Nick's demanding one—she mumbled, "Okay, I'll do it."

Nicholas opened his wallet without comment and Janet gave him a big smile.

Prudence grumbled, "You're wasting a dollar."

"A dollar to find you a husband is money well spent," he replied.

Feeling foolish, Prudence picked up an apple and peeled it. Throwing down the knife, she quickly mumbled the chant, circled the apple skin over her head and let it go.

"I think it's a flower," said one of the little girls, squatting next to it.

Prudence leaned over her to get a better look. Sure enough, the peel had landed in a big looping circle. It looked like one of Aunt Barbara's smaller snakes, sunning in the dirt. "An *o?*" she said doubtfully.

"More like a zero," Nicholas said, straight-faced. She glanced at him and he added, "Maybe it means you won't have a husband. Or that he isn't worth much." He sent a significant glance in Edmund's direction.

Prudence clenched her fists. "If that's supposed to be funny…"

He lifted his brows. "Did it sound humorous?"

"It sounded like you're making fun of my future husband."

"Who is?"

"Try…it…again," Janet intoned.

Familiar with the drill, Nicholas plunked down another two dollars. But Prudence was too incensed to take the time to peel another apple. She salvaged the first peel off the ground, gingerly trying to shake off the worst of the sawdust clinging to its sticky length. Grimly she began circling it over her head, shutting her eyes to concentrate and biting out the rhyme.

"…'So my lover's letter can be *read*,'" she chanted, releasing the peel on the final word.

"Oh, my God," gasped Rhonda.

Something in the other woman's voice caused Prudence's muscles to tighten in apprehension. What had the peel predicted? Was it an *e?* Or…an *n?*

Opening her eyes, she slowly looked around.

Mrs. Swain stood about ten feet behind her with Mrs. Watson by her side. The peel had caught on Mrs. Swain's high prim bun and dangled rakishly over her eyes.

Pru's eyes widened in horror. Rhonda's narrowed in satisfaction. Nicholas covered his mouth, coughing to hide a laugh.

Edmund, however, stepped bravely forward. "Hello, Mother, Mrs. Watson," he said. "I believe Mother, you have, er…intercepted Prudence's peel."

His mother didn't answer. Mrs. Watson rewarded him with a look of loathing. Reaching up to her bun, Mrs. Swain pulled off the apple peel and with a contemptuous gesture tossed it over her shoulder.

The little girls scampered after it.

The two older women had turned to march on

when one of the girls said with awe in her voice, "Look at that, Nikki. It broke and made a perfect *m, o* and *s.*"

"It sure did, Danielle," her friend answered.

"Michael…O'…Sullivan," Janet intoned.

Mrs. Swain's step faltered. She hesitated. She turned around. "It's a shame to litter," she said haughtily. Walking back to the broken apple skins, she bent down and studied them. A pleased smile flitted across her thin lips, then she picked the peels up and dropped them in the trash. With a nod to her friend, the two continued regally on their way.

Remembering the gossip about Mrs. Watson's pursuit of Michael, Pru's mouth twitched. She glanced at Edmund, but he was frowning, counting the money in his wallet. As she turned away, her gaze met Nick's. His eyes were gleaming with amusement, and before she could prevent it, Prudence smiled.

His white teeth flashed in response. "Going to try again?" he asked.

"I don't think so," Pru replied.

"It's the men's turn," Rhonda decreed.

"But I don't know how to peel an apple," Edmund protested. "I'll probably just cut myself."

Rhonda sighed. "You have to do the bowl method, silly. That's the one the men use."

She gave him a small push toward the tent. Janet obligingly lifted the flap and the four ducked inside. Filtered through the thick canvas, the light inside the tent was murky white and thick, reminding Prudence of being underwater.

Virgil, Janet's husband, stood in one shadowy corner. Dressed as a gypsy king in a bright red shirt, the violin he was holding imbued the simple outfit with a sense of authenticity.

Everyone gathered around the small table in the middle of the tent. On the table were three bowls—red, yellow and blue—each covered with a pristine white linen napkin.

Virgil drew his bow across his violin. Silvery notes hung in the white light. "Greetings, seekers of the truth," Virgil said, his rich voice making the words ring.

He worked the bow again. More crystal notes glistened, the sweet sound mingling with his voice. "Choose the bowl that will indicate your future mate," Virgil chanted softly. "Clear water in the bowl means your wife will be as pure as the snow-filled stream above the mountain. If the water is muddy, then a more...experienced woman will be your bride. But if the bowl you choose is empty, then your future will be equally so. Your days will be filled with sorrow. Never will you have a warm and willing woman to fill your bed...."

His voice trailed off, but the music lingered, dancing in the air. The apparently random notes had a haunting, almost hypnotic, quality. Prudence felt a little sleepy. Tension eased out of her, and she leaned back against Nicholas, unconsciously relying on his warm strength to hold her up. He wrapped his arms around her waist and pulled her securely against him.

Rhonda's brown eyes were wide and glittering with excitement. She clutched at Edmund's arm. "Come on, Eddie. Try it."

"Okay." Edmund reached for his wallet as the notes twinkled on. He pulled out a dollar.

The music stopped abruptly.

"Five dollars," Virgil said.

Edmund's eyes bugged out. *"Five dollars!"*

The notes danced in the air again.

"Damn," Edmund said. He plunked down a five.

The notes chased each other gaily as Edmund stepped toward the table. He studied the bowls intently. He reached out for the blue bowl, hesitated, and then pulled the napkin off the yellow one.

The water was a muddy brown.

The notes faded away. Silence filled the tent. Prudence blinked and straightened. Feeling as if she'd just awakened, she moved away from Nicholas's arms.

Edmund seemed to shake himself as if coming out of a trance. He stared at the dirty water in bewilderment, saying, "But this can't be…it *can't* be right."

The fierce excitement faded from Rhonda's face.

"The bowl never lies," Virgil intoned.

Edmund looked up. "But I would never marry a woman who was…impure."

"Impure! You…you *idiot,* you!" Rhonda burst out.

Startled, Prudence glanced over at the redhead. Rhonda stood with her hands clenched into fists, her eyes blazing as she looked at Edmund.

"Who are you to judge if a person is pure or not?" Rhonda demanded. "Just because a woman has had a relationship or two doesn't mean she isn't worth marrying."

Edmund stammered, "But…but, Rhonda—"

"But nothing," Rhonda said. She picked up the bowl full of muddy water. "It's what's in a person's heart that matters, you sanctimonious jerk!"

The gypsy king saw what was coming sooner than Edmund did. Adroitly Virgil moved away, leaving Edmund alone to receive the muddy water—directly in his face.

Edmund gasped, staggering backward, arms wind-milling wildly. He landed on his rear, knocking the table with his head.

Bowls jiggled, bounced and tipped. Clear water from the blue bowl spilled across the table and down the front of his pants. He gasped at the fresh shock. "Oh, my… But, Rhonda!"

But Rhonda didn't hear him—she'd run out of the tent. Dirty water dripping down his face, Edmund struggled to his feet and followed.

The flap closed behind him. Again silence filled the tent. The others remained frozen, standing amidst the wet sawdust, broken bowls and overturned table.

Then Virgil drew his bow again. Notes quivered beguilingly. "Would you like to try?" he asked Nicholas.

"I don't think so," Nick said.

11

THEY EMERGED from the tent to find that Edmund and Rhonda had disappeared.

"Where could they be?" Pru asked. She rubbed her arms, feeling cold and still shaken by Rhonda's actions. "Don't you think we should go find them? Rhonda seemed very upset."

The shadows were lengthening now and she wrapped her arms around herself, shivering a little at the increased chill in the air. The playful breeze had become more earnest, making the maples trees shiver and shake.

Janet had begun packing up her apples, while Virgil dumped the extra nuts into the cash box. Vendors at the other booths were closing up, too.

Nicholas shrugged, glancing around at the thinning crowd. "They probably went up the hill—like everyone else." Wrapping a hand around her nape, he urged her to join the general exodus heading toward Spook's Hill. "Let's go check at the bonfire."

Like most of the Faire goers, Nick had parked in the dirt field at the bottom of the hill. As they passed his car, he paused to retrieve two woolen blankets, a thermos and a thick hooded black sweatshirt.

"You use it," Prudence said when he held the sweatshirt out to her.

"I'm not cold. You are," he answered, and despite

her protests, bundled her up. He zipped the jacket up, lifting her chin and even tucked her hair carefully under the hood.

The small task completed, he took her hand again and set off up the hill. The sweatshirt fell well below Prudence's knees. She probably looked like a gnome, she thought, as she trudged beside him. A gnome with a pointed head who was already huffing and puffing.

Spook's Hill wasn't especially high; the walk to the top was just under a mile. But the incline was steep enough for her to feel the pull on the backs of her calves and to be grateful for the strong grasp of Nicholas's hand tugging her along.

She didn't see Edmund and Rhonda anywhere among the teenagers and adults grouped on top of the hill's bald pate. Traditionally children didn't attend the bonfire. Not only was the climb a bit hard on little legs, but on this night the town's younger citizens were too busy trick-or-treating or handing out candy to gather around a fire. Since most parents remained in town with their offspring, the bonfire had evolved into something of a singles event, with enough childless young couples attending to add variety.

The fire itself was always built directly on the bare summit and was visible from the town below. Woods covered one side of the hill, and an old graveyard sloped down the other. The cemetery was small, not even a tenth as large as the newer one at the other side of town, but this one had the distinction of serving as the final resting place of the town's founders. Aunt Barbara was the last resident to be buried there, more than fifty years ago.

Most of the couples had placed their blankets on the tree side of the hill, but Nicholas headed in the opposite direction. It had been seven years since he'd last attended a Cauldron bonfire, but without a word he led Prudence to "their" spot—a shallow hollow right behind Aunt Barbara's pink marble headstone.

When she saw where he was headed, Prudence slowed her steps. "I doubt Edmund and Rhonda are over here. Don't you want to get closer to the fire?"

"No. I'm tired of crowds."

"But what about Edmund and Rhonda?"

"If they're up here, they'll know this is where to find us. Everyone in town knows this is where we always used to sit, and this is where we're going to sit tonight."

His tone told her he wasn't going to change his mind, and aware of the people walking past who could possibly overhear, Prudence quit arguing. He'd find out he wasn't going to have everything his way.

While Nicholas spread out one of the blankets, she walked around to the front of the grave and pressed her palm against the polished tombstone. The marble still felt warm from the sun's heat, and seemed to glow faintly pink in the gathering dusk. The darkness was too thick now to read the inscription engraved there, but Prudence didn't need light to know what the epitaph said. She repeated softly, "'Here lies Barbara McClure, beloved aunt and friend, who died young at heart at the age of 103.'"

Crouched down beside the blanket, Nicholas glanced up at her. "I'd always thought she sounded a lot like Heppy."

Prudence nodded. "Me, too. I wish I could have known her. She took Heppy and my father in, you know, when my grandparents died. Just like Heppy did with me.''

A small snake was etched at the top edge of the marble. Watching as she ran her slender finger along its curving length, Nicholas asked, ''Why was she so fond of snakes?''

Prudence smiled. ''Heppy says it was because Aunt Barbara loved Ireland so much she couldn't help but pity any creature banished from its shores.''

She dropped her hand and scanned the shadowy ground, adding half seriously, ''But I hope none are lingering nearby. I certainly don't share her fondness.''

Sitting down on the blanket, Nick held out his arms to her. ''I'll keep you safe.''

Sure he would. ''It's not the snakes in the *grass* I'm most worried about.''

''Come on,'' he coaxed. ''What are you afraid of? It's not like we're alone out here.''

That was true. Only thirty feet away, other people milled around the growing bonfire. The football team was in charge of feeding the voracious flame, and the husky teenagers took the job seriously, throwing log after log into its smoldering jowls.

Still, Nicholas and she hadn't been alone out here seven years ago, either, and yet the intimacies they'd shared then were as clear in Prudence's mind and heart as if they'd happened yesterday.

But she'd been young then, and convinced they were in love. This sham engagement wasn't the same at all. To prove the point, at least to herself, she walked over and sat down—a good two feet from him.

He chuckled a little, the sound deepening as he

reached across her to pick up the thermos and she jumped. "Relax. I'm not one of Heppy's snakes—I won't sneak up on you. You'll be able to see me coming."

Using the lid for a cup, he poured some coffee. He took a drink, then handed it to her. "Here, have some. It'll warm you up."

Prudence accepted the cup, welcoming the warmth of the cup against her chilled fingers. She looked toward the bonfire. Rhonda and Edmund were still nowhere in sight. The fire was growing brighter and brighter as the evening light waned. Most of the couples had settled now, some near the fire, others—like Nicholas—outside the warm circle of light. The cheerleaders were gathering in a group, getting ready to perform.

She watched the activity, unwillingly aware that Nicholas was watching her. She gave him a discreet sidelong glance. Sure enough, those golden eyes were fixed on her as he sprawled lazily against the headstone.

Trying to distract herself from his intent perusal, Prudence took a sip from the cup in her hands. The coffee tasted creamy and nutty, with an added flavor she couldn't identify. The warm liquid slid down her throat, settling with a heated glow in her tummy.

She drank some more, saying between sips, "This is really good. What did you put in it? It tastes a little different."

She took another sample.

He shrugged. "I don't know. Rhonda brought it with her. She said Heppy gave it to her to give to me."

Prudence choked, spewing out liquid as she

lurched forward. She coughed, trying to catch her breath, and Nicholas reached over to pat her on the back.

"Don't drink any more," she gasped as soon as she was able.

He paused in his gentle pounding. "Why not?"

"I, uh, think it's gone bad—the cream, that is. Yuck, nothing worse than soured cream."

While he watched with interest, she crawled to the edge of the blanket and emptied the cup and thermos into the grass, shaking them a little to make sure all the liquid was gone.

Then she crawled back to him. This time he didn't let her settle primly beside him but pulled her back against his chest, wrapping his arms firmly around her.

"Nick!" she protested, trying to squirm away. "I don't need to sit this close to you."

He held her tight. "Yes, you do. People are watching and we're supposed to be engaged. Besides, I'm cold and I need you to keep me warm."

The night air *was* getting chillier. She was cold, too. "Okay," she said grudgingly. "Just behave yourself."

He widened his eyes in innocent amazement. "Don't I always?" he asked, and immediately pulled her even closer.

She knew she should protest some more, but was too relieved at having averted a possible disaster to want to start another argument. She leaned her head on his shoulder, watching the bonfire leap in the darkness, contentment seeping through her at the feeling of his arms linked across her stomach. Thank goodness she'd found out in time that Heppy had made that coffee. She wouldn't put it past her aunt to try to slip another love potion into the brew.

Nicholas shifted, leaning forward with her to wrap the second blanket around them. Prudence was faintly amazed that he was still cold. His body seemed to radiate heat. It seared through her clothes—even the thick sweatshirt—keeping her so warm she didn't even protest when he tugged down the hood of her sweatshirt to rest his chin on her hair as he settled back again.

She hated to admit it, but she'd enjoyed the day— some of it, at least. She'd forgotten how much fun Nicholas could be, even when he was annoying the hell out of her. And now, resting against him like this, she felt safe and warm.

More logs were sacrificed to the blaze. The flames leaped higher, reaching toward the full moon. The breeze captured the rising sparks and sent them spiraling upward like a small, transient flurry of shooting stars. Back lit by the bright blaze, the cheerleaders' lithe figures were flattened to dark silhouettes. They pranced against the light, exhorting the mighty gopher to "go, go, go!" in an unconscious imitation of those primitive people in faraway lands who had once danced and chanted to distant gods in savage celebration of the pagan new year.

The cheers and laughter around the fire grew ever louder, while the silent stillness in Nicholas and Prudence's small hollow deepened. On this side of the hill it was shadowy and still. The wind that rustled noisily through the trees on the far side of the circle, glided silently here between the stolid stones.

The chilly breeze blew a strand of Pru's hair against her mouth, and she lifted her hand from the blanket's warmth to push it away, then snuggled back under the cover again. Her cheeks and nose were cold, but inside their blanket cocoon it was nice and cozy with Nick's hard chest supporting her, and his long legs bracketing hers on either side.

Through lowered lashes she watched the bonfire. The half circle of tombstones nearby seemed to be watching, too, the cold slabs tilting toward the flames as if seeking their fluid heat.

The darkness grew deeper, more intimate, more intense. Pru stared at the flickering light on the hill, her mind drifting between the present and a similar night seven years ago, when she and Nicholas had held hands and climbed to this same spot. She'd been happy and excited nestled next to him watching the celebration. She'd felt entranced by the sparkling night, the dancing flames and, most of all, his warm hand gently, tentatively sliding beneath the blanket, beneath her shirt, to cup her breast over her bra.

She'd been alarmed by his gesture—never before had he attempted such an intimacy. But he'd soothed her faint distress with adoring kisses scattered along her cheek to her lips. For a while, she'd succumbed to his caresses, but fright had overcome desire when his hand had stroked down over her stomach to the waistband of her pants. Breaking away from his embrace, she'd hurried down the hill with him not far behind.

He'd never touched her like that again; only two days later they'd broken up. But the memory of his touch had remained like a brand on her heart, marking her clearly and distinctly forever his.

She stirred a little, trying to push away the disturbing thought, and his arm tightened around her.

She settled back against him with a faint sigh. She was positive now that Heppy had put a potion in the coffee. She was also sure she'd drunk too much of it. She felt drugged by the sandpapery rasp of his chin against her temple, the slow rise and fall of his chest, the heavy warmth of his arms linked across her stomach.

Every slight movement he made, every breath he took, was imprinted so distinctly on her heightened senses that when he slowly turned her in his arms, she felt as if she'd willed the action, so intensely had she yearned for it.

She lay sideways across his lap, with one of his arms supporting her back while his other hand tilted her face up to his. Her eyes fluttered shut as his warm lips roved across her skin, dropping soft kisses on her cheeks, brow and eyelids.

Then his mouth closed over hers, and she reached her arms up to encircle his neck, clinging to him in convulsive response to the sweet intimacy of his tongue stroking hers. He tasted like Heppy's coffee, dangerous and enticing. His kiss deepened and she trembled in response, her hands sliding into his hair in her effort to draw him closer.

In a move worthy of the mighty gopher, his hand burrowed beneath the blanket and beneath her clothes, searching for bare skin. His fingers slid over her ribs and Prudence shivered with delight. He reached higher, cupping her breast beneath her bra.

His hand felt hot against her skin. Prudence stirred, aware that she should protest the intimacy but unable to resist the aching pleasure of his thumb brushing her peaked nipple. She'd missed his touch. She'd yearned for it. They were pretending to be engaged, after all, she thought hazily. She'd simply pretend his hand wasn't there.

But that proved impossible. She moaned against his mouth, her body quivering, instinctively seeking more of his tantalizing caresses. She shivered in the enveloping darkness. The heat he was generating with his mouth and hands was seeping into her, trailing through her veins and leaving her body pliant and liquid.

His hand exploring her beneath the blankets was like a secret. No one but she and Nicholas knew that he was gently circling her nipple with his finger, coaxing the peak to tighten even more. When he tugged gently on it with his finger and thumb, her stomach dropped, then clenched in fierce excitement, the feeling echoed between her thighs.

So enthralled was she by his deep searching kisses and enticing caresses it was a shock when he suddenly lifted his mouth from hers and removed his hand from her breast.

Prudence blinked, becoming aware that her lips were swollen and sensitive, that her breath was coming in little gasps. She looked at Nick's face above her. His features were bronzed, gilded by the firelight to a pagan cast. He was breathing hard, too, she realized, but his gaze was fixed on the small knot of people heading past them on their way down the hill.

With easy strength he rose and helped her up beside him, holding her steady until her shaky legs supported her again.

Feeling as if she'd just awakened, Prudence glanced about, clutching the blanket around her shoulders. She trembled in the cold. The bonfire was dying; everyone was leaving. Nicholas gathered up the thermos and the other blanket, and they joined the procession walking down the hill.

He didn't say a word and Prudence remained silent also, unsure what to say. Even when they reached the car, neither had spoken and the silence thickened as they drove home. Prudence's mind whirled with conjecture. What was he thinking? His mouth was set in a rather stern line. His dark hair was tousled. His gaze met hers fleetingly and she shivered a little at the desire she saw in his eyes.

They were nearing her house, and her pulse beat faster in anticipation. No doubt he'd try to take advantage of the situation, the closeness they were both feeling after the intimacy they'd shared by the bonfire. He'd probably try coaxing her into finishing what they had started.

She wouldn't, she thought resolutely, although her pulse raced at the thought. If he imagined this engagement was more than a simple pretense, he had another think coming!

True, she'd teased and flirted and cuddled with him all evening, but that was just to keep up appearances. And so, as soon as he made his move, she would let him know.

He stopped the car and opened her door. Silently they walked up to the porch. She turned to face him, glancing up at him beneath lowered lashes. His eyes held a restless hunger as they roved over her face. His skin seemed to be pulled more tautly over his high cheekbones. Her mouth grew dry in anticipation. She ran her tongue across her lips and lifted her face to his.

He stared down at her. Her eyelids drifted half-closed. His mouth was lowering to hers when from inside the house a sweet, if slightly off-key, soprano suddenly warbled in air. Heppy, Prudence realized hazily.

Nick's hands tightened on her shoulders, then just as quickly released her. "Good night, Prudence," he said, his tone edged with frustration. "I'll talk to you tomorrow."

In the next second he'd opened the front door and thrust her inside. The door shut in her face.

12

PRU BLINKED. Well! So he wasn't going to make a pass. Obviously all the teasing and flirting and cuddling he had done this evening had only been for appearances, too. She was very glad to know it; very glad, indeed.

Her gladness caused her to stomp into the kitchen. She needed a drink.

Heppy was there and looked up with a welcoming smile. "Hello, dear! How was your evening?"

"Fine. Just great." Prudence walked over to the refrigerator and grasped the handle. Maybe she'd gotten a little carried away, but she was certain that was because of… Memory pricked and she paused, giving her aunt a considering look. "By the way, about that coffee you gave Nicholas…"

"Yes, dear?"

"Did you add anything to it?"

"Of course."

"Aha. I thought so." Prudence's eyes narrowed in satisfaction. "What did you put in it?"

"A half teaspoon of vanilla."

"Vanilla?" Prudence repeated blankly. "Is that all?"

Heppy nodded and Prudence frowned, her disgruntlement returning. She just wished she'd had a chance to tell Nicholas that she'd only let him kiss

her and touch her breasts for Edmund's sake. She
opened the refrigerator door and peered inside. An
old bottle of champagne was on one shelf, a pitcher
of Heppy's cider on another. No way was she going
to touch either of those. A soothing glass of hot
milk—that was the answer. Pulling out the milk car-
ton, she slammed the door shut and reached into the
cupboard for a glass.

Her fingers closed around the snake glass, and she
changed her mind. Forget hot milk; she needed it
cold to quench the unfulfilled anticipation still simmering inside her. After filling up the goblet, she
downed a slug. There. That was a little better.

Sighing, she wiped the excess milk from her lips
with the back of her hand. "I thought we might see
you at the bonfire," she said to Heppy.

"The trick-or-treaters kept me too busy," her aunt
replied. "Also, Kristie was having a few labor pains,
so I thought I'd stick around in case Tim had to rush
her to the hospital and I'd have to baby-sit little
Timmy."

Prudence's eyebrows arched when she noticed
Heppy had a knife in her hands. A plump pumpkin
squatted in front of her on newspapers spread across
the kitchen table. Judging by the scraggly-toothed
face penciled on one side, the squash was obviously
destined for sacrifice.

"Isn't it a little late to be carving a pumpkin?"
Prudence asked.

"Not at all."

"But all the trick-or-treaters must be in bed by
now—or out tipping over trash cans."

Heppy gave her a reproving look. "Children aren't
the only ones out on Halloween night, you know.

This is the evening of lost souls, when spirits are abroad seeking repose. This jack-o'-lantern I'm making will scare the unwanted ones away.''

"They're all unwanted in my opinion," Prudence said, taking another drink. She added curiously, "You don't really believe in all those superstitions, do you?"

Heppy wielded her knife, plunging it into the top of the squash. "Oh, I don't know…it seems to me loneliness ails so many of the living, why not the dead?" The knife rose and fell as she hacked a small circle around the stem. "What about you, dear? Didn't you or your friends try any fortune-telling at the Faire?"

Pru wrinkled her nose. "Of course we did, but that was just for fun. If I believed in it, I'd really be in trouble. Edmund spilled his bowl of 'divining' water, and when I threw an apple peel over my shoulder, it didn't look like an *n* at all. Just a big fat zero."

Heppy looked up from her hacking. "An *n,* dear? Don't you mean an *e*—for Edmund?"

"No, I— Yes, of course I do!" A flush warmed Pru's cheeks and she took another sip of milk to cover her reaction. "I simply meant it didn't resemble any letters in the alphabet. We didn't even bother to try the 'know-it-all' nuts."

"I think that was wise, dear." Setting down her knife, Heppy grasped the stem and yanked on it. The top came off with a faint sucking sound, strewing gooey strings of orange pulp everywhere. Heppy put down Jack's "hat." Picking up a spoon, she began to scrape happily away at the pumpkin's innards, adding, "Those methods really aren't the most reliable. It's usually better to seek the truth—especially about love—from inside yourself. Now there's one method that I've heard is almost infallible.''

Orange gore plopped on the papers.

"You swallow a thimbleful of salt before going to sleep, and in your dreams, your future husband will bring you a drink to ease your thirst. If the cup he carries is made of gold, it means he'll be rich. Silver means he'll have average wealth, and if the cup is clay, he'll be a poor man.''

Thirsty just at the thought of all that salt, Pru took another healthy swallow of her milk. "What if he's holding a clear glass?''

Heppy frowned. "Oh, dear. That would be a problem, wouldn't it? Well, maybe you should try the yarn method, instead. You take some yarn and you walk around the house while winding it into a ball, saying, 'Whoever will my husband be,/ come wind this ball of yarn with me.' Aunt Barbara tried that one once.''

"It couldn't have worked. You told me she never married.''

"You're right, it didn't. The old barn cat came up and tugged on it, which gave her hope, but she said even if the cat had turned out to be a man in disguise, she wouldn't have married him. He'd been neutered.''

"A definite disadvantage in a husband," Pru conceded, rinsing out her glass. The little snake-worm seemed to grin at her as she set the goblet on the shelf. "Besides which, we don't have any yarn.''

"How true. Why didn't I ever take up knitting?'' Obviously peeved at her lack of foresight, Heppy jabbed at the pumpkin's nose. The little orange triangle fell out onto the table. She sighed, then brightened. "Well, the yarn really doesn't matter, because the very best, never-fail, can't-miss method to discover your future husband is with the candle and the mirror."

"The candle and the mirror?" Pru repeated. She leaned back against the counter, patting a yawn. It had been a long day.

"Surely you've heard of it. You light a candle, and at the stroke of midnight on All Hallows' Eve, stand in front of a mirror with your eyes shut and say, 'Reflective glass, make the future past,/ Show my husband, don't make him an ass.'"

Heppy frowned. "No, wait. That not quite right. Now I remember! You say, 'Reflective glass, make the future past,/ Show the husband of this lass,' and then you lift the candle up and look in the mirror, and there you will see the face of your future husband." Heppy threw her hands out dramatically as if the prospective groom had suddenly appeared in the kitchen. Pumpkin goo flew everywhere.

One sticky orange patch landed on Pru's sweatshirt. Resignedly she picked up the dishcloth and wiped at the glob.

Heppy didn't notice. She'd hurried to a cupboard with a look of determination on her face. Opening the door, she began excavating. "I think I have a couple... Yes, I do! Here are the candles!" she exclaimed, pulling out two white tapers.

Using the stove's pilot light, she lit one of the candles and popped it in a brass holder. She held it out to Prudence, saying, "Take this upstairs with you and try it with the gilt mirror on the wall."

Prudence shook her head. "It would be a waste of

time, Heppy. My future husband is going to be Edmund.''

"I don't think so, dear."

Prudence's gaze narrowed suspiciously on her aunt's face. "You don't like Edmund, do you?"

"Of course…well, no, dear. I'm afraid I just don't believe he's the right man for you. And so I think you'll discover if you take this candle and try the mirror method."

Prudence accepted the candle without further comment, feeling sleepier by the minute. Somehow it just seemed easier to take the thing than to argue with her aunt. "Are you going to try it, too?" she asked in mild curiosity, eyeing the remaining lit taper in her aunt's hand.

Heppy laughed merrily. "Goodness, no. This one is for Jack. Doesn't he look scary?" she asked, turning the orange globe around.

Actually the plump little pumpkin looked rather wistful, as if he hoped a couple of wandering souls *would* come visit.

But Prudence said dutifully, "Very frightening, indeed." Kissing her aunt on her soft cheek, she added, "Don't forget to lock up after you put him on the porch."

"I won't, dear," Heppy replied, tenderly returning the salute. "And don't you forget to try the poem."

Prudence promised and headed toward the stairs. She smiled a little as she passed Heppy's bedroom. A jaunty paper skeleton dangled on her aunt's door. How Heppy loved Halloween, with all its stories and symbols and silly superstitions.

Holding the candle carefully to avoid dripping hot wax, Prudence mounted the stairs to her bedroom on the second floor. The long hallway leading to her room was dark, but the candle threw enough light to make turning on the electric switch unnecessary. As she passed the ornate gilt mirror on the hallway wall, Prudence hesitated. The mirror looked mysterious in the candlelight. It glinted invitingly, as if its silvered surface really could reflect the future.

Shaking her head at the fanciful notion, she walked on and then paused. She tilted her head, listening. It sounded quiet downstairs—her aunt had probably already retired. But still, a promise was a promise. She *had* told Heppy she would try the method.

Returning to the mirror, she stood before it and shut her eyes. "Reflective glass, make the future past,/ Show the husband of this lass," she mumbled. She opened her eyes.

Her own solemn face stared back at her.

Feeling like the ass her aunt had mentioned earlier, she turned and walked on to her room. *Who did you expect to see, anyway?* she scolded herself. *Edmund? Oh, please, who do you think you're fooling? You hoped to see Nicholas of course.*

She wanted to want Edmund, but despite all they shared—a love of family and community, a vision of what Cauldron's future could be—they didn't love each other, and after today she knew their future wouldn't be together. At the Faire—and by agreeing to this engagement as Nicholas had pointed out— Edmund had made it very apparent he cared more about his campaign than he did about her. And she wasn't much better, with this yearning she had for Nicholas Ware.

She set the candle on the nightstand and pulled her

white cotton nightgown from a hook on the closet door. A hopeless yearning that would lead nowhere. He'd never settle in Cauldron. And she'd never desert Heppy, not when her aunt needed her so much. It was time to forget Heppy's foolish rituals and her secret hopes that she and Nicholas would get together again.

It was time to forget Nicholas, for good this time.

For the past three days she'd been swept up by the foolish fire of desire—that legendary "*ignis fatuus* that bewitches, and leads one into pools and ditches." But she was through following her foolish desire for Nicholas, through with responding to the tiny flames that beckoned in his eyes. She didn't know why he'd bought land in Cauldron, but any hopes she had that he planned to build a home here would be foolish, too. He'd stated just today that he wasn't staying—and Nicholas always meant what he said. He'd gotten rid of all his father's furniture. Soon he would be gone again, and the fierce excitement that gripped her whenever she was with him would leave, too.

She slipped her gown over her head. Nicholas didn't love her. He didn't need her, either. But Heppy needed her; Prudence had a place in this town. She'd been content with that before and she'd learn to be again.

She climbed into bed and lay down. But tonight, contentment seemed very far away. She shifted restlessly on the cool sheets. Her body still hummed from the joy of being in Nicholas's arms. The sweet smoky smell of the bonfire lingered in her hair, and her blood still felt heated. She licked her lips, almost tasting again the passion of his kiss.

She turned onto her side, her cheek cradled on her palm, and tried to fight off the sadness sweeping over her. She wouldn't cry over him, she simply wouldn't. She wouldn't even think about him. It was just that the night was so dark, so mournful—and so terribly lonely.

It was also a little scary, she realized as a sound reached her ears. The noise was stealthy, furtive—like the faint hush of tip-toeing footsteps creeping down the hall.

"Heppy?" she called.

No answer. Not Heppy, then.

A tinge of apprehension crept in along with her grief. She stayed still, primal instincts holding her frozen, like a small animal hoping a predator would pass it by. Her heart beat faster. She wished she wasn't alone. Okay, she wished Nicholas was with her. His strong solid body would be very welcome reassurance right now. She'd cuddle up to him and— Damn, she was thinking of him again! Gathering her courage, she sat up, gave her pillow a thump and turned on to her other side. This was silly. Her imagination was getting the best of her. She needed to forget these fanciful notions about strange noises, forget about Nicholas and get some sleep—

Dark wings beat frantically, fluttering at the window.

Pru's heart fluttered equally as frantically. Just a bat, she told herself as the creature disappeared into the night. Certainly not one of Heppy's forlorn spirits seeking shelter.

Still, her pulse refused to calm and she lay on her back, blankets clutched beneath her chin, her senses on alert. She suddenly remembered that Aunt Barbara had died in this house. Many people believed a person's spirit lingered in the place where they'd died.

Prudence's throat went dry at the thought. She tried to swallow. She had always wished she could have met Aunt Barbara—but she really didn't want to do it tonight. She just wasn't in the mood for ghostly visitors. Not even related ones.

She struggled to see into the darkness, to identify the hulking shadows of wardrobe and dresser, and the long dark shape on the floor. Her ears strained to catch the slightest whisper, the merest rustle outside her room.

Creeeaaak.

Her clutch on the bedclothes tightened. That sounded like the low keening creak the loose board at the top of the stairs always made when someone stepped on it.

"Heppy?" she tried again. Again no answer.

She tensed, straining to hear other sounds. Only the faint scratch of a twig against the window reached her ears. The darkness seemed to press in closer; the hairs at the nape of her neck lifted. Slowly, she sat up again and reached for the lamp by her bed. She turned the switch.

Click. Click, click.

Nothing. Her heart beat faster.

Cauldron was probably just experiencing a blackout, she told herself. The wind often blew down the electric wires that ran through the woods. But suddenly, having light was a necessity, not an option. She picked up the candle from the nightstand and fumbled in the drawer, her fingers finally closing around the box of matches she always stored there.

She pulled a match from the box and struck it, the smell of sulfur strong in her nostrils, her fingers trembling as she tried to hold the flickering flame to the wick.

The wick caught. The flame flared. A welcome golden glow warmed the room, chasing the shadows back to the corners.

The wardrobe was a wardrobe again, not a hulking beast. The long dark shape on the floor was merely her discarded pants, which had fallen from the chair, not one of her great aunt's snakes. Aunt Barbara herself wasn't anywhere in sight. Breathing a small sigh of relief, Pru climbed out of bed and padded to the window, the carpet soft under her bare feet. She peered out.

Through the ragged clouds, the full moon cast an orange glow over the lawn and street, an appropriate backdrop for the lace-edged wings of the bats circling the old oak in search of prey. A black cat streaked across the lawn with a high-school mascot dangling from its jaws.

From the corner of her eye Pru caught a glimpse of a blurry white form floating slowly across the dark sky. Her pulse jumped. A soft hooting reached her ears and again she sighed in relief. Not a ghost— simply one of the white owls that so infuriated the lumbermen in the area.

As her gaze roamed the scene, Prudence frowned. Not a blackout, as she'd first thought. The lighted porches of the other houses on the street showed that the power outage existed at their house alone.

A fuse must have blown. Prudence hesitated, resisting the desire to just go back to bed. She didn't want to venture downstairs in the dark, but if Heppy awoke and realized what had happened, her aunt might try to go down to the basement to change the fuse herself. And that would be dangerous for the older woman.

Resolutely Prudence gripped her candle more tightly and moved to the door and opened it. A wayward draft caused the flame to flicker. Cupping her hand around the light, she stepped into the hall. After the nubby warmth of her bedroom carpet, the wooden floor in the hall felt icy beneath her bare feet. Her fingers felt cold, too, the faint heat from the small flame barely noticeable against her palm.

She slowly moved forward. Her gown brushed her ankles and feet, the tickling feeling unpleasantly reminiscent of scampering mice and creeping spiders. Biting her lip, she walked a little faster.

Suddenly she paused, an unreasonable but unmistakable panic holding her in place. Her nape tingled.

Someone was watching her.

Forcing herself to move, she turned, holding the candle high.

No one was near. But melting faces with hollow eyes and gaping mouths seemed to stare mournfully at her from the walls. The effect was caused, she knew, by the knotty-pine grain of the paneling. During the day the faces were interesting; in the dark on Halloween night they were spooky.

Still, they weren't real; they couldn't hurt anyone. Darn Heppy and her scary stories, anyway. Pru took another halting step forward, drawing a deep breath to steady herself. Heppy was the reason for this overwhelming feeling of uneasiness. Heppy with her talk of ghosts and goblins, lost spirits seeking repose, of warnings from the past and divinations of the future.

Nonsense, all of it. Pru walked faster, trying to smile at her own susceptibility. As for Heppy's suggestions for divining a future husband…well, Prudence didn't think so. All she'd get if she swallowed a thimbleful of salt would be a tremendous tummy ache. As for the mirror…

She glanced into its shining surface as she passed. Nicholas stared back.

13

PRUDENCE FROZE, her eyes widening, a scream hovering on her lips.

Instinctively she whirled around, expecting to find Nicholas standing behind her. But the hallway loomed empty and silent.

Fearfully she closed her eyes. It must have been her imagination. She turned back around and opened them again, taking another peek at the mirror. Good Lord, his face was still there—his tousled hair, his golden eyes staring knowingly at her. As clear as a picture.

Prudence frowned and leaned forward, holding the candle closer to the mirror. Not as *clear* as a picture—*exactly* like a picture. As if someone had cut around a photograph of his head and then pasted the image on the glass.

Her fingers clenched in the folds of her gown. *"Heppy!"* she whispered fiercely.

"Heppy isn't here," a deep voice said.

Prudence screamed and turned, pressing her hand to her pounding heart. For a terrifying moment all she could see was Heppy's jack-o'-lantern hovering in the air. A second later she realized Nicholas—the real Nicholas this time—was holding the little pumpkin cradled in one big hand as he stood at the head of the stairs. The top of the squash had been removed and the light from the candle inside streamed upward, highlighting Nick's prominent cheekbones and jaw, but leaving his eyes and hair shadowed.

"What are you doing here?" she gasped.

His eyebrows rose at her tone. "I was hoping you could tell me." He lifted the pumpkin higher in an effort to cast the light in her direction. She could see his eyes narrow as his gaze roved over her from her face to her bare feet.

He said absently, "Hepzibah called and told me she had to go to the Dazas' to baby-sit their little boy—seems Kristie had gone into labor and Tim rushed her to the hospital. Your aunt asked me to come over here right away, said that you needed me, but hung up before I could ask her any questions."

"Oh! How could she!" Prudence said. What a troublemaker Heppy was! Her crafty aunt had known Pru would come looking for her once she discovered the mirror trick—and as usual fate had helped Heppy escape the consequences. Already Prudence could feel her anger at her aunt fading, replaced by mere annoyance. By morning she'd probably be chuckling at the trick her aunt had pulled.

But right now she was just glad to know it *was* a trick. That no magic mirror existed. That Nicholas was here and she was safe.

She glanced up to tell him so, but then paused, the words dying on her lips. Because suddenly she didn't feel safe at all.

It was there again—that hungry desire in his eyes. The look that made her flush with responsive heat from the top of her head to the tip of her chilled toes. A few minutes ago she'd craved the light, but now she felt exposed in its soft glow, vulnerable to the raw passion on Nicholas's lean face. Instinctively she clutched the V-shaped neckline of her nightgown closed, the candle wavering in her other hand.

Nicholas saw the revealing gesture, the trembling of the candlelight against the wall. He knew she was scared. But he couldn't move or look away. He was enthralled by the sight of her in the soft candlelight. She was a vision he'd conjured up again and again through the years, an image of how he'd always imagined she would have looked on their wedding night.

Her gown was a thin white cotton, with just a touch of lace at the hem above her bare toes and along the neckline, now clenched so tightly in her tense little hand. The sheer material covered her completely but couldn't disguise the roundness of her hips, the deadman's curve of her waist, the small peaks of her nipples.

His gaze lingered there, then slowly lifted to meet hers. Her eyes were huge, her pupils so dilated that only a faint rim of smoky gray remained. Her hair tumbled around her shoulders in a dark cloud, framing the kitten shape of her face. Her mouth was rosy pink.

He took a step toward her, and her bottom lip quivered before she caught it in her teeth to steady it. His heart ached a little at the fear and uncertainty in her eyes. "Prudence," he said huskily, "don't be afraid. It's only me."

He held out his hand. She hesitated, then to his profound relief, put hers into it. He gently tugged on her fingers and she came closer, stepping into his embrace. Bending, he blew out her candle and the flame disappeared in a puff of spiraling smoke. Then his arms closed tightly around her. He could feel her hugging him in return, her breasts flattened against his chest, her face hidden in the curve of his neck. He lowered his face to her hair and breathed in her smoky sweet scent.

Prudence could feel his heart beating heavily in his chest. The beat of her own heart quickened in response. For a second he simply stood there in the hall, holding her. The house was dark and silent.

He pulled away a little. She could feel him looking down at her, but his expression remained hidden by the shadows. "You're not scared, are you?" he asked. His husky voice was soothing, but his arm tightened possessively around her waist.

Prudence shook her head, but knew she was lying. She *was* scared—not of him but the feelings he aroused in her. This was it. This was what she'd been afraid of ever since he'd returned. She'd tried so hard to forget what it felt like to be in his arms—the excitement, the pleasure of his touch. The feeling of rightness she had never had with anyone else, not even Edmund. She knew she should be running in the opposite direction, but she was so tired of running. She wanted this. She wanted Nicholas. No matter what happened in the future, she wanted to know just once what it was like to truly belong to him.

Her heart pounded, her stomach muscles clenched. Excitement caused a fine tremor to begin deep inside her that she couldn't control. She trembled in his arms.

He set her away from him and offered her the little pumpkin. Prudence automatically took it, then gasped as Nicholas lifted her in his arms. She held the pumpkin high so its flickering light illuminated their way to her bedroom.

Once inside he set her on her feet, then took the jack-o'-lantern and set it on the bedside table. He put her extinguished candle beside it.

He turned back to where she silently waited. He cradled her face in his hands, tilting her face up to his. "Prudence," he said softly, his warm breath caressing her cheeks. "Prudence..."

His mouth closed over hers, his tongue lightly stroking her lips, persuading her to part them. With a low moan, she did, opening to receive the slow penetration of his tongue. He tasted so good, he felt so good—solid and real against her. She pressed closer, sliding her hands up into his vibrant hair, enjoying the way the soft strands curled around her fingers. She snuggled closer, savoring the feel of his hard chest rubbing against her sensitive breasts.

One of his arms locked around her waist, arching her into him while he kissed her. His other hand moved up and down her back, tracing the bones of her shoulders and spine. It should have felt soothing, that slow exploring touch, but the drag of her nightgown against her skin as his hand glided up to her shoulder and then down in a long slow stroke to her bottom set her skin on fire.

Lightly circling the resilient curves of her bottom, he closed his hands around her, lifting her and spreading his legs to nestle her lower body tightly against his thighs.

The night air was cold, but she didn't feel it. He was making her burn. She couldn't stay still—restless desire caused her hips to shift, to rub against him. Instinctively she pressed herself more firmly against the hardness in the front of his jeans. She lifted her bare foot to run it along the back of his calf.

"Prudence..." he rasped again. His mouth trailed hotly down her cheek to the sensitive cord on the side of her neck. She shivered as he sucked gently on her skin.

Nicholas felt her response and shuddered, nuzzling along her throat to find the pulse he'd wanted to kiss earlier that day. He found the small beating rhythm, and opened his mouth against her delicate skin to stroke it with his tongue. She moaned, and the sound caused his muscles to flex, his arousal to grow even harder.

He felt as if he was in a dream, a fantasy he'd replayed over and over in his mind. When he'd been younger, his imaginings had always been about the sex act itself. How would it feel? What would it be like? But now he was a man, and sex was no longer a mystery. Prudence was the mystery, with her silky skin and soft sighs. For a long time now—too long— his dreams had all been about her. What was *she* like? How would *she* feel in his arms?

Now he knew. She felt pliant, warm, giving. And he wanted even more. He lifted his head slightly to coax, "Take off your gown, sweetheart. I need to see you."

She stilled for a second. Then she moved away and his arms dropped to his sides. His eyes fixed on her face, half-hidden behind her tangled curls. She lifted her head and her hair fell back around her shoulders. He sucked in a breath. The candlelight flickered over her face, revealing the heavy-lidded passion in her eyes and the pink flush rising on her skin.

Reaching down, she grasped the hem of her gown. Slowly she raised it over her head and pulled it off. She dropped the garment, standing there in the candlelight. And the vision of the girl Nick had carried in his mind, altered to encompass the woman he now carried in his heart.

He knew she couldn't be perfect...yet, he couldn't see any flaws. She was simply...Prudence.

Her small round breasts were topped by tight brown nipples, which he longed to take in his mouth. He wanted to feel her slender arms and legs wrapped around him, trail kisses across the slight roundness of her tummy, explore the enticing dark curls between her thighs.

His loins swelled and grew heavier as his gaze moved over her. He wanted to simply stare at her forever, but then she lifted her arms, crossing them self-consciously.

His gaze met hers. Her eyes held a faint anxiousness, and his heart melted with tenderness. "You're beautiful, sweetheart," he told her, and some of the tension in her expression relaxed. "Get into bed while I undress so you don't catch cold."

Obediently she climbed beneath the covers and pulled them up under her chin as she sat, hugging her knees. Watching him unfasten his shirt, she whispered, "Hurry, Nicholas."

He'd never taken off his clothes so quickly in his life.

Naked, he turned to find she was still looking at him, her eyes half-closed. A small smile curved her lips as her gaze moved over him. "You're beautiful, too."

He smiled and blew out the candle in the pumpkin, then climbed into bed beside her.

He drew her into his arms, almost groaning at the heavenly feel of her bare skin against his. He slid his thigh between her legs and kissed her deeply, plundering and exploring her mouth while he stroked her soft skin, down her arm and around to her breast.

She gave a little gasp as he circled her nipple with a finger, arching her back to thrust it into his palm the way she had at the bonfire. She'd had him so aroused, so hungry there, that he'd almost forgotten the people around them.

And he was even hungrier for her now. He kissed the slope of her breast and then took her nipple into his mouth, pressing on the nub with his tongue. She jumped and groaned, pulling his head tighter to her. He kissed his way to the other one and accorded it the same treatment.

"Oh, Nicholas," she moaned. "Oh, please..."

She didn't tell him what she longed for, but he knew. He slid his fingers into the soft curls between her thighs, gently teasing, probing, exploring her until she was writhing in his arms. He'd never touched her so intimately all those years ago. He'd always sensed she was holding something back.

He didn't want her to hold anything back—not with him, not anymore. Seven years ago he'd had her love, but not her body. Now she was offering her body, but not her love. He wanted both.

"Who do you love, Prudence?" he asked, his fingers touching her in a place that made her pant and cling more tightly.

She didn't answer. Her eyes were closed, and she twisted, straining upward against him, against his hand, silently begging for release.

But he wanted the words. "Who do you love, Prudence?" he repeated, his voice, his hand, firmer now.

She moaned. "Oh, Nicholas. Nicholas... please..."

He didn't cease the aching torment, the movement of his fingers, the demand in his voice, "Who do you love?"

"You...I want you," she almost sobbed.

They weren't exactly the words he wanted—but his body wouldn't wait any longer. He moved over her, settling between her thighs. Slowly, inexorably, he pushed into her. Her fingers bit into his shoulder. A cry broke from her lips as he pressed past the small barrier and slid deeply into her body.

He paused, breathing deeply, trying to hold still, wanting to give her a chance to adjust to him. He kissed her temple, tasting the salty tears that seeped from the corners of her eyes. He wasn't surprised that he was the first, the only man to have ever possessed her. Because whether she'd admit it or not, he knew—he'd always known somewhere deep inside—that she was his, a part of him. She always had been and always would be.

He thrust his fingers into her hair, holding her still as he took her mouth, again and again, kissing her deeply, until the inner muscles clenching him so tightly relaxed a little, and she began to move beneath him, echoing the rhythm of his body and tongue.

Her hands stroked his back now, clutching at his buttocks, urging him faster and faster as together they rode through the dark night, spiraling higher and higher like the sparks from the bonfire.

And when they were as high as they could go, they hung there for one exquisite excruciating second. Then they burst into flame.

And slowly, so slowly, drifted back down to earth.

14

THEY LAY ENTWINED together during the deepest part
of night, when the darkness seems eternal, yet the
promise of dawn hovers only a heartbeat away. Prudence snuggled next to Nicholas, her head on the
pillow while he lay propped up on one elbow facing
her, his head supported by his hand, a heavy thigh
thrown across her legs.

The darkness no longer bothered Prudence; it
seemed warm and friendly now, cloaking them with
softening shadows. She knew the bewitching hour
had long passed, but its spell lingered on in the mag-
ical touch of his fingers against her skin as he slowly
traced along her ribs, down to her tender belly, tickling her gently.

Prudence half chuckled, half sighed. She knew he
watched her as his hand slid along her skin, leaving
little shimmers of sensation behind.

She stretched lazily and his hand flattened on her
stomach, holding her in place as he lay down again
with his head beside hers on the pillow. She picked
his hand up and idly played with his fingers, tracing
the lines on his palm that marked his future, com-
paring the length of his fingers to her own. Her fingers looked small, slender and white next to his long
tanned ones. He was a big man, big all over. She
knew that intimately now.

Linking their fingers together, she let them drop back on her tummy and said huskily, "Well. That was something."

She could feel his smile against her hair. It echoed in his deep voice as he said, "Is that the best you can do?" He nuzzled her curls.

"What do you expect? Paeans of praise for your sexual prowess?"

He smiled again, nipping her earlobe. "I dare you to say that ten times without making a mistake."

"Make love to me ten times more and I'll try," she promised.

His hand slid up her body to cup her breast possessively, his skin dark against the whiteness of hers. "Sounds like a deal," he said.

He kissed her ear, outlining the shell with his tongue. "We should be able to get in at least one more time now, maybe two," he said huskily, "before I have to head out to Portland. And then later..."

Her heart sank. "You have to go to Portland? Today? When will you be back?"

"Next week. I figure I can fly back in on Tuesday and help you pack up your things. Then we'll go to my apartment and get you settled, take care of a few pressing items—" he nudged one of the pressing items against her hip "—and then we'll go out and do the town. I can't wait to show you the city—and my office. It's kind of—"

"Wait a minute, Nick." She placed her fingers against his lips. He nibbled at them, and she pulled them away, saying, "You're not making sense. Why would I pack up? I think we should get our home set up here first before we take a trip together to Port-

land. We need to figure out where we want to live—
if we'll be keeping your father's house or maybe
building another on that land you bought.''

He tensed. ''What are you talking about? I'm not
planning on building a house. I'm not even planning
on staying here. And neither are you. You're coming
with me.''

Prudence felt as if she'd stepped from a dream into
a nightmare. She swallowed, trying to ease the tightness in her throat. This was all so painfully familiar.
She said huskily, ''We've had this conversation before, Nick, seven years ago. I told you then and I'm
telling you now—I'm not leaving Cauldron. Nothing's changed.''

Behind him, the dawn was breaking outside the
window. Gray light seeped into the room, illuminat-
ing the hard angry planes of his face. He moved
away, turning to sit on the edge of the bed. ''How
can you say nothing's changed?'' he demanded.
''We just made love—we're bound together now,
Prudence. You know it's true. You can't lie about
that.''

She didn't try. Reaching out, she smoothed her
hand along his warm back. ''But I'm bound to Cauldron, too.''

He stood up and stepped away from her touch. Her
hand dropped. ''Don't even say that.'' He paced to
the window and looked out at the town. ''There're
other places, other towns, where we can be happy
together. How can you compare the importance of
what we feel for each other to this…this place.''

The disgust in his voice pricked her. Her own anger began to rise. ''Our families have lived in this
place—as you call it—for over a century. This town

is rich in traditions begun by our ancestors. My mother and father were raised here—*you* were raised here. Your father is buried here.''

"So what? Am I supposed to set up camp next to his grave site?'' He stalked back to glare down at her. "I don't need to go to a special place to remember my father, Prudence—any more than you need to visit her grave to remember your great aunt Barbara. You know her because Heppy shared her memories with you. And I remember my father every time I look in the mirror and see the color of my eyes and hair. My father is in my flesh and bones. Unlike the Swains, I don't need to donate a building as a tribute to his memory. *I'm* the tribute to his memory.''

He picked up his pants and yanked them on.

Prudence watched him. The vehemence of his tone caused a fine trembling to begin inside her. Her own voice sounded harsh as she replied, "Oh, yes, that sounds really noble. And it conveniently gives you the excuse to do whatever you want without any ties or responsibilities. It certainly gave you a reason to leave before—and how many times did you actually see your father in these past seven years? Once? Or was it twice that you flew him down to Portland for a few days? Big deal. Well, I don't plan to desert Heppy. She needs me and I'm going to be here for her.''

He laughed without humor. He picked up his shirt and shrugged into it. "Don't kid yourself, babe. You're staying in Cauldron for you, not Heppy.''

She stiffened. "What do you mean by that?''

"Heppy doesn't need you.'' He bent down to retrieve his shoes and socks. He sat down on the side of the bed to pull them on.

The bed dipped under his weight. Prudence sucked in a breath, feeling as if he'd punched her in the stomach. "How can you say that? You have no idea of the kind of trouble she can get into. Her finances were a mess before I took over, she gets crazy ideas, she even makes potions—"

"So what? Heppy can take care of herself—she's not a child or an idiot." He tied one shoelace and started on the other. "You're simply using her as an excuse for not taking a chance—for not going out into the world and trying to make a living with your art, for not having children or getting married, for not even loving, damn it! You tell yourself it's okay to marry Swain, a man you don't even love, because it gives you an excuse to stay in this town. That's wrong, Prudence, and you know it."

"It's not like that!"

"Isn't it? Then why is it you never noticed Swain before I came back? I'll tell you why. Because you were using him as a barrier to keep me away from you. You don't love Swain. You love *me*."

"I've never said I love you."

"But you do. Why else would you wait so long for me to return? Why else would you wait to make love with me—and *only* me?"

"People make love for a lot of reasons other than being in love," Prudence said.

"But not you."

"Oh? Why should I be any different from you? You don't love me. You proved that seven years ago and again now. If you really loved me, you'd understand about Heppy, and Cauldron. You'd stay here."

"And once again the opposite is true. If you loved me enough, you'd come with me."

He looked at her for a long moment. She didn't move.

His mouth twisted wryly. "Well, déjà vu. This was my cue to get out of town the last time, and I guess nothing's changed."

Turning on his heel, he strode from the room, slamming the door behind him.

15

FOR THE BAREST SECOND Prudence didn't move, but remained in bed, stunned. She felt as if the tornado she'd been whirling in for the past few days had finally stopped and sent her crashing to the ground.

How could he say what he had? How could he plan to leave Cauldron—and her—after what they'd experienced last night? She waited, half expecting him to come back, to finish the argument. Surely he wasn't going to leave things as they were, was he?

But it seemed he was. She heard a door slam downstairs. Her anger flared higher. Fine. Let him leave. She never wanted to see him again.

She jumped out of bed, hurrying to the window to watch him go. She held aside the curtain to find a cold, foggy dawn. Against the cloudy sky, the bare limbs of the trees looked naked and vulnerable. Winter had stolen in during the night, stripping away all their bright leaves. The faint mist covering the ground leached the color from the landscape, diluting everything to a dull gray as Nicholas disappeared down the street.

He never once looked back.

Prudence let the curtain fall. Good. She wouldn't look back, either. She'd forge ahead with all the plans she'd made before he disrupted them. She was very happy with the way things had turned out, so happy, in fact, that she climbed back into bed to shed some happy tears into her pillow.

When the storm had passed, she lay there awhile, feeling too exhausted to get up. The morning light grew progressively brighter, her mood progressively darker. She heard Heppy come in, but couldn't find the energy to go down to greet her. It wasn't until she heard a deep, masculine voice in the kitchen that the inertia holding her in its grip suddenly lifted.

She sat straight up in bed. Nick had returned, had he? Well, he needn't think she was eager to talk to him after the terrible things he'd said.

She swung her feet to the floor. Hurrying into the bathroom, she took a two-minute shower, then quickly dressed. She only chose her red sweater and gray pants because they were warm, she told herself, yanking them on, not because they were the most becoming items she owned.

Ruthlessly dragging a brush through her curls, she put on some lipstick and walked casually down the stairs. She could no longer hear anyone talking, and she hesitated, then pushed open the kitchen door.

Heppy was sitting alone, wearing a gray linen dress with a broad white collar. A teacup and saucer were on the table. She had her hands clasped loosely before her as she stared absently at the calendar on the far wall, now turned to a page featuring a fat red turkey wearing a pilgrim's hat.

"Heppy?" Prudence said. "Did I hear Nicholas down here with you?"

Her aunt glanced up, startled. "Oh, no, dear." She still seemed preoccupied. "That was the sheriff. He was here questioning me about the vandalism to Edmund's campaign posters."

"The sheriff!" Prudence repeated, stunned. "What happened?"

Heppy sighed. "Issie Swain told the sheriff I'd destroyed them." Heppy frowned at the turkey, her brow wrinkling in thought.

Dismay filled Prudence. She knew Heppy didn't like Edmund and she knew her aunt's solutions to problems were often harebrained, but she'd never expected her to pull a stunt like this.

Or hadn't she? Pru frowned, uncomfortably aware that along with the dismay and alarm she was feeling was also the tiniest bit of satisfaction. Because this proved Nicholas was wrong; Heppy did need looking after. Here was the proof, as well as a problem she could handle.

"Don't worry," Pru said firmly. "The sheriff certainly can't prove anything if Mrs. Swain didn't actually see you."

Aunt Heppy glanced up, faint surprise in her blue eyes. "Oh, I know he can't. Which is why he came here. To ask me about it."

Prudence's heart sank. Surely her aunt hadn't confessed? "You didn't say anything, did you?" she asked, dropping into a chair.

A troubled look crossed over Heppy's face. She closed her fingers around the teacup, as if taking comfort from its warmth. "I had to, dear. I couldn't lie to the police."

"No, but—"

"Of course, I realize many people are going to be very angry at me—"

"Yes, but—"

"Sally Watson is going to have a fit! But that

doesn't matter. I had to do what I had to do. I didn't mean to hurt anyone—''

''No, but—''

''Sally will just have to learn she can't go around destroying other people's property.''

''Yes, but—'' Prudence paused. ''Sally Watson?''

''Yes, dear. Oh, didn't I mention that? Sally's the one who destroyed the posters with black paint. I saw her last night when I was on my way to the Dazas. She changed 'Swain' to 'Swine,' called Eddie 'a pig man' instead of 'a big man,' and gave him a mustache on every single one.'' Heppy frowned, her brow wrinkling as she added thoughtfully, ''Actually, Eddie looks rather good with a mustache—kind of hides his weak mouth. But that's beside the point,'' she continued more briskly. ''Sally just can't do things like that simply because she's mad at Eddie's mother.''

Prudence felt bewildered. ''But why would she be mad at Mrs. Swain?''

''Why? Because Michael O'Sullivan is courting Issie, of course. And Sally hoped he'd be looking *her* way. She's kept her feelings hidden from Issie until now, but I don't see that she can any longer after what she's done. Sally always has been a menace when she gets a spray can in her hand.''

''Oh.'' Prudence slumped back in her chair, trying to cope with this latest turn of events—and the way she'd so misjudged her aunt. She couldn't believe she'd ever thought Heppy capable of doing such a thing.

Heppy might be a little eccentric at times, but her love of people was deep and true. Why else would all the children flock to her, and parents trust her to baby-sit? Because Heppy was so kind to the people around her, of course.

Nicholas's words echoed in Prudence's mind. "Oh, good Lord," she said slowly. "It was all an illusion. Nicholas was right."

"He often is, dear," Heppy said. "What was it this time?"

"He said I was fooling myself, that you don't need me. That I just need to think you do."

Heppy looked indignant. "How unlike him to make such a silly statement. I need you. You're my niece!"

"But that's all you need me for—to be your niece. You don't need me to be your keeper or help you with the bookstore."

Clearly concerned by the distress in Prudence's voice, Heppy leaned across the table and reached for her hand. "That's only partly true, dear. Maybe I don't need you for those things anymore—that's not to say I never did. You've helped me get on a firm financial footing at the bookstore. And maybe I don't need a keeper right now, but I might in the future. Who's to say?"

Prudence's troubled expression didn't alter, and Heppy patted her hand, saying gently, "People change. Circumstances change. You can't foresee the future, dear. You can only do what's right for you at the time and place you're at."

And where was she now? Prudence wondered. She glanced around the kitchen. All the Halloween decorations had been put away—the skeleton on her aunt's door, Heppy's witch hat and cape, construction-paper cats and ghosts. All that sat on the counter was a box of plain old oatmeal. Everything looked blessedly normal again. Even her aunt.

Prudence should have been pleased. Yet she felt strangely bereft. The tantalizing promise of the unexpected was gone. The magic in the air had evaporated. And it had nothing to do with Halloween or decorations, Heppy, love potions, or anything else...except Nicholas.

He was leaving. There'd be no more stolen kisses or shared desire. No teasing or laughter or hungry passion. Once again everything would be flat and predictable, normal and unexciting.

Prudence clasped her hands together. She'd thought that was exactly what she wanted. Now she wasn't so sure. She felt as if she was at a crossroads, uncertain which way to go. He'd moved on—and for the first time she considered how it might feel to move on, too. She'd miss Aunt Heppy, of course, and her friends, but she could always come back to visit. She remembered what Nicholas had said about seeing famous cities, about selling her art, about being happy in other towns, other places. Could he be right about that, too?

She wasn't sure anymore, not about anything. The only thing she was sure of was that she needed to talk to him. He could help her find the answers.

She straightened in her chair. But he might be leaving even now. He'd been gone in less than an hour seven years ago. She just hoped practice hadn't made him faster.

Jumping up, she gave her aunt a kiss. "I'll talk to you later, Heppy. I need to—"

"I know, dear," her aunt said, waving her on her way. "Just hurry."

Waving back, Pru headed out the door and down the walk. Heppy was right; she needed to hurry. If she did, surely she could catch him, at least talk to him a bit before—

"Ooof!"

She ran smack into Jimmy Burrows, delivering newspapers on his skateboard, at the end of Heppy's walkway.

She caught the boy's shoulders, preventing him from falling, while barely managing to retain her own balance. Jimmy wasn't fazed in the least by the incident.

"Hi, Prudence!" he sang out, his freckled face lighting up with a big smile.

"Hello, Jimmy," she answered, stepping around him. "Can't talk now—I have to hurry."

He flung a newspaper at Heppy's door. It landed with a loud thump. Prudence kept walking and Jimmy rode his board along on the sidewalk beside her, weaving from side to side and forcing her to sidestep whenever he swerved her way.

"Say, Prudence, where are you going in such a rush? Are you having another party?" he asked, a hopeful note in his voice. Another paper went flying. It landed neatly on the stoop.

"No," she said.

"Oh." His freckles bunched together as he screwed his face up in disappointment, then spread out again as he added, "But hey, wasn't it a good Halloween? With someone messin' up Eddie Swain's posters and all, and him and my dumb sister getting engaged? And I got tons of candy trick-or-treating—"

"Jimmy—"

"Lots more than Tyler Decker. I got jelly beans, candy corn, jawbreakers, pencils—Stephanie Roosen gave me those. She started crying when I said they were stupid—candy bars, suckers—"

"Jimmy!"

"Sour straws, bubble gum, a candy apple—I dropped it in the dirt, but Tyler says I can eat around the rocks and hair and stuff—cinnamon sticks, corn nuts—"

"*Jimmy!*"

He glanced up, innocently surprised at her loud tone. "Yeah?"

"What do you mean Edmund and Rhonda are engaged?"

He rolled his eyes. "Didn't you know? She came home from the Faire, crying all over the place, and my dad said he'd shoot the son of a you-know-what who made his little girl cry, and then Eddie showed up, and somehow he and Rhonda got engaged. He's going to be sorry, though, when he sees her without her makeup," Jimmy added, satisfaction in his voice as he sent another paper winging. "Man, does she look bad."

Shock ran through Prudence. "I don't believe it."

"It's true. Her face looks all weird and kinda white—"

"I mean, I can't believe Rhonda and Edmund are engaged."

A shock of red hair fell over his eyes as he nodded his head in agreement. "I know. Kinda gross, isn't it? Imagine kissing Rhonda—yuck! And what if they have kids!" He screwed up his face in disgust, then brightened again, adding, "There's one good thing, though. My mom says Rhonda gets to be a mayor's wife now that Tim Daza's dropped out of the race."

"Tim Daza dropped out?"

"Yeah. He decided not to do it 'cause he'll be too busy with his new job. He's going to be the manager of the new electronics plant they're building on the south end of town."

"But—"

"Hey! There's Tyler! Gotta go, Prudence. See ya." With the toss of one last paper, Jimmy jumped the curb and swooped away in graceful arcs.

Prudence stood there a minute staring unseeingly after him, almost unable to take it all in. Rhonda...and Edmund? No wonder they hadn't gone to the bonfire. Why hadn't she noticed something was going on between those two? Because she hadn't wanted to, she realized, biting her lip. Like Nicholas had said, Edmund had been a convenient barrier to keep him at a distance, and she hadn't seen anything else.

She started walking again. Well, she was glad for Rhonda and Edmund, and glad she didn't have to feel guilty about Edmund in any way. As for the news about the new plant...could she have misjudged Nicholas there, also? He might not be planning to stay, but he had helped Cauldron. The new plant would be a shot in the arm for the town's economy.

She only hoped she had the chance to tell him so, and to thank him. Prudence walked on, half bracing herself for an encounter with Mrs. Watson as she passed her house, but thankfully, the shutters remained closed. No beady-eyed, old graffiti artist heckled her as she passed.

She hurried to Nicholas's house. But on his walkway, her steps slowed. The house looked quiet, deserted. Surely he hadn't already left?

She continued almost tentatively to his door. She knocked. No one answered. Her throat tightening, she knocked again and then tried the handle. The door swung open.

"Nicholas?" she called, stepping inside. Again no answer.

Her footsteps echoing hollowly on the wood floor, Prudence went into the study. The room looked exactly the same as it had the day before. The tired armchair and scratched-up desk sat in the middle of the threadbare rug. The boxes of family memorabilia were piled in a corner.

He'd obviously decided to leave them behind, she thought, her shoulders drooping. Along with her.

Sad, desperate grief had started building inside her again when suddenly, she heard a door closing down the hallway.

Her heart lifted with hope. She whirled around. "Nicholas?" she called.

A second later he appeared in the doorway. When he caught sight of her, he stilled, and Prudence glimpsed stunned surprise in his eyes before it disappeared, replaced by his usual unrevealing expression. He must have just taken a shower because his dark hair was damp. He was wearing suit pants and a white shirt.

His gaze dropped to his unbuttoned cuffs. He started fastening them before he glanced up again.

"Hello, Prudence," he said. "What are you doing here?"

She swallowed, feeling a little nauseated, wondering what to do. He didn't seem to be the same man who'd held her so tenderly only a few hours earlier. He sounded completely uninterested, and the distant expression he wore made her heart ache. She'd seen the expression often years ago when he'd been around other people in the town. She'd never before had it directed at herself.

She didn't know where to start, how to break through his remoteness. "I came because I think we need…to talk," she managed to choke out.

He shrugged. "Okay, let's talk." He leaned back against the desk, folding his arms across his chest.

He nodded toward the chair, indicating she should sit down, but Prudence remained standing. She felt too tense to sit. She clasped her hands together in front of her to hide their trembling.

Last night she'd stood naked before this man. Now she felt more frightened than she had then—more frightened than she ever had in her life. Why?

Because nothing had ever been as important to her as Nicholas, she realized.

She glanced at his stern mouth, his steady eyes. It should have been easy to explain with his full attention. It wasn't. So often he'd seemed to know what was in her mind, almost before she did. This time— when she so desperately wanted his understanding— he seemed to have retreated to a place she couldn't reach. He might as well have already left, so remote did he seem.

Unconsciously she gripped her hands more tightly, and glanced desperately around for inspiration on how to start explaining. Her gaze fell on the boxes. "I never did finish sorting all that out," she said. "I can work on it…until you get back."

"Get back?"

She nodded, her voice husky as she reminded him, "You said you'd be back in about a week."

His mouth twisted wryly. "We said a lot of things this morning."

"I know." She swallowed past the tightness in her throat. "But I don't think all of them were true."

He straightened and his gaze pinned her. "Are you saying you wish you had left with me seven years ago?"

"No, not exactly..." She faltered as some emotion—could it be pain?—flashed in his eyes before his expression once again became flat and unrevealing.

Hurriedly she continued, struggling to explain, "Heppy says you can only make decisions based on present circumstances. That's what I think I did. I made the best decision I could at that time, for me."

He didn't say anything and she added almost desperately, "I wasn't ready to start traveling or to move again. My whole childhood was spent traipsing from one country to another or sitting alone in a boarding school, waiting for my parents to return to drag me to yet another new place. I needed some time to stay here with Heppy, to concentrate on getting my degree, to absorb traditions, to meet—really meet—and get to know people. I think I simply needed to...nest here awhile."

He made an impatient gesture. "Fine. I understand."

"But I don't think you do, Nicholas," she said. "I made the only decision I could for me, and you did the same. You were right—there was nothing for you in Cauldron. You needed to get away to build your future. But if I'd gone with you, I don't think our marriage would have lasted. You hardly had time to visit your father, much less any to devote to a wife.''

Nicholas ran a hand tiredly through his hair. She was right; he *hadn't* had much time for a wife. The reason he'd gotten ahead so fast was that he'd devoted so much time to his job. But that was then and this was now. ''It's not the same anymore, Prudence,'' he said quietly. ''I do have time for a wife now.''

She said simply, ''And I'm ready to leave Cauldron.''

For just a second his breath caught. She was saying everything he'd once hoped to hear. But now he knew that wasn't enough. Cauldron wasn't truly the issue between them. Maybe it never had been. The issue was whether or not she loved him. More than any thing, any place, any person.

His gaze locked with hers. ''So what do you want?''

She gestured helplessly. ''I want to be with you.''

''You know I want that, too,'' he answered quietly.

Prudence's heart leaped to her throat and she waited—for him to come to her, to kiss her, to take her in his arms. But still he didn't move. He said, ''Just last week you were planning to marry Edmund.''

''I know. I made a mistake.''

''And I don't want you to make another one simply because of last night.'' He took a deep breath. ''I need to know, Prudence, once and for all. Who do you love?''

It was a simple question, and yet the answer meant so much. But only one response filled Prudence's heart. She stepped forward and the coldness in his eyes seemed to thaw a little. It gave her courage. "You, Nicholas. I love you."

As his eyes heated to a burning liquid gold, a flush of warmth washed over Prudence. He opened his arms and she flew into them.

He kissed her searchingly, passionately and so tenderly that once again magic shimmered inside her. She clung to him tightly.

Finally he lifted his mouth from hers and rested his cheek against her hair. His hand stroked lightly down her back as he asked huskily, "Why was that so hard to tell me?"

"I don't know. Maybe because you are the most important person in my life," she said, and almost gasped at how fiercely his hold tightened. After another long kiss, she added, her voice muffled, "It would have been easier if you'd said the words to me first."

"I did say them. Seven years ago. And I meant them forever, even though for a long time I tried to deny it to myself." He trailed his mouth along her temple and down her cheek to her mouth. "I loved you from the moment I first saw you, and I love you even more now." He pressed a hard quick kiss on her lips. "I came back to get you, and I wasn't going to leave without you this time—in spite of the fact that you've been driving me crazy."

His mouth took hers again in a kiss that made Prudence a little crazy, too.

She sighed against his lips. "Thank goodness, I

didn't let you get away this time." Her fingers worked busily, undoing his shirt buttons.

He teased her ear with his tongue, then whispered, "I wasn't going away for long. I've learned that no matter how far I am away from you, you are always with me."

Tears stung her eyes. "Oh, Nicholas. That's so sweet."

"I know," he said smugly, dropping a kiss on the tip of her nose. "Kind of poetic, too. Maybe I should start writing campaign slogans for Swain."

"I wish you would," she said, sliding her hands inside his now open shirt. "I even liked Mrs. Watson's versions better than the one he originally came up with. At least hers caught people's attention. Oh—" she lifted her head "—I forgot to tell you. Edmund and Rhonda are getting married."

"Good Lord," he said, the disgust in his voice very similar to Jimmy Burrows's. "Just think of those two together..."

"I don't want to think of it. I'd rather know about this new plant you're building and why you gave Tim Daza a job."

He shrugged. "Because he needed one and he did a good job as manager of the mill before it closed. I expect he'll do an equally good job here, and I thought he'd be the most knowledgeable about the people in Cauldron—who to hire and such."

"But why didn't you tell me?"

He tilted her chin. "I was tired of Cauldron being an issue between us, and I didn't want my actions to influence you in any way."

"And to think I accused you of not caring about Cauldron," she said, hugging him contritely.

He returned the hug, but admitted, "To a certain extent I don't. One place is much like another to me. What I care about is you." He traced the curve of her cheek with his finger. "I never want to take anything away from you, sweetheart—not your family or your friends. I just want to add to your life."

His tone was so tender Prudence could feel her insides melting. She whispered, "In that case, I guess I'll have to become accustomed to how unsentimental you are about mementos and stuff."

She gave a significant nod toward the boxes.

He followed her gaze but said, "You know, I did save one memento from our past."

He released her and she watched in puzzlement as he reached into the back pocket of his pants. He pulled out his wallet and extracted something from the coin pouch. He held it out to her.

Prudence stared at the circle of gold resting on his palm. The shank consisted of two hands, holding a glinting diamond heart.

"My ring!" she said in wonderment. "You still have it."

"Yeah. I thought about tossing it, but I could never quite do it." He picked up her hand, toying with her fingers a moment. "I kept hoping that somehow I'd have the chance to put it back where it belongs." He slowly slipped it on her finger. "For seven long years I've kept it in my wallet."

Tears burned behind Prudence's eyes. To think, all these years her unsentimental lover had carried her ring next to his...well, not next to his heart exactly, but the sentiment was the same. And her ring felt so good, so right, on her hand again.

She lifted her hand to admire the sparkle of the

diamond, and Nicholas caught her hand in his. Opening her fingers, he dropped a burning kiss on her palm.

"You are the magic in my life, Prudence," he said, his breath warm against her skin. "I love you. I never want to be without you again."

He looked up, cradling her hand against his cheek, and a slow smile crossed Prudence's face. She didn't need a magic mirror, bowl or potion to know what the future would bring.

Her future—*their* future—was as clear as the love and happiness in Nicholas's eyes.

CHERYL ANNE PORTER

Puppy Love

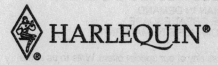

HARLEQUIN®

TORONTO • NEW YORK • LONDON
AMSTERDAM • PARIS • SYDNEY • HAMBURG
STOCKHOLM • ATHENS • TOKYO • MILAN • MADRID
PRAGUE • WARSAW • BUDAPEST • AUCKLAND

Dear Reader,

Well, I finally got it right! I've wanted to write this dog's story for years, but each incarnation—until this one—didn't quite make it. But I *knew* Godzilla deserved to be in a book, so I kept trying. My editor agreed. Twice she told me, when turning down an idea, "We love the dog. Knock off the people." And off I'd go to find new owners and a new story for Godzilla. But now I've done it. So, here is Godzilla, in all her nasty little-dog radiance. Long may she and Kafka love!

Cheryl Anne Porter

Books by Cheryl Anne Porter
HARLEQUIN LOVE & LAUGHTER
21—A MAN IN DEMAND
44—THE GREAT ESCAPE
63—FROM HERE TO MATERNITY

To Gertie, Jordan, Jag and Buster,
Patti, Brittanie and Paige—some of the best dogs
and people I know.

1

"YOU HAVE GOT to be kidding me, Mr. Trenton. Her entire estate? She left it to *me?*" David tightened his grip on the telephone. Clearly, the attorney at the other end of the line had to be mistaken. "But I don't even know an Amelia Stanfield. Why would she leave me *millions* of dollars? Are you certain you have the right person—David Andrew Sullivan? CPA in D.C.?"

By way of an answer, the attorney then read David a litany of his own life's data, forcing him finally to concede, "That's me. But I don't get it. It doesn't— Well, I'm sure you do want to clear this up. So do I, but I can't drive to Virginia— What? No, I really can't. I have a full afternoon. And then I've got a flight to Colorado this evening. What? Alive? What's alive?"

David yanked the handset away from his ear and stared at it as if it had just licked him. Then, frowning in disbelief, he repositioned it and spoke to the waiting attorney, "Define, if you will, Mr. Trenton, 'alive'— as you're using it."

But Mr. Trenton wouldn't. Instead, he embarked on some fancy verbal footwork, saying he couldn't...not over the phone...the will was specific in this regard...yada-yada-yada. As the man droned on, David resorted to half-listening, waiting only for a chance to interrupt and reaffirm his unavailability today. He checked his watch. One-thirty. And then his desk calendar, Friday, October twenty-seventh. He studied his afternoon schedule. Three longtime clients. Busy, but no major problems. Nothing to keep him here late. For once.

Murmuring noncommital responses to the lawyer on the other end of the line, David used the time to study the jotted-down reminder of that evening's flight out of Dulles to Denver. Alicia, his kid sister, was all grown-up getting married next Thursday afternoon. *But not without you there, David,* she'd warned. David grinned, shaking his head. Alicia had always called him a dull boy, a workaholic. Either he closed down shop for a week and came home to Denver for her wedding and all the festivities leading up to it, she'd threatened, or she was bringing the whole affair—crazy family and all—to him. It was his choice. He'd wisely chosen to close up shop. And now, here it was. Time to put up or shut up.

Besides, Alicia was right. He hadn't been home in over a year, so he was overdue for a visit. He could definitely use some downtime. A change in scenery. Maybe a little excitement. Why not? Hell, his packed luggage already sat in his car. All he had to do was get through this afternoon's clients, make sure everything in the office was buttoned down—the home front was no problem...no one and nothing waited there—and then go straight from work to the airport. Otherwise, his family would show up at this airport. And that was the last thing he wanted. So nothing Mr. Trenton could say would influence him to change his plans.

May as well break in and tell him so. "Mr.—Hello? Yes. Sorry to cut you off. But the bottom line is I have a flight to catch later, and I won't be back until the third. So how about Monday, November sixth? I can— What? Will I hold?'' And apparently he would, judging by the recorded violin music now playing in his ear.

David's jaw tightened. *All right, buddy—two minutes. And then you hear the dial tone.* He glanced at his wristwatch, marked when two minutes would be up and then focused on the weather drama unfolding outside the picture window across the room from him. Wind-driven rain pinged against the glass panes and showed no sign of letting up. *Drive to Virginia in this? Not for a million bucks.*

Then David remembered—it really *was* for a million bucks. For *more* than a million bucks. His stomach flip-flopped. What was he thinking? Not drive there? Was he just in shock, or what? Because, hell, he ought to have already broken all land-speed records sprinting down the road…with a fresh ink pen in his hand, ready to sign. Why was he arguing? So what if he didn't remember the lady who'd left him all her money—*and something alive, Dave. Don't forget that part.* All right…so it was alive. He'd have millions of dollars to deal with it—if he'd just get up off his butt and forget about work for one afternoon. Then he'd never have to work again. Except at managing his new wealth.

Really and belatedly excited now, hardly able to sit still until Mr. Trenton came back on the line, David sent up a silent but no less whopping, *Thank you, Mrs. Amelia Stanfield, you sweetheart, no matter who you are! But, yeah, you've got me curious. Were you a client, once? Or just some eccentric old lady who closed your eyes and stabbed a finger at a name—my name—in the phone book? Why not? Stranger things have happened.*

With that thought, David found himself expanding on his theories regarding his benefactress...the lovely, the beautiful, the benevolent Mrs. Stanfield. He was pretty sure she wasn't a relative. Not the way Grandma Sullivan loved to research and discuss family genealogy. *Everybody* in the family's genealogy. Whether you were a Sullivan by birth or marriage, it didn't matter. Your entire life...under the guise of "for the permanent record"...was fodder for her stories around the dinner table. She'd blithely and innocently set about making you squirm.

It happened all the time to Mom and Dad, didn't it? David's chuckle held great affection. There was a reason he handled all the family's financial and legal affairs from afar. His entire family, except for him and Alicia, was totally and sweetly nuts. Need proof? Even now, the folks—those living relics of the hippie era—were off in England, absorbing...how had they put it? Oh, yeah—the cosmic vibes of Stonehenge. With a shake of his head, David recalled himself chiding them before they left. *This is all real groovy, folks, but how about an itinerary?* Which had earned him their oft-repeated lament. *We've raised a child of the Establishment. Where did we go wrong?*

David sighed, remaining certain that only by threats issued by both sets of grandparents that they'd have heart attacks on demand had he and Alicia escaped such names as Human Delight and Daisy Freedom. *Far out, man.* Speaking of far out, David mused, how about the serendipitous timing of this phone call, coupled with the family gathering for Alicia's wedding? Grams and Grampa were RV-ing in to Denver, and Mom and Dad would fly in tomorrow night from London. David could just picture himself telling them all, right in the middle of the festivities, about this unbelievable turn of events in his—Mr. Sensible, as they called him—life.

They'd all flip. Just like he would—and not in a good way—if this…*alive* thing somehow prevented him from going home. Naw, that shouldn't happen. Well, there was no law that said he had to get…*it* today, was there? So maybe he'd just pick it up when he got back. After all, he was rich now—or he would be when Mr. Trenton came back on the line so David could tell him he'd be right there. But still…the darned thing was *alive*. Scary thought.

What could it be? A little kid? *No, seriously.* An exotic lizard? A rare bird? A fungus? A virus with the potential to rid the planet of all its life-forms? David shook his head, thinking, *No, germ warfare wouldn't just be sitting around for some little old lady to pass on to an heir.* Okay, he was letting his imagination get the better of him. So he was curious. Big deal. But he had to admit this was pretty exciting stuff—unlike his staid and predictable existence in the cut-and-dried world of finance.

That thought sat him up straight. Now where had that come from? Mom's and Dad's errant genes? *Don't knock 'em,* an inner voice warned. *Look at you, man. An office on Massachusetts Avenue in the big D.C. You're a suit. A buttoned-down kind of guy. Boring. Come on, Dave, go get the money. And see what that alive thing is. What can it hurt?*

Don't listen to him, the sensible side of him countered, reminding David that's how he got into that running-the-rapids thing last summer. *Remember that? And your former girlfriend? Oh, bring that up,* the adventurous side of him argued. *That cast came off her leg two months ago. And who knew Philippa couldn't swim? It's not like she drowned. And what kinda name for a girl is that, anyway? Forget her. Come on, Dave—you're thirty, man. Getting old. Getting soft—*

Mr. Trenton—finally!—came back on the line with an apology for having put David on hold. "It's okay," David said, cutting him off—*We'll see who's old, who's soft*—and taking the plunge. "I changed my mind. I'll be right there. I just need time to rearrange my clients—Sir, are you crying? You're not? Because it sounded like—No, I wouldn't *toy* with you. I said I'd be there. Only I can't take the alive thing right now. What? Don't worry because it's safely contained?"

Safely contained? As in radioactive material? David scrubbed a hand over his face. *I'm a dead man.* Then, at the lawyer's out-and-out insistence that he do so, David promised, "I *swear* to you, Mr. Trenton, that I will be there. Yes—Tysons Corner. I'm writing down your address now. What? Oh, um, God bless you, too. Yeah. Goodbye."

Frowning, David hung up the phone and stared at it. Then he swung his gaze to his closed office door. His gut clenched. Mrs. Hopemore—secretary extraordinaire, Grandma Sullivan's friend and a woman who took delight in telling all his clients that she'd babysat him and changed his diapers—would not be amused. She was as bad as him about working. Getting her to change his schedule was akin to hand-to-hand combat with a squadron of Marines.

Telling himself he was ready to face her, yet not ready to tell her why he was changing his plans—his natural caution in all things monetary had him wanting first to verify his good fortune before she spread the word, and he knew she would via Grandma Sullivan—he sat back and yelled, "Mrs. Hopemore? Can you come in here, please?"

And then, as always, he waited, silently counting. One one-thousand, two one-thousand, up to ten one-thousand before the door finally swung open. And into the room stepped the tiny, gray-haired, outrageously dressed and totally terrifying Mrs. Hopemore. Already, her red-painted lips were pursed in disapproval. "You bellowed, Mr. Sullivan?"

"I did." She insisted on calling him Mr. Sullivan. Even though she'd known him since birth.

"Well, what do you want? I've got work to do."

David narrowed his eyes at the thousand-year-old lady. Despite all her connections to him and his family, he really ought to fire her. And had. Twice. But both times, when he'd come in to work the next day, there she was. At her desk. Typing. And telling him he was late. And both times that he'd terminated her employment she'd given herself a raise. If he fired her again, her salary would exceed his. He couldn't afford that. So, he said, "I need you to cancel my afternoon appointments and reschedule them for when I get back. That last call you put through to me was about an…urgent matter up in Tysons Corner."

Her penciled-in black eyebrows rose like McDonald's arches above her tortoiseshell eyeglasses. "Tysons Corner, is it? Did somebody die?"

Death—excluding his own—David knew, was the only reason she would accept for a disruption in their workday. Hell, she was barely allowing him to be gone for his own sister's wedding. Even though she herself had been off last week because of a friend's illness and then sudden demise. But now he was thankful for that because he had the same excuse. "Yes, someone died."

And then he waited...for her permission, essentially. Sure enough, Mrs. Hopemore's expression pruned, became that of a warden weighing the parole-worthiness of a particularly heinous inmate. But finally she waved an age-spotted hand in dismissal. "Fine. Go. Just leave me here with all this work. It's enough that I can't go to Alicia's wedding because I have to hold down the fort here while you're gone for a week."

"Now that's not true. And you know it. You were invited, too. I told you we could just close the office and go, didn't I? Grandma would love to see you."

Her chin came up. "I know all that, young man. But it's just not possible. Someone has to keep this place going. And speaking of that, I don't know where I'm supposed to move your afternoon appointments to. I already moved these clients from next week to today because of that wedding. Now I've got to change them to a date later than their original times. You do know what's going to happen, don't you? You'll lose their business, and we'll both starve to death."

David glared at her. "You're secretly in love with me, aren't you, Mrs. Hopemore?"

"Ha!" She was already swinging the door closed behind herself. "I used to change your diapers. Besides, you should be so lucky." The office door slammed closed.

One one-thousand. Two one-thousand. Three— The door opened. Mrs. Hopemore again. Knowing what was coming, David fought a grin. He'd lived in D.C.

for nearly seven years and knew all the ins and outs of getting around this maze that was the capitol city. But try telling her that. Or even Grandma Sullivan, who'd insisted, years ago and all the way from Ohio, that he hire her friend. So she could keep an eye on him, see to it that he didn't get himself killed. They both treated him as if he just fell off the turnip truck.

Sure enough, standing in the doorway, her hand on the knob, Mrs. Hopemore fussed. "Wear your raincoat. And use your umbrella. No sense catching cold and missing more work. And stay off I-395 at this time of day. Instead, go across the Key Bridge and north on G.W. Parkway to Chain Bridge Road, which is Highway 123. Then stay on that, past the CIA Headquarters on your right, all the way to Tysons Corner."

That settled, she turned to go, but stopped and again pivoted to face him. "And don't pick up a hitchhiking ax murderer. It'd be just like you to get yourself killed. And if you did, do you know what that'd make me? Unemployed, that's what." Again, she slammed the door behind herself.

Grinning, staring at the door, David nodded. "Yep. She loves me."

IT WAS HIM. He was the right one. The money was his. It was mind-boggling, the amount of money. So all David wanted to do was sign the papers, deal with the money matters and get the heck out of here to go celebrate. But first things first, Mr. Trenton had insisted before he left the room. He'd said he had to get something first, before anything was signed. Something that was David's.

Well, whatever that Something was in the next room with Mr. Trenton, it was kicking the man's tail big-time. And David didn't want it. Yelling, cursing, window-rattling, banging…all that filtered through to his hearing. Seated in the lawyer's elegant outer office and giving a wary stare to the wainscoted wall that separated him from the melee, David wondered if he should go help Mr. Trenton. Just then, another yelp— decidedly human and followed by a curse—helped him make up his mind. Naw. It sounded like the lawyer was holding his own.

With that thought, David sank back into the maroon leather wing chair and, with no other choice but to wait, made a determined effort to thumb through a dog-eared magazine he'd picked up off the cherrywood table perched at his elbow. But then came a "Yowtch!" The cry snapped David's head up, and he inadvertently crumpled the glossy copy of *Today's Lawyer* as he listened to the muffled battle.

"Don't you bite me, you little demon. Behave yourself. Come *here*." The man's voice then changed to a wheedling, begging tone. "There now, that's better. Yes, that's nice. Come to Mr. Trenton. No one's going to hurt— Ouch! Why, you little—I ought to— Ow, ow, ow!"

David eyed the closed door and wondered, *So why am I still sitting here? The inheritance will still stand a week from now.* "That's right," he said out loud to himself. "Game over. Goodbye," he further and cheerily announced to the furniture as he tossed the ruined magazine onto the ornately carved desk and stood up.

But an angry yip brought him back to his seat, had him gripping the armrests. Then all was silence. Ominous silence. David cocked his head, listening, and was rewarded with the sudden and renewed sounds of battle. Cried warnings, running feet, scraping and banging and…was that growling? Whatever it was, it was getting louder, as if it meant to come in here. David's heart thumped. Then it stopped. The noise, that is. Not his heart. Well, maybe his heart. He put a hand over it, checked. Still beating. And while it was, he was leaving.

As he levered himself up again, David kept his wary gaze locked on the labeled private door. *If that door opens—* It opened. The lawyer entered. Too late for escape. And he wasn't alone. Or unscathed. Gaping at the man's appearance, David leaped up from his seat. "What the hell happened to you? And what's in that cage? Why's it snarling?"

"Because it doesn't wish to *be* in this cage, Mr. Sullivan. Now, clear a path. And then get out of the way, I beg you."

Not needing to be begged, David got out of the way in only two giant steps, taking up his last-ditch position behind his chair. Clutching at its high back, he eyed the short, paunchy attorney's stiff-legged and cautious approach. For his part, the older man paid strict attention to the wildly pitching Pet Porter he held out at arm's length…with both gauze-wrapped hands.

Gauze-wrapped? The man hadn't been bandaged when they shook hands, David recalled. Nor had he been pasty-faced with fear. This turn of events, then, was decidedly *not* good. As Mr. Trenton neared his desk—his concentration still that of a man carrying enough nitroglycerin to obliterate all of Western civilization—David flicked his gaze to The Occupant.

Inside the small, hard-sided carrier, the wildly whirling and howling little critter suddenly stilled and glared at David with beady eyes. Then it lunged at the

open-weave mesh of the—*Thank you*—securely gated
door. David jerked into a reactionary crouch, but immediately felt pretty silly. So he straightened up and,
pointing at the critter, called out over its unholy din,
"Is that a badger, Mr. Trenton? Because it looks like
a badger."

"I assure you, sir, it is *not* a badger. We couldn't
be so lucky." The balding, red-faced and wheezing
attorney gritted out as he plunked the carrier on his
desk and jumped back from it.

David wasn't appeased. "Why's it so mad? What
did you do to it?"

Jerking toward David, his bandaged hands held up
as if they were Exhibit A submitted into evidence, Mr.
Trenton bleated, "Look at me, Mr. Sullivan. I'm the
wounded one here. And you ask what did *I* do to *it?*
That 'it' in the cage is a dog. A very spoiled and nasty-
tempered little dog, to be sure. But—and you have no
idea how greatly it pleases me to say this—it is now
your very spoiled and nasty-tempered little dog, Mr.
Sullivan."

As ticked off as he was surprised by the man's obvious—he hated using one of Mrs. Hopemore's out-
dated words, but it fit here—*glee,* David jutted his jaw
out, saying, "I'm not sure I like your attitude, Mr.
Trenton."

The old guy's brown eyes widened, his lips
twitched and he said, "No doubt, Mr. Sullivan—and
favors for an old friend aside—you'll be surprised to
find that I don't give a cat's fur ball if you do or
don't."

It was then, into the ensuing silence, and much to
David's openmouthed distress, that the elegant little
attorney simply came undone. He began crying. For

real, honest to God tears. Alarm gripped David as he fought another overwhelming urge to turn and flee. He had no clue what to say, what to do, who to call to bring a net.

But just then, Mr. Trenton sobered…some. He pulled his potbellied self erect and awkwardly—given his bandaged state—pulled a handkerchief from a pocket. Holding his eyeglasses up, he mopped at his eyes. "I do apologize, Mr. Sullivan. I assure you that I am not normally rude to my clients. But I have been through a living hell with this dog."

"Yeah, I can see that," David conceded.

As if encouraged by David's response, Mr. Trenton nodded, replacing his wadded hanky in his pocket. "But my good fortune in your actually coming here today only proves to me that there *is* a supreme and infinitely compassionate deity who, despite what the general public believes, does look in favor upon those who choose to practice law."

Frowning, David slogged through the man's elevated language, tossing the wheat from the chaff, until he believed he'd found the important words. Then, ignoring all else—cat's fur balls, rudeness and deities— he chose to point at the beast in question and stare at the attorney. "So, what you're telling me is that's a dog, and it's mine? As in my dog? You're kidding me, right?"

The attorney's eyebrows rose menacingly. "Do I look to you as if I'm kidding, Mr. Sullivan? I assure you, I am not. But go ahead—" he nodded toward the carrier "—take a peek. See for yourself. I dare you."

Really not liking the little man now, David ducked his chin. Then eyed the carrier. And swallowed. *Come on, Dave, you played four years of college football.*

You can do this. "Fine." Thus steeled, David stalked to the desk, grasped the Pet Porter by its handle and lifted it to his eye level. Peering inside, he saw—sure enough—a wiry-haired and wildly yapping… "Dog. Sweet Mary, a dog." He turned to Mr. Sullivan. "I can't keep a dog. I don't know the first thing about them. I've never—"

Cutting off his own words, David set the carrier on the desk and confirmed, "No way." Then he launched into a full retreat, striding purposefully for the brass coatrack and ceramic umbrella stand to one side of the hallway door. He grabbed his raincoat and turned to the sputtering attorney. "I'm sorry, Mr. Trenton, but I'm not your man. Someone's made a big mistake." He pulled his dripping umbrella from the stand. "I don't have room for a dog. Not in my condo or in my life. Like I told you on the phone, I've got a flight out of town in—" he looked at his watch "—less than three hours. I'm already late, so if you'll excuse me, I'm leaving."

"You're leaving? What about the money, Mr. Sullivan? No dog, no money. It's a stipulation of the will."

"You're lying." The words were out before David could think.

Mr. Trenton stiffened with insult. "I'm doing no such thing. You'll see when you sign the papers. But to do that, you have to take the dog. And keep it. You can't give it away. Or sell it. It's yours. And I am *not* keeping this…this *demon* for even one more day. Two weeks is enough." His voice broke on a sob. "Look at my condition, sir, and have pity. I too am leaving this very afternoon—for a much-deserved month-long rest." Then the attorney narrowed his eyes. "Do you know what I mean when I say rest?"

David stared at the wide-eyed, scratched up, undone little man, and said, "I think so, Mr. Trenton, after that cat's fur ball speech. And, yeah, I'd love to have all the money. But that dog…I don't think so. Can't you just kennel it somewhere for now? I can't take it with me, either."

Mr. Trenton all but jumped up and down in place, so agitated was he. "No, no, no! You have to. You *are* taking it. Right now. This dog is yours. And you are taking it." Fired up, Mr. Trenton charged across the room toward David. "You are not to leave here without that dog, Mr. Sullivan. Miss Stanfield's will—"

"—could be a diabolical plot by a foreign government, for all I know." David finished the sentence for him. "I'll sign the papers but that…that—" David pointed to it "—dog is *not* leaving here with me tonight. I'm warning you, stop right there."

But Mr. Trenton kept coming at David. Why, the little man meant to attack him. Righteous conviction and determination to have his way, when combined with the heat of the moment and the stumpy little man's crazed advance, had David brandishing, swordlike, his closed and sopping umbrella. Droplets of water from it flew about willy-nilly, spotting the expensive carpet.

Boink. Too late, Mr. Trenton stopped. Much to David's distress, the umbrella's pointy tip poked hard into the chubby folds of the suddenly sick-looking and outraged attorney's belly. Who now cocked his heavy-jowled head, looked David right in the eyes and said, "You've poked my person, Mr. Sullivan. As a result,

I'm suffering great pain and anguish. Why, I believe
you have just committed assault and battery upon my
person. Unless..."

"So. YOU'RE A DOG, HUH?" David glanced over, feeling pretty silly for questioning the suspiciously sub-
dued inhabitant of the Pet Porter that perched on his
car's passenger seat. Outside, the sky steadily darkened with rain and approaching dusk. The windshield
wipers chased each other across the wet streaked glass,
keeping time as David drove to D.C.

Getting no answer from the furry part of his huge
windfall, for which he'd just had to sign a lot of papers
in Mr. Trenton's office, David watched the road and
added, "Look, I'm not any happier about this than you
are. My choices were keeping you for the rest of your
life and all the money you come with—or a lawsuit.
So, here's the deal. I'm exiting at Reston, since it's
on the way to the airport, and hunting a kennel there
for you. When I get back, I'll...I don't know...keep
you, et cetera, but just not with me. Maybe I'll pay
someone to keep you for me."

He thought about that and then chuckled. "Maybe
not. Poor, unsuspecting people. Okay, so I don't know
what to do with you. You got any ideas?" With his
question, David again glanced over at the animal carrier. Black eyes glittered at him from behind the wire-
mesh door. Refusing to feel like a heel—none of this
was his fault—David shook his head as he divided his
attention between the traffic and his inheritance.
"Knock it off. The cute-little-puppy act isn't working," he assured the dog...and himself.

"Because I've seen you in action. You trashed Mr.
Trenton's office worse than Godzilla did Tokyo. So

don't think you can make me feel guilty with those big, dark eyes.'' He glanced over again—yep, big, dark eyes. He was a sucker for big, dark eyes. ''Look, it's nothing personal. It's just that I work odd hours. And tax season is coming up. Besides, I date, I travel, I entertain. I'm a single guy. I'm not home a lot. I don't have the time or the patience for a pet. Or anything else that needs me to walk it and feed it and care for it. That's not me. Understand?''

No answer. So they rode on in silence for long moments. Then David blurted, ''Did I say yet that I live in a high-rise no-pets-allowed condo? See? I can't keep you with me. Now I know your…mama died and you're sad. And I'm sorry for that. But think what it'd be like for you with me, alone and cooped up all day in a condo. What you need is a yard and kids.'' Another vision of the bloodied and desperate Mr. Trenton presented itself. ''Well, maybe not kids, but someone. Anyone. Except me.''

At the turnoff to Reston, Virginia, David exited from the stop-and-go flow of the motorized ocean surrounding him. Then, and accepting it as the sign from above that it was, his gaze immediately lit upon a proud neon sign proclaiming a veterinarian's clinic and kennel. ''Hallelujah,'' David said. ''Life is good.''

The Wright Choice Clinic and Kennel. What more did he need to know? Thinking he may as well break the news to his dog—that got a fatalistic sigh out of him—David ducked his head to peer into the carrier. A thumping tail and a pathetic whine greeted him. A tiny pink tongue tipped against the cold metal bars of the gratelike door. David's shoulders and his resolve slumped. All that fatal cuteness. He suspected he was done for, even as he straightened up, gripped the steering wheel with both hands and edged his car over to the right lane. "Great. Just what I need. A dog."

2

THAT DISMAYING THOUGHT accompanied David until he got to the clinic's driveway. But when he pulled into a parking space and flipped the gearshift to park, his spirits lifted. Because hanging in the doorway was an Open sign. Further evidence of a divine providence, David decided as he turned off the windshield wipers, lights and finally the car's engine. First unbelting himself, he then reached over, gripped the Pet Porter handle, lifted the carrier onto his lap, then opened the car door. "Let's go, pal. Time to get rained on."

Proving his point, David dashed through the driving rain to the clinic. He skidded to a halt under the overhanging eave of the narrow porch's roof. Just then, and inside, a slender, white-coated, dark-haired woman—whose attention was otherwise directed over her shoulder—casually flipped the sign to Closed and flicked off the outside lights.

Never one to be left in the dark, much less out in the rain, David knocked on the glass. "Hey, wait a minute. Ma'am? Doctor? Hello!"

The woman jerked and spun to face him, a hand to her chest, her long, dark hair swirling poetically about her shoulders. Under a fringe of bangs, her big, dark eyes, set in an angelic face, widened in startlement. David's insides tightened…then he groaned. *More big, dark eyes*. Instantly, she unlocked and opened the door, stepping aside to allow the immensely relieved and soaked David to enter.

Then she hurriedly closed the door behind him, shutting out the wind and the rain, and met his gaze. "I am *so* sorry. I didn't see you out there. Rodney said something that distracted me and—"

"Wr-rack, go away. It's suppertime."

The woman gasped as David, in the act of running a hand through his sopping hair and staring appreciatively at her, jerked toward the sound of the raspy, definitely not human voice. And *really* stared. Slowly, he lowered his hand. And raised his eyebrows at the biggest, whitest, most…*plumed* bird he'd ever seen. The sucker was two feet tall, if it was an inch. Its black feet gripped a wooden stand that perched in a corner of the waiting room.

The bird, with its head lowered, eyed him right back and squawked, "Wr-rack, not polite to stare, mate."

Blinking, David turned to the pretty, dark-haired and embarrassed woman and jerked his thumb toward the bird. "Rodney, I presume?"

She nodded, looking even more attractive somehow as she rolled her eyes in an apologetic gesture and confirmed, "Yeah. Rodney." Then, she stared wordlessly at him, almost as if he were a long-lost friend. Or lover. The very air between them seemed to thicken.

Caught up in this shared moment, David stared at her, noting her features. Like her eyes. He'd been wrong. They weren't brown. Or black. They were blue. A deep, dark blue…like twilight. And luminous. As luminous as her dark brown hair. But it was her mouth—

"Oh, I'm sorry. I'm…staring, aren't I?" Then she

became all business, which somehow gave her away. Dare he hope she was as captivated by him as he was by her? "I was just closing for the day. But if this is an emergency—"

"It is." David rushed in, rousing himself from his decidedly warm thoughts.

"It is?" she repeated, reaching for the carrier and looking ready to go into veterinarial action.

"Okay, it isn't," David confessed, swinging the Pet Porter away from her grasp. She stopped short, put her hands in her lab coat pockets and stared at him, her eyebrows arching. David caved. "Well, not the usual blood-and-guts emergency you probably see. It's more of a desperate-situation emergency."

"I see." A silence followed, into which she at last said, "Go on."

What's wrong with me, David wondered. He wasn't usually this wishy-washy around women. Could it be the doctor's good looks were at the root of his indecisiveness? *Doctor?* Wait a minute. She *was* the doctor, right? David looked her up and down. "You are the Dr. Emily Wright listed on the sign outside, aren't you?"

"Oh. Yes. Of course. I'm sorry. I should have said so right off." But then she glanced at her watch— another sign she was anxious to leave—and focused again on David. "Now, how can I help you?"

"By not throwing me out, for one thing," he said, giving her a hopeful grin. "I appreciate your letting me in, even though I don't have an appointment. Well, *he* doesn't have an appointment, I mean." He hoped Dr. Wright was as nice and understanding as she was attractive. But for good measure, he added, "Please. I really am desperate here."

"Yes. You've said that." Then the woman frowned, her gaze again flitting to the animal carrier and back to David. "I don't mean to sound rude, but is something, or is something not, wrong with your dog?"

Caught off guard, David blurted, "What dog? I don't have a dog."

EMILY STIFFENED, fisting her hands in her white lab coat's pockets. *Extremely attractive man. And insane.* Apparently just her type, if one went by her recent romantic track record. But still, she heard herself saying, "Excuse me?"

The tall, dark and handsome man shrugged his broad shoulders as a red flush crept up his neck and cheeks. "Well, obviously, I *have* a dog. I mean, here it is. I just meant it's not *my* dog."

"I see," she said, but she didn't really. Then, when he didn't offer any explanation, Emily felt compelled to ask, "Is it your mother's? A friend's or a neighbor's?" Then, although she had a feeling she already knew the answer, she added, "Your wife's, maybe?"

"Wife? No. None of the above."

"Good." Emily heard the triumph in her voice. Immediately, a flush claimed her cheeks, telling her she was turning as red as he still was. "Well, I mean…good that you— Um, just tell me what it is you need from me."

The man said nothing. Just stared at her, his eyebrows slowly arching. But to Emily, her words hung like weighted piñatas between them. Dying fourteen kinds of death inside, she heard them again. *Tell me what it is you need from me. Great, Emily. Has a woman anywhere in the course of human history ever given a man a more perfect opening?* Okay, so she'd broken up with Jeff over six months ago. And it had been a long dry spell since. But why did her body have to pick this moment to rediscover its libido?

Finally, the man, his raincoat dripping onto the bare linoleum floor, saved them both by repeating, "What do I need from you? I guess the safest answer is a doggy bed. For the next week or so."

Such a diplomatic response. What a relief. But then, Emily caught his meaning. "A doggy bed? You mean…you want me to board your pet?" Her expression drooped. "Oh, I'm sorry, but I don't have any openings. There's nothing I can—"

He reached out and gripped her arm, startling her, but not unpleasantly so. "Please. I have a plane to catch, and I can't take this dog with me. I'm desperate, Dr. Wright. I'll pay you whatever you say."

"It's not the money," she assured him, her gaze lowering to his hand on her forearm. His fingers were lean and strong, his touch warm and reassuring somehow. Emily looked up, met his slate-gray eyes and felt her heart leap. Drawing in a steadying breath, she rushed on. "The problem is your eyes are gray." Her heart stopped. "No, my kennels are gray." Her heart stopped again. "No—occupied! They're occupied. They're not gray at all. They have dogs in them."

Near to bursting into tears, so embarrassed was she that even when he released her to hold his hand up and assure her, "Whoa. It's okay. Really. It's not your fault. If you're full, you're full," it didn't help. Not one bit. She still wanted to crawl into a corner somewhere.

But it was his expression that kept her in place, that had her looking outside herself. His look mirrored his obvious disappointment at this turn of events as he set the small animal carrier down. Then sounding as if he were merely thinking aloud, he grumbled, "Great. Now what do I do? I'm going to miss my flight home. Talk about stuck."

Talk about awkward. Not knowing what else to do, Emily crossed her arms under her bosom and took the concerned and friendly route. "A plane home, huh? Please don't tell me it's a family emergency because then I'm really going to feel bad."

The man's gaze brightened. Hope sparked in those deep-set eyes of his. "Start feeling bad. It is a family emergency. Of the worst kind. A wedding—one that's been put off too long already. And if I don't show, there won't be one."

"Oh. That sounds awful." Then she heard herself. "Well, not the wedding. I didn't mean that." Emily watched his gaze rove over her face as she spoke and felt her pulse pick up. Fatalistically, she told herself, *Emily, meet the groom. Wonderful*. The first man to make her pulse race in what seemed like decades—and all he had to do was stand there to do it—was trying to get home to his beloved. Great. "I meant about the bad things, of course," she added when the silence between them began to stretch out.

He blinked. "Yeah. Thanks." Then, changing the subject and the mood, he said, "Listen, I need a minute to think this through, preferably out of the rain. Can I impose on you a little bit longer while I do that?"

"Sure," Emily said. "Take your time."

A nod and a flash of a grin thanked her. He then rubbed his chin and turned his back to her, staring out into the dark and stormy night.

For her part, Emily melted, standing there, admiring

his broad shoulders…and realized she was trying to picture what he'd look like without his clothes on. *Quit ogling the guy, Emily. And do the right thing. Jeez. How would you feel?* All right, fine, she fussed at her conscience. Then, mustering all her polite and false detachment, she said, "So, a wedding, huh? That sounds, um, romantic."

His first response was a chuckle. Then, without turning around, he said, "Romantic? Not under these circumstances."

"No. I guess not." Then Emily had a brilliant idea, one that would mean she might *see* him again, married or not. "If you like, I can call some other kennels in the area and see if one of them has an opening."

The man spun around to face her, his expression lit by a dazzling grin that all but brought Emily to her knees. He opened his mouth—no doubt, to express his gratitude. But Rodney cut him off with a wolf whistle and a screech. "Wr-rack…knew you'd cave. Sucker!"

Emily felt the blood drain from her face as she stared wide-eyed at the equally startled man in front of her. "Rodney means me, I'm sure. Not you. After all, I'm the one…who offered…and…oh, never mind." Emily covered her eyes with a hand and took a deep breath. Then she again faced the rain-soaked, now clearly amused man on a romantic mission, and said, "I'll just go make those calls."

He chuckled and said, "Thanks. You're more than kind."

"Aren't I, though?" she mumbled as she turned away, heading for the partitioned area of the waiting room that housed the neat clutter of her assistant's desk. As she passed Rodney, she shot him a look that had him edging to the far end of his perch and warning, "Wr-rack, watch out, I'm armed."

Emily rolled her eyes. Just her luck to inherit the only cockatoo in the world with the IQ of a smart-aleck ten-year-old. *Thanks, Grandpa,* she thought, arrowing her comment heavenward, but not the least bit sure she shouldn't send it directly to the big white bird on the perch. *It'd be just like you to find a way to inhabit Rodney's feathered body so you can keep an eye on me, you stinker.* Behind the desk, flipping through the Rolodex and reaching for the phone, Emily looked up. "I need to get some— Oh, you startled me."

The man stood directly in front of her, placing the Pet Porter on the receptionist's counter. "You need to get some what?" he prompted, obviously waiting for her to fill in the blanks.

"Information," Emily blurted. "On the dog. So if we get lucky—" *If we get lucky?* A blazing heat claimed her cheeks, but she kept right on talking. "—and find a kennel who'll take your dog, I can give them the answers they'll need to plan for his stay."

Apparently oblivious to her suggestive slip of the tongue, he frowned. "Information? Like what?"

Emily managed a smile. "Nothing hard. Like the dog's age."

"His age?" He shrugged his broad shoulders. "I'm not sure. I—"

"Oh, that's all right," Emily assured him. "They'd just need to know if he's a nursing puppy or a really old dog." She peeked into the carrier. "No. He's not either of those. Good." She then focused on the handsome hunk of man and heard herself say, "So, how about sex?"

The guy's eyes popped open wide. "Excuse me?"

Emily wanted nothing more than to unzip her skin, step out of it and walk away. "*His* sex. I meant his— Wait. Duh. *His.* So you said…and so did I." She huffed out a pained breath. "Okay, he's male. Breed?"

The man's expression drooped. "Breed? I guess he can. I haven't checked. Oh, wait. You mean *what's* his breed and not *can* he, right? My mistake. But again…I don't know." It was his turn to peek into the carrier. "Mutt, I suppose."

"Mutt," Emily intoned, as if this were the password that opened a door to another universe. "Okay, good. So, do you know his vaccination history or feeding habits and general health? What about his dog tag number?"

"None of the above. A dog tag number?" The man's expression had glazed over. He stared at her now…without blinking.

Emily nodded. "Yes. His dog tag. He *is* registered with the county, isn't he? He *has* had his shots, right? I can't place him at any reputable kennel unless he's—"

"He's registered," the drop-dead gorgeous man assured her. "I'm sure of it."

But he didn't sound sure of it, just as he hadn't been with any of his answers thus far. One thing was clear. This man knew nothing about this dog. And proved it, as far as Emily was concerned, when he again peered into the carrier's depths, as if to verify for himself that the dog indeed had a tag on its collar. Warning bells—very belated ones—sounded in Emily's head as she watched him glance at his watch. What was going on here? Had she been so caught up with his handsome presence that she'd missed something important? Something dangerous? Even illegal?

Feeling suddenly very alone with this man, Emily was glad for the wood partition and desk that separated them. If the need arose, she could…what? Yell for Rodney? *As if.* Maybe sic the German shepherd kenneled out back on him? She'd never make it to his run before being grabbed. Then, what? Fling the man's own portered pet at him? No, wait…he'd said it wasn't his. It now occurred to her that he'd never said just whose it was, either.

Fright licked at Emily's insides. Maybe she'd be best served by quickly finding a kennel with an opening and sending this stranger on his way. What had she been thinking to let him in after hours, when she was alone? How many times had she warned Karen, her assistant, about this exact thing? After all, good looks and nice clothes were no guarantees of sanity and honesty.

"Is something wrong?" the man asked, frowning. "I appreciate your offer to help, but I am in a hurry. If you don't wish to—"

"Oh, but I do," Emily countered, softening her words with a smile. No sense letting him know she was onto him. Whatever that meant. "Um, let me just go ahead with that call."

"Thank you."

Polite, but not forthcoming. This was getting more and more curious. Emily ached to ask him point-blank just whose the dog was, if not his. But instead, taking the nonchallenging road, she prompted, "Still, I guess you know his name." She managed a grin, a chuckle—and then just blurted her growing suspicion. "I mean, you didn't steal him or anything, did you?"

The man's gray eyes widened. "No, of course not. It's, um, Godzilla."

A struck-dumb moment passed before Emily said, "What is?"

He nodded, looking suddenly pleased with himself. "The dog. Godzilla. That's his name."

Emily found herself nodding right along with him. But she couldn't have said why. "Godzilla? Like the dinosaur monster in the Japanese movies?" She leaned forward over the desk and peered into the carrier. Then she faced the man. "That tiny little dog's name is Godzilla?"

"Yes."

"Because...?"

"Try taking him out of there."

Emily pulled back at the man's challenge and met his gaze. He was serious. She glanced again at the Pet Porter. Just then, the man, whatever his name was, brushed back his sleeve and again checked his watch. Then he shifted his attention to her, sending her a pleading can-we-speed-this-up look. Her thought exactly. Thinking she'd call the Reston Pet Hotel for him, Emily spun the Rolodex with more force than necessary.

The stirred air sent a curled fax into a lazy swirl to the floor. Grimacing her exasperation, Emily reached to pick it up, glanced at the headline and froze as the words invaded her consciousness.

Dognappers! Karen had mentioned this fax had come from the police department. They warned area vets to be on the lookout for suspicious activity. Her assistant had said that rich peoples' beloved pets were being nabbed from their homes, boarded with unwitting veterinarians, essentially being held captive, until a "reward" came through. Read "ransom." And if the owners didn't pay, the pets were taken out and— *No!*

Yes. And the odds were she had one of them right here in her office. In a sweat, Emily angled a glance in the man's direction—why had she ever thought he was attractive, the snake?—and watched him stroking a finger along the wire-mesh door of the animal carrier. He spoke in a low voice to the caged dog and said something that made it whimper. In fear, no doubt.

Well, not this puppy, mister. And not this vet. Emily squatted on the other side of the desk, out of the man's view, and chirped, "Uh-oh, silly me. Look what I've dropped. I'll only be a moment." She stayed there, her knees scrunched to her chest, her arms around her legs, and plotted. She had to save this dog, Godzilla. What a stupid fake name. She should have known right then. *Okay, first things first. Don't provoke him. Stay healthy. Can't help if I'm dead.* Emily bit back her whimper by stuffing a knuckle in her mouth.

All right, next—don't do anything to arouse his suspicions that you're onto him. She looked at herself. *Like squatting down behind this desk for an extended period of time.* She risked a glance up, her gaze lighting on the telephone. She had to call the police. Darn it, he'd never allow her to complete that call unless— her eyes narrowed in calculation—he wasn't here when she called them. Yeah, *he* wasn't here, but the *dog* was.

Good idea, Emily. Okay, how to separate him from the dog. She stared at the fax as she thought. Then...of course! It was brilliant. She sprung up—somewhat like a jack-in-the-box, she suspected, given the man's start of surprise. "You know what? I just remembered that I *can* keep your dog."

"Wr-rack, here we go."

"Rodney!" Emily shrieked as she spun toward the bird. "One more word out of you, and I'll ship you off to the rain forest." She waited. Rodney cocked his head, stretching his neck out at her in a challenge. But finally he ducked his head under a wing. Only then did Emily pivot to face the handsome, horrid man. "Like I said, I'll keep your dog."

A brilliant smile lit his face. "You will? That'd be great. Thanks." Then he sobered some. "But I thought your kennels were full. Did something change while you were down there on the floor?"

A guilty flush washed over Emily. "Yes, something did. But you shouldn't worry about it." Immediately she picked up a clipboard and a form, pushing them and a pen at the despicable stranger. "Here. Fill out this owner information form. And then you can be on your way. I'll take care of everything else."

And, boy, would she! She could already see the coming week's various headlines. Quick-Thinking Local Veterinarian Saves the Dog and the Day. Foils Suspected Ring of Dognappers. Parade in Her Honor on Saturday. Grateful Owners Lavish Rewards on Beautiful Doctor. Local Hero, Dr. Emily Wright, to Wed Mel Gibson.

It could happen. Emily folded her hands and smiled as the unsuspecting criminal began filling out the form. Certain he was cooperating, she implemented part two of her plan: get the dog safely away from its napper. Bravely, she stretched across the counter and took hold of the carrier, pulling it toward her, saying, "While you're doing that, I'll just take, um, Godzilla to the back and—''

''No, don't do that.'' His expression as alarmed as his words, the man dropped the clipboard and the pen to grab the Pet Porter. His hands atop hers, he easily resisted her tugging efforts.

''Okay. I won't.'' Emily fought to overcome her wildly thumping heart and her suddenly weak knees. Her hands, all but lost under his, ached at the strength evident in his grip. One good yank and he'd have her dragged right over the counter. Swallowing hard and striving for the same soothing tone she used on large, agitated dogs, she said, ''I'll just leave him right here where everyone can see him. All nice and safe now. No problems.''

The man met her gaze and relaxed his grip. When he did, Emily exhaled, blinked several times…but didn't move. Not even when the man spoke. ''I didn't mean to startle you. It's just that Godzilla bites. He's not a very nice little dog.''

''No dog is when its scared.'' The words just popped out of her mouth. The alleged dognapper cocked his head à la Rodney and frowned at her. Emily offered a conciliatory grin. But powerless to do anything until the man released her, she further assured him. ''I promise I'll be very careful with Godzilla. I'm a trained professional, you know.'' She glanced at her watch. ''Besides it's not getting any earlier. I'm talking about your flight, the plane you have to catch.''

That worked. ''You're right.'' He let go of her, again checked the time, then grabbed the clipboard and pen. ''I'll work on this. Go ahead and take him back to the kennels. But, seriously, be careful—that dog is vicious.''

''So you said.'' Emily pulled the Pet Porter off the counter and held the hard plastic shell in her arms like she would a baby. With its weight thus balanced, she began backing toward the door to the kennels. ''Don't worry about a thing,'' she told the man. ''Godzilla will be just fine. I'll be right back. You work on the form.''

Her voice trailed off as she felt the doorknob bump against her kidney. She fumbled behind herself one-handedly and finally got the door open and herself and Godzilla across the threshold and into the kennel area. Sure enough, once they saw her, every dog in its run set up a happy, howling cacophony. Suppertime. But forced to ignore them, given that she was gasping and shuddering, Emily turned and slammed the door shut, punching in the lock button on the knob.

Only then did she collapse and stare mindlessly at her paying guests. She'd done it! They were safe. So far. Now call the police. *Can't. The phone's out there on Karen's desk. Doggone it.* How many times had Karen asked her to get an extension and a second phone? *Okay, so go to the examining rooms and see to the dog. It might have been hurt when it was nabbed.*

Good plan. Emily pushed away from the door and hurried to the right, to the operating room, closed that door behind her, then set the carrier on the surgical table. Bending down, ignoring the leaden thump of her fearful heart, she put her finger to her lips, shushing the whining, glittery-eyed canine inside. ''It's okay, Godzilla. Or whatever your real name is. You're going to be fine. You just have to trust me.''

With that, she lifted the latch on the wire-mesh door

and opened it. The dog scooted to the back of its carrier and cowered there, shivering. Instant anger washed over Emily, its object the person who'd reduced this poor little creature to such a state. Carefully, she reached inside and drew the short-legged, brown, spiky-haired, ten-pounds-or-so doggy out and into her arms. Around its neck was a blue-leather, fake-jewel-studded collar. But no dog tag by which to trace its owners. No doubt, the criminal had removed it for exactly that reason. Darn him.

"Well, look at you," Emily cooed as she petted the pup, ignoring for the moment the need to act quickly. First things first. The little creature in her arms needed to trust her before she could examine it. But beyond that, it was a victim and needed reassuring. "What a sweet boy you are. Yes, you are. You don't bite, do you? No, you're a good boy—" Cutting off her words was what she didn't feel against her palm. "Wait a minute." In one deft but gentle motion, she flipped the dog over in her arms and looked. "Why, Godzilla—you're a girl."

And that proved it—this was a stolen dog. The man out there, that rotten scum, hadn't even had its sex right. Emily again cradled Godzilla in her arms and rubbed between her pointy ears as she thought about her next move. Something moved against her palm. Emily's heart sank. "Oh, don't tell me—let me guess."

But she didn't need to guess. Setting the dog on the operating table, she poked and prodded the too-fat belly. And confirmed her escalating fears. Squatting to put herself at the dog's eye level, Emily crossed her arms on the gray metal of the surgical table, sighed, accepted a pink-tongued, slurpy kiss to her nose and said, "This probably won't come as any surprise to you, Godzilla, but congratulations. You're going to be a mother."

3

THERE WAS NOW more than one life at stake. Emily's. Godzilla's. And now Godzilla's puppies. And all of them were now in Emily's hands. *Literally,* she added, again picking up the shuddering little mother-to-be and holding her close.

Looking at her charge, stroking the dog's coarse and spiky fur, she whispered, "What are you caught up in, little girl? Were you taken because your mommy and daddy are rich?" Emily sighed. "This is so scary and so important that I wish you could talk, sweetie. Like in a Walt Disney movie. Did you ever see *101 Dalmatians?*"

As if answering her, Godzilla barked, a sharp, yapping retort that startled Emily out of her reverie.

"You're right," she conceded to the canine. "Where would you have seen it? Okay, Emily, focus. Especially since there's an impatient criminal right outside there." She looked around her operating room and hefted the dog to eye level. "You don't seem to be any worse for wear. And I guess you'll be safe enough back here while I go deal with *him.*" Emily stopped, considering her words and the implied bravery behind them. "Will you listen to me? Who do I think I am? Wonder Woman? All right, in you go."

With that, and using soft, soothing tones and nonsense words to reassure the animal, Emily put Godzilla into the carrier. As she locked the mesh grate, she said, "I'm going to put you in the kennel area with the other dogs. You know, just for the company. Don't be scared. They're all very nice, once you get to know them."

With that, she picked up the carrier by its top-mounted handle and took it with her into the kennel area. Again, the dogs set up a racket. Emily put a finger to her lips to shush them. Of course, it didn't work. She set the carrier down by the first dog run. An ancient schnauzer poked his nose through the fencing and wagged his tail. Emily rubbed his head and told Godzilla, "This is Mr. Edgar. He's about a hundred years old—in dog years. Just listen to everything he tells you and you won't go wrong. Now, wish me luck."

Godzilla looked at her as if she'd just thrown her into a pit of vipers. "Oh, now don't do that. You'll be fine. And I'll be back as soon as I can. I promise." With that, Emily straightened and drew a deep breath. Then, exhaling, she turned to face the closed doors. "Okay, here I go. One foot in front of the other."

All too soon, she was turning the cold brass knob to the door that, when she opened it, would again expose her to danger. But nevertheless, and thinking of Godzilla, Emily did what she had to do. She opened the door and walked into harm's way, falsely chirping. "Well, she—um, *he's* settled in now. So all I need from you is—"

Emily stopped and stared. Her waiting room was empty. The man was gone. And the front door was wide open to the night and to the rain. But in her mind, momentary confusion reigned. Then Rodney cleared things up. "Wr-rack, the chicken bailed."

"He bailed?" Emily repeated stupidly. "Are you serious?"

"Wr-rack, are you?" Rodney challenged.

Emily ignored him as she cautiously stepped to the open door and peered out, all the while praying she wasn't walking into some sort of trap. A shiver assailed her at the thought. But she quickly dismissed it when she reminded herself that the man was in a hurry, and she had told him he could be on his way. So, maybe he took her literally. Yeah, that made sense. With the form done, the chicken bailed.

But just then, her attention was captured by the squealing tires of a fishtailing white sports car and its red taillights—as it exited her parking lot and sped off down the rain-slick street. Gasping in terror, her heart thumping, Emily pulled back and slammed the door closed, quickly locking it. *The getaway car!*

This confirmed it. Criminal activity. Emily crossed the room and grabbed the owner information sheet she'd given the man to fill out. But he hardly had. Blank spaces stared at her. But unbelievably, the two things he had written down were his name, David Sullivan, and his car's D.C. license tag number. How careless of him—unless the name and number were as fake as the moniker he'd stuck that little dog with. But then again, maybe in his haste to be away, he'd forgotten. Either way, she had to call the police.

Tucking the clipboard under her arm, Emily rounded Karen's desk, grabbed the phone, and dialed emergency. Within two rings, help was on the line. In her breathless fear, Emily began babbling and, no doubt, thoroughly confusing the calm woman at the other end who asked her what the nature of her emergency was. "Dognapping. I mean—police emergency.

He's getting away. Who? The dognapper! What? Oh. I'm Dr. Emily Wright, of the Wright Choice Clinic and Kennel in Reston. No, with a *W*. I just had one of those dognappers here. Like in that fax the police sent out. Yes. Right here. I've got the dog, but the man left.''

As she spoke, Emily peered into the night, trying to see past the watery glass that protected against the rainy darkness outside. She looked this way and that, half afraid that—she pulled the clipboard from under her arm and read the name again—David Sullivan— would burst back in and— ''What? Yes. Something about a wedding. And flying out of Dulles. But I guess that could be a lie. I mean, he *is* a criminal. But he did leave his name and car tag number. David Sullivan. White. A sports car. I don't know the make or the model. But here's his tag number.'' She read that to the dispatcher.

The dispatcher's next question tightened Emily's grip on the phone. ''What's he look like? Um, kinda handsome, sorta tall, blackish hair, grayish eyes. An expensive overcoat. Intelligent. Nice manners. Broad-shouldered. You know, your basic gorgeous male.'' *Great. I'm waxing rhapsodic about a criminal.* She cleared her throat. ''Not that I got that good a look at him.''

''I see,'' the dispatcher said, and then chuckled. She told Emily to sit tight, she'd send two uniforms to take a report and to question her. She said she would also alert the airport to check their passenger rosters and have security officers stop any and all David Sullivans. As well as any and all men fitting the, ahem, good description Emily had given. She told her not to touch anything the suspect had. Fingerprints, you know.

"Oh. Right." Emily grimaced in guilt as she tossed the clipboard onto the desk. *Great. The clipboard and the Pet Porter. I've already manhandled everything the man…handled.* A sigh escaped Emily. Even words were tripping her up. Then she responded to the dispatcher again. "Yes, the doors are locked. Yes, I'll wait here with the dog. Okay. Oh, and please hurry. I'm alone here, and he could come back at any moment."

"WR-RACK, CHEESE IT! The cops!"

"Cute parrot," the huge and rain-dripping cop deadpanned as he stood facing Emily—but glaring at Rodney, who nimbly stepped along his perch, screeching and flailing his wings.

Emily glared at the white-plumed brat, too, and spoke above his din. "He's a cockatoo. Not that you care about an ornithology lesson at this point." It was just as well, given that her stated fear had turned out to be both founded and unfounded. Meaning the dognapper *had* come back. But not at any given moment.

No, it was about two hours later, time enough for her to have fed her charges, given medicine to those who required it, and generally prepared the animals for the night, making sure, in the interest of peace, that everyone had his or her own favorite toy or piece of blanket.

And again fortunately for her, the dognapper hadn't come back alone. Instead, two uniformed police officers said they had, in the back of their squad car, a David Sullivan who fit her description. And that they hadn't arrested him yet, since he'd said he would cooperate and had accompanied them here of his own free will. If she identified him as the man who'd brought the allegedly stolen canine in, they would then arrest him.

"Identify him?" Emily blurted, shaking her head. "No. I don't want to see him again."

"I understand," the bigger and burlier of the two cops said. "But if you don't make a positive ID, then we can't hold him."

What he didn't say, Emily knew, was that the man would then be free to return here without them. So what choice did she have? She took a deep breath. "All right. I guess it's my civic duty. And I did make the call. Bring him in. But I won't give Godzilla back to him."

"Godzilla, ma'am?" the smaller of the big, burly cops asked as he looked up from writing his report.

"Yes," Emily said, nodding and jamming her fists deeper into her lab coat pockets. "The dog. Godzilla. He's not getting her back, is he?"

"Godzilla is a *her*?" The smaller cop turned to his partner. "I always thought Godzilla was a he."

"Yeah," the big guy agreed. "Me, too. Hollywood. Go figure." Then he turned to Emily. "No, ma'am, the dog goes with us. Evidence. We'll take it down to the city pound and—"

"No!" Emily bleated, not able to stand the thought of the scared little dog being locked up. Since the cops just stared at her, she continued. "She's going to have puppies, you know." Emily crossed her fingers against the little white lie in her next words. "And soon. Very soon. Maybe right in the back of your police car. What a mess that would be, huh?"

The two men exchanged less-than-thrilled glances and turned to her, both speaking at the same time. "Puppies?"

"Uh-huh" Emily rushed on. "Godzilla's in a *very* family-way. But I wouldn't mind keeping her until you find her owners. *If* you find her owners. Which will be hard since she doesn't have a tag on her collar." They didn't look convinced. So Emily added, "I am a veterinarian, you know."

The uniformed men again exchanged glances. Then the bigger one said to the littler one, "She makes some good points. Call the station. See if we can leave the dog here. Make the arrangements. And I'll go get the perp."

Emily figured her triumphant grin held more wattage than a searchlight. She watched the big cop wheel around and head for the front door, leaving the other one to ask Emily if he could use her phone. Emily nodded, pointing the way for him. "Sure. On the other side of that partition. While you're doing that, I'm going to take Rodney to the back and put him in his cage."

As the officer rounded the desk, Emily stepped over to Rodney and, using a treat she pulled from her lab coat breast pocket, coaxed the big bird onto her arm. As she passed by the officer, she hesitated long enough to ask, "What's a…perp?"

The man—well over six feet tall, but still smaller than his big partner—said, over his shoulder, as he dialed, "It's short for 'perpetrator.' You know, the bad guy. Who's not any too happy, for all his cooperating. He's been yelling about how the dog is his, about how he's missed his flight and some wedding. So, I hope you're right about him. Because he could sue you, you know."

Emily's heart lurched. "Sue me? For what?"

The policeman shrugged. "Oh, things like public

humiliation, defamation of character. That sort of thing. No, your bad guy is not a happy camper.''

My bad guy? Emily swallowed and exchanged a look with Rodney, who flared his considerable plumage and remarked, ''Wr-rack, your goose is cooked.''

AS HE WAS HAULED out of the squad car by a big cop and forced to sprint alongside the armed man, in the driving rain, no less, right back into the Wright Choice Clinic, David had a sudden ironic appreciation for the kennel's name. *The right choice? Ha.* He could not, would not believe this. *Dognapping? Who even knew there was such a thing? This is insane.*

But apparently only to him. Because here he was, lacking only the reading of his rights and the applying of handcuffs to be under actual arrest. Like a common criminal. But these officers—and about three hundred people at Dulles International Airport—already believed him to be a common criminal. Or uncommon, if the charge was for real. Again…dognapping?

In a scene all too soon repeated, a rain-soaked, hopeful and desperate David again stood in front of the still gorgeous but clearly deluded Dr. Emily Wright. This time, though, it was to listen to her tell the policemen, ''Yes. That's him. That's the man.''

David's temper snapped. ''What do you mean 'that's the man'?''

She stiffened. ''Just what I said. You're the man who brought that poor little scared dog in here. It hasn't quit shaking and whining yet.''

''What?'' David shouted. ''Shaking and whining? That dog's a killer!''

The officer to his left gripped David's arm and

warned, "All right, that's enough. Don't shout at the lady."

David twisted to face the uniformed man. "Don't shout at her? She accuses me of stealing someone's dog, calls the police on me, gets me all but arrested and makes me miss my flight home—and *I'm* not to yell at *her?*"

The officer was unmoved. "That's what I said. Now, maybe if everybody calms down here, we can clear this up."

David stared at the man, then exhaled. "Fine. I won't yell at the lady. But this is nuts. Do I *look* like a dognapper?"

The officer's shrug told David that he might. So he turned his attention to the finger-pointing vet. "Dr. Wright, will you please tell me what it was I did or said to make you even remotely believe that I go around stealing people's dogs and holding them for ransom? I don't even *want* the dog I brought in."

The accusatory silence and solemn expressions that met his words caused David to hear them again. A guilty flush washed up his neck. "What I meant was the dog was given to me. In a legal matter. I didn't ask for it or buy it. But neither did I steal it. Believe me, I'm the victim here. And *not* the dog. Can't you see that?"

Apparently she couldn't. "I called the police, Mr. Sullivan, or whatever your real name is, because I—"

"What? That *is* my real name. What makes you think it's not?" David turned to the officer nearest to him. "Tell her my name. I showed you my driver's license. Tell her."

The policeman nodded. "Yeah, he showed me. It says David Sullivan. But it could be stolen or fake."

"See?" David confirmed—then denied, as he jerked to face the man. "No. It's not fake. Or stolen. It's real. I *am* David Sullivan. I'm a CPA, I own my own firm and I'm a law-abiding citizen. A *taxpaying* citizen. Believe me, if I was going to steal something, it wouldn't be a dog. It'd be money." Three sets of sharply rounded eyes had David all but shouting. "Not that I'd steal money. I wouldn't do that."

"I know," the cop deadpanned. "Because you're a law-abiding, taypaying citizen. For what it's worth, sir, if I were you and I found myself in a hole this deep, I'd quit shoveling."

David fumed, but could see the sense in that. Then he had an idea. "Look, I know how we can clear this whole thing up. Just call Mr. Trenton in Tysons Corner. He's the attorney who gave me the dog. I'm sure he'll be more than glad to tell you it's mine, that it was a bequest to me from the late Mrs. Amelia Stanfield."

The shorter of the two officers was writing all this down. He looked up to ask, "This Mrs. Stanfield…who is she to you?"

Too late realizing this dead end, David just stared at the armed man, who stared right back at him in such a way that David confessed, "I have no idea. I never met her before."

The officer nodded his head. "I see. So why'd she leave you her dog?"

David didn't even blink. "Believe me, Officer, I have no idea."

"I see. And what was that attorney's name? Tyson?"

"No. Trenton. In Tysons Corner."

"I see. And you think if I call him, he can clear this whole thing up?"

David was beginning to hate this officer's doggedness. "Yes, I do." Then he remembered. "Or would, if you could reach him. Which you can't. He left this afternoon for a month's rest and relaxation."

The officer's eyebrows rose. "Convenient. Did he say where?"

"No, of course not. That would be too easy, wouldn't it?" In his mind, David saw an executioner putting a blindfold on him and standing him against a bullet-riddled wall. Ready, aim— Wait! A governor's pardon of a thought popped into David's mind. "How about my family? They'll vouch for me. And my secretary. I can call them—"

"Are they here local? Could we verify who they are...you know, go see them for ourselves?" The officer with the notepad looked almost apologetic. "Not that we don't trust you, sir."

David's stomach knotted. "Of course. But no, they're in Colorado. And London. And somewhere on the road between Ohio and Denver. But my secretary—" *What?* raged his sensible side. *Involve Mrs. Hopemore in this ridiculous situation? She'll never let you out of her sight again.* David knew the truth of that. Just as he knew he'd rather face that firing squad. "Never mind."

At an impasse, everyone stood around. Then, "I have a good idea." The words rang out into the silence. It was the lovely, meddling veterinarian.

"Great," David said evenly. "Any more of your good ideas, Dr. Wright, and I could end up on death row."

Her expression crumpled. David's breath caught, and he hurt somewhere in his chest region. What a face. As if she were Bambi and he'd just zapped her with an electric cattle prod—right in front of a kindergarten class. Now he was done for. Especially with these two big cops who couldn't take their eyes off her, either.

Sure enough, the big policeman intervened, encouraging. "I'd like to hear your idea, Doc, if it'll help clear this up."

She gave the man a tremulous smile, and looked so fragile doing it, that David wanted to save them all the trouble and shoot himself. He may as well. Because no matter what she said, she looked like an angel saying it.

"Thank you," Dr. Wright said to the officer. Then she turned to David, pinning him with those widened midnight-blue eyes. "I recalled seeing an old movie— I think it was a Lassie movie—where a judge brought Lassie into the court and had both boys who claimed him call to him. And—"

"Lassie's a he?" blurted the shorter of the two policemen.

"I thought he was a she," opined his partner.

"Does it matter?" This was David, whose crankiness was eating away at the edges of his mood.

"Yeah, it matters—to Lassie," the big one argued. "Especially in that episode where *he* had puppies."

David took a deep breath preparatory to howling his frustration with this sidebar, but the vet saved him. "Okay, *she* went to Timmy when *he* called her and he got to keep her. There. That's it."

"That's it?" Not seeing the first good idea in there

anywhere, David ventured, "So, you're saying what, exactly?"

"That we get Godzilla out here and see what happens. Like with Lassie."

Silence followed her words. A silence that escalated David's horror at such an idea. Increasing his sweat factor were the gee-I-never-thought-of-that looks the two cops were beaming the veterinarian's way. David looked her up and down. How could she, pretty woman that she was, be so right on target when it came to ruining his life?

"No. Not good." David's outburst earned him center-of-attention status. He knew how it looked. An innocent man wouldn't be concerned. But they didn't know Godzilla like he did. Which was why he needed to nip this in the bud before he got nipped in the butt. And arrested. "No," he said again, trying to ignore the guilty-as-charged stares coming his way. "That dog is too unpredictable. Anything could happen. And probably will."

"But I think I like it," said the big cop. "Go get the dog in question, Doc." Then he, along with his partner and David, watched in appreciation as the doctor walked away. Only when she was out of view did the big cop turn to David. "If the dog knows you and acts friendly, then the way I see it, sir, you're free to go, dog and all."

David plunged his hands into his overcoat's deep pockets and rocked back on his heels. "Meet my character witness—a dog. Him, you'll believe. But not me." To himself, he added, *I'm a dead man.*

As if to prove it, out came Dr. Wright with Godzilla. *Great,* was David's thought with an accompanying grimace. *Just lovely.* Un-Pet Portered, tucked under the doctor's arm, riding next to her side, against her breast, the dog looked downright adorable. Or was it triumphant? Could that glittery gleam in its eyes bode well for David? Not the way this evening was going. Just the same, David stood taller and pasted a brave but welcoming grin on his face as he reached out a hand toward the dog and said, "Hey, there you are, buddy. Come to…papa—" he felt stupid even saying that "—come on, Godzilla, old pal, oh, please."

The dog darned near jumped out of the vet's arms in its haste to snap and snarl and bite at David's extended hand. Sucking in air, David jerked his hand back. At the same time—and raising an unholy din that had the lady veterinarian and the police officers gasping and drawing back—the wretched beast, still held securely by Dr. Wright, curled its lips back to show those baby-shark teeth that had earlier shredded Mr. Trenton's flesh.

"Wow," Officer Number One—the big one—offered as he turned to David. "He hates you."

"You think?" David asked, his own lip wanting to curl.

"She," the meddlesome veterinarian said.

David and his escorts turned to her. To a man they asked, "What?"

Dr. Wright's gaze flitted from one to another of them, finally lighting on the officers. "The dog. He's a she. Remember?"

But it was David who gave himself away. "He is?"

Dr. Wright nodded, her fluttering gaze showing reluctance to meet his eyes. "Yes. He is. He's also going to be a mother."

Again. "He is?" David heard himself ask.

"Yes. And soon." She looked squarely at David.

"Which is why *I'm* going to keep him—her—for now." She turned to the big cop. "Right?"

"Wrong," David argued again, cutting off any reply the officer might have made. Everyone stared at him. "That is *my* dog, and he—she—goes where I say." He couldn't believe he'd just said that. Not an hour ago, he couldn't wait to be rid of the mutt.

"I'm afraid you can't do that," said the smaller of two policemen. "We already checked. The pound's full. Dr. Wright here has been okayed to keep the animal—on the city's tab—until this thing is cleared up."

The good doctor nodded, even smiled. David opened his mouth to protest, but got cut off by the big cop. "And what's more, sir, you're not going anywhere, either."

The fight went out of David. He felt suddenly cold and hollow inside. "Are you putting me in jail?"

The uniformed man shrugged. "I could. But it's not too clear yet what's going on. I called the precinct. The sergeant says to release you to your own recognizance and advise you to maybe retain legal counsel. And for sure, to stay away from the lady here and the dog. You're to have no contact with them, understand?"

David couldn't believe this. He looked from the lady of the midnight-blue eyes to the dog—his dog. And back to the waiting policeman. "Yeah, I understand. But I don't—"

"There's no 'but,' sir. And, you have to stay in town until we—"

"I know...clear this thing up." David grimaced, seeing his week's plans go down the tubes. He turned to Dr. Wright, forcing himself not to react to her good looks. "Thanks. I hope you're happy. I've missed my flight. And now I'm probably going to miss my sister's wedding in Colorado. All because you think I stole this dog. May I just say, it's been nice meeting you, Dr. Wright. The pleasure has been all mine."

Cheryl Anne Porter   247

looks. "Thanks, Loma. Vm so happy." He raised my hands and... [illegible faded text]
wedding. I'd thought... [illegible faded text] ...ance since c...
his day. Also, I just say... [illegible faded text] ...be proud of you...
to Mom. You... [illegible faded text] ...ll miss...

4

HE COULDN'T HAVE meant it, last night, when he'd said the pleasure was all his. Although Emily could again, on this bright and clear Saturday morning, hear him saying it. Well, she admitted to herself, under the circumstances, she could understand if he hadn't been thrilled to see her again.

Way to go, Em, she chastised herself. The first really nice-looking, obviously successful man you meet in months—since you broke it off with Jeff—and what do you do? Get the guy arrested. And you wonder why you're still single?

Emily set the carafe on the coffeemaker and absently stared out the window over her kitchen sink. Shying away from her self-induced problems with men, she occupied herself with thoughts of slipping into her clothes and maybe stepping over to help Karen clean the kennels. *What the—*

Emily's hand, holding a coffee cup, halted in midair. She couldn't believe what she was seeing. In the driveway, her car sat tilted at a crazy angle. *Oh, great. A flat tire.* She narrowed her eyes in consternation. Was that her mail strewn across the front yard? *Now, why—*

Emily frowned as she sat her cup atop the tiled counter. "What is going on around here?" she asked aloud, knowing she was alone in the house. *Alone in the house.* The words echoed in her mind. She was, wasn't she, alone in the house? That thought froze her in position, standing there, leaning against the countertop, gripping its edges. *Oh, come on, Emily. Of course there's no one here but you.*

Well, it sounded good on paper, but convince the shiver running down her spine, she thought, as she mentally poked into each quiet room, trying to discover where alleged criminals might be lurking. After all, she'd seen that movie. The girl turns around, only to find some warped and degenerate mutant standing behind her. With a raised and bloodied ax.

"Oh, stop it," Emily chided herself, stepping back from the counter and wrapping her arms around her. "This is silly," she added, looking all around her familiar kitchen. But maybe it wasn't silly, she finally had to admit. Especially when she lumped together the tire and the mail with the two telephone hang-ups that had awakened her earlier.

Refusing to believe anything diabolical, Emily quickly blamed everything on early Halloween pranks by neighborhood kids. It just had to be. Then she let out a breath. *Face it, Em, you don't believe that. You're being harassed, plain and simple.* But why? Who would have reason to do these things to her?

And suddenly, there he was. In her mind's eye. A handsome face, complete with gray eyes, a strong jaw and a generous mouth. Emily wanted to die. Oh, surely not. Not David Sullivan. Not those broad shoulders. He was just too good-looking to be evil. Yeah, in a perfect world, maybe. Well, maybe even in this one, Emily conceded. Okay, so she'd been wrong about him. That man wouldn't kidnap a dog or bedevil her thoughts— *No! He doesn't bedevil my thoughts. He doesn't. Oh, what is wrong with me?*

"As if I have time to go into that," Emily muttered, totally disgusted with herself. She stepped out of the kitchen, intent on getting a robe, then going outside to retrieve her mail and take a look at that flat tire. But when she pulled even with her telephone, which sat on a round-topped antique table, she had another thought. She really ought to call David Sullivan and apologize. After all, she'd ruined the man's weekend. If not his life.

She got as far as lifting the receiver before remembering she had no idea what his telephone number was. "Damn." She replaced the phone in its cradle and eyed the thick phone book. Then she frowned. *Like there won't be a thousand David Sullivans in the listings.* Was she prepared to call them all? *No,* she admitted.

Okay, so maybe calling him wouldn't be the smart thing to do, given everything she'd already done to him. After all, what if it *was* him harassing her? What if she was right, and he was guilty? She made a face, not wanting to believe it of him but recalling how mad he'd been at her. And, truly, who knew what evil lurked in the hearts of men?

Hadn't she seen that movie, too? Some gorgeous hunk, the last one you'd believe could be evil, and yet he was? Only the heroine didn't realize it until it was too late? A frisson of fear rolled over Emily. *Oh, that'd be—*

"Yap-yap-yap!"

Emily shrieked, and jerked around. "God—" She bit back the curse, substituting the dog's name. "Godzilla, you little…schmuck," she finished lamely. "I nearly jumped out of my clothes, you scared me so bad. What were you thinking?''

Apparently something. Because, with her vicious overbite revealing tiny little serrated teeth, the fat mama-to-be grimaced and wagged her tail and jumped stiff-legged. Then she set about running in tight little circles, the long tufts of hair on her pointy ears waving in the breeze she created. ''Forget it,'' Emily advised. ''You've eaten everything in the house, including a piece of wooden fruit and one of my bedroom slippers. You simply cannot be hungry.''

The dog stilled, slumping as she frowned at Emily, as if to say, *stupid human,* then stared at the front door and immediately set about another round of jumping and yapping. Emily divided her attention between the front door and the frenetic dog, finally asking, ''What now?''

As if to show her, the doorbell rang. Emily stiffened at the sound, pivoted to face the door, then turned back, staring at Godzilla. ''So, what you're trying to say is, someone's at the door, right?'' Godzilla stared wide-eyed at Emily and then tore off down the hallway toward the back of the house. ''Great,'' Emily called after the wiry-haired dog's waddling behind, with its stub of a tail held high. ''What a wonderful watchdog you are.''

Totally unrepentant, Godzilla veered to her left. Into Emily's bedroom. Which made her groan because Rodney—who hated Godzilla with a purple passion— was in there. Besides that, no one had to tell Emily that something of hers, something she held precious and dear, was about to be sacrificed on the altar of Godzilla's pregnant I-need-to-chew-on-everything-in-sight cravings.

Shaking her head, dog-indulgent to the end, Emily advanced on the front door, and again found she was reduced to muttering. "This had better be good," she warned the closed door as she unlocked the dead bolt and twisted the knob. Using the door's solidness to block as much of her state of undress as she could, Emily held her long hair back with one hand, ignored the dog and bird rantings coming from the vicinity of her bedroom and opened the door, peering around its edge to see who was paying a call.

"Yes?" Already wary because of the morning's unsettling events, Emily blatantly and carefully looked her visitor up and down. And pronounced him suspicious. Well, she had no one to blame but herself, she decided. She'd just said this had better be good. And it was. "Can I help you?"

Outside, with shoulders hunched up, stood a scrawny, unshaven little man with a prominent Adam's apple. His ratty ball cap was pulled down low over his forehead, his denim jacket's frayed collar was turned up and his hands were plunged into his pockets. At his side sat what appeared to be a salesman's sample case. "Uh, good morning, um…ma'am. I'm selling a complete line of, um, dog care products. Do you have a dog?"

Emily stared at the man. His halting speech, as much as its content, threw her reaction off a good second or two. Veterinary products salespersons never came to her home. They paid their calls next door at her clinic. And never on a Saturday. Before she could form a response, from behind her, somewhere in the bowels of her home, she heard Rodney the cockatoo cuss in a particularly virulent, eye-watering manner.

Mortified, Emily begged, "Will you excuse me a moment?"

But before she could do anything more than jerk around, Godzilla roared down the hall, her ears laid back, her butt tucked under as she made a guilty, speedy retreat toward the living room and safety. Emily took no more than a step toward her before Godzilla came to a doggy-toenails-on-the-wood-flooring screech of a halt. Standing immobile, the dog stared at the stranger at the door. Her pointy ears stood straight up, as did the hair down her spine, and she erupted into a yappy, snarling tirade.

Before Emily could move or even chastise Godzilla, the alleged dog-care-products salesman at her door growled, "There you are, you lousy mutt," and bounded across the threshold, nearly knocking into Emily as he lurched past her. Shocked, Emily screamed and jumped back. But in the next second, when the intruder attempted to grab the yelping, retreating Godzilla, an adrenaline rush made Emily yell "No!" as she ran toward the melee.

But she was beaten to the punch by— She couldn't believe it. A big masculine blur brushed by her, all but spinning her around. A big masculine blur that looked remarkably like David Sullivan. *Because it is,* her stupefied mind finally registered.

Sure enough, David Sullivan himself clutched the scrawny interloper's shoulder and spun him around. The two men—David struggling for a handhold, the other guy gyrating frantically—grappled while Godzilla renewed her yapping.

Finally, by shrugging out of his unbuttoned jacket and leaving David holding it, the intruder freed himself and took off, fleeing past Emily, who screamed and pulled back. Out the front door the ugly little man fled, grabbing his alleged samples case and tearing down the driveway. His spraddle-legged gait carried him to an engine-revving white sports car. He leaped inside—right through the open passenger-side window. The screaming machine took off, tires squealing, the sound shattering the quiet of the suburban neighborhood street.

In a state of shock, still standing in the open doorway, Emily suddenly realized she wasn't alone. No. David Sullivan had crowded in next to her and had an arm around her waist. Protectively? She couldn't say. So, not sure whether to be comforted or afraid, she stiffened warily and stared at him. David, his breathing ragged from his recent exertion, asked, "Are you all right?"

Emily nodded, since she found it hard to get words past the lump of fear clogging her throat. "I think so," she said shakily.

"Good." His arm around her tightened, increasing Emily's heart rate. Then he nodded in the direction of the fleeing car. "Who the hell was that? Do you know?"

"I have no idea," Emily breathed, shaken to her core. Then a realization hit her. "Wait a minute! That's the same car I saw last night. At the clinic. It's the one that took off—"

She swallowed the rest of her words. *Oh, no.* Pivoting to face him, tugging free of his comforting embrace, she stared at the finely formed man standing next to her—which was the key issue. He was standing here. With her. As the car she'd believed to be his disappeared from sight. A hot and guilty flush claimed her cheeks. "I thought that was *your* car."

Frowning, he looked at her. "My car? What made you think that?"

"Because last night, at my clinic, when I came out of the back room, you were gone and that same car was pulling away, just like now, and——" She couldn't help it…she burst into tears. "I called the cops on you. I am *so* sorry."

"Ah, for…" David Sullivan muttered as he reached out and awkwardly patted her shoulder. "It's okay. Really." Then he pulled her into his all-weather-jacketed embrace. Holding her close, he rubbed a hand up and down her back and stroked her hair. "Look, it's okay. But for the record, I'm not a dognapper. Or any other kind of criminal. I'm a CPA. And *that's* my car. Over there. In your driveway."

Reluctant to leave the shelter of his arms but left with no choice, Emily pulled back, wiped at her tear-streaked cheeks and looked to where he pointed. Sure enough, behind her gimpy little blue sedan hunkered a shiny, fire-engine-red, expensive foreign car. Like a Thoroughbred at a starting gate. Emily swallowed, forcing herself to look at David Sullivan. Her breath and her heart caught in her chest. *Dear God, could he be better looking?* "You must hate me."

He shrugged. "Not so much as you'd think. Or deserve." Then he grinned, taking the sting out of his words, as he released her and stepped inside, tossing the other man's jacket onto a nearby upholstered chair behind them. He turned to her. "Mind if I use your facilities? I'd like to wash my hands." He held them up. Long, strong fingers, square palms. "I feel dirty after handling that guy."

"Oh, sure," Emily blurted, polite to the end. She

pointed the way. "Right down the hall there. On the right. Help yourself."

He nodded and started down the hall. Emily unabashedly watched him walk away from her, thoroughly enjoying his…hindsight. He turned to his right, into the washroom, and closed the door. Emily shook her head appreciatively, sighing. *Whew.* But beyond that, and more important, the man was a good guy. Obviously. After all, he'd just saved her. From exactly what, she didn't know. But he had.

And Godzilla, his dog. He'd saved her, too. Emily grimaced. *Great.* David Sullivan's dog. No doubt about it. He'd been telling the truth. This morning's events were proof of that. So, David Sullivan was exactly who and what he said he was. A rich CPA and the dog's owner. And as much an intended victim as she'd just been.

Now, that makes sense, Emily conceded as she began an agitated pacing of the room. After all, the guys in the white car had tried to steal the dog from her today. Maybe last night they'd been tailing David, waiting for a chance to take Godzilla from him. But then he'd dropped the dog off at the clinic. And maybe they'd followed him, not being sure if he still had her. And then they saw him at the airport and realized he had left Godzilla behind. And maybe they drove back and got scared off when they saw her looking out. Or maybe—

The door to the washroom opened. Emily turned toward the sound. David stepped out and, with an easy, confident saunter, started down the hall toward her. Emily's breath caught. He was so brave. And forgiving. And selfless. *And gorgeous.* It was true. He'd seen her in trouble and had jumped in with no apparent thought to his own safety. For all they knew, that dog-napper guy could have had a gun. So that made David Sullivan a selfless hero.

What else was he? How about not supposed to be here at all—according to that policeman last night. So, before she could stop herself, Emily blurted, "What *are* you doing here?"

David Sullivan stopped in front of her. "Well, the obvious answer is…saving your life."

Struck anew with the realization of the danger she'd been in, Emily put a hand to her chest. "You're right. And I haven't even thanked you, have I? Well, thank you. You saved my life." Finally, she offered him a grin, one she hoped softened her abrupt behavior to this point.

And it was then that she remembered—because he was returning her warm look for warm look—that all she wore was her nightshirt. Which, though too big and shapeless, only made it to mid-thigh on her. She tugged at its hem and, hoping to derail his overt attention from her semi-clad body, she persisted. "So, before you were saving my life, Mr. Sullivan—"

"David," he said. "Call me David. And, yeah, it's my *real* name."

Flushing at yet another reminder of her erroneous conclusions about him, Emily still felt her nerve endings sit up and beg. He wanted her to call him by his first name. How…intimate. Almost breathlessly, she nodded.

"Okay…David." It fit him, that name. A fresh, clean name. An all-American name. Everything you could ever want in a man— *Name.* In a name.

Blinking, awash with a mishmash of conflicting emotions regarding him—even Jeff, to whom she'd been engaged until six months ago hadn't elicited such feelings in her—Emily whirled away from David's assessing gray eyes. "So…David. Again, before you were saving my life, what brought you here? I mean, it's not like I sent up a bat signal or anything."

With that, Emily pivoted, facing him again, not giving him a chance to answer before she continued. "I mean, I guess it was obvious, with my clinic sitting on the same piece of fenced property as this house, that I live here. But still, last night the, um, police said you were supposed to…stay away from me and—" she took a deep, guilty breath "—your dog. Oh, my God, I am so sorry."

"Don't worry about it. And you're right. That's how I figured it out. About your living here. And the police…I know. I'm not supposed to be here. But—" he made a helpless gesture "—here I am. I got up this morning and, with nothing else to do, went in to work for a while. But the longer I sat there, the more I got to thinking about you—um, got concerned about you…and my dog being here. I mean, I didn't know if you were alone. Or married."

"I'm not," Emily rushed to tell him…and felt her cheeks heat up. "Married, that is. I'm not. I'm… alone." Not able to look away from his face, totally mesmerized by the sound of his voice and his nearness, Emily suddenly realized she was still twisting her fingers together and immediately stopped. "Sounds pathetic, huh?"

He shook his head and went on with his halting, somehow endearing narrative. "So I got in my car and drove here. I just needed to see for myself that you were okay. Both of you. Good thing I did, huh?"

"Yeah. I'll say."

Silence ensued while he stared at her and she at him. "I never thought I'd say those words...about missing a dog," he added "Or that I'd even have one." Another pregnant silence stretched between them. "Your turn," he said.

Basking in his slip-ups, which to Emily meant she had the same effect on him as he had on her—or so she hoped—she said, "So. Your dog. Well..."

And then, once again, Emily's heart all but stopped. Forgetting her state of near nakedness, even forgetting the warming up going on between herself and this nice CPA, she stared wide-eyed at David. Whose own panicked expression told her he'd probably just had the same thought she had. "Your dog, David. Oh my God, where's Godzilla?"

David thumped himself in the forehead. "Son of a—probably out leveling Tokyo. She must've slipped out when the door was open. You don't think—"

"—the dognappers got her?" Emily finished, her knees weak, her hands pressed to her warm cheeks. "David, what are we going to do?"

"Look for her," came his grim assessment, his expression matching his tone of voice. He started across the room, his long strides eating up the distance between him and the front door.

"I'll get dressed and be right out to help you," Emily said, already starting for her bedroom. As she passed David, he clutched at her arm, stopping her.

"If she's not right outside, Emily, I'm going to go find those guys in the white car. If I do, you call the cops, okay?"

Noting that he'd called her Emily, that his grip on her arm was warm and firm, Emily shook her head and said, "No. I really don't think that's a good idea,

David. Because, innocent or not, you're not supposed to be here, remember?''

His expression clouded. "Damn. That's right."

"Besides," Emily continued, "that's my tire out there they slashed. And my mail all over the lawn. So, if anyone's going after them, it's going to be me."

David pulled back, but didn't loosen his hold on her. In fact, his grip tightened. "What? *They* did all that? I saw the tire and the—" He pursed his lips and looked away from her, arrowing a glance toward the door. "Low-life scum. Rotten little..." he muttered, his voice trailing off. Then he focused again on Emily, frowning as his gaze slipped to his hand on her arm. He let her go. Abruptly. As if she were hot. "I'm sorry. I didn't mean to—"

"It's okay," Emily said, putting a hand on his chest before she realized she was going to...and felt certain that electricity sparked between them. But still, her focus was on the missing dog. "You go ahead and start looking for Godzilla. I'll call Karen—she's my assistant—to make sure she's okay. Maybe she saw or heard something. Then I'll join you when I'm decent."

Surprising her, he covered her hand with one of his and squeezed. "Thanks for helping." Then his gray eyes warmed as his gaze traveled over her face. "By the way, you're already more than decent. Dressed or not. Even getting me arrested or not."

Loving his touch, Emily shrugged. "Well...thank you. That's very gracious of you, especially under the circumstances. The least I can do is help you look for your dog, don't you think?"

"The least? Yeah. Maybe so. But I'll give some thought to what the *most* you can do is," he said, grinning. "Then...we'll see."

5

AND SEE THEY DID. Sort of. In about five minutes, with Emily clad in jeans and a sweater and having assured herself that Karen was safe, that Godzilla wasn't with her, she and David scooped up her mail, deposited it in her mailbox for the time being, and then were off and running all over creation. Well, all around Emily's part of it, anyway.

First they checked the back part of her property, where the various kenneled dogs, outside in their runs, added their barking encouragement but little in the way of constructive help. Godzilla was nowhere to be found.

However, search they did. All the while calling, "Godzilla! Where are you?" And all too painfully aware of the insane picture they presented to the few of Emily's wide-eyed neighbors who stopped to watch them as they swooped down on other people's totally tamed shrubberies and elegant trees, calling "Godzilla! Where are you, girl?"

As if that great big lizard could hide behind a stubby little Japanese holly shrub. But then, just when Emily met David in the middle of her own half-acre front yard, their sides heaving, their breathing labored, the rotten little stinker of a dog shot out from under a shrub almost at their feet—and fled.

Startled beyond measure, all they could do was grab

for the fat brown blur with the waddling behind and stubby tail held high. But Godzilla was too quick for them. She made a beeline for the street. Right toward a man who was walking his dog.

Both of whom Emily immediately recognized. Groaning in disbelief, she grabbed David's arm. "This cannot be worse, David. That's Kafka. Mr. Smith-Hill will just die. Or worse, sue me. He wants me to get my clinic out of the neighborhood." With that, Emily took off at a run, heading for the street. "Run!" she called over her shoulder. "We have *got* to get to Godzilla before she gets to Kafka."

David fell in beside her, easily loping along at her elbow. "Kafka? The Russian writer? What's he—"

"Not that Kafka. The dog, David. With Mr. Smith-Hill. He's an Afghan hound. The dog is. Not the man." Emily's breathing and speech became ragged as she ran, trying all the while to keep Godzilla's churning little self in view. "The breed's...not technically...Russian. But neither is Kafka—the writer. I mean was. He's dead. But don't tell Mr. Smith-Hill. About the dog. Not the writer. He's a lawyer. Mr. Smith-Hill is. And he thinks...the name is very clever. And that...my clinic is...a blight on the neighborhood."

"He does?"

Emily cut her gaze to David and saw his frown. "Yes. We're too...lowbrow, I guess. But that dog...is his whole life. Pampers it. A show dog. Worth...a fortune. A top stud."

"Great." It was David's fatalistic observation. "We'll never catch her."

No, they wouldn't. Emily could see that for herself. Because Godzilla, moving with the speed of a lovesick puppy—which proved to be only slightly slower than the speed of sound—remained out of their reach and was, even now, homing in on Kafka's tall, well-built, aloof and silky golden self. A burst of renewed fright had Emily flapping her arms as she, still on the run, cried out, "Mr. Smith-Hill! Look out! Save yourself—and Kafka! Godzilla's coming! Godzilla's coming!"

He heard her, at least. Out on the street, at the rounded curb, Mr. Smith-Hill, a short and portly, dapperly dressed, mustachioed little man, stared Emily's and David's way. And then he stopped, frozen, no doubt disbelieving. Kafka did the same, but with a show of class and bored curiosity. His regal head rose an elegant notch, one long ear arched quizzically.

But Mr. Smith-Hill wasn't so noble. Or so blasé. His bespectacled eyes widened as his focus moved from the wildly fluttering figures of Emily and David to the brown spiky-furred guided missile even then homing in on him and his prized companion. And that got David to yelling. "Godzilla! Stop! Come here! Bad dog!"

Too little, too late. All Emily and David could do was watch the scene play itself out in seeming slow motion. Knowing they were done for, they stopped as Godzilla, yapping jubilantly, pounced lovingly right on the snooty and aghast Afghan hound. Which startled the show-dog composure out of him and sent him reeling right into his owner. Who, with his legs knocked out from under him, belly-flopped onto Emily's dry and browning lawn with both leash-entangled dogs atop him. A perfect example of the domino effect.

"Dear God," Emily said aloud, her voice flat as she envisioned her tiny savings account scattering with the thrashing, in her yard, of arms and legs, lawyer and canine.

At her side, David drawled, "Damn. I bet that hurt."

"Oh, yeah," Emily agreed, sounding to her own ears like a coach on the sidelines watching a busted play. "You can bet it did. But not as much as it's going to, come my day in court." She looked at David. "And yours."

David looked at her, his expression souring. "Mine?"

Her lips firm, Emily nodded. "Yep. My property. Your dog. *Our* day in court."

David stared at her. And blinked. "Great. Have I said yet how nice it's been to meet you?"

"I think you have."

"Did I mean it the last time?"

"No. Or this time, either, I'd bet."

"And you'd win," he assured her. Then, grimacing as he took her elbow and drew her with him across the lawn, he added, "Come on. Let's go untangle the spaghetti from the sauce."

Emily frowned. But not because of his tugging on her. More at that spaghetti and sauce thing. "Isn't that impossible, once they're mixed?"

David nodded, his square jaw tightening. "Yep. My point exactly."

AND DAVID SOON REALIZED he was right. There was no separating the attorney from the show dog and mutt. No sooner would they free one, in most instances the happily writhing Godzilla—who, intent on greeting Kafka, insistently poked her cold nose right up against his person, than she'd launch herself right back onto the wide-eyed and shuddering Afghan hound. Which had him in a snit and hunkering down in a most inelegant pose, all but obscenely atop his master. Who, on his back and still on the ground, was screaming lawsuit. In a decidedly British accent. With his wire-rimmed spectacles askew.

Finally, David got Godzilla corraled and held her wriggling self tightly against his side as he backed away and allowed Emily to apologize profusely as she helped the outraged elderly gentleman to his feet.

"I am so sorry, Mr. Smith-Hill," she said as she brushed him off and helped him with his glasses. David enjoyed every movement, noticed every detail of her, every line of her body. *Whew.* He warmed right up, deciding she was one well-put-together woman, one he could watch indefinitely. But besides that, and besides her penchant for getting him arrested, she was a nice person. Even now, she was asking the older man, "Are you hurt anywhere?"

"I'm certain of it, Miss Wright." The red-faced man fussed as he patted himself down, no doubt searching for bruises or broken bones. "I assure you my dignity is injured, if not my actual person." Then, his voice all but breaking as he gestured toward his dog, Mr. Smith-Hill complained, "And my Kafka. Look at him."

Indeed, following the plaintive attorney's instructions and the swing of Emily's long, dark hair as she turned her attention to the show dog, David saw what they did, and gulped. Great. Kafka was—what archaic word would Mrs. Hopemore use? Disheveled? Yep. That was it...if it meant anything close to the animal's hairy fur being grimly awry. Which it was, and riddled with bits of grass and dirt and moldy leaves. No one had to tell David that this couldn't be good. Especially given the frown on the top stud's face as he stared narrow-eyed at Godzilla. Whom David was still holding. And at whom Emily and Mr. Smith-Hill were also staring.

"What?" David heard himself saying, squashing an inordinately childish need to tell everyone, "I didn't do anything."

The ruffled attorney broke the silent staring contest by pointing at David. "I say, sir, is that your—and I use the term loosely here—*dog* you're holding? Or is it one of Miss Wright's errant charges?"

At once offended at this slur against Godzilla's very canineness, and surprised that he was, David's jaw tightened. He might think she was an obnoxious little dog, but dammit, she was *his* obnoxious little dog. That notwithstanding, and feeling as if he were in the witness hot seat with a judge only two seconds from instructing him to please answer the question, David heard himself say, "She's my dog, all right. And the lady is Dr. Wright to you. Not Miss Wright."

Around the attorney's blustering harrumphs and assurances that he meant no disrespect, David caught Dr. Wright's beaming smile, one meant for him. Right then, David was won over. He stood taller and even forgot himself enough to stroke Godzilla's coarse and spiky fur. But the dog hadn't forgotten herself. To prove it, she jerked her head around and snapped irritably at David's fingers. Which he promptly jerked away.

"Great heavens, that animal is vicious." He took a step back, hauling Kafka with him.

"Oh, no. No, she's not," Emily instantly soothed, a reassuring hand on the attorney's coat-covered arm.

Which made David jealous. He wanted her hand on him again, as it had been, inside when she was wearing next to nothing. And had caused his breath to catch. Feeling sour that it wasn't him she was touching now, David rushed in. "Oh, yes, she is vicious. But I bet you would be, too, if a ring of dognappers had just tried to steal you away."

Again, Mr. Smith-Hill gasped and prodded Kafka back yet another step with him, as if David himself were one of the alleged dognappers. *As if I don't know that feeling,* came his grim thought.

"You don't mean the very ones in all the news features?" Emily's neighbor blurted. "Why, it's my worst fear, Kafka being the prime candidate he is for such a ring of evildoers."

David couldn't resist. "The very same. And just think—" he hefted his scruffy little dog, so adorably perched over his arm, her stubby paws crossed lady-like as she stared bright-eyed and adoringly at the aloof Afghan hound in Mr. Smith-Hill's clutches "—they wanted *my* Godzilla."

Mr. Smith-Hill raised a disbelieving eyebrow—almost to his receding hairline. "Your *what,* sir?"

Emily apparently took this turn in the conversation as her cue. "Why don't we all step inside my house for a talk and some nice, relaxing tea? It's just occurred to me, Mr. Smith-Hill, that you can possibly be of some help to Mr. Sullivan."

David bristled. The last thing he wanted was this guy's—

"Mr. who?" the formerly dapper little man asked. "I don't know any Mr. Sullivan."

David spoke, again drawing their glances his way. "Sure you do. That would be me." But still, he could only wonder what Emily was up to. Along those lines, he gave her a what-are-you-doing look.

Which she ignored, except to signal him to follow her and her neighbor and his silky-coated top stud of a dog. Still toting Godzilla, David followed along, content enough for this chance to watch Emily's denim-clad behind swaying provocatively in front of him. But that didn't mean he had to otherwise like this turn of events. What was she up to?

At this point, his adventurous side checked in. *Man, she is one nice-looking animal doctor. Whew, buddy, good choice. Much better than that prissy Philippa chick. But hey, don't take that old dude's insults to your dog. Godzilla could kick that show dog's butt any day. And…Kafka? What kind of a name is that for a dog? As if that long-haired mutt could ever write anything worth reading.*

And then they were inside Emily's house, in the living room, where she was closing the door behind them all, only to find that big white bird of hers had taken up residence on the sofa. And was only too eager to greet them. He stalked across the cushions, his wings spread out. "Wr-rack. Look what the cat dragged in."

"Rodney!" Emily sharply warned. "Mind your manners." And then she waited. So did they all. Finally, Rodney the bird, with a fine show of resetting his impressive plumage…plopped down on his clawed feet and sat there, eyes narrowed. Apparently satisfied with this behavior, Emily turned to Mr. Smith-Hill. "Why don't you make yourself comfortable on the sofa? I'll make a pot of tea. That ought to warm us up. And never mind Rodney. He'll behave."

David wasn't so sure. And apparently neither was

Mr. Smith-Hill. Because with a wary eye—as if he expected the cockatoo to peck his eyes out at any moment—the older man carefully arrayed himself on the furniture and sat perfectly still, Kafka nobly pressed against his leg.

With the older man settled in, David figured he was next. Sure enough, Emily turned to him. With a raised and questioning eyebrow, he silently asked her what she was about, bringing the attorney inside with them. With a lot of nodding and an encouraging expression, she just as silently pleaded with him to trust her on this. Well, she was so damned cute, what choice did he have? And so, David shrugged his intent to give her secret plan a chance.

Emily's radiant smile was his reward. And his undoing. Basking in her attention and feeling silly that he was—after all, he wasn't some schoolboy who had a crush on the teacher—David's nerve endings frittered. And they hadn't done that in a long time. Maybe not ever, he decided as he reflected a moment on his past responses to all the women he'd ever been involved with. No. None of them had ever made him feel this way. Whatever "this way" was.

At any rate, his physical reaction to Emily's beaming smile, as she walked past him on her way to the kitchen, almost caused him to drop Godzilla, whom he'd all but forgotten he was holding. However, with a yelp and a snarl—and renewed gasps from Mr. Smith-Hill—she was all too happy to remind him.

With a care for the exposed flesh of his hands, David gingerly set Godzilla on the floor. She immediately flitted over to Kakfa and plopped her pregnant self down at his side, staring adoringly at him. The heroic-looking AKC champion spared her a glance down his long, elegant nose and then made a studied show of ignoring her. She didn't seem to mind that. However, Rodney did. And said so. "Wr-rack, puppy love. Makes me wanna puke."

Startled, David locked gazes with the equally disconcerted Mr. Smith-Hill, as they heard Emily warn, from the kitchen, "Rodney! One more word out of you and I'll put you in your cage. And do you know what that'd make you?"

"Wr-rack...bitter," the bird called, much to David's further stunned surprise.

"Exactly," Emily called back. "So knock it off."

David stared at Rodney. Apparently the bird and Emily held intelligent conversations on a regular basis. And in somewhat the same vein as the ones he had with Mrs. Hopemore. That being so, not for one minute did David believe that Rodney would allow Emily to have the last word. And the cockatoo did not disappoint him. Rodney glanced at David and—he'd swear to it in a court of law—winked, and said quietly, "Wr-rack...women, huh?"

"Yeah," David heard himself agreeing—out loud, before he could stop himself. Noticing Mr. Smith-Hill's attention, David felt compelled to say, "I know it's a bird."

"Of course, you do," Mr. Smith-Hill quickly soothed, his knuckles nevertheless whitening around Kafka's leather leash.

Great. The man thinks I'm a bird, too—a loon. David berated himself, wondering what the hell was taking Emily so long. And if he was supposed to stand here the whole time. Or sit down. Or what. The minutes ticked by. No one said anything. And Emily didn't return. Mr. Smith-Hill resorted to fussing over

Kafka, straightening the dog's collar, stroking his head, ignoring Godzilla. The quiet became downright grim.

David caved first. Shoving his hands in his coat pockets and pasting a polite smile on his face, he got the conversational ball rolling. "So. You're a lawyer, huh?"

At the sound of David's voice, Mr. Smith-Hill jumped and Kafka's eyes widened. Which irritated David. Had they forgotten he was here? To add insult to injury, even Godzilla cocked her head, staring at him with her overbite comically catching her upper lip. "I said," David repeated, intending by sheer dint of will to wring a response out of the other man, "so, you're a lawyer, huh?"

"Yes, he is," Emily said from behind David, making it his turn to be startled. She walked around him, a silver tray of tea trappings held in her hands. Then shooing Rodney away, she set down her load. "We have a lot to discuss with Mr. Smith-Hill. I think he can be of great help to us. So, sit down, please, David."

To his own surprise, David immediately angled for an upholstered chair that faced the sofa and sat down. "He can?"

"I can?" Mr. Smith-Hill echoed.

"Wr-rack, he can, you can, a toucan can can-can," Rodney sang as he waddled off down the hall.

David, along with the British lawyer and the two dogs, turned to Emily. Whose face was turning red. "My grandfather taught him that," she offered, and then added, as if it explained everything, "He was a merchant marine. My grandfather, I mean." This, too, was met with silence. "Just be glad Rodney didn't sing the second verse. It's quite obscene,'' she blurted. ''Tea, anyone?''

And that, during the next hour, and over tea in Emily's living room, was how it came to pass, once the situation had been explained to her neighbor, that Mr. Smith-Hill announced he could indeed help them. But, he was very careful to say, that didn't mean he'd changed his stance on having a—sniff—veterinary clinic marring the neighborhood, you understand. David frowned, wanting to call the man on his snooty opinion. But Emily agreed readily enough, so David kept his silence. After all, it wasn't any of his business. Nor was she…any of his business. To his surprise, David found he didn't like that notion one bit.

But still, David listened, interested in Mr. Smith-Hill's legal take on the matter. That certainly was his business, since he could be the one going to jail. So, what did the British lawyer think? Well, number one, they should not, at this point, further involve the police. Why? Because David's story thus far was ''already squirrelly enough,'' in Mr. Smith-Hill's esteemed opinion, without regaling the local constabulary with this morning's bizarre events.

Two, they should instead spend their time gathering concrete facts about Amelia Stanfield and the reasons behind her leaving Godzilla and her money to David. Mr. Smith-Hill felt those answers could shed some light on the attempted dognapping. It had to be something about this dog in particular and not merely a random attack, he was convinced.

So, that being the case, they should now take steps to secure the safety of ''that hideous little cur''—Mr. Smith-Hill's words—since two attempts—possibly last night at the clinic and then again this morning—

had already been made to abduct her. Which meant
the dognappers knew the dog's whereabouts. Nobody
was safe. Not Emily. Not Godzilla. Not David. Not
here. They must make arrangements to stay elsewhere.
And certainly not at David's condo, either. Most likely
the criminal element knew his address, too. So, any
suggestions?

While they thought, Mr. Smith-Hill suddenly had a
realization that, "Dear me, I'm not even safe. Those
hard-looking men eyed me steadily as they made their
getaway earlier in that hideously loud car." Then he
gasped. "They saw Kafka! A prize any evil-minded
dognapper would simply cherish. And there I was, involved quite unwittingly. It appears now I *have* to
help. For Kafka's sake."

And for truth, justice and the American way, David
groused. Nothing like a good mystery to stir the juices,
he thought, looking at the older man wryly. A bit of
danger, a dash of clandestine chicanery. Or whatever
the British would say. As for himself, David was more
concerned about what Mrs. Hopemore would say
when they—surprise!—swooped down on her when
she thought he, her dear friend's grandson and her
boss, was out of town.

Man, this will teach me not to pay attention, he
fumed, while Emily packed a few things and then
spoke on the phone with Karen, apprising her of the
situation and instructing her on the care for the kenneled animals. All David knew was he'd been innocently sipping his tea—which he hated—and watching
Godzilla put the moves on Kafka. The next thing he
knew, and in response to Mr. Smith-Hill's question of
where could they stay, somewhere private, somewhere
the villains wouldn't think to look...

He—or at least his adventurous side—had blurted, "I know. With my secretary, Mrs. Hopemore. She lives in Georgetown. Close to the university and above a coffee bar. They'd never think to look there. Besides, she lives alone, loves dogs and could vouch for me with the police, should the need arise."

"Oh?" Emily had asked, looking—for some reason David couldn't fathom—sour. "Do you think she'd mind?"

"No, she won't mind," he'd continued stupidly. "She'll do anything for me."

"Will she?" Emily said, eyes narrowed, her voice flat. "Gee, I'd love to meet her."

And so it had been decided—over David's vehement attempts to get them to forget his suggestion—to simply descend on the woman, thus giving her less of a chance to say no to their scheme. Yes, it was deceptive, but desperate times called for desperate measures, according to Mr. Smith-Hill. And David had to admit, this was pretty desperate, all right. Especially since they all needed to stay with the poor woman. All being defined as Emily, Godzilla, Rodney and David.

A fate worse than death. But Mr. Smith-Hill had called it a splendid idea, which had made it a done deal. Okay, fine. A done deal, it is. Maybe for them. But David knew what it would make his ancient secretary. To use Rodney's words—Wr-rack…bitter.

6

"SO TELL ME about your secretary," Emily said on their way into Georgetown, riding in the front seat of David's Euro-machine as he drove. In the back seat, restrained appropriately in their respective birdcage and Pet Porter, were the unusually quiet Rodney and Godzilla. Behind David's car, in a battleship-size American luxury car, were Mr. Smith-Hill and, of course, Kafka.

But still, aware though Emily was of the potential for danger in this course of action they'd set themselves on—that of essentially taking the law into their own hands—she was proud that she managed to sound nonchalant as she interrogated David, especially when her real motives were to assess the competition. "Is Mrs. Hopemore *happily* married?"

David glanced at her, his gray eyes hidden behind his sunglasses. Fortunately, the weather remained bright and sunny, not too cold. And his closeness was wonderfully titillating, if not disconcerting. Which meant Emily was obligated to hate this perfect Mrs. Hopemore, who would do anything for him. *Yeah. I'll just bet she would.*

"Happily married?" he repeated. "Mrs. Hopemore? She might have been. She was widowed at a young age."

"Oh, that's too bad." Frowning at his answer and

not wanting him to see, Emily pivoted until she was peering between the bucket seats to check on Rodney and Godzilla. They were dozing. Thanking the stars for small favors, she turned and gave her feminine jealousies their moment. *So, not only does this Mrs. Hopemore see him every day at work, she's got a heavy sympathy factor going for her. Why couldn't she be an unfulfilled wife or some sexy divorcee I don't have to feel sorry for? But no. She's got to be a widow. A gorgeous merry widow, no doubt.*

Emily's frown deepened. Why was she acting like this? She had no claim on the man. *Get that through your head, Emily. He's here because he has to be. Otherwise, he'd be in Denver with his family. And you'd never see him again. Get over it.*

As if. She was a free agent. And for all she knew, so was he. Time to find out. So she turned toward David and, acting like she hadn't been silent this long, said, neutrally enough, "So...this Mrs. Hopemore. How long has she worked for you?"

"Seven years. This is her first job."

"Oh, her first job. How...nice," Emily commented. *Her first job. Lovely. And she's young. How old could she be, about twenty-seven? Great. Younger than me. With some horrid heart-wrenching reason for being widowed, too, no doubt.* "So, is she any good?"

David looked at her. "Excuse me?"

Emily's stare was unwavering. "Her job. Is she any good at it?"

"Oh. Yeah. Sure." Then he shrugged. "I guess."

Aha! At last, a chink in the woman's armor of perfection. "What do you mean, you guess?"

"Well, I've fired her twice."

Emily sat up and beamed. "You have? Twice? Why?"

David shrugged. "I forget. But it never takes. She just keeps showing up the next day to work. And giving herself raises."

A chuckle escaped Emily. Now, *that* was funny. And the last thing she needed—to admire the woman's spirit. But, "She does? That seems a little cheeky." It was all Emily would admit.

"Yeah," David agreed. "I thought so, too."

You did? Then why do you put up with her? Do you have no control over this overbearing woman? Emily could only wonder. Because if she actually said it, she'd sound like a shrew. Just then, David saved her from herself by putting her under the gun with his own interrogation.

"So, Emily," he said, keeping his gaze on the road, his black-haired profile making Emily's stomach tighten in reaction. "Tell me how come a gorgeous woman like you isn't married."

Stars burst before her eyes. Her nerve endings frayed with giddiness. *He thinks I'm gorgeous. Mrs. Perfect Hopemore, you are so outta here.* But maintaining an air of cool collectedness, Emily replied, "Thanks for that 'gorgeous' thing. And I very nearly was. Married, that is. About six months ago."

"Yeah?" David glanced at her as he changed lanes and then checked the rearview mirror, apparently looking to see if Mr. Smith-Hill had jockeyed his way in behind them. "What happened? If you don't mind my asking."

"I don't." And the funny thing was, she really didn't. Which surprised her. Because she certainly minded when her parents got on the subject of her "losing" Jeff. She'd been quick to tell them that she hadn't lost him. She'd cut him loose. "It turned out, that Jeff—my on-again off-again fiancé—was allergic to animal dander. Sneezed all the time. Finally, he was told he'd have to take shots if he wanted to be around me, since I'm with animals all the time. Well, he didn't want to go through that, so he issued me an ultimatum. Either him or my profession."

David looked at her, an expression of disbelief on his face. "That's what he said? Him or your career? He had no right to ask you that."

"I know," Emily agreed, grinning, realizing she was being pretty adult—for the first time—about her breakup with Jeff. So maybe she was over it. Which made her really warm up to David. "Guess which one I chose."

David chuckled, even as he kept his gaze on the traffic. "Oh, I'd say you made—excuse the pun—the *right* choice—Dr. Wright." He gave her a blazing grin that scorched her. "The guy sounds like a jerk."

Around her happily thumping heart, Emily managed a shrug. And even managed to be magnanimous in regard to poor old Jeff. "Oh, he wasn't always a jerk. He just got that way toward the end. And I guess he's not totally to blame. He said I always put the animals first. Maybe I did."

"You probably did," David agreed, serious. "But from what I've seen, you have to. Which makes you that dreaded of all things—a dedicated professional. Now, I'm not much of a pet lover myself—which I'm sure comes as no surprise to you—but I do know that anyone practicing medicine has to be on the job constantly. It comes with the territory. And this Jeff guy should've understood that. If he loved you."

If he loved me. Emily stared unblinkingly at David. "Where were you when I needed you?" she said in a deadpan tone. He lowered his sunglasses and winked at her, which made Emily's heart trip over itself. "That was my entire argument to Jeff. And one I've continued to give my folks. I could kiss you for that."

"Yeah?" David quipped, actually sounding hopeful. Emily felt her pulse flutter. "Go ahead. I won't stop you," he added.

She could barely swallow. But she managed to lighten the moment with a chuckle. Surely, he was kidding. But still, given the opening—if not the go-ahead—she found herself wondering what that would be like. To kiss David Sullivan. Even the mere thought of a quick thank-you peck on his clean-shaven cheek excited the heck out of her. But she didn't dare try. "You say that to all the girls, don't you?"

David's grin became a leer. "Of course I do. I even say it to Mrs. Hopemore. I think she's secretly in love with me."

Well, how nice. Emily soured right up. He'd just put a screeching halt to her burgeoning desire for him. Clouds came out. It rained. Poured. Flooded everything. Drowned everyone. The whole world was lost. Or was, in her mind. But outside, in the real world, the awful day remained sunny and cloudless. Emily pushed back against her seat, crossing her arms tightly over her chest. But still couldn't stop herself from persisting. "You do? You think she's secretly in love with you? Why do you think that?"

Again, David chuckled. A sound that was beginning to grate on Emily's nerves, she decided. And when had this car gotten so small? The man was practically sitting on top of her. "Because, of the way she treats me," he said. "See for yourself when you meet her. Tell me what you think."

"Oh, I will," Emily heard herself say, somewhat peevishly. And suddenly felt like an idiot. *What is wrong with me?* How many times had she already asked herself that since she'd met this man less than twenty-four hours ago? She was definitely not herself around him. That realization got her to thinking and finally deciding that yes, that was it. Being around him made her different. But good different? Or bad different? Well, she didn't know. Nor did she know how she felt about that.

"What's the matter?" David suddenly asked. "You're too quiet. Did I say something wrong?"

He looked so repentant that, despite her emotional upheaval, Emily dismissed her jealous mood with a wave of her hand. "No. No, of course not. It's just me. Never mind. I'm being ridiculous." Then she lobbed the ball into his court. "So, David, it's your turn. Tell me why you're not married."

He grinned. "Well, assuming I'm not—" Emily's expression fell. "No, I'm just teasing. I'm not. So you must mean…a gorgeous guy like me, why aren't I married?"

Shaking her head, Emily continued, "Yeah. A gorgeous guy like you. Why aren't you married?"

He shrugged, his expression sobering. "I don't know. Lots of reasons. Like you, there was college. Then a career. Setting up my own practice, getting it going. I've dated a lot, had a few serious relationships. My last one ended a couple months ago. I think I'm like you about work. Always at it. Relationships seem to come in second. Which costs me, in the long run.

But since Philippa—my last girfriend—well, I don't know. Maybe I just never met the right one.''

There wasn't anything about his last statement that Emily liked. After all, he knew *her* now. So, had he already eliminated her as a candidate for the right one? Talk about not giving someone a chance. *Great.* Managing to sound conversational, if not philosophical, Emily repeated, "The right one. Do you really think there's a right one out there for each of us?''

He looked at her, his gaze lingering a second or two on her. "I don't know about out there. But I like the one I have right here.''

She was elated, thrilled, triumphant. Emily's breath caught. She didn't know what to say. "I don't know what to say.''

"Hey, I want that in writing. That's a first for you, isn't it?''

Emily smacked at his arm. "You're politically incorrect, you know. And funny. I've never thought of accountants as funny before.''

David grinned. "Yeah, we bean counters are a pretty humorless lot, by and large.''

Loving anew this somehow intimate banter between them, especially in light of his *liking the one he had right here* remark, Emily kept it going. "And why is that, do you suppose?''

"Ah. Two questions.''

"What?''

"Why is that. And do I suppose. You asked two questions. And I have two answers. One, I don't know. And two, yes, I do.''

Thoroughly lost, Emily asked again, "What?''

"Never mind," David urged. "Tell me about your parents. Where do they live?''

Allowing the change in subject, Emily waved a hand at him. "That's easy. The same place where everyone else's parents live. In Florida."

"Ah. The Sunshine State. Retired, huh?"

"Yes. But even more importantly, they're far away."

David glanced at her. "They make you nuts, right?"

"Like it was their profession," Emily quipped.

David nodded. "I hear you. I keep my family half a continent away on purpose. My folks are leftover hippies. And my grandparents are RV gypsies."

"Wow. Hippies and gypsies. You're almost nobility."

"Darned near. My sister, Alicia, and I are the only two true adults in the whole family."

Eww. His sister. Emily grimaced with guilt. "I guess I owe you an apology on Alicia's behalf, David. I made you miss her wedding."

"No, you didn't. At least, not yet. The wedding's not until Thursday, and today's only Saturday. I called her last night and told her what's up. I'm thinking if we clear up this dognapping thing pretty quick, I can still make it."

"Oh, good. I'm glad to hear that." While genuinely relieved on that score, Emily still couldn't quite forgive herself. "Your sister must think I'm a big jerk."

"She does," David assured her.

Emily's belly plunged. "Great. She really does?"

"I'm teasing you. She said she thinks this whole situation is funny and that I needed someone like you to shake me up."

Shake him up good? Or shake him up bad? He

hadn't said. That got another grimace from Emily. "I shake you up?"

"You do. But try not to sound so happy about it."

His tone sounded teasing to Emily's ear, but she couldn't really be sure. After all—and she had to keep reminding herself of this—she hardly knew him. Even if being with him and riding comfortably in his car like this, and talking this easily with him, made it seem as if they had always known each other. She glanced at him, so big and handsome. And such a good sport through all the craziness she'd heaped on him when she'd called the police.

She realized that David was quiet. And not paying her the least bit of attention. Emily could only laugh at herself for being such scintillating company. She vowed that from here on out, she would hold his attention. Starting with the coming confrontation with his secretary.

Confrontation? That word stopped her. It had her blinking in surprise. This was getting way out of hand. She had no right to confront anybody about him. But even if she did, just what would she accuse the woman of? Working for him? Being loyal enough to stay on for seven years? *How dare she, the hussy,* Emily mocked herself. *Come on, Em, the woman could be as ugly as homemade sin and have a sweet, unthreatening nature. As well as three little barefoot children to feed. Doesn't she have enough problems, living over a store with all of them, without you intending to give her such a hard time?*

Emily narrowed her eyes, not liking herself right now. Was she really jealous of the man's secretary? Did she really care enough about him already to warrant such diabolical thoughts? Exhaling grumpily, she took a moment to examine her motives. Yes, as it turned out, she *was* jealous. And, yes, she *did* care that much already. How did she know? Because she quite simply was throughly jealous of any woman who even saw him, much less had contact with him. And because she wanted to rip his clothes off him and kiss him all over and brand him with her touch and make him hers and—

Emily gasped. What was she thinking? She'd never had such gut-level cravings for any man before. But she did now for David. Glancing covertly at her intended conquest and feeling her pulse leap at the sight of him, Emily stiffened her resolve. *Watch out Mrs. Hopemore.*

FROM DOWNSTAIRS, the heady smell of fresh-ground coffee wafted up to Emily's nostrils. She stood on the carpeted second floor landing over the popular coffee bar below with David, Mr. Smith-Hill, Kafka, Rodney and Godzilla. David had knocked and they were waiting for the apartment door to be opened. And unbeknownst to the men, Emily was also waiting for her first glimpse of Mrs. Hopemore, that man-trapping vixen.

Finally, around David's enigmatic and monotonal counting—"Seventeen one-thousand, eighteen one—"

The door opened. A bespectacled, gray-bunned little old lady wearing too much makeup but not quite enough clothing for a woman her age—bare feet, black leggings and a white, oversize man's Oxford shirt—stood there, a full wineglass in her hand. She sized them up, not appearing to be the least bit surprised to find them here. Behind her came the steady rise and fall of lively debate. All male voices. All young male voices.

Emily, her arms wrapped around Rodney's cage, found she couldn't look away from the, um, vision the woman was. But apparently it didn't bother Rodney any. In that charming cockatoo way of his, he wolf whistled. "Wr-rack, give us a kiss, sweetie."

Emily stiffened, wide-eyed with embarrassment. "He's a cockatoo." She blurted. "A very expensive bird. My grandfather—"

"I am not amused, Mr. Sullivan," the little old lady said, cutting Emily off. "Not one little bit. I am hosting my Saturday Afternoon Literary Society meeting, which I am now missing because of all this commotion out here with you and this little honey here and these caged animals."

This little honey here? Me? Emily could only stand there, offended.

Just then, the lady of the house's gaze lit on Mr. Smith-Hill. She sized him up. And down. "However, you seem like a nice sort," she pronounced, lasciviously enough. Then she squared off again with David and continued her tirade. "And just why aren't you in Colorado, Mr. Sullivan? You missed the plane, didn't you? I knew you would."

"I did not miss the plane," David instantly protested. "I got—"

"You didn't? So what'd you do—take another one back?"

David pushed his hand through his hair. "No, I didn't. I never—"

"Did you go to the airport on the route I laid out for you? You didn't, did you? That explains this, doesn't it?"

David tried to protest, but the chattering old woman gave him no chance. She narrowed her gaze. "Are these people hitchhikers?"

"No, they're not," David managed to say. "We're here because—"

"Your sister decided not to get married, didn't she? Good. Then I'll expect you in to work on Monday."

"Will you please listen to me, Mrs. Hopemore?" David begged.

Emily's spirits soared. *This* was Mrs. Hopemore? *The* Mrs. Hopemore? This crotchety old woman dressed like a beatnik from the fifties? *She* was who Emily had been worried about? *Ha! Life is good.*

Tell that to David. He embarked on introducing them all and apologizing to his secretary, explaining their uninvited presence in her hallway. He did an admirable job of it, too, Emily had to admit. Even if he didn't take a discernible breath—no doubt, knowing that if he did, he'd be raked over the coals. But it turned out all right. Mrs. Hopemore—who couldn't take her gaze off Mr. Smith-Hill, that debonair little specimen—was finally won over.

She understood their predicament, she said, even finally admitting she'd just known something like this would happen. *She'd known? How could she know?* But the outlandish older woman offered no explanation. All she said was it all sounded wonderfully adventurous and deserving of her special skills. Emily cringed to think what exactly those skills might turn out to be. But eventually, the surprising number of handsome young men comprising the literary society meeting were promptly ushered out. And the motley hallway contingency, each holding on to a pet, was ushered in.

The door behind them closed. Loudly. Forcefully. Uneasiness settled over the group as they exchanged glances. Their avenue of escape was cut off. Mrs. Hopemore had them in her clutches.

Emily blinked, uncertain what to do next. She could only look around and stare at the older woman's, um, hip bachelorette pad, for lack of a better phrase. All chrome and glass tables and big splotchy paintings and oddly shaped furniture. Not to mention beanbag chairs. And gaudy plastic flowers. And lots of empty wine bottles and glasses. Lots. Yes, lazy academia and Art Deco ruled the room.

But Mrs. Hopemore ruled the roost. And set about proving it. "Before we devise a plan of attack, we need to get everyone settled. Down the hall there," she said to Emily, pointing a lacquered fingernail in the direction she indicated, "is a spare bedroom. The first one on the left. You and that bird will sleep in there. So make yourself at home. He can be loose in here if he needs to be. But if he makes a mess, you clean it up."

Emily found herself nodding and was almost inclined to curtsy to the imperious Mrs. Hopemore. "Okay. I will. If he does. But I don't think he—"

"Okay. You." Again the tiny woman cut Emily off, turning to David. "Since you're the reason we women are in danger, you're staying here, too. If anyone is going to stop a bullet, it'll be you. Besides, knowing you, if I let you out of my sight, you'll just wander off and get yourself killed. And where would that leave me?"

Emily looked at David. "Unemployed," he said, grinning. Then, as if she were watching a tennis match, Emily swung her attention to Mrs. Hopemore. Who didn't disappoint.

"That's right. So, it's settled. Except where you're going to sleep. Not in the spare bedroom with her, I can tell you that much. So forget that—"

"Hey," David broke in, stiff with offense. "I hardly know Dr. Wright. I wasn't even thinking of—" He cut himself off and turned to Emily, whose eyebrows had raised at his words. "Well, I have to confess. I was...I mean, at some point, I figured—"

"Never mind, David." Emily rushed in, flushed with a mixture of joy and embarrassment. "I understand what you mean."

Mrs. Hopemore saved them from embarrassment by declaring, "Good. We all understand each other. You get the sofa, Mr. Sullivan. And the same rule goes for you. If that dog you've got there—wait. You did say it was a dog in that carrier, didn't you?"

"She's a dog," David assured his secretary.

"I'll just bet she is." With that, she adjusted her huge glasses and narrowed her eyes as she peered into the Pet Porter. Surprisingly, her voice warmed, and she waggled her painted fingertips in greeting to the dog. "Hello, Contessa. Good to see you." She straightened. "If she forgets herself on the floor, you clean it up."

Then the thousand-year-old lady became all smiles as she directed her attention to Mr. Smith-Hill. "Now, where do you and your beautiful hunk of leashed canine want to sleep, handsome?" she asked, simpering.

Emily gulped. David made a strangled noise. Kafka regally raised an eyebrow, as if acknowledging his beautiful hunk status. But poor, sputtering Mr. Smith-Hill. His face turned crimson. Beyond blustering disjointedly about his own bed at home, madam, to be sure…not one further or intelligible word came out of his mouth.

But the same couldn't be said of Rodney, who picked up the slack—and addressed Mrs. Hopemore. ''Wr-rack, you the man, honey.''

YOU THE MAN, HELL, was David's sour thought late that
afternoon as, with his shaving kit and a change of
clothes thrown together, he drove to Mrs. Hopemore's
Georgetown apartment from his high-rise condo across
town. Truth to tell, he'd been troubled ever since Mrs.
Hopemore had made that statement about stopping a
bullet. He hadn't really thought about the danger. Especially since the bad guys—assuming the yo-yos in
the white sports car who showed up this morning at
Emily's were indeed the true dognappers—had
seemed so bumbling.

But now that David thought about it, he had to admit that real trouble could be a possibility. Because
the guy at Emily's door had shoved past her—obviously not caring if he hurt her—in his determination
to get to the dog. David's sense of uneasiness heightened, and had him pressing down on the accelerator,
needing to see for himself that Emily was okay.

Not surprisingly, his heart gave a great big tender
lurch. *Emily.* Just thinking her name did that, elevated
his pulse, made him want to take her in his arms and
make love to her…slowly, passionately. With a lot of
heat and noise and deep, deep kisses. *Whew. Down,
boy,* David told himself, forcing his attention to the
traffic, always a tricky thing in the capitol city. *Yeah,
traffic and this predicament we're in. Think about*

those things. And how he was beginning to think of this predicament as a godsend that had brought Emliy into his life in such a fast and furious way. His adventurous side was having fun, David thought, grinning.

But beyond that, he was rethinking Mr. Smith-Hill's advice about not involving the police. Because adventure and mystery were good—on TV. But this wasn't TV. *Why the heck did I leave Emily there alone?*

Then he remembered. She wasn't alone. Aside from the animal kingdom, Mrs. Hopemore and Mr. Smith-Hill were also there. David grimaced, thinking that didn't make him feel any better. Because how much of a deterrent would those two oldsters be against seasoned criminals? Which led David to wonder, why *were* those men—the two in the white car—so determined to get Godzilla? She certainly wasn't anything special, certainly not show-dog quality, like Kafka.

Which meant the bad guys somehow knew about the obscene amount of money Mrs. Stanfield—whoever the heck she was—had and he now controlled on Godzilla's behalf. And for that matter, what the heck *was* the dog's real name? It was probably in the will, but he hadn't asked or cared, since he hadn't intended to keep her. He decided her real name didn't matter. And despite Mrs. Hopemore's out of the blue dubbing the dog Contessa, Godzilla she was, and Godzilla she would remain.

Suddenly hearing himself and the conviction in his last thought, David quirked his mouth and chuckled. *Great. I have a dog.* Well, a canine juvenile delinquent. Which meant he'd have to sell his condo, given their no-pets policy.

His sensible side was instantly outraged. *Don't do*

*anything rash, David. We've worked hard to get where
we are now. Life is finally easy, and the future is predictable.* Not to be outdone, his adventurous side
checked in. *Don't listen, man. Think of the fun. It
doesn't get any better than this, Dave. We're on the
edge, buddy…living large, got a dog, some pocket
change and running from the outlaws. And maybe, just
maybe we can get the girl, too. Cool, huh?*

David parked in an alleyway beside Mrs. Hopemore's car and chuckled. Well, here he was. So, obviously, and once again, his adventurous side had won.
Cool. David gathered his things and—after looking
around and not spying any suspicious sorts—got out
of his car and locked it. Slinging his canvas bag over
his shoulder, he thought, *Was it only yesterday that
my life was on track?*

Sounded like his sensible side was making a come-
back. And it wanted to know, what he was doing here,
tangled up with dangerously idiotic felons, a British
lawyer, his cranky, quirky secretary, two ungrateful
canines, a foulmouthed bird and— *Oh, yes. Emily.*
With a low whistle and an appreciative shake of his
head, David acknowledged his response to the
woman's sweet face and even sweeter figure. Feeling
his body tighten in response, which made him glad to
be alone in the alley, David strode to the private entry
and, using the key Mrs. Hopemore had given him earlier and told him not to lose, let himself in to the
narrow hallway. He made sure the door behind him
closed securely and the lock engaged, then started up
the stairs.

Dr. Emily Wright. The cute one. The funny one.
The crazy one who'd thought he'd stolen Godzilla and
had called the cops on him. *Oh, yeah, that's why I*

can't call the police now. I'm the suspect. And I'm not supposed to be in contact with Emily. David thought a moment and decided, *No way. I'm not backing out now.* So, there it was—if Rodney should be calling anybody "the man," it was Emily.

Because she'd been very brave last night at her clinic when he'd shown up on a dark and stormy night. No, that irony wasn't lost on David. But she risked her own life—she had, after all, believed him to be a dangerous criminal—and all for the sake of a dog she didn't even know. Wow. That was character.

And that was when it hit David. He was doing the exact same thing Emily had done—namely, the right thing. He was getting involved, being part of the solution. Well, even if it had taken some umbrella jousting with Mr. Trenton to get him involved. Still, he was doing the right thing now. David realized he liked this aspect of his character. And wouldn't his parents be happy at this turn of events? Their son, the activist.

Talk about your warm fuzzies. David inserted the key in the slot and turned it. He was staying. He was in this for the long haul. Right up to his eyeballs. He opened the door. It creaked eerily on its unoiled hinges. He stepped over the threshhold. And *why* was he staying? Because he cared. About Emily. About Godzilla. About—

Fur, feathers and a frying pan all attacked David. Dropping his overnight bag, he flailed his arms, trying to ward off the blows and the growls and the screeches and the bites. Finally, he remembered to yell, "It's me! It's me! Wait a minute! Hold on! It's me—David!"

The attack stopped as abruptly as it had begun. But it took David a moment to believe it. Cautiously, he lowered his arms, only to see a loose white feather floating to the ground. Beyond that, there stood Emily. With a frying pan. And Rodney. And Godzilla. Kafka, for his part, sat dispassionately aside. But the berserk trio in front of David was breathing heavily, Emily's face was red with exertion, and the two animals were ruffled.

David felt pretty much the same way. "What the hell was that all about? Why'd you attack me?"

To a critter, the animals all looked to Emily, effectively designating her as their official spokeswoman. Looking sheepish, she explained, "You scared us, coming in so suddenly. We thought you were the dognappers."

David didn't even know where to begin. "The dog— Again you thought I was the dognappers? And coming in so suddenly? Emily, I had a key. I let myself in. I came in slowly—wait a minute." David crouched into a defensive posture, his gaze searching the apartment. "Where're Mrs. Hopemore and Mr. Smith-Hill? They're not going to jump out at me, are they?"

"No. It's safe. They're gone," she said, tossing the frying pan onto the nearby shape-tormented sofa.

David relaxed his stance but felt less than reassured by her answer. "They're gone, Emily? Gone where?" He snatched up his canvas bag and closed the apartment door behind him. It then occurred to him that Emily hadn't answered his simple question. Ominous. Tossing his bag onto the same hulking stump of a sofa as she had the frying pan, he turned to her. Her dark blue eyes were wide and shiny...as if she were getting ready to cry.

Great. Women. They attack you. You scare them.

They cry. You apologize. "Hey, what's wrong? You all right?"

Sniffing, she put a shaking hand to her mouth. Tears welled up in her eyes. "David, I am so sorry. I was just scared. And I—you must hate me. I didn't—"

"Come here." He stepped over to her—scattering the assorted wildlife, all of whom rearranged themselves nearby—and took her in his arms, holding her close. She felt so right. "It's okay," he crooned, rubbing her back as she shook with sobs. "I shouldn't have scared you like that. I should have let you know it was me first. You did the right thing to protect yourself." With that, he pulled back, looking into her tear-streaked face. His heart melted. Damn, but she was beautiful. "You okay?"

She nodded. "Yes. But I'm...I'm sorry." She hiccupped. "I could have really hurt you with that frying pan."

"Ah, don't worry about it, I'm fine," David soothed. But his adventurous side wasn't buying it. *Whadda ya mean you're fine, Dave? She just about made hash out of your brain. And Big Bird over there—he tried to make shish kebab out of your eyeballs. And Godzilla—your own dog, let me remind you—all but shredded your ankles.* But as it turned out, when David took a physical inventory of himself, he realized that their attack had essentially been all sound, fury and little else. Because he didn't really hurt anywhere. So, about all they'd done was scare the hell out of him.

Then suddenly it was funny. David chuckled and shook his head, thinking this woman in his arms was the bravest person he'd ever run across.

She blinked, her chin still quivering. "What's so funny?"

"You are," he told her. "You're funny and brave and good-looking as hell. And you've turned my entire life upside down."

She sniffed, nodding. "I know. I guess you hate me for turning your life upside down."

"I should," he agreed. "But I don't. Far from it." With that, acting only on impulse and desire for her, David lowered his head, capturing her mouth with his. Her initial start of surprise quickly melted into acquiescence, further igniting David's passion. Could it be that she felt it, too, the spark that crackled across his lips? He hoped so. And he hoped she realized, as he did, that their mouths fit together perfectly, that this feeling between them was maybe more than simple need. Or desire. Or lust. It was much more.

Finally, she slipped her arms around his neck, pressed herself against him and moaned into his mouth. And some dammed-up response inside David broke, telling him she was the one. It was her. They'd been doing this all their lives with one another. At least, that's how it felt. Especially when the kiss deepened, became hungry, insistent, demanding—

And Godzilla howled. And Kafka barked. And Rodney crowed out, "Wr-rack, get a room."

As if they were teenagers caught in the act, David jerked back the same second Emily did. Holding her by her arms, he stared at her. Her mouth was open, still wet with his kiss, but surprised embarrassment rode her features. Shaken from their first kiss—and figuring she was, too—David resorted to humor, hoping to smooth over the moment. "So, Emily, just how attached *are* you to that bird?"

"Not especially," she answered, shrugging and looking delicious. "Why? Would you like to kill him?"

David nodded. "I think I would. I really do."

"Okay. I'll help. On that sofa, there's a nice frying pan you can use."

Still playing along, David grimaced. "I'll need a weapon?"

Her thick black hair swinging with her movement, Emily cut her gaze to the bird. David looked, too. Rodney's wings were spread and his head lowered as he eyed them right back. And not in a nice way. "Oh, yes," she assured David. "Definitely. In fact, you might also need a whip."

David snapped his fingers. "Darn. I left mine back at my condo."

Emily quirked her mouth. "Didn't your mother ever tell you to think ahead?"

"No. She said live for today. And don't worry about tomorrow. For tomorrow may never come."

Emily's nose wrinkled. "That's it?"

David pretended to think about it. "Well, there was also don't trust anyone over thirty."

"Oh, that's right. The make love, not war generation, right?"

"Right. Although, you know, that's not such a bad credo to live by. Especially that part about making love."

Emily opened her mouth. "I…" She stared at him, blinking. And then closed her mouth.

"You what, Emily?" David murmured as the moment deepened, as he lessened the distance between their bodies by again pulling Emily to him, intent on repeating that sweet kiss they'd just shared.

But as their lips edged ever closer, Emily suddenly pulled back and put a restraining hand on David's chest. "Oh, my God, David. Wait. In all the excitement, I forgot. Earlier you asked me about Mrs. Hopemore and Mr. Smith-Hill. Remember I said they were gone? Well, gone in a bad way, David. The worst kind of gone there could possibly be."

David frowned. What was she saying? Then it hit him. "Define gone."

Her blue eyes widened. "Handguns, David. Gone with handguns. They armed themselves and left. Said they were going out on a scouting mission."

David stared at Emily. None of what she said made any sense. However, in the next and blinding second, it did. Distressingly, her words sunk in and took on meaning. Horrible meaning. Then, much as if he'd just seen a shark fin coming at him in his own bathtub, reaction exploded through David, stiffening his whole body. "Handguns? Those two—?"

He let go of Emily and began pacing back and forth in front of her. "When, Emily? When did they leave? And why didn't you tell me?"

Wringing her hands, she reminded him, "I did. Just now."

David stopped his pacing to stare at her. A part of his brain noted exactly how beautiful she was, but the rest of him said, "Sooner. I meant sooner than just now. When I came through the door, for example."

"I know. I meant to. But you scared me when you came in. And then I was crying. And then you kissed me, and I forgot. And then Rodney—"

"Emily," David said, putting a hand on her arm, squeezing gently. "Never mind. It's okay. I'm sorry.

Just tell me what happened. Start with the handguns. Where'd they get handguns?''

"*Your* secretary—'' Her accusatory tone flashed David back to his childhood. Neighborhood parents had sounded much the same way when tattling on him. Your son yada-yada-yada. "Opened a drawer in that…whatever that strange piece of furniture is over there and just pulled them out like they were silverware or something. I swear to you, David, it was like a John Wayne Western. She tossed—*tossed*—a gun to poor Mr. Smith-Hill and as much as told the man to mount up. Which he did. And they…left.''

As he stared at Emily, a sudden vision assailed David. Those two old codgers loose in D.C. With handguns. Can you say six o'clock news and film at eleven? *Where in the world*— "Where in the world could they be going? How would they know where to start? You and I don't even know where to look, much less who we're looking for.''

Emily nodded. "I tried to tell them that, too. I even tried to stop them. But…well, they *were* armed, David.''

"True,'' he conceded. "And dangerous. More to themselves than anyone else.'' He blinked and added fervently, "I hope.''

Her expression serious, Emily quirked her mouth. "Me, too.'' Her mood brightened a little. "David, I just have to tell you. That secretary of yours. She is some piece of work.''

"I know. I told you so. Cranky old thing, isn't she?''

Emily's distressing response was a grin—a really big grin. Figuring he knew why, and pretending it upset him, David slumped where he stood. "Oh, no. You like her, don't you?'' David shook his head, feigning defeat. ''Great. You like her.''

''I do. I think she's a trip. I mean, look at this place. It's absolutely wild. And all those young guys who were here, David. At her age! I love it. And come on yourself. Admit it. You like her, too.''

David stood taller. ''I don't have any choice. I've known her all my life.''

She was clearly startled. ''What?'' Emily said. ''All your life? I thought—''

''That she just worked for me, right? Wrong. As silly as it sounds, when I moved here and opened my firm, my grandmother—Mrs. Hopemore's lifelong friend—called her and told her I was here. And asked her to keep an eye on me. Only I didn't know it at the time.''

Emily put her hands to her hips. ''And here I was ready to—never mind. Still, that explains a lot. Like why you'd be comfortable just showing up here with all of us and our descending upon the poor woman.''

David snorted at that. ''I was not the least bit comfortable, if you'll recall. And poor woman? That's the last thing she is.''

Emily eyed him…and saw right through him. ''You like her.''

David caved. ''Fine. I do. But if she even suspected that, she'd ask for a raise. And right now, all I want to know is where she is. Every time she gets loose, it either costs me money or weakens the nation. Hell, I ought to be sending out a squadron of fighter jets in our defense.''

Emily grimaced. ''Think we'll need them?''

''Does Godzilla have an overbite? Yeah, I think we'll need them. If they don't show up soon—''

The door behind David burst open. He jumped, Emily shrieked, Godzilla yapped. Kafka merely watched them, an elegant ear raised, while Rodney flew over to an indescribable piece of furniture that had glass thingies on it and perched there, squawking, "Wrrack, battle stations! Man the torpedoes!"

NOT A BAD IDEA, was Emily's thought when the two runaways exploded into the room much like thrown hand grenades—ones scented with a mingling of smoky autumn air, stale perfume and Italian sausage.

Stopping short—no doubt surprised by their welcoming committee—Mrs. Hopemore and Mr. Smith-Hill, their faces flushed, a huge square of a pizza box and a bottle of red wine clutched in their hands, said, "Oops." And then hung all over each other…tipsily.

Which had a quieting effect on the remainder of the room's occupants. Disbelief had Emily raising an eyebrow. She sought David's gaze. And got it. He exchanged a look with her and then focused on the duo. "Well, you two seem to have bonded."

"Bonded." Mr. Smith-Hill pronounced the word carefully, his bespectacled eyes bright as he pulled himself up into an elegant posture, hoisted the wine bottle and amended, "*James* Bonded."

At that, Mrs. Hopemore shrieked merrily, nearly folding the pizza box in half. Galvanized, Emily and David made an emergency dash to rescue the pizza and the wine from the older couple's precarious clutches. With the food and drink safe, Emily couldn't help but ask, "What happened to you two? Did you fall into a vat of laughing gas or something?"

"Even better," Mrs. Hopemore assured her. "An afternoon wine tasting."

Emily gasped, reflexively clutching the wine bottle tighter. "Don't tell me you drove a car in this condition," she challenged.

The odd old couple stared at Emily, then looked at each other, shrugged, turned to her and said "Okay" in unison. Thus unrepentant, they shed their coats and closed the door behind them, finally tossing their garments over to the sofa, atop David's canvas bag and Emily's frying pan, which resulted in a heavy clunk or two. *The handguns,* was Emily's hope. Having no idea how to handle this recalcitrant duo, who now put their heads together and whispered secretively, she stood there, defeated. What now? Did they just let these two get away with their antics?

I don't think so. Reacting like a mother whose deep-seated conviction is that her children's bad habits are all inherited from their father's side, she pivoted to face David. "Did you hear that?"

Looking blank, obviously caught off guard, David lowered the pizza box he'd been sniffing. "Hear what?"

Emily exhaled loudly. "They were carrying handguns—"

"For heaven's sake, kiddo," Mrs. Hopemore chimed in, waving a hand at Emily. "Lighten up. They're not loaded, you know."

Emily could only stare at the older woman. "Like that makes it okay to carry a concealed weapon?"

"I have a license. Tell her, Hubert."

Hubert—who turned out to be Mr. Smith-Hill—verified this. "She does. I saw it. And it's quite lovely."

Outraged, embarrassed and not even knowing why, Emily turned to David, who looked like he'd just been gut punched. Apparently he'd learned something new about Mrs. Hopemore. But that didn't get him off the hook. "They were drinking and driving, David." She instantly pivoted to the old folks. "You don't have a license for *that*, do you?" They shook their heads. Satisfied, Emily focused again on David. "Do something."

She watched and waited while he sought other gazes and additional help. None was forthcoming because everyone was looking everywhere but at him. *Poor guy.* Suddenly tickled and upset with herself—when had she become so uptight?—Emily struggled to keep the solemn expression on her face. And almost lost her battle before David, acting as if it were a peace offering, held out the pizza box and said, "Look. They brought supper."

His silly gesture took her by surprise. And touched her heart. He could have been a little boy holding out a bunch of flowers he'd just pulled from a neighbor's garden. And because he *was* so cute, and she was so overwrought—not to mention hungry—Emily caved, forgiving everybody in the room for the day's antics. To prove it, she held up the wine bottle. "Not only that, they also brought nerve tonic."

Instantly, the tension was broken. Barking, swooping, cheering and wr-racking ensued. In a few short moments, the handguns were retrieved from the two oldsters' coat pockets, their unloadedness verified, and they were replaced in their cases in a drawer. Next, the animals were fed, and plates and napkins and wineglasses—clean ones—were brought out and everyone gathered around the table, talking and eating and drinking. And asking questions. Pointed questions. Such as this conversation stopper from Mrs. Hopemore to David... "So, Mr. Sullivan, what if I said that all our lives now depend on Contessa over there participating in an obedience trial in a public dog show tomorrow out on the grassy mall in front of the White House?''

8

THIS WAS ONE SATURDAY that Emily had, at one point, thought would never end. And now, close to midnight, she found herself hoping it wouldn't. Because this was the best part of the day. For several reasons. Such as the noisy coffee bar downstairs. It was closed. And Mr. Smith-Hill. He'd sobered up by mid-evening and had left for home with Kafka. Which meant that Mrs. Hopemore's apartment was, at long last, quiet. And so was she. Even now, snoring came from behind the closed door of the older woman's bedroom down the hall.

But what—or who—really made this time the best part for Emily was David. He was here in the living room with her. Such a sweet, warm feeling it was, this cocoonish intimacy they'd been weaving together all day. As if they'd known each other for years. Just the two of them. Well, okay, the two of them plus Rodney and Godzilla. But at this point—lying on her side on the oddball sofa with a sleepy Godzilla tucked up against her—Emily philosophically reminded herself that getting what you want in life isn't always easy.

Meaning, sometimes the handsome Prince Charming is accompanied by dognappers and a canine in a delicate way. But that was okay because, in this case, the lovely Princess Charming herself owned a foul-mouthed cockatoo, as well as various other assorted and opinionated critters. Sighing, so aware of David's masculine presence that she ached with wanting to touch him, and indeed could, he was so close—*if only I had the guts*—Emily kept her hands to herself and admired his well-toned and muscled physique.

Apparently oblivious to the sculpted and seductive picture he made in the room's low light, he was lying on the carpeted floor, on his back, his knees bent, his hands behind his head. Incongruously, Rodney was perched on one of David's denim-covered knees. Even more frightening, the bird was behaving. Well, behaving for Rodney, meaning he offered only the occasional barbed comment.

Which now centered on the odds of getting Godzilla to behave in general, much less in particular. Particular being defined as at tomorrow's dog show. An open-air dog show. An open-air dog show free to the general public—a large and ready-made audience for Godzilla's antics. Antics at a time when their very lives depended on her unwitting cooperation. Which had Emily asking herself again—just why *did* their lives depend on the outcome of Godzilla's performance in an obedience demonstration?

It seemed she wasn't the only one wondering. "So, Emily, let's see if I have this straight. Mrs. Hopemore and Mr. Smith-Hill, while they were out this afternoon doing whatever it was they were doing—" He turned to look at her. "Beyond the wine tasting, they never did say just what they'd really been doing, did they?"

She heard his question and wished she had the answer. Not that she could have responded...not this second, anyway. Because the look in his eyes had captivated her senses. Every time he gazed at her, she tingled. The glances that passed between them seemed to intensify to a sizzle in only seconds. And right now, Emily felt herself heating up significantly—

"Emily? Did you hear me?"

"Oh. Yes. I heard you," she blurted. "And, um, you're right. I don't think they said." *Great. I sound like an idiot.* She took a calming breath and added, more slowly and in her normal tone of voice, "But we'll probably sleep better not knowing."

"Yeah. Not knowing is definitely better," David agreed, sounding a little breathless himself. Had he, too, Emily wondered, been aware of the sensual spell mushrooming between them? Then, as if working to keep the conversation impersonal, if not innocuous, he added, "Wasn't it supposed to be something to do with gathering evidence?"

"Yes. But apparently the only things they gathered were wine and pizza."

Chuckling, settling into his former position, David said, "Nothing wrong with that. So they just ran across this dog show thing and signed up Godzilla in the obedience trial?"

Now it was the sound of his voice causing Emily to sigh. A delicious shiver slipped over her skin, and a smile came to her lips as she savored the feeling. Just then Godzilla perked up and stared into Emily's face, as if to say, *Answer the man.* Blinking out of yet another David reverie, Emily blurted, "Correct." And hoped it was—her answer, that is. Because by now she'd forgotten his question.

"Great. Too bad they couldn't have signed up Kafka instead."

Oh, yeah. Whew. Godzilla and the obedience thing. "I know," Emily agreed readily. "But it's Godzilla they're after—much to Mr. Smith-Hill's amazement.

But anyway, he couldn't have signed up Kafka. This is an amateur show. And Kafka is a registered show dog and a champion, so he can't participate. He'd lose his professional standing.''

"Well, jeez, we wouldn't want that," David said, heavy on the irony, "especially since our *lives* depend on it."

And that brought her back to her original question. Emily raised up on an elbow. "They keep saying that. Our lives depend on it. How, David? How do our lives depend on it?"

He shrugged. "Maybe in a number of ways. For one thing, we'll be vulnerable since we'll all be in public with Godzilla in tow. Like bait. And they'll recognize her, for sure, if not the rest of us."

"Still, David," she persisted, "our lives?"

"Well, Em. You never know. That guy this morning didn't think twice about shoving you out of the way to get to Godzilla. So why would he hesitate to do more than shove any of us, given the right provocation?"

He called me Em. Like a pet name. As happy as she was at this intimacy, Emily still grimaced at his words. "I hadn't thought of it that way. I was just afraid for Godzilla. Not myself."

"Exactly. Which explains me being here right now. Your safety. I won't have you hurt over something to do with my dog. Or for any other reason."

Hugging his words, words of caring, to her heart, Emily took up her end of the conversation—anything to keep from saying good-night and ending this time alone with him. "In light of that, I guess Mr. Smith-Hill's reasoning *is* sound. I mean, where else would dognappers be but at a dog show?"

"I agree. So, it's the perfect opportunity to see if they come after Godzilla in particular. Or if they now pass her by for easier—not to mention more rational—choices."

"Aw, nothing personal, girl. We love you," Emily told Godzilla as she petted her. Then she focused on David. "Okay, all that's true. And I know this is a serious situation. But life or death? That's just so bizarre. Like something in a movie. But not real life, at least not mine."

David turned to her, also going up on an elbow like she had. Which dislodged Rodney, who squawked. "Wr-rack, watch your step, boy-o." He fluttered to the carpet and stalked around à la Groucho Marx.

David shot the ruffled bird a shut-your-beak look and then focused on Emily. Again, she thought her heart would stop at the serious look in his mesmerizing eyes. "Yeah, in your life, Emily. And the scariest part for me is she's—" he pointed to Godzilla "—the bait to draw out the dognappers. And I know you well enough already to know that if she got nabbed, you'd be right behind her and prepared to give up your life to protect her. Tell me that's not true."

Emily chuckled. "I can't. Because it is true." No doubt exasperated with her, David shook his head. Emily scratched the dog in question between the ears. "Oh, come on, David. You'd be right behind me, prepared to go the distance for her. Admit it. She's so sweet."

David grunted. "I admit nothing. And try telling that sweet stuff to Mr. Trenton. After two days with her, he was bloodied and ready for a mental home."

"Wait. Mr. Trenton? That's the woman's attorney, the one who left you Godzilla, right?"

David nodded. "The very same. And that's another thing. I still don't know who Amelia Stanfield is. I mean, what did I ever do to her to make her retaliate like this?" Again he pointed to Godzilla of the black, narrowed eyes and the flattened ears. Clearly, she remained insulted.

Emily continued to stroke the maligned mama-to-be—as much to keep her in place as anything—and said, "Be nice, David. We're talking about Godzilla's previous owner. What's her name again?"

"Amelia Stanfield."

"That's right. I've heard you say that before, about not knowing why'd she name you her heir. Odd, isn't it, that she'd just pick you? Like out of the phone book or something."

David's expression sobered. "I thought the same thing. Maybe I ought to ask Mrs. Hopemore—since she has a filing system known only to her—to go to the office and search through our old cases. Amelia Stanfield could be someone I did a financial thing for on a one-time basis years ago, and I just don't remember her."

"That could be. But—no offense, David—a woman as rich as you've said she was would have had a slew of private accountants to take care of her finances for her."

"I agree. But rich old people can be pretty eccentric. Who knows? She may have had me do something for her that she didn't want her people to know about."

Emily's interest quickened. "Oh, I like the sound of that. Maybe she didn't use her real name. And that's why you don't remember her."

David shook his head. "I doubt it. I ask for all kinds

of legal ID. Which she most likely wouldn't have. And an incident like that I would have remembered.'' He wagged a finger at Emily. ''You know what really intrigues me? Why the dognappers want Godzilla. You'd think they'd kidnap me and not her, since I control the money. Hell, they can *have* Godzilla. I'll be glad to meet them somewhere and give her to them.''

''David Sullivan, shame on you,'' Emily railed. ''You don't mean that.''

''I do, too.''

''You do not. Just this morning at my house you rushed in to save her.''

''Did not. I rushed in to save *you*.''

Well, that got her. Emily brightened. ''I guess you did,'' she finally admitted. ''That's—'' *the most wonderful thing anyone's ever said to me or done for me, you great big heroic hunk of sweet, gorgeous male* ''—nice.''

Looking a little sheepish, as if embarrassed that he'd just told on himself, David resettled into his former position and stared at the ceiling. ''Yeah, well, don't let it get around. It'd ruin my reputation.''

Emily grinned at him, loving the frowning tilt of his mouth and his feigned gruffness. Then deciding that as long as everyone was confessing… ''David, I have something to tell you.''

Without looking at her, he said in a deadpan voice, ''Let me guess. You're pregnant, unmarried and running away from kidnappers.''

''No!'' Emily gave a surprised gasp, which unsettled Godzilla enough to make her get up and turn around three times, within the close confines of the sofa cushion, before settling again and glaring at Emily. Who immediately clamped a hand over her own mouth, belatedly mindful of awakening Mrs. Hopemore. Then she whispered, "That's a terrible thing to say."

David shrugged, but Emily could see the smile tugging at his lips. "Well, it's just been that kind of a day."

"Oh, really? Well, what if I *was* all those things you said? What would you do then?"

David immediately rolled onto his side and faced her. "I'd marry you, give your child a name, keep you safely tucked away and spend all my money on you."

Taken aback, Emily breathed, "You would?"

"Sure," he confirmed easily enough. "Either that, or go shopping for a new car. I can't decide which."

That comment had a throw pillow living up to its name. Reaching for one behind her, Emily hurled it at him, smacking him in the shoulder. "David Sullivan, you were teasing me. I hate you."

Chuckling, he held onto the pillow. "No, you don't." Then his expression became what Emily could only term baiting. "But you had yourself worked up into believing you'd hate Mrs. Hopemore, didn't you?"

"I did—" Emily gulped. "No, I—" Embarrassed heat exploded in her cheeks. "Hate her? You think—? I did *not*," she finally said, wanting to run to her room. If only her muscles hadn't locked and held her in place. In the hot seat.

Which that grinning stinker of a David Sullivan took full advantage of. "Did too. Earlier, in my car, all those questions about her? You thought I had something going with her, didn't you? And you were jealous."

"Was not," Emily sputtered, intending to leave it at that. "Well, you let me think that, didn't you? You led me to believe there was something there. All that merry widow stuff—"

"Merry widow?" In one smooth movement, David sat up, his expression purely quizzical, despite Godzilla's low and warning growl for him not to come any closer. "Emily Wright, I have never said anything about a merry widow."

"Maybe not. But I am right, aren't I? You timed your comments and slanted it that way. So tell me why."

Completely unrepentant, David answered her. "To see if you'd get jealous."

With no throw pillows left at her disposal, Emily confessed, "Well, it worked. I got jealous. So there."

"No," David said, rising and crawling over to her. "Not so there. So *here*." With that, he lifted a squirming, snarling Godzilla off the sofa cushion, set her on the carpet, cupped Emily's face in his hands...and kissed her silly.

She melted. Never before had she been kissed like this, with a wealth of desire and tenderness and hunger all rolled into one. Jeff had never made her feel this way. All tingly and weak and yearning. She slipped her arms around David's neck, held him close and felt herself being lifted in his arms and carried with him to the thick carpet. Once there, he gently laid her on her back and hovered above her, a leg thrown over both of hers.

Emily moaned. This was so delicious. She could stay here all night, in this man's embrace, and give herself to him. Forget convention. Forget that they'd known each other only twenty-four hours. Who cared?

Not her. Not when his touch, his kiss, even a simple smile from him made a mishmash of her emotions—not to mention her body. So probing was his gaze that Emily wished she had deep, dark secrets she could confess to him. Riches she could give up to him. Anything. State secrets. Family jewels…

"Emily," David whispered, his lips lightly brushing hers.

"David," she whispered right back.

"Emily," he breathed. "We're not alone. Get up."

"Oh, David, I really—" *What?* Emily stiffened. Her eyes popped open. She stared up at David, who had only a tight smile and raised eyebrows to show her. "David," she began cautiously, "when you say we're not alone, you mean in the larger sense, right? Like…lovers everywhere, we're not alone?"

"I wish I did. But no." It was David's measured response as, with a nod of his head, he indicated someone—or something—to his left. "I mean we're not alone in the immediate sense. We need to get up."

Emily could only stare at him. Get up *now?* When she really, really didn't want to? After all, the man's arms were wrapped around her. And his body was stretched out on top of hers. But he wasn't looking down at her, his heart in his eyes. No. He was still looking over to his left. Reluctantly, Emily followed his gaze.

Sure enough, they weren't alone.

Little black and beady eyes—fake ones—set in fuzzy pink bunny slippers, which in turn were attached to two spindly legs and an uneven negligee hemline, all about two feet away, stared back at them. If she looked up just a tad, Emily knew, she'd see Mrs. Hopemore.

Sure enough, the older woman said, "Mr. Sullivan, I came out here to get a glass of water. But I never thought I'd live long enough to see a sight like this. And in my own living room. Do you know what this makes me?"

David slumped, resting his forehead against Emily's. "Oh, I don't know. What *does* it make you? A witness? Maybe mad? Or sleepwalking? Bitter? Drunk? Unemployed? Any or all of the above, Mrs. Hopemore?"

"None of the above," she remarked, calmly stepping over their intertwined bodies and continuing on her way to her kitchen, an empty glass in her hand. "What this makes me is…happy for you. It's about time. All you do is work, work, work. So, this is good, and I'm happy for you. But by the time the sun comes up, I won't even remember I said it. Which makes me senile."

To which Rodney—who sidled along in her wake—apparently felt compelled to add, "Wr-rack, I'm with you, sister."

"OH, I SAY. Past midnight? And right there on your living room floor?"

"The very same one, Hubert. Why, I practically tripped over their entwined bodies trying to get to my own kitchen."

"My word. Young folks are rather cheeky nowadays, don't you think, Lavinia?"

Emily rolled her eyes. Hubert and Lavinia—aka Mr. Smith-Hill and Mrs. Hopemore—along with the well-behaved if not bored Kafka, preceded her and David and Godzilla as, following a late lunch, they weaved their way through the dog-show crowd the next day.

Emily had thought that the four of them were supposed to be keeping an eye out for suspicious-looking characters. But apparently her and David's activities of late last evening were of more interest today than looking for criminals. Not to mention the main subject of conversation, since Mr. Smith-Hill had met up with them for lunch. And, true to her word, Mrs. Hopemore hadn't once mentioned today the part about her being happy for David. Yet she was more than happy to regale Mr. Smith-Hill with all the other details. But the part about being happy for David? Naw. And happy for what? Emily wondered. That he'd found...well, love, maybe? Could that be what she'd meant?

With that thought, that hope, guiding her, Emily leaned in to speak in private with David, who was busy trying to keep the bright-eyed and wriggling Godzilla tucked into the crook of his arm. The rambunctious little dog obviously wanted down—probably so she could stir up all the other dogs. Indicating the two seniors walking ahead of them, Emily said, "You'd think they'd be more concerned with finding the darned tent where we check in for the obedience thing, wouldn't you?"

"I would," he agreed. "But I'll just be glad if they don't make an announcement over the PA system about you and me last night."

Emily clutched at David's coat-covered arm. "Tell me you don't think they would."

David looked at her, grinning. "Can't. I think they would. In a heartbeat." Then his grin warmed to a smile. A seductive smile. "Which is about how far away we were last night from giving them something really newsworthy to report.'' His voice became husky. ''Am I right? Or was it only me?''

Not knowing how to react, Emily stopped and got bumped from behind. She ignored the stranger's apology in favor of staring at David. She only hoped her heart wasn't in her eyes. ''No. It wasn't only you, David. I—''

''Oh, *now* look at them, Hubert. We can't even take them out in public. It's like they're in heat.'' Mrs. Hopemore's loud comment drew the curious attention of every nearby stranger, human and canine.

Emily, along with David, jerked toward the two oldsters and saw them standing there, hands on their hips, staring disapprovingly. As always, Kafka looked away, no doubt in an effort to distance himself from this very crass moment. But Emily had no such qualms. She glared at Mr. Smith-Hill and Mrs. Hopemore as she informed David, ''I am personally and cheerfully going to kill her.''

''Oh, hell—don't,'' he pleaded. ''Her ghost would show up Monday for work and scare me to death.''

Emily could only stare at David—and believe him, especially when he winked at her. Darn him. She wanted to be mad at Mrs. Hopemore. Then she sighed and let it go. Given the woman's penchant for mischief and her basically warm heart—as well as her dramatically made up appearance—how could anyone stay mad at her? She was like a human Godzilla. The dog. Not the lizard.

''Well,'' Emily finally quipped, ''Tuesday *is* Halloween. If she scared you to death, you could go out as a ghost. You wouldn't even need to buy a costume.''

David's eyebrows rose. ''*Buy* a costume? I'd never

buy one. I just borrow something from Mrs. Hopemore. You know, a feather boa, some glitzy high heels, a bit of makeup and I'd be ready for trick-or-treating.''

Surely he— Emily couldn't even finish the thought.

Finally, David—admitting nothing—took her arm and propelled her forward. "Come on. Let's go find that tent. And catch us some dognappers.''

9

THE OBEDIENCE DEMONSTRATION ground to a halt—
Again. Again the crowd—including David and Mr.
Smith-Hill, Kafka and Mrs. Hopemore—laughed. And
again the official ringmaster—a big scary lady in a
tweed suit and sensible shoes—pointed accusingly. In
her heavy German accent, she called out, "*Fraulein?*
Zuh one whis the naughty spiky little doggy? *Ja,*
you!"

"Yes, ma'am, I know it's me," Emily called, helplessly watching Godzilla cheerfully wind herself
around Emily's ankles. Out of the side of her mouth,
Emily murmured, "Stop it, Godzilla. Seriously. Stop,
or I'll—"

Or I'll what? And there it was. The despicable little
canine knew there was no "or what." Emily sighed,
as she eyed the stubby-legged critter making this moment in her life a living hell. What else could she do—
with so many witnesses—but laugh? However, once
she got out of this ring, she decided, she was going to
throttle David Sullivan. After all, he was the one
who'd stuck her here, saying he needed to be free in
case the dognappers made a move. A likely story.

"Ve haf been through zhis, *Fraulein,*" the drill sergeant of the year was saying. "You must show zuh
doggy you are not afraid of her."

Insulted, Emily raised an eyebrow and said perhaps

a bit too loudly, "I'll have you know that I am not afraid of her. I'm a veterinarian, for crying out loud." *Great, Emily. Good advertising.* But not done humiliating herself, she pointed to Godzilla, and added, "And *she's* pregnant and hormonal. So lighten up, okay?"

Everyone in the show ring got quiet. Well, got quieter. Except for the professional dog trainer. Whose smile tightened. "Even zo," the woman chided, "unvind yourself and then schtand zuh doggy beside you. Go ahead. Ve vill vait…again. And remember, be firm whis her."

You can vait all day for all I care, was Emily's sullen thought as she bent and untangled Godzilla and then realigned the naughty spiky little dog's bottom with some stupid white line that the woman had, only moments ago, finally spray painted in the grass to mark their place. As if they were too simple to figure it out. Okay, so they *were* the only one of the twelve dog-owner teams who'd had to have their space so marked. Still, Emily's way of thinking, that whole paint thing was just spiteful and unnecessary.

"Come on, Godzilla," she begged. "Behave, will you? And keep that cold nose to yourself. You're wreaking havoc here. Just how long do you think that nice bulldog is going to be patient with you?"

Of course, Godzilla only grinned, thus showing her overbite off to its best advantage. Then she gave Emily a cheerful bark. Which Emily, her heart melting with affection for the little turkey, desperately chose to take as a hopeful sign. Grinning, rubbing Godzilla's head, Emily straightened, standing tall and proud, woman and canine, united against…

Godzilla jerked away, taking the leash with her.

With Emily in frenzied pursuit and the crowd once again in a merry uproar, the furry terror zipped over and yet again greeted—in the time-honored tradition of one polite dog to another—the startled English bull-dog. But apparently someone had failed to inform the brindled gentleman that Godzilla's was a mannerly display. Because he yelped and ducked his hind end down and scooted about ten feet across the grass before his outraged owner could take up enough leash to stop him. The man then asked for another spot away from "that rabid dog and its alleged veterinarian."

Emily felt compelled to loudly tell the departing snotty man, "Your dog's scooting like that because he's infested with worms, sir."

In a twinkling, another man—a balding, cheerful guy with thick glasses and horsey teeth—stood next to Emily and Godzilla. With him, on a thick leather lead and eyeing them as if they were his dinner, was a big shepherd-husky mix of a dog. Emily gripped Godzilla's leash tighter and sidestepped a few discreet feet as she focused on the dog handler in the middle of the circle. But, sure enough, just as the woman launched into an explanation to the crowd of the next maneuver she would have these rank beginners attempt, the new guy next to Emily chirped hello, apparently as pleased as punch to be here.

Emily merely nodded at him, reluctant to get to know him, since she didn't know how long he would last.

But the middle-aged guy's grin never faded. Nor did his muscular dog's serious eyeing of Godzilla. Godzilla whined and shrank against Emily's ankle. Which of course meant that Emily now loved this new big dog. Anybody who could intimidate Godzilla was a friend of hers. In that vein, she gamely asked the toothy man, "So. What's his name?"

"Ask him," the man said.

"Excuse me?" Emily looked from man to dog and back again.

"Ask him," the guy repeated.

Not knowing what to think—was the man nuts or what?—Emily looked around and caught sight of David on the sidelines. Staring at her, he had a hand over his mouth. No doubt he hid a smirk. *Yeah, it's real funny, isn't it, Sullivan?* But still she grinned at him. Because it *was* funny. Then she saw David pointing beside himself. Emily looked to where he indicated. Surprise! Kafka had stood up, adopting a challenging posture aimed at the brawny shepherd husky next to Godzilla. Could it be our boy was jealous?

Emily looked again to David, who gave her a shrug, the international symbol for *Who knew?* Then he pointed to the trainer, as if telling Emily to pay attention. Which she did. Or tried to. Because the big-toothed man next to her said, out of the blue, "It's a joke, you know."

Despite her best instincts to the contrary, Emily glanced at him. "What is?"

"His name." He pointed to the very unfunny animal he had tethered on that thick length of leather.

"Yeah. I'll bet it is," Emily said.

"No. Seriously. That's his name."

Defeated, figuring the guy wouldn't let it go if she didn't bite, Emily again asked, "All right. Fine. What's his name?"

The very annoying man grinned and again said, "Ask him."

Emily narrowed her eyes, hating this goofy guy

more than she did the trainer. But knowing when she was whipped, she focused on the staring, unblinking dog. Feeling really silly, she asked, "So. What's your name?"

Of course, the animal said nothing. But his owner hee-hawed with laughter, startling the chihuahua next to him into shivering violently and the toy poodle on the other side of the chihuahua into wetting itself. "That's the joke," the husky's owner laughed. "His name is Askim. A-S-K-I-M."

"Oh. Ha, ha. I get it," Emily said. *The only thing I want to ask Askim is if he'd like a new owner.*

Just then, the crowd behind Emily shifted, people fussed, someone said, "Hey, watch it, buddy," and Godzilla yelped. Startled, Emily sidestepped, thinking she'd accidentally trounced on some canine toes. But she was more confused when the leash in her hand suddenly went limp. Reflexively, she pulled on it, expecting it to be attached to the dog's fake jewel collar. But it wasn't. She looked down—and gasped.

The only thing fastened to Godzilla were two claw-like hands, which seemingly had leached from the crowd to close around the wide-eyed and terrified dog's pregnant belly. *The dognappers!* In a flash, even before Emily could scream, Godzilla was yanked backward. And was gone, whisked away through a crowd that flowed together and innocently blocked the departing criminal from Emily's view.

"David!" she finally remembered to scream, her legs weak, her heart fluttering. Emily saw David— despite his being across the way—tense at the sound of her voice. She raised the empty, dangling leash and saw him grab Mr. Smith-Hill's arm and point in her direction. "They've got Godzilla! Help me!" she cried.

With that, she turned, fighting her way through the jungle of startled people, tangled leashes and barking dogs. Through it all, Emily thought she heard Godzilla's distinctive little yap. But with all the animals, she couldn't really tell. Panic-stricken, she shouldered her way through, yelling, "Dognappers! They've got my dog! Stop them!"

That gained the immediate attention of the surrounding crowd. People looked all around, craning their necks, trying to see whatever they should be looking for. But beyond that, no one seemed to know what to do. Because, after all, almost everyone here had a hold on a dog. Who, then, should they grab? So instead of actively helping Emily in her pursuit, they collectively did the next best thing—they held on more tightly to their own dogs. And got out of Emily's way.

Which cleared the path for her. At least this way, maybe the only ones running would be her and the dognappers, making both of them more obvious. Someone grabbed Emily's arm and hauled her to a stop. Startled but prepared to fight, she swung around, her hand fisted—and saw David. "Oh, thank God," she breathed, collapsing against him and clutching at his coat front.

Holding her by both arms to steady her, David asked, "Was it him—the guy from yesterday?" At Emily's corroborating nod, he said, "I thought as much. Which way did he go?"

Trying to catch her breath, she shook her head. "I don't know. He could be anywhere. This crowd—"

"I know. They're everywhere—like roaches. Come

on. All we can do is keep looking." With that, he turned her loose, and they set off on the trail again.

As they scooted through the crowds, David divided his time between navigating and looking over his shoulder at her. "Maybe we should look for the white car instead. I'm betting it's close by and revving up right now. Let's try to work our way to the street and see if we can spot it."

Hurrying along beside David, Emily nodded. "Where're Mr. Smith-Hill and Mrs. Hopemore?"

Before David could answer, they were at the fringe of the grassy mall. Breathing hard, Emily came to a stop beside David. And began looking all around, her senses honed in on every white car they spotted. Frustratingly, none of them was the right one.

Shaking his head as if disgusted with their findings, David responded to her question. "I told them to stay together. And to put Kafka on the trail. It's what those hounds were originally bred to do, isn't it—hunt?"

Intent though she was on noticing everything around her, Emily spared a glance at David. What a calm mind the man had under pressure. "Yeah. It sure is. But do you think he'll do it? Do you think he cares?"

"You saw him earlier. He wanted that husky that was next to Godzilla. He wanted him bad. So...oh, yeah, he cares. I don't think he likes it—we are talking Godzilla here—but he cares."

And right there, in the middle of this huge crisis, Emily felt her heart warm. *How sweet. Kafka, the big lug, is in love.* "Care or not, David, it's possible that his pampered life may have bred the hunter's instinct out of him."

At that, David shot her a look. Emily gasped. There,

under his civilized veneer, was the ancient hunter, every pure instinct honed in on the prey. "You think it's possible to do that?" he asked.

Emily swallowed, at once shivering deliciously with the irresistible sight he made—and with a bit of fear for the dognapper, should David catch up to the man first. "No, I don't," she told him. "Not with that look on your face. I only hope Kafka catches the guy first."

David further narrowed his eyes, looking more dangerous than ever. "It'd be the best thing that could happen to him, trust me."

"I do, David. I trust you," Emily quietly said.

For an instant, David's expression softened. Then he turned away, again scanning the street full of cars— an inordinate number of them white.

Emily did likewise, but still found time to berate herself. What had she been thinking to say that, about Kafka's instincts not being intact? It just showed how upset she was. Because, as a doctor of veterinary medicine, she knew better. Hadn't she'd seen it before? Certainly every species—humanity included—was capable of quickly reverting to its heritage when presented with the right set of circumstances. Like these.

Just then a screeching, growling cacophony arose. Emily whipped around toward the sound. So did David. They spoke as one. "Godzilla."

Emily added, "Kafka."

David continued, "Lavinia and Hubert."

Then again, they spoke as one. "Oh, no." With that, they took off toward what sounded like a pitched battle, if you counted human bellowing and cursing and canine growling and snarling. And the odd yelp or two. All of which spurred Emily on, right after David.

Only through desperate effort did she keep up with him as he pushed his way into the crowd. On the opposite side ran one empty-handed scrawny man with a tattered pant leg. Emily gasped, tugging on David's arm.

"I see him," David said, his muscles under Emily's hand bunching, telling her he was preparing to chase the guy. Adding to this was a familiar background noise—a revving engine. Probably that of a white sports car. David tensed.

But Emily hauled him back, holding him in place. "No, David, wait! Let him go. Think of Godzilla. Where's Godzilla?"

He whipped around, staring at her, almost as if he didn't know her. Emily attributed it to their high state of anxiety. Then David's vision cleared, became less glazed as he covered her hand with one of his and squeezed reassuringly. "You're right. Godzilla." He looked around, scanning the area with her, and suddenly tensed. "What the—"

Emily knew exactly what he meant. Because she, too, couldn't believe what she finally realized she was seeing.

Unbelievably, there, in a grassy clearing—in front of Mr. Smith-Hill and Mrs. Hopemore, both of whose mouths were agape with either shock or surprise, maybe both—stood the proud, the triumphant Kafka. Tall and aloof, his silky hair flowing. Every inch the hero. In his mouth, a ragged bit of pant leg dangled.

But the biggest surprise of all was that hard at Kafka's side was his adoring yet stubby-legged, wire-haired...well, woman. Godzilla.

Emily exchanged a look with David. His expression showed him to be as amazed as she was. "My God,

David, Kafka did it. He rescued Godzilla. I don't believe this.''

"Me, either." With that, David freed himself from her grip and took her arm, directing her across the broad circle to where the dogs and the older couple were. "Come on, let's go get them and get out of here before the guy who lost his pant leg decides to come back."

A shiver of fright went down Emily's spine. "Do you think he would?" The sound of tires squealing told them that a car had just sped away. No doubt, *the* car. Emily stared at David.

"That doesn't mean our guy was actually in the car, Emily," David said. "Yeah, it'd be pretty brazen for him to come back right now. But, hell, he did just make a daylight attempt in front of hundreds of people. And he was almost successful. When better to try again, when everyone thinks it's safe?"

Wide-eyed, Emily met his gaze. "You're right, David," she conceded. "I don't know about you, but this does it for me. Enough with the trying to do things ourselves. I've had it. We need to involve the police. And we need to do it right now." With that, she stalked toward the dogs and the older couple, who were busily gesturing and no doubt embellishing events for the surrounding crowd.

Beside her, David said, "No, Emily. No cops. Not yet."

Confused—why would he not want the police involved, given everything that had just happened?— Emily stopped. "Why not? What are you thinking?"

David's mouth was no more than a grim line. "I'm thinking it's obvious now that Godzilla is their specific target. Which means that Mr. Smith-Hill's plan worked. This attempt to snatch her, and not one of these pampered pooches, proves it. There's something about *her*. And I want to know what it is. It's personal now.''

She could hardly argue with that. Or could she? "David, I understand how you feel. But we can't take the law into our own hands."

"I'm aware of that. But think about it another way. I'm not supposed to have any contact with you or Godzilla. And yet here I am. At the same time and place when there's another attempt to steal the dog. What will the cops think?"

Emily made a face. For more than one reason. One, he was right about the cops. And two, she hated his reminder that he wasn't supposed to be around her. He'd be put in jail if they went to the police at this point. But still, she felt compelled to try reason. "The difference now is, David, the police would have to listen to our story. We have hard evidence that it wasn't you."

"By 'evidence' do you mean the shredded pant leg that the esteemed Mr. James Bonded Smith-Hill is wagging around in the air right now?"

That characterization of her neighbor—the little man was sweetly dotty, but would seem beyond eccentric to the police—had Emily's resolve faltering. Still, she persisted. "Yes, I do. But there's also Mrs. Hopemore. She could vouch—"

David abruptly pointed to his secretary. "Look at my character witness, Emily. Really look at her."

She did. And swallowed hopelessly. She'd forgotten the woman was wearing a leopard-print cape over a flowing purple caftan. Emily slumped. "Oh yeah. Right. I forgot." Then her next thought brightened her.

"What about me? I know what I saw. And it *was* my house yesterday that the bad guy—"

"—showed up at. With me there. And you knew I wasn't supposed to be around you. And yet, you didn't inform them. Can't you just hear yourself telling *that* story, Em? Especially with Lavinia and Hubert backing you up? Face it—the cops would put us all away. In an asylum somewhere. With white jackets that close in the back."

The man was right. Emily chuckled. "Maybe they *should* put us away, David. Maybe we *are* just plain nuts. Stuff like this doesn't happen to ordinary people. I mean, how did life get so crazy?"

"How?" He shrugged. "I don't know about how. But I do know when." A sudden grin lit his features as he made a point of staring deeply, accusingly into her eyes.

Emily rolled her eyes in a self-deprecating way. "Go ahead. Tell me when. As if I don't know."

Those grin lines on either side of his mouth deepened. "About the time I met you."

Well, there it was. Emily made a dramatic *ta-da!* gesture with her hands. "I deserve that. It's true. Every bizarre thing in your life happened after you met me. You poor man."

With those gray eyes of his softening like cashmere, David slowly shook his head, heating up the moment. "Not so poor as you'd think. It's not been *all* bad. I liked kissing you. And holding you."

Caught off guard, Emily could barely breathe. So it was no wonder her voice was thin and reedy. "You did?"

David nodded. "I sure as hell did. And I'd like to do it again. A lot."

"You would?" Emily breathed.

With a slow and easy motion, David reached out to smooth her hair off her forehead. "Yeah. I would. Wouldn't you?"

With his hand in her hair and cupping her cheek, it was all Emily could do not to purr like a cat and rub her face against his square palm. "Oh...yeah. I would. So very much I would."

David's grin became lopsided. "Good." He withdrew his hand, causing Emily to practically fall over, so entrenched was she in his touch. Embarrassed, even though he didn't seem to notice her stumbling, she jerked herself upright. "Let's get the dogs and the old folks and get out of here," he said. "I don't know about you, but to me this whole situation with Godzilla proves the old saying that truth is stranger than fiction."

"Definitely," Emily quickly agreed. "But I have to say, somewhat like Patrick Henry, give me fiction or give me death."

"Hell," David quipped, "just give me an alibi."

NIGHT HAD FALLEN...hard. The good news was, no deaths loomed. The bad news was, neither did any alibis. Or solutions. But that didn't mean that tensions weren't running high in Mrs. Hopemore's apartment as the four humans—with the two dogs and the lone cockatoo in attendance—sat around her dining room table, arguing over what their next course of action should be.

David's head was reeling. Whether it was from the overheated air in the apartment or the spicy Chinese food or the outrageous plotting going on, he couldn't have said. But still, he tried to inject some sense, if not decorum, into the situation. "No, I'm not strapping on a sidearm, Mrs. Hopemore. And I don't care if it does make you bitter. Sorry, but I'm willing to take the law into my own hands only to a certain extent. And I think I speak for Emily, too, when I say that."

With his words, David glanced at Emily and caught her nod. His heart instantly picked up its pace. He could look at her all night. Her black hair and midnight-blue eyes shone in the reflected light of the honest-to-God crystal chandelier that hung above the table.

"David's right," Emily said, blinking him out of his admiring reverie. "We need to do something concrete. Find something, or someone, somewhere, that can tell us why all this is happening."

Mr. Smith-Hill snorted. "I dare say we know the why of it, Dr. Wright. It's because of that nasty little dog who's enamored of my Kafka. Much to my horror."

"And mine," David cut in, instantly on the defensive and drawing all gazes his way. He'd been through too much in the past few days on Godzilla's behalf to take any more guff from this snooty guy. "You think I want that prissy, overgrown dust mop you call a dog hanging all over my Godzilla?"

Well, that did it. Chairs were shoved back and the men stood up, faced each other, challenge evident in their stances.

"Wr-rack, take cover, take cover." The dogs were convinced. They quickly scooted out of range as Rodney stalked around, flapping his wings, which sent knickknacks flying off low tables, onto the unforgiving hardwood floors. All heads turned his unrepentant way at the first crash. The darned bird eyed them right back and deliberately—David would swear it—swiped at the next breakable and sent it tumbling, as well. Instant smithereens. Rodney merely blinked at it and then stared at them. "Wr-rack, told you so."

"Why, you little Thanksgiving dinner on the hoof." This was Mrs. Hopemore. She turned to Emily. "Will you please clip that bird's wings—and his beak? Before I cook him up in a dish of cock-a-doodle noodles?"

Emily stood up, her hands fisted, her expression grim. "I'll have you know that bird is my grandfather."

Into the deeply confused silence that followed, David could only stare at Emily, even as she amended, "I mean he was my grandfather's bird. And *nobody* is going to put his doodle into noodles of any kind. Not while I'm alive to do anything about it."

David looked at Mr. Smith-Hill, whose mustache was twitching. "I say," he said. "Doodles and noodles? You Americans are rather droll."

They all turned to stare at Rodney. Who was glaring and apparently highly indignant at being the butt of this joke. Plumping himself down like a nesting owl, he buried his beaky chin in his breast feathers to prove it. David, Emily and Mr. Smith-Hill plopped heavily down onto their chairs. And looked all around at each other.

"Truce?" Mrs. Hopemore asked. "No more insults about anyone's pets or doodles?"

David shrugged, looked around the table. It appeared to him that they were all waiting for someone to make the first move. So David extended his hand to Mr. Smith-Hill, who took it and shook it enthusiastically, saying no harm done, he supposed. Follow-

ing suit, Emily leaned over and shook Mrs. Hopemore's hand. Then, feeling as if they were past it,
David said, "Emily was right earlier. About hunting
down some concrete answers."

Emily shifted in her chair, crossing her legs. "I
was?"

Watching her, David grinned, nodded that she was
indeed right, then turned to his secretary. "What I'd
like for you to do, Mrs. Hopemore, is go to the office—"

"Tonight? On a Sunday?" she squawked.

Well, he hadn't really meant tonight, but now that
she mentioned it—and wanting some time alone with
Emily like he did—David glanced at his watch. Seven
o'clock. Not so late. He continued. "Sure. Why not?
Maybe Mr. Smith-Hill could go along." That foxy little man's entire demeanor brightened, along with Mrs.
Hopemore's. "To help you hunt through the files, see
if you can find some work I might have done for Amelia Stanfield."

Mrs. Hopemore's initial silence, coupled with a
Mona Lisa smile, set off warning bells in David's
head. This was never good. Then she grinned. "I
could do that. But there won't be anything there."

Now, see? Just plain irritating, she was. "How can
you be so sure without even looking?" David asked.

Mrs. Hopemore's face pruned as she adjusted her
tortoiseshell glasses on the bridge of her nose. "Because, Mr. Smarty Pants, I just happen to know that
she—"

"Lavinia!"

The warning bells became true alarm bells. *What's
going on here?* David turned from his guilty-looking
secretary to stare at Mr. Smith-Hill, who had inter-

rupted her. Before he could think further about what she'd almost blurted, Mrs. Hopemore hurried on.

"I *mean* I can be sure there won't be anything there because I do the filing, so I would know. That's how." And then she blatantly changed tactics. "And anyway, I always said the old girl who left you that Godzilla of a dog wasn't any too smart for having the hairy little thing in the first place."

Oh, really? David leaned over the table and pointedly asked, "You did? You always said that? Who did you *always* say that to, Mrs. Hopemore?"

Scrunching her lips belligerently, the old girl crossed her arms. "Why, to…to Mr. Smith-Hill, of course."

"Of course. To Mr. Smith-Hill. Whom you met only yesterday."

Into the ensuing accusatory silence, Mrs. Hopemore said, "So? You wanna make something of it?"

"Yeah, I do." But only to an extent. "I just can't believe she pulled my name out of a hat or a phone book, Mrs. Hopemore. Can you? She had to know me, don't you think?"

"Maybe. Or maybe she knew someone who knows you," Mrs. Hopemore said, which elicited another gasp from Mr. Smith-Hill.

Certain he was on the trail of something meaningful, David was inclined to get to the bottom of the whole thing when Emily recaptured his attention. "Or maybe she just knew of you, David. Like by your reputation."

David turned to the gorgeous veterinarian and shook his head. "I don't know how she would know *of* me. I mean, I am a good accountant, and I have a successful practice. But this is D.C. Unless you're a politico, you don't draw much notice.''

Emily sighed. ''You're right. And this is pointless. It could be anything.''

''Which has been my point all along,'' Mrs. Hopemore chided. ''We're just treading water here. You've got the dog. You've got the money. So just get—'' Mrs. Hopemore stopped. As if another thought had occurred to her, she leaned over the table and pointed a long and lacquered fingernail at David. ''By the way, you're not quitting work. Because I need my job. I'm a senior citizen, and I have rights.'' She turned to Mr. Smith-Hill. ''Isn't that right, Hubert?''

''That's absolutely true, Lavinia.''

Hearing Emily's chuckle next to him, David grinned and shook his head with amused defeat.

It seemed that Mr. Smith-Hill wanted to add his two cents, as well. ''Being a barrister, Mr. Sullivan, far be it from me to suggest breaking the law. But as I have already suggested, I do believe that your answers lie in a file somewhere in Mr. Trenton's office. And not in your own.''

''I agree,'' Mrs. Hopemore said. ''So why don't Hubert and I stay here with the wildlife, while you and Emily go—''

''No.'' Rubbing his forehead, David exhaled. ''I told you, Mr. Trenton's not in town. And won't be for a month. And I'm not going to break into the man's office and go through his papers.'' Sitting up straight, David mustered the sternest look he could. They'd been through this before. And he wasn't yielding. They could sit here all night, and his answer would remain the same. ''I'm not going to do it,'' he said again. ''So forget it. I'm serious. No.''

10

EMILY COULDN'T BELIEVE David had talked their way past the cleaning ladies and into the building at Tysons Corner. Glancing at him in the elevator car as it effortlessly glided up to the twelfth floor to Mr. Trenton's office, she decided she really had to hand it to him. He might be innocently watching the digital numbers ticking off the passing floors, but that was quite a story he'd told that group of non-English-speaking, cleaning-cart-pushing women downstairs.

Emily bit her bottom lip, seeing the two of them again as they'd been only moments ago. Outside. But that was before David had grinned disarmingly through the glass doors at the inquisitive women and really turned on the charm, saying he'd forgotten his pass card. Couldn't they just let them in so he didn't have to go all the way back home for it? With lots of nodding and gesturing, the women had not only opened the tall doors, but they'd waved and grinned as Emily and David strolled past.

And now here they were. Getting ready to compound their crime when the elevator spit them out on the twelfth floor. Suddenly, and admittedly somewhat too late, the whole thing seemed pretty bizarre to her. She turned to David, preparatory to telling him all this—

Only to have him turn to her at the same moment

and say, "Have we lost our minds, Emily? What the hell are we doing here?"

"Oh, thank God, David." Relief coursed through her. She clutched his coat sleeve. "I am so glad you said that. I was thinking the same thing. How did this happen? We could go to jail just for being here. Don't buildings like this have a security guard? I mean, where is he? For all we know, he could be waiting to greet us, his gun drawn, when these doors open, David. And those nice, innocent women downstairs—"

"Could identify us in a lineup. We've got to get the hell out of here. Now."

"We can't, David. We're in an elevator."

He looked at her, frowning. "I know that. I meant when it stops."

Emily nodded rather disjointedly, given her sudden fit of the shakes. "Of course. I knew that. I mean, I knew that you knew that."

The elevator stopped. Smoothly. Glibly. A bell sounded. Emily gasped at the sudden noise and, pivoted to look at the red-digited panel. Sure enough, a big blinking twelve shone there. The doors whooshed open to...

Silence. And emptiness. No security guard. No drawn gun pointed at them. No nothing. Just dark and orderly quiet. Awash with relief, Emily let out her breath. And heard David do the same. "Will you look at us?" she whispered loud enough to capture his attention. "We're acting as if this is the gateway to a life of sin and degradation."

David was quiet for a moment, then said, "Maybe it is."

She thought she knew what he meant, for beyond the large square opening created by the elevator doors,

It beckoned. *It* being the carpeted and darkened hall-way, which seemed to urge unsuspecting fools into its depths. Urging them into criminal acts, all because they lacked the moral fiber to say no to David's thou-sand-year-old secretary.

Without looking away from the darkness beyond—as if she feared it could come alive and bite her—Emily asked, "So, what should we do?"

"I'll show you," David said bravely. Then he took the two steps he needed to reach the car's panel of floor numbers and stabbed the one marked L. Lobby. Immediately stepping beside her again, David sur-prised her by taking her hand and holding it. Much as if they'd been doing this all their lives.

Her heart floated in warm joy, but following his restrained lead, Emily stood facing forward, not speak-ing, awaiting the closing of the doors on their lives of crime. Finally, the doors closed. Without hideous in-cident. Only then did Emily exhale and allow herself to feel things. Like David's hand holding hers. It was cold. Maybe from a little bit more than the cool weather outside. She smiled, liking him all the more for that, for having a conscience, for being a little scared. His cold hand foretold a warm heart. A warm, law-abiding heart.

All the way down to the lobby, Emily didn't say a word. Neither did David. She was content just to stand there, holding David's hand, feeling him reassuringly squeeze her palm as the elevator car winged them away from darkness. And back to a life in the sun-shine. At last, the elevator car stopped smoothly, the bell sounded, the big red L lit up on the panel, and the doors opened. They'd done it. They'd escaped. Okay, so it wasn't sunshine that greeted them when they stepped out of the car. So it was recessed over-head lighting and faux marble flooring. It still felt good. And safe.

With a few stiff and hurried steps, and without drawing the notice of the cleaning women, they were outside. Outside in the brisk night air of personal responsibility and freedom. Behind them, the glass doors—the kind that freely let you out but not in without a pass card—whooshed closed and locked.

"Come on. Let's get out of here," David said.

"I'm right behind you," Emily answered.

And then, running away while trying not to look as if they were running away—there was that whole unseen security guard business to worry about—Emily had no trouble keeping up with David as they hot-footed it to the visitors' parking lot and his big foreign car. She practically hugged the passenger side door as David sprinted around to the driver's side. Emily thought she was over the fright until a sudden electronic chirp split the quiet—and made her scream.

David's head popped up from his side of the car. "Sh. That was me. Well, my key, anyway. Come on, get in. We need to get the hell out of here."

Moments later, the tires squealed as they exited the parking lot and sped down a highway access road. Only when they were safely away from Tysons Corner did Emily turn to David. "Explain to me exactly how all this—" she gestured to indicate that *this* meant the immediately preceding and lunatic activities "—happened. I mean, what are we doing here, David? How did we get talked into even *attempting* to do something this stupid?"

David glanced over at her and grinned. "Two words. Male hormones."

Straining against her confining seat belt, Emily leaned toward him. Surely she'd heard him wrong. "What? Male hormones? I would've thought the two words would be *Mrs.* and *Hopemore.*

"No. It's all me. Male hormones," he repeated. Then he conceded, "All right, Mrs. Hopemore suggested we do this. But the truth is, I wanted to be alone with you. And this was the way to do it."

So, should she be thrilled that he wanted to be alone with her? Or should she bop him on the head for getting them involved in such a harebrained scheme that could have landed them in prison? She decided to take the neutral route. "All of this was because you wanted to be alone with me?"

"Yep. Still do. That's why I wanted to send the oldsters off to my office."

Still trying to assess this information, Emily considered his answer. And found she was flattered, but still…she was leaning toward the bop on the head. Except he was driving. "Again…so you could be alone with me?"

His grin turned into a chuckle. "You don't sound happy about that."

"I'm trying to get there, David. But here we are—hurtling guiltily down the highway after attempting an illegal entry into Mr. Trenton's office."

"We almost did it, too, didn't we?"

Emily shook her head at that. "No, we didn't. And don't sound so smug. You were just as scared as I was."

David's unrepentant grin became a grimace. "No, I wasn't. And while we're on the subject, we wouldn't have been alone even if Mrs. Hopemore and Mr.

Smith-Hill had gone instead of us. Remember Rodney and his big mouth?''

Emily slumped against her seat. ''Oh, yeah. Like he wouldn't broadcast everything we—'' Emily stopped, capable only of staring at David. Finally, she asked, ''What exactly would he be broadcasting?''

A lazy, disarming smile claimed David's features. Emily's breathing faltered. She felt hot all over. Especially when David managed to look her up and down in that one heated moment as he reached out to stroke her cheek. ''Want to see where I live?''

Now it was Emily's turn to grin. And to nod. Yes.

''Wow. This is great, David. What a view.'' Emily was staring out at the night, at the Washington, D.C., skyline as seen through the wall of plate-glass windows in David's fancy high-rise condo. She was trying desperately to think of something to say. Because he'd just called Mrs. Hopemore to see if things were quiet there. And as David had told her, the woman hadn't wanted to talk. But she *had* sounded breathless. And giggly, as she shrieked at Mr. Smith-Hill to take his hands away from...there.

His face red, David had hung up and retreated to the safety of the wet bar. Emily turned to see him preparing their drinks. He was very quiet. So she tried again. ''You must love it here. This whole place is fabulous.''

David shrugged, setting down a crystal decanter of rum. ''It's home.''

''Home?'' Emily persisted, overcome with the pristine wealth of the place as she walked across the thick champagne-colored carpet, past richly upholstered overstuffed furniture, over to David. ''No, my house is what people call a home, David. Old furniture. In need of repairs. Animals everywhere. Big lawn. While this place is…I don't know. A showplace.''

David frowned, stopping in the act of plopping ice cubes into two glasses. He looked around his living room as if he'd just seen it for the first time. And didn't like it.

Seeing his response, Emily sobered. ''I meant that in a nice way. I like your place. I wish I had something like this.''

Finishing with their drinks, pouring cola over the measured rum already in the glasses, he said, ''No, you don't. You'd hate it. No private place outside you can go. No sounds of life going on around you. No animals allowed.''

Emily made a face. ''Eww. Not good.'' Then she remembered. ''Eww. Worse for you. So what are you going to do? About Godzilla, I mean.''

The drinks in his hands, David came from behind the wet bar and handed Emily hers. ''Well, my choices are buy the building—the mysterious Mrs. Stanfield left me enough money to do that—and change the no-pets policy. Or—and I think this is an easier route—I can move. And sell this place.''

His words, like everything else about him, warmed Emily to her core. ''You'd do that? Give up all this…for a dog?''

David sipped his drink and eyed her over the glass's rim. ''Yeah. That surprise you?''

''Not as much as it surprises you, I'm betting,'' she said, eyeing him back as she sipped her drink.

David hoisted his glass to her in a salute. ''You're right.'' He clinked his glass with hers. ''As early as last Friday, I wouldn't have said that. Or even have thought it.''

"But now?" she persisted, again sampling her drink.

"But now I have a legal responsibility towards a warm-blooded creature."

Emily abruptly lowered her glass, feeling the rum warm her belly, unlike his words. She gave a mock shiver. "Brr. Is it chilly in here? That sounded unbelievably warm and heartfelt, David."

His expression soured. "All right. Fine." Then, fighting a grin, he added, "So now I like the damned little dog. And, having already put my life on the line for her, I'm not going to give her up. Besides, she's going to have puppies. What am I supposed to do—put her out on the street? I don't think so. Which means she's mine. For better or worse. There. You happy now?"

Emily wanted to kiss him. "Yes. You're an absolutely wonderful man, do you know that?"

David's answering tough-guy look didn't fool her for a minute. "You know, your going around saying that could ruin my reputation."

"Well, we wouldn't want that, now would we?"

"No. I'd just have to say it was a lie."

"Oh, really?" Then some leftover something from her childhood had her using a fingertip to sketch an X over her heart and saying, "Kiss a frog and hope to die, I promise not to tell a lie."

David chuckled, but something very adult sparked in his eyes and pricked her attention, as well as her nerve endings. She swallowed and reminded herself—as well as her suddenly stiff fingers—that she still held a drink in her hand. "That was a silly thing to say, wasn't it?" she said, her voice low and honeyed.

David shrugged…and reached for her glass. "Maybe. But instead of a frog, I wish you'd kiss me. And promise not to die, by the way."

Her heart pounding with anticipation, Emily handed over her drink. "Well, I didn't mean right now. Some day, sure. But not now…I hope. I mean, I promise."

"Good." David set the glasses down on an end table and turned to her, his expression intent, shadowed, serious. "I want you, Emily. I think I have since I first saw you."

A frisson of desire coursed through Emily, weakening her knees. But still, she couldn't resist teasing him. "Even when I was getting you arrested and making you miss your flight home?"

David nodded. "Even then. But especially now. Emily, everything about you just sets me on fire. The way you walk. Your scent. The sound of your voice. Your laugh. In fact, you're pure magic to my senses."

Her thoughts suspended, her emotions hanging on his every word, Emily could only stand there. And wait.

Then, and mercifully, he took a deep breath, rubbed a hand through his hair and said, "I want to make love to you."

There it was. Her breath left her in stuttering gasps. She tipped her tongue out to wet her suddenly dry lips. "I want that, too, David. I do. I feel…well, a lot of things, but mostly as if I've known you all my life. And—I know it's crazy—but I really believe that our…first time won't even feel that way. I think we'll just *know* each other. Does that sound crazy?"

He reached out and caressed her cheek, his gaze

roving over her face. "No. It doesn't. In fact, it sounds as if you've given this a lot of thought."

Flames of embarrassed heat leaped up her cheeks. Tears sparked her eyes. "I...well, I—"

"Sh. It's okay. I feel the same way. I've been thinking about it a lot, too. Come here. Let me show you."

Emily stepped into his embrace, watched as his expression tightened, his color heightened. Instantly, David's mouth slanted toward hers. "I think I could come to love you, Emily Wright," he whispered, just before his lips claimed hers and took her surprised gasp into his mouth.

In only moments, they were without clothes and in David's bedroom, where he'd carried her. He deposited her on the quilt-covered bed and instantly joined her there. A lamp beside the bed cast a soft glow over the scene as Emily made room for David to stretch out beside her. She opened her arms to him, and he slipped into her embrace, rolling until he was atop her, staring at her, his warm body touching every burning-for-him inch of hers.

"Emily, I meant what I said." His voice was pure whiskey. Soft and husky. Then he kissed her temple, her forehead. "You are the most wonderfully easy woman to be with," he murmured.

Taken aback, Emily bit at her bottom lip. "You think I'm easy?"

David pulled back, stared into her eyes. "What?" Then he seemed to catch on. "Oh, wait. Hell, no, Em. Easy to be with. Comfortable. You know, like I can talk to you. Hang out with you. We fit together. I don't think you're easy *that* way. Not at all. Damn, I'm sorry."

Reassured, Emily tried to lighten the mood. "So you'll still respect me in the morning?"

"Respect you? Hell, I'll probably revere you by morning. I mean, if you make love with the same passion and dedication you give to everything else I've seen you do, then I am one lucky man. And I will *more* than respect you. Sweetheart, I'll erect a statue in your honor."

That made her laugh. Gaining confidence, Emily playfully bumped her hips against his. "Speaking of erecting things, David…"

And that was all it took. Within moments of touching each other, of kissing, of exploring each other—and with only a pause for David to pull protection out of his nightstand drawer—they joined their bodies into one loving, thrusting embrace. And it was as they'd said, as they'd hoped. They did fit together. Comfortably. Easily. Like two longtime dance partners. But with a burning fire that, in the end, left them both gasping.

When things quieted, David rolled off her, and gathered her into his arms. Happier than she'd ever been before, with her head on his chest, the fine hairs there tickling her nose, and hearing his pounding heart under her ear, Emily knew complete contentment. And figured he did, too, when, breathing hard, he simply said, "Wow."

She looked at him with a smile. "I told you we'd be good at this. That we'd know each other."

David's chuckle rumbled through his broad and muscular chest. Emily splayed her hand across his warm, taut skin to feel the comforting vibrations it caused. "And damn if you're not right," he said. "Hey, want to do it again?"

Emily smacked his chest and heard his grunt. She pulled herself up on an elbow, flipped her hair from her face and took his chin in her hand, turning his face to hers. "Well, I don't know, Mr. Smooth Guy. Got any more of those condoms you so nonchalantly pulled out of that drawer right there by your bed?"

His unrepentant grin was broad and beaming. "So I'm a healthy, red-blooded American male. And a conscientious one, too. What's not to like?"

Emily narrowed her eyes at him. "I'll let you know—if this drawer is full of those things."

Laughing at her, David gave her a quick and smacking kiss before he again rolled them, covering her with his weight and reaching for the drawer beside the bed. Raising himself up so she could do the same and see for herself, he opened the drawer. "See? Just a few. That's my whole stash."

Emily gave him a playful look and said, "Well, then, we'd better use them wisely, now, hadn't we?"

MONDAY MORNING dawned bright and early. And like every other Monday morning, traffic was a bumper-to-bumper nightmare. No one wanted to be out in it, least of all David and Emily. But here they were. And it appeared that everyone except them—freshly scrubbed, holding hands and possibly falling in love—was cranky.

They'd stayed at David's the whole night. With Mrs. Hopemore's blessing. And no doubt, Mr. Smith-Hill's, too. But that didn't bear thinking about. Unfortunately, that was *all* Emily and David could think about. Having breakfasted on buttered toast and coffee that David had prepared, they were on their way to Georgetown. To Mrs. Hopemore's. Breaking into the comfortable silence between them, Emily said, "God, please let those two be up and dressed."

David looked at her. His gray eyes sparked with humor. "Was that a rhetorical question to me? Or a for-real out-loud prayer?"

"A for-real prayer," Emily assured him. "I just hope they are."

"Me, too. Anything else would put me off my feet for a year."

Emily nodded. "I also hope that we can put a quick end to this dognapping mess. I feel so bad for making you miss your flight on Friday. It's just not fair."

David let go of her hand long enough to squeeze her shoulder affectionately. "Don't be so hard on yourself, Em. I'll get there. I feel certain of it. The wedding's not even until Thursday. Besides, I wouldn't have missed a minute of this for anything."

Her heart in her eyes, Emily said. "Seriously, David? You are such a good sport."

"I am, aren't I? But I'm serious, Em. These past few days with you have changed my life. In a good way. And who could have known that?"

"Well, speaking as the cause of it all, certainly not me." But warmed by his admission, and desperate to hear every last little detail of how she'd changed his life for the better—but not really having the courage to ask him—she settled for saying, "Still, I'm glad you feel that way. I guess it's everything else—besides you and me—that has me worried."

David grimaced. "The scary part is, I understood that. So about everything else. Care to share it?"

Emily took a moment to wallow in her deepening pool of affection for David. "What would I do without you?" she asked him. "It's really no wonder I—"

Sudden caution had her swallowing her words, like bad-tasting medicine.

Too late. David's eyebrows rose. "It's no wonder you what?"

Trapped, Emily looked everywhere but at him as she confessed, "Care about you."

David chuckled. "Well, after last night, I sure as hell hope you do." Then his expression sobered. "Look, I understand your hesitation, not wanting to rush in and just blurt things out. I know all about that. I've done my share of it. With disastrous results. All I can tell you is I care about you, too, Emily. I care a lot. And I'm not playing with your heart here. I hate morning-after games, so I don't play them. Or get myself into situations where I have to. I'm not a casual person. And I don't think you are, either. Am I right?"

Heartened, Emily answered, "You are. Very right." Then, fiddling with her fingers, she added, "It's just that…well, like you said, you never know. And it's so stupid. Sex just complicates everything, doesn't it?"

"Yeah. But it also clears up the complexion."

"David!" Startled and titillated by his quick sense of humor, Emily smacked his arm. "You say the most outrageous things."

"And you love me for that, don't you?" Giving her no chance to say yes or no, he continued. "Okay, back to everything else that's worrying you. Lay it on me."

Feeling on target now, what with all that relationship stuff pretty much cleared up—not to mention their complexions—Emily embarked on her litany of worries. "All right. My clinic, for one. I know your office is closed, since you were supposed to be gone. But mine isn't. I'm just lucky that Karen works on Mondays and can see to the kenneled animals and reschedule my appointments. But tomorrow is another story. I'm usually by myself on Tuesdays. And to make things more complicated, it's Halloween.''

David moved his car ahead about a foot when the other cars moved. ''I understand about your clinic. But Halloween?''

''You've obviously never been to my neighborhood on October thirty-first. There are about a zillion kids in it. And I don't have anything to give out.''

''Hell, give them doggy biscuits. I'll bet you have a lot of those. Or maybe a real dog or two. Or a bird. Give them a bird. One named Rodney.''

''I could never be that cruel.''

''You're right. So, what if I help you?''

''Help me what?''

''I'll help you pick up all the candy you need. And then I'll come by your clinic and give you a hand. Doing exactly what, I don't know. You can direct me. But I'll stay over and help you with the trick-or-treaters. If you want me to.''

Why, the big wonderful lug. ''I do. You'd really do all that?''

He frowned, as if seriously considering her question. Finally, he turned to her. ''Well, I'll be darned. It turns out I would.'' He grinned at her. ''I must be in love. But here's a promise—if we don't make any headway today on this dognapping thing, we'll go to the police. We'll just spill our guts and let them handle it. Deal?''

''Deal,'' Emily breathed. *He must be in love?* She felt giddy. *He must be in love? With me? He must be in love with me.* She looked over at him, to admire his profile. The black hair, neatly cut. The strong jaw, the straight nose, high forehead. And sighed. It was true.

He was handsome and wonderful. And she'd just bet she was falling in love with him, too.

Hugging that realization to herself, Emily sat quietly and soaked up the joy of just being with David. He was just the cutest thing. And so masterful as he inched the car forward, finally finding an opening in a faster moving lane and shooting into the space, propeling them toward Georgetown—and, no doubt, the end of their quest.

They must have been thinking the same thing. "So, was it just me, Em? Or do you think that maybe Mrs. Hopemore knows more about what's going on than she's letting on?"

11

EMILY COULD ONLY laugh as she adjusted her seat belt. "David, I think your secretary knows more about everything—including the Loch Ness monster and the Abominable Snowman—than she lets on. What specifically do you mean?"

Traffic slowed. David braked to allow for it, then adjusted his speed. "Like how Godzilla seems to know her. When Mrs. Hopemore calls her Contessa, Godzilla responds as if it's her real name."

Emily frowned. "You know, I thought the same thing. But I figured it was just—and excuse the expression here—a pet name. But shame on you anyway for naming that sweet little dog Godzilla."

David snorted. "Sweet?" He checked the rearview mirror, then again changed lanes. "You didn't see her level Mr. Trenton like Godzilla did Tokyo."

"Oh, please. The poor thing was just scared."

"Ha. Not half as scared as Mr. Trenton." David sent her a pointed look. "Emily, the man committed himself to an institution after only two weeks in her sweet company."

Emily's scoffed at that. "Well, how silly. Maybe he just wasn't tough enough."

David eyed her skeptically. "He was tough enough to hunt me down."

"Hunt you down?" Her interest piqued, Emily leaning toward him. "How do you mean?"

"Well, he called me out of the blue and seemed to know everything about me."

Emily tucked a lock of her hair behind her ear as she sat back against the leather seat. "Hmm. And you didn't think that was odd? Didn't you ask him how he knew where to reach you?"

"No. I should have. But last Friday, when he called me, I was too stunned by what he was telling me to think about anything else. After all, it's not every day someone leaves you millions of dollars. Much less a dog."

"I guess not. So, anyway, what did you think, when you had time to think about it?"

"Nothing concrete. I just assumed that since Mr. Trenton was a lawyer, he had ways of finding these things out. But now that we're talking about it, it does seem kind of fishy."

"Yeah, David. Big-time fishy. Moby Dick fishy. So what do you think is really going on?"

Clearly amused, David glanced at her. "Did you ever consider becoming a police detective? You're great at grilling people."

Emily made a self-deprecating face and shrugged. "I'm sorry. It's a skill I had to cultivate as a veterinarian. My patients can't talk, so I have to close-question the owners. Am I making you crazy?"

David reached over to her, squeezing her hand and rubbing his thumb over the back of it. "Oh, yeah. Extremely so. But in a good way, Doctor. A very good way."

Suddenly shy, she looked at her lap, at his hand

covering hers, and pretended she couldn't feel herself blushing.

"Look at you," David said. Emily looked at him. "You're blushing. If that's not the cutest damned thing. Anyway, ask away. Your questions are right on target. They make me realize I really don't have any idea in hell what's going on around me. Well, except for how I feel about you. That much I know."

Emily grinned and covered his hand with her other one. "Thank you for that. I'd hate to think my more obnoxious habits chased you away before I had a chance to prove how truly wonderful I really am."

David grinned, shaking his head. "You're as funny as you are good-looking, do you know that?" Then he released her hand to brush his fingers over her cheek. "See why I like you?" He adopted a mock-serious expression and, gripping the steering wheel with both hands, said, "Go ahead, Doc. Fire away. I, David Andrew Sullivan, stand ready to answer."

Emily raised an eyebrow. "Andrew? That's your middle name?"

David narrowed his eyes, then grinned. "Yeah. You wanna make something of it?"

"No. I think it's cute. Like Godzilla. Which brings us back to your interesting point about Mrs. Hopemore knowing the dog."

"Exactly. Which has to mean she knew Mrs. Stanfield. And probably Mr. Trenton."

Emily's eyes widened. "Wow. You're right. That explains—" Emily's breath caught on a gasp of sudden realization. "Oh, my God. Last night, David, didn't she almost say as much, as if she wanted you to realize that very thing, that *she* knew Mrs. Stanfield?"

"Exactly what I've been thinking. And all her talk about how maybe Mrs. Stanfield knew someone who knew me. Ha. Pretty cagey old girl, huh?"

"You bet she is." Then Emily frowned. "But wait—not everything makes sense."

"You'll have to be more specific," David remarked drolly.

"Okay. Even assuming Mrs. Hopemore did know her, why would Mrs. Stanfield leave you—someone she *doesn't* know—her dog and her fortune? Why not leave it all to her friend—again, Mrs. Hopemore?"

David glanced at her. "Good point. I don't know. But who *does* know, with Mrs. Hopemore involved?"

"No lie. She could make anyone act kooky."

"We're perfect testimonials to that statement. Hell, she had us trying to break into Mr. Trenton's office last night. Which is another thing—if she knew him, and we had broken in, she probably knew, too, that he wouldn't have pressed charges against us."

"This is insane. Do you hear us? Who would have thought? But anyway, if Mrs. Stanfield— Wait. She *was* a Mrs., David. Which means she was probably a widow and she and her husband evidently didn't have any children or other family to leave everything to—"

"Or maybe she did, but they're jerks and she liked her dog better—"

"And then her friend, meaning Mrs. Hopemore—"

"Liked me and convinced her friend to leave everything to me."

Emily's breath left her in a rush. "Oh, my God, David. That's it."

He looked just as excited as she felt. "You think?"

"I do. You said yourself that Mrs. Hopemore is secretly in love with you."

"Oh, hell, Emily, that's a joke."

"It's not. She loves you. But like a mother would."

David's expression soured. "That's what I need. Another mother."

"Which is exactly what you have in her. I'm telling you, David, she's the key. Think about it. She's a family friend, right? And has been all your life?"

"Yeah. But for even longer than that. She went to school with my grandmother. But what's that—"

"Does she have any children of her own?"

He shook his head, saying, "No."

"Okay. On Saturday you said that her job with you is her first one. And then yesterday you told me you hired her because your grandmother made you."

David shook his head. "Not exactly. I said I didn't know at the time that my grandmother had called her. But she had. And I hadn't seen Mrs. Hopemore in years. Even though Grandma had given me her number and told me to call her. But on the day when my ad for a secretary appeared in the paper, Mrs. Hopemore bopped in told all the other applicants to leave because she'd gotten the job."

"Wow. You hired her right there?"

"I never did. She just told them I had."

"That is outrageous, David. What happened then?"

"What do you think? They left."

Emily stared at the car in front of them, one also exiting with them in Georgetown. "Well, I'll be damned."

"Exactly."

She pivoted to face David. "So what'd she say? I mean, did you at least ask her why she wanted to work at this time in her life? Was it because of money? Did she need it?''

''Who knows? She's a very private person in some ways. For example, I'd never, in seven years, been to her apartment before. Remember how I had to hunt for it? And I certainly had no idea *how* she lived before then.''

''You mean that wild furniture and all those young guys?''

David looked pained. ''Exactly. Bizarre, huh? Anyway, she's certainly kept her own secrets all these years. Even if *my* life was an open book to her.''

''You discussed your personal business with her?''

David slowed the car to a stop at a red light, ''No. Didn't have to. My Grandma Sullivan did…in fact, she still does, I'm sure. How else would she know to show up at my office and sit down at the receptionist's desk? Which is where she's been ever since. And running my life from there. Or telling me how to live it.''

Emily shook her head in sympathy. ''Women just completely undo you, don't they?''

He grinned. ''It's a curse I bear.''

Emily patted his hand. ''Don't worry. We'll be gentle.'' Then something else occurred to her. She sat up straighter and grabbed David's hand. ''Oh my God, David, you don't think Mrs. Hopemore could actually *be* the mysterious Mrs. Stanfield, do you?''

David locked gazes with her. And froze. From behind them, car horns blared. He quickly checked the rearview mirror and then glanced ahead. Emily looked, too. The light was green. David accelerated through the intersection, then moved to the right lane and said, rather grimly, ''I'll cheerfully kill her if she is. But I doubt it. I mean, we're dealing with a will. And Mr.

Trenton, friend of hers or not, wouldn't he have to say?"

Emily shrugged, shaking her head. "You're right. I was just throwing things out. But on second thought, no, I guess she couldn't be involved. I mean, I don't think she would have orchestrated this whole dognapping thing. Do you?"

Frowning, David checked his speed and finally shook his head. "I don't think she'd go that far. Sure, she's loony, all right, but not diabolically so. And besides, why would she?"

"I don't know. Maybe she thinks you need something more in your life than work."

"Yeah, she says that all the time. She always tells me I need to get out of the office more often."

Emily nodded. "Well, that's certainly what you've been doing for the past couple of days, isn't it?" She clutched at David's arm. "We're wrong. That's *it*."

Frowning, he stared at her—as much as was possible, given the ebb and flow of traffic. "What's it?"

"Mrs. Hopemore. She *did* do all this. Everything. She set it up. Even the dognappers."

A stunned expression claimed David's features. "You can't be serious."

"Oh, but I am. You were the first one to realize they specifically wanted Godzilla, right? And not the more expensive breeds of dogs with wealthier owners, even dogs easier to get at. Like Kafka would have been on Saturday, right?"

"Well, yeah, okay. I admit that. But still, Emily, the danger—"

"What danger, David? Think about it. Those guys in the white car haven't hurt anybody. Not even when that one whipped by me into my house. He never touched me. And he could have. And then yesterday at the dog show? Nothing really happened.''

"But what about Kafka biting that guy?"

"Hm." Emily thought about that a second or two. And then remembered. "We didn't *see* Kafka bite the guy, David. All we saw was the guy running away and Mr. Smith-Hill pulling that pant leg from the dog's mouth. Who's to say how it got there? And Kafka was sitting down, not the least bit hyper. And there stood Hubert and Lavinia, with the dogs already on their leashes. Ta-da!"

"I'll be damned," David fumed. "But wait, what about Mr. Smith-Hill? Mrs. Hopemore didn't even know him before Saturday."

"True. But that didn't stop her from getting him alone and drunk and enlisting his help, did it? See? All I'm saying is Mrs. Hopemore could have set up the initial events, hired those thugs…and then things took on a life of their own from there. Is that so far-fetched?"

"Yeah. It is. And perfectly logical. You think I've been set up?"

Emily nodded. "I do. I think Mrs. Hopemore talked Mrs. Stanfield into leaving you all her money and her dog. And then had Mr. Trenton hang onto Godzilla until she'd hired those guys to scare you into caring about her—her being the dog. See? She gave you an instant life."

David's expression puckered. "No. No way, Emily. I can't believe that. I nearly beat that guy up at your house—and would have, too, if he hadn't gotten away. There are too many unknowns here, too many times when someone could have gotten hurt. I mean, how do you hire someone to go to those extremes?"

Emily shrugged. "I don't know. Hit men do it all the time."

David spared her a pointed glance. "Hit men? Do you hear yourself?" Then his expression suddenly soured. "Well, I'll be—Emily, guess who was off work all last week because a friend passed away?"

"Oh, you're kidding. Mrs. Hopemore?"

"Exactly. Now who could that friend have been?"

"Wow." Emily thought about the whole thing for a moment and came to a heartwarming conclusion. "Maybe a wonderfully generous old woman who loved her dog and her friend and trusted her to find it a good and loving home. Oh, David, maybe Mrs. Hopemore's methods are suspect, at best, but her heart is in the right place."

David's expression softened. "I don't believe any of this. But...you're right. I'm just sorry you got sucked into it, Emily. Hell, anything could have happened. And still might. I'm serious. If Mrs. Hopemore went to the lengths you've said, then the old girl is clearly off her rocker. And if she is, what am I going to do with her?"

Emily smiled at him. He was so sweet. And generous. And forgiving. "I don't think you have to do anything, David. Just think of her as quirky and eccentric. She just charges at life. I have to admire that. And you know what? I'm not the least bit sorry any of this happened. Especially the part about—well, meeting you."

David returned her smile as he reached over to take her hand in his and hold it. "You're a wonderful woman, you know that? And I feel the same way you do. No matter what the truth is, it led me straight to you. And I couldn't be happier about that."

Emily's heart swelled. "So, Mrs. Hopemore's plan worked, huh?"

David's smile puckered into a disbelieving grin. "Yeah, it did—if she had one. But still I am going to kill her. Care to join me?"

Emily perked right up. "Why, I would love to."

"WAIT." At the top of the stairs, in the shadowy hallway that led to Mrs. Hopemore's apartment, David grabbed Emily's coat sleeve, startling her and forcing her to stop. She looked up to see him pointing down the hallway. "Look at that," he said, cautiously lowering his voice.

She did. And found the problem. Her heart thumped. The door to Mrs. Hopemore's apartment was open. And it was quiet. Ominously so. Emily didn't know whether to be afraid or not. It depended on what she believed. Either Mrs. Hopemore had set everything up. Or she hadn't. "What do you make of it?" she whispered.

Not taking his gaze off the open door down the hallway, David whispered back. "Nothing. Or everything. Depending on what we believe about Mrs. Hopemore. But with the downstairs door also unlocked…"

"Maybe they just forgot to close it."

"Maybe."

His voice was taut with wariness, which did nothing to allay Emily's fears. It was one thing to suspect a setup. And quite another to walk into a trap. "Well, maybe they stepped out for a moment. To check the mail or take out the garbage or something."

"We'd have seen them. The mail drop and the trash bins are both out back, the way we came in."

"True. Well, maybe they're walking the dogs. We might've missed seeing them then."

"Okay. So where's Rodney?"

Emily exhaled loudly. Would he allow her no hope? "In his cage?"

"Without raising hell about it?"

Fine. She slumped, giving up. "No. You're right. He'd squawk and cuss to high heavens."

"Exactly. So, assuming they're all in there and accounted for, and with the door open, why isn't the hallway littered with critters? And why don't we at least hear them? Again, not good."

"You're right. Rodney loves to explore, especially where and when he isn't supposed to."

"Great. Then again, this means…nothing at all. Or big trouble. Right?"

Emily hated her own stupid assessment of this weekend's events. "Yes. So, what *do* we know?"

"We know that Mr. Smith-Hill and Mrs. Hopemore are here. Their cars are parked out back."

"Right." And that meant, Emily knew, that action was called for. *Great*. She took a deep breath and whispered, "So, do we call the cops?"

"We could. But they might not get here in time."

She slumped. "So *we're* going in, right?"

David swung his gaze to her. "We? There's no we to it." He tugged her back and stationed himself in front of her. "*I'm* going in. *You're* staying here." With that, he turned his back to her and started down the hall.

Instantly stubborn, Emily grabbed his sleeve, stopping him and using her momentum to propel herself in front of him. "I am not staying here."

David freed himself, grabbed her arm and stepped in front of her. "Yes, you are."

Emily freed herself and stepped in front of David. "No, I'm not."

David gripped her arm and turned her to face him. "A few more of these synchronized dance steps and we're going to be completely past the door, Emily. Now, stop it."

"You stop it. I'm going in there with you. That's my bird and my neighbor and his dog in there, you know."

"And my grandmother's friend—my secretary—and my dog."

"Well..." He had her there. But still, Emily was determined. "So we're going in together, right?"

David glared at her. "I didn't know about this stubborn streak."

Emily's bottom lip poked out—stubbornly. "Yeah. So?"

"So..." David shook his head. "So...good for you. Will you at least let me go in first?"

Emily looked him up and down, concluding that discretion was, after all, the better part of valor. And David was bigger than the better part of the doorway into Mrs. Hopemore's apartment. Which meant he stood a greater chance than she did of dealing with any physical threat that might await them. Or might not. Either way, she didn't believe there was really any way he'd stand for her going in first. He was too much of a guy for that. "Sure," she said. "I don't have a problem with that."

"Good." With that, he turned, starting off down the hall. "Stay behind me."

Right on his heels, Emily reminded him, "I said I would, didn't I?"

David stopped short, and Emily nearly ran into him. He turned around. "Shh. Since we might need it, I'd like to keep the element of surprise on our side."

Emily mouthed *I'm sorry* and put an index finger to her lips. *I'll be quiet,* she mouthed. Well, quiet until the need to scream arose. If it should. She felt certain it would. And that she'd do a good job of it when it did. But no sense telling him that. He already had his hands full. And he was still staring at her. Emily offered him an innocent enough Stan Laurel smile.

Again David gave a disbelieving shake of his head as he turned and once again started down the long hallway. And, again on his heels, this time staring at those football shoulders of his, Emily realized that for such a big man, she sure could make him shake his head a lot. Poor guy had a lot to learn about women. And she meant to teach him. If they lived through the next few minutes.

They reached the slightly open door. True to her word, Emily remained behind David. She even held her breath as he nudged it open enough to see inside the apartment. But then all he did was stand there. With no overt reaction. For a long time. Finally he said, "I don't believe this."

12

EMILY FROWNED. *Believe what?*

"Well, it's about time you two got here."

Mrs. Hopemore! All Emily could do was offer up thanks that the cantankerous older woman was okay. If she was, then most likely everyone else was, too.

"You may as well come on in," David's secretary was saying. "As you can see, you missed all the fun. But it's not as bad as it looks. Before these two got the drop on us, we'd called the police."

These two who? And—the police? Had something really happened? Agog with curiosity, Emily quickly edged her way around David. He tried to stop her but was too late. Because surprise stopped her first and had her stiffening in response. Facing her were Mrs. Hopemore and Mr. Smith-Hill. And they weren't alone. *Oh, please.*

As David put an arm around her shoulder, urging her to his side, Emily rolled her eyes. She'd been right about Mrs. Hopemore. And this proved it. The scene before her was so obviously set up that she had trouble taking it all in at once. Such as the giant pistols in the hands of the scruffy-looking bad guys. The same bad guys and, no doubt, the same unloaded guns that belonged to Mrs. Hopemore. Who, along with Mr. Smith-Hill, was at the business end of those guns...

with hands reaching for the sky. Or the ceiling, as it were.

To Emily, it looked like a scene out of a 1930s gangster movie. *Talk about your setups. And your classic bad guys.* She recognized the scrawny one. The other one was some tubby guy she'd never seen before. No doubt, he was the driver of the white sports car. *And get a load of the animals. Such drama queens.* They'd arrayed themselves around the bad guys. With low, rumbling growls and feathers or fur ruffled, the critters were certainly doing their part to look threateningly realistic.

Only Emily wasn't buying any of it. If this was real, then the armed and dangerous felons could simply have snatched Godzilla and taken off. And yet they hadn't. So what was going on here? The big finale? *Enough is enough.* Emily found she was hard-pressed to decide who actually was doing a better acting job here, the old folks or the gangsters. Fine. She'd play her part—the frightened heroine, Polly Pureheart—until they all confessed. "Oh, David, look," she wailed. "The dognappers!" She pointed to the scrawny one. "He's the one who shoved his way into my house and nearly ran me down."

"I recognize him," David assured her, his voice flat, his gaze trained on the guns the two men held.

Having fun, Emily went on. "And the other one. Why, I'll bet he's the driver of the getaway car."

David covered her hand on his arm. "Can we talk about all this later, Em? Just calm down. It's over now. And the police will be here soon to take these two away."

The scrawny one yelled, "You don't scare us with no talk about cops. They'd already be here if these old coots had really called 'em. And besides, we ain't no dognappers. Me and Ned here been trying to tell these two that we don't want Contessa. Just her collar.''

That did it. Emily threw her hands up. ''How long are we going to play this out? David already loves the dog. He's going to keep her. And you, Bad Guy Number One, just slipped up. Hello…you called Godzilla Contessa.''

Bad Guy Number One—along with everyone else in the room—stared at Emily. ''Lady,'' he said, ''you do see these guns, don't you?''

Well, apparently the game wasn't over yet. ''Fine,'' Emily fussed. ''Sorry. Go ahead. What am I supposed to be doing? Looking at the dog's collar?''

She moved toward Godzilla, but not before David whispered to her, ''What are you doing?''

''The same thing you are,'' she whispered right back. ''Taking a really good look at the fake jewel collar around Godzilla's furry little neck.''

Before David could say anything else, Bad Guy Number Two—Ned, wasn't it?—swung their way, gun and all. ''The jewels on there is what's special. They ain't fakes. They're real. And worth a small fortune— one that's owed us, the way we see it. All me and Billy wanted was what was owed us.''

''Owed you? Who owed you? And who the hell are you?''

Good, David. Put him through his paces, was Emily's smug thought.

Billy, the skinny one, blurted, ''Mrs. Stanfield owed us. That's who. Me and Ned worked for her. An' she didn't leave us a dime when she died. Not one. An' after all them years. She was the meanest old lady—''

"Easy there, Billy boy," Mrs. Hopemore warned. "If my friend didn't leave you two hooligans anything, it was probably because you'd been stealing from her for years. And that mean old lady, as you call her, was my best friend."

Oh my God, I was right. Just as I suspected. Emily poked her elbow into David's ribs. He didn't even flinch.

"We never stole nothing," Ned continued. "For years, I done the repairs on the old house whenever she called. And my partner here done the yard work. And not a bit of kindness from her to show for it."

"You got paid, didn't you?" David asked. All heads turned his way. "I said, she paid you, didn't she? Enough maybe to buy that sporty car you like peeling out in?"

Billy narrowed his eyes at David. "You the one she left everything to, ain't you?"

"I am. And if you had any complaints about your treatment at the hands of the deceased, or a legitimate claim against her estate, there were avenues open to you for lodging them formally and legally."

Silence followed that declarative statement. Then Billy and Ned said in unison, "Whut?"

"All we wanted was the jewels." Ned added. So we could sell 'em quick and keep the money which was due us. That's all. We never meant no harm."

"Ha!" Emily said, having most of the answers she needed and tiring of this bad acting.

"I jolly well concur with my esteemed neighbor. Ha!"

Emily cocked her head at Mr. Smith-Hill. *He holds me in esteem? Since when?*

David sighed. Apparently he, too, was tiring of this

game. "Why didn't you just contact me?" he asked Ned and Billy...although Emily didn't really know why he asked. They *were* only actors Mrs. Hopemore had hired, right? "Wouldn't that have been a lot easier?" David continued. "Hell, to avoid all this trouble, I probably would have given you the damned collar."

"You would have?" Billy sounded incredulous. Emily was impressed with his acting skill.

But not Ned. Frowning fiercely, he lowered a chubby hand to smack at the back of his skinny friend's head—which elicited a whining yelp from his partner. "I told you so, you moron. I told you all's we needed to do was say something. Didn't I say these was decent folks?"

"Like hell you did! You called the old lady there a—*gwaak!*"

Before he could finish, Emily stepped up and snatched the unloaded guns out of the men's hands. Then she aimlessly pointed the weapons at the shocked-as-hell acting partners. "End of the play. Enough," she said. "Bravo. You've all been wonderful. Great job. Take your bows. But I have office hours. And you—" leading with the gun in her left hand, Emily swung to Mrs Hopemore and Mr. Smith-Hill, both of whom took two startled steps back "—have a lot of explaining to do."

About that time, David walked into her eyesight as he joined his secretary and Mr. Smith-Hill. "Emily, what are you doing, honey?"

Grinning—he'd called her honey—she said, "We were right. It was Mrs. Hopemore. She knew Mrs. Stanfield." Emily focused on David's wide-eyed secretary. "Right?"

"You bet, sister," Mrs. Hopemore babbled, her

gaze never leaving the guns. "She was my dear friend and had all that money. And no one in the world to leave it or Contessa to. So I told her all about David. And we even followed him a time or two, before she got too sick, so she could see what he was like."

"You did?" That was David.

"Shut up, David," Mrs. Hopemore said, never looking away from Emily. "We did. I was just trying to do a good thing, girlfriend. Thought he needed something outside of work to love. And I never did like all those women he hung around with—"

"*All* those women?" Emily asked, looking at David.

Like Mrs. Hopemore, David was eyeing the guns warily. "I don't know what she's talking about. There weren't all those women in my life. I swear it. Only one recently. Philippa. Which is a stupid name. And anyway, that was months ago. I didn't even really care about her, and since I met you I—"

"Uh, can we go now?"

Oh, right. Emily had completely forgotten Ned and Billy. She looked at them…standing there, stiff-legged and scared, eyeing the gun trained on them. "What's wrong? You did a great job."

They exchanged looks with each other. "Um, thanks, ma'am," Ned offered.

"I'm sure Mrs. Hopemore is paying you well."

Again they exchanged looks between themselves. "Um, yes ma'am," Billy said respectfully. "We can see you folks have a lot of talking to do. So, if you don't mind, can we go now?"

Emily shrugged, turning to Mrs. Hopemore. "You through with them?"

Mrs. Hopemore, looking totally lost, finally gestured

helplessly. "Sure, honey. Whatever you say. You got the guns."

"What? The guns?" She looked at her hands. "Oh—stupid me. I forgot I was holding them. Did I scare everyone?" They all silently nodded at her. "I'm sorry. Don't worry. They're not loaded. Remember?"

Everyone looked at her, good guys and bad guys and peeking-around-the-corner critters alike. But it was left to David to tell her, "Emily, honey. Don't let these two go, okay?"

"Why are you talking to me like that, David? Like I'm some demented child."

David's eyes widened. "I didn't—" He cleared his throat. "I didn't mean to sound any such way, honey. But why don't you give me the guns and I'll keep an eye on these two—" he pointed to Billy and Ned "until the police come."

Emily frowned. "Why are the police coming? Everyone's just acting, remember? Like we discussed on the way here? You know, Mrs. Hopemore hiring these guys."

"What?" Mrs. Hopemore said. "I never saw these men before in my life."

Something in her voice told Emily the older woman wasn't kidding. Emily began to feel sick. "You haven't?" Mrs. Hopemore shook her head. Emily turned to Billy and Ned. "Who are you?"

Billy's shifty-eyed gaze...shifted. "We're who we said we were, ma'am. Employees of the late Mrs. Stanfield."

Emily's arms dropped to her sides. She turned to David. "I don't feel so well."

"I'm coming, honey." David headed over to her,

keeping his eyes on Ned and Billy. "Don't you two move. Not one step." Then he focused on her again. "Try not to drop those guns, Em. They're loaded, baby."

Emily suddenly got sicker. None of this was happening. "They are? They aren't Mrs. Hopemore's unloaded ones?" David took the guns away from her—and immediately pointed them at Ned and Billy.

"No, sweetie, they aren't," Mrs. Hopemore assured her. "Mine are in the cabinet over there. I don't know what you thought was going on, but those two brought the guns with them. And no one here is acting. Except maybe you."

And that was when there was a knock on the doorway and someone called out, "Police! We're coming in."

And that was when Emily passed out.

When she came to Emily found herself stretched out on Mrs. Hopemore's gnarly couch, her head resting on David's lap. Across the room, the *real* bad guys were being hauled away in *real* handcuffs. By three *real* policemen. Mrs. Hopemore closed the door behind the cops…but not before inviting them to attend her Saturday Afternoon Literary Society meeting next weekend.

Finally, alone with her friends, as well as Rodney, Godzilla and Kafka, all of whom arrayed themselves in front of the couch and made sympathetic noises over her, Emily tried to sit up. David immediately helped her, then squatted in front of her and tenderly brushed her hair out of her face. Feeling pouty and sweaty—she hated passing out—Emily said, "What happened?"

"Emily," David said, his voice soft, his expression

tender. "Honey." He took her hands in his. "What the hell were you thinking?"

Loving the feel of his strong, capable hands holding hers, Emily could only stare at him. Not all her mental faculties were up and operating yet. Then it finally came to her. "I was thinking I was getting tired of the games. I just wanted it over."

"Oh. Well, then, dear," Mr. Smith-Hill said, capturing her attention, "you were most effective. Most effective. It's very decidedly over now."

Emily gave him a shaky grin. "Thank you, Mr. Smith-Hill. It's nice of you to say."

"Dear girl, it was nice of you to do. You quite saved all our lives, you know. Our neighborhood is blessed to have such a brave, strong girl as you in our midst. But those hooligans! Why, they were about to shoot that poor nasty little dog just to get her collar. I say, such crassness."

Emily sucked in a breath. "They were?"

"You bet," Mrs. Hopemore told her. "While Billy boy kept a gun on us, that big one—Ned, wasn't it?— chased her all over this apartment. But what with Rodney and Kafka on her side, he didn't have a chance. They'd just decided to shoot her when you two showed up."

Emily frowned. This was horrible. "How'd they get in?"

Mrs. Hopemore shrugged. "They surprised us when we came back from walking the dogs this morning. And the rest you know."

At that point, David affectionately smoothed Emily's wildly tossed hair from her face again. "Sweetheart, you are the wackiest and the bravest person I know. And I can't wait for my family to meet you because you are *so* right for me.''

Emily stared into those gray eyes of his. And her heart did a joyful back flip. ''I am?''

He nodded, still smiling at her. ''Oh, yeah. You are.''

From behind David, Mrs. Hopemore said, ''I knew this would work. I told George—Mr. Trenton, an old flame of mine—that it would.'' Emily, along with David, looked at her. Beaming, with her arm around Mr. Smith-Hill's shoulder, Mrs. Hopemore added, ''I also told Mellie—Mrs. Stanfield, to you—that Contessa—Godzilla's real name, by the way—was just the thing you needed, David. I knew that wild and crazy little dog could lead you to love.''

David chuckled. ''She sure as hell did that. Along with quite a few merry chases.'' He reached out, petting and stroking Godzilla-Contessa. For once, the wiry-haired little mama-to-be allowed it. She even licked his hand.

Everyone sighed. It was all so heartwarming. Except to Rodney.

''Wr-rack, young love. Worse than puppy love. Makes me wanna hurl.''

Epilogue

"WR-RACK, disgusting. Shoot me now."

Emily looked over her shoulder at her cockatoo, who gripped his perch in a corner of her clinic's operating room sporting a miniature black tuxedo tie around his neck. "Not a bad idea, Rodney. Don't give me any ideas."

With that she turned to her task. And decided she couldn't believe this. Well, maybe she could. After all, why should today be any different than any other wonderfully insane day she'd spent since first meeting David a little over two months ago?

Just because it was her wedding day, and yet here she stood—garbed beautifully in her white and lacy gown, complete with seed pearls and covered protectively by a green surgical scrub gown, while a blizzard raged outside—instead of at the church, where most of their family and friends were already gathered, including David's sister, Alicia, and her new husband. And just because David stood helpfully beside her, handsome in his black tuxedo…and Karen, her assistant and maid of honor, was here, too, looking smashing in her wintergreen bridesmaid dress and matching scrub gown and latex gloves…and both her father and David's father sat disgruntledly in her waiting room but couldn't stand to be in the same room with each other—political disagreements—and their mothers were out there, too, and after realizing they'd both been at Woodstock had hit it off...

And just because also adding to the general confusion and cacophony in the waiting room was the older set—David's RV-ing grandparents and Emily's feisty little grandmother and the dapper Mr. Smith-Hill and the effervescent Mrs. Hopemore—an *extremely* rich widow, as it turned out, who worked and lived where she did simply because she felt like it—also in their, well, eccentric if not Victorian finery and telling the other old folks God alone knew what. And just because...all that was going on, what better time for Godzilla to choose to deliver her puppies than now? Who didn't know it would happen this way?

And who couldn't guess, given Godzilla's penchant for big strapping male dogs, that her four squirmy newborns would all be different breeds? It was appalling. But mostly so to David. "Good God, Emily, tie her tubes or something."

Peeling off her gloves and surgical gown, Emily grinned at him. "I think she's a little busy right now, David. Don't you?" Emily pointed to the new mother, who with Kafka proudly at her side—as if he'd had anything to do with this litter—was recovering from the births and was licking affectionately at her nursing little babies.

"So, what do you think, Dr. Wright?" Karen asked as she shed her surgical gown and smoothed her velvet dress. "What breeds were the papas?"

David tsked. "Do we have to talk about this in front of Kafka? I think he thinks they're all his."

Emily laughed. "David, he doesn't have the slightest idea." Then, tilting her head at a thoughtful angle, Emily leaned over the blanket-filled wicker basket on the floor and scrutinized the litter. "Well, I'd say there were a couple of fence jumpers and a traveling man or two. And maybe it's a little early to tell, but I think that one—" she pointed to the tiny brown and spiky-furred runt of the litter "—will be just like her mama."

"That's it," David complained, his hands braced against his knees. "She's going to be raised in a convent."

Karen laughed at him and excused herself to go inform the family that mother and daughter and daughter and son and son were all fine.

Alone with her groom—well, alone if she didn't count Mama Godzilla and Kafka and their brood—and loving David with all her heart, Emily straightened. David followed suit and, with his handsome face puckered in earnest fatherly vexation, as if he had something else to say about the varied paternity of this litter, he turned to Emily—and got a fierce hug and a big kiss from his wife-to-be. "Then I guess we're keeping all of them?" she teased him.

"What? Well, hell, yeah, we are. What did you think—that I'd just give them away? I don't think so. These are my puppies, too, you know." Then he frowned, as if he'd just heard his own words. "Well, not actually my puppies. You know what I mean. Mrs. Stanfield's will. The money. Godzilla's my dog, et cetera, et cetera."

With her arms still wrapped around his neck, Emily assured him, "I know what you meant, David. And do you know how much I love you?"

He grinned. "I think so. And I love you, too—enough to sell my condo and live here with you in the middle of Critter Land."

"And that's another thing. You've turned into a wonderful papa, you know."

He scoffed. "What choice did I have but to become a wonderful papa? There I was, on the receiving end of Mrs. Hopemore's good intentions. What else could I do?"

"Wr-rack, take a hike."

Startled, the happy couple, soon to be on their way to the church and a life together, turned as one and yelled, "Rodney!"

The bird raised his magnificent head plumage. "Wr-rack, that's Best Man Rodney to you."

"This book is DYNAMITE!"
—Kristine Rolofson

"A riveting page turner..."
—Joan Elliott Pickart

"Enough twists and turns to keep everyone
guessing... What a ride!"
—Jule McBride

See what all your favorite authors
are talking about.

Coming October 1999 to a retail store near you.

 **HARLEQUIN®**
Makes any time special ™

In celebration of Harlequin®'s golden anniversary

Enter to win a *dream!* You could win:

- A luxurious trip for two to
  The Renaissance Cottonwoods Resort
  in Scottsdale, Arizona, or

- A bouquet of flowers once a week for a year
  from FTD, or

- A $500 shopping spree, or

- A fabulous bath & body gift basket, including
  K-tel's *Candlelight and Romance* 5-CD set.

Look for **WIN A DREAM** flash on
specially marked Harlequin® titles by
Penny Jordan, Dallas Schulze,
Anne Stuart and Kristine Rolofson
in October 1999*.

FTD

RENAISSANCE. COTTONWOODS RESORT
SCOTTSDALE, ARIZONA

K·TEL

HARLEQUIN WIN A NEW BEETLE® CONTEST
OFFICIAL RULES
NO PURCHASE NECESSARY TO ENTER

1. To enter, access the Harlequin romance web site (http://www.romance.net) and follow the on-screen instructions: Enter your name, address (including zip code), e-mail address (optional), and in 200 words or fewer your own original story concept—which has not won a previous prize/award nor has previously been reproduced/published—for a Harlequin Duets romantic comedy novel that features a Volkswagon® New Beetle®. OR hand-print or type the same requested information for on-line entry on an Official Entry Form or 8 1/2" x 11" plain piece of paper and mail it (limit: one entry per person per outer mailing envelope) via first-class mail to: Harlequin Win A New Beetle® Contest. In the U.S.: P.O. Box 9069, Buffalo, NY 14269-9069. In Canada: P.O. Box 637, Fort Erie, Ontario, Canada L2A 5X3.

    For eligibility, entries must be submitted through a completed Internet transmission—or if mailed, postmarked—no later than November 30, 1999. Mail-in entries must be received by December 7, 1999.

2. Story concepts will be judged by a panel of members of the Harlequin editorial and marketing staff based on the following criteria:

    - Originality and Creativity—40%
    - Appropriateness to Subject Matter—35%
    - Romantic Comedy/Humor—25%

    Decision of the judges is final.

3. All entries become the property of Torstar Corp., will not be returned, and may be published. No responsibility is assumed for incomplete, lost, late, damaged, illegible or misdirected e-mail, for technical, hardware or software failures of any kind, lost or unavailable network connections, or failed, incomplete, garbled or delayed computer transmission which may limit user's ability to participate in the contest, or for non- or illegibly postmarked, lost, late nondelivered or misdirected mail. Rules are subject to any requirements/limitations imposed by the FCC. Winners will be determined no later than January 31, 2000, and will be notified by mail. Winners will be required to sign and return an Affidavit of Eligibility, and a Release of Royalty/Ownership of submitted story concept within 15 days after receipt of same certifying his/her eligibility, that entry is his/her own original work, has not won a previous prize/award nor previously been reproduced/published. Noncompliance within that time period may result in disqualification and an alternate winner may be selected. All federal, state and local laws and regulations apply. Contest open only to residents of the U.S. and Canada who are 18 years of age or older, and is void wherever prohibited by law. Any litigation within the Province of Quebec respecting the conduct and awarding of a prize may be submitted to the Régie des alcools, des courses et des jeux. Employees of Torstar Corp., their affiliates, agents and members of their immediate families are not eligible. Taxes on prizes are the sole responsibility of winners. Entry and acceptance of any prize offered constitutes permission to use winner's name, photograph or other likeness for the purposes of advertising, trade and promotion on behalf of Torstar Corp. without further compensation to the winner, unless prohibited by law.

4. Prizes: Grand Prize—a brand-new Volkswagon yellow New Beetle® (approx. value: $17, 000 U.S.) and a Harlequin Duets novel (approx. value: $6 U.S.). Taxes, licensing and registration fees are the sole responsibility of the winner; 2 Runner-Up Prizes—a Harlequin Duets novel (approx. value: $6 U.S. each).

5. For a list of winners (available after March 31, 2000), send a self-addressed, stamped envelope to Harlequin Win A Beetle® Contest 8219 Winners, P.O. Box 4200 Blair, NE 68009-4200.

Sweepstakes sponsored by Torstar Corp., P.O. Box 9042, Buffalo, NY 14269-9042
Volkswagon and New Beetle registered trademarks are used with permission of Volkswagon of America, Inc.

HARLEQUIN
Duets™ Win a New Beetle® Contest!

Starting September 1999, Harlequin Duets is offering you the chance to drive away in a Volkswagen® New Beetle®!

In addition to our grand prize winner, two more lucky entrants will also have their winning stories published in Harlequin Duets™ series and on our web site!

To enter our "WIN A NEW BEETLE®" contest, fill out this entry form and in 200 words or less write a romantic comedy short story for Harlequin Duets that features a New Beetle®.

See previous page for contest rules.
Contest ends November 30, 1999.

Be witty, be romantic, have fun!

Name

Address

City   State/Province

Zip/Postal Code

Mail to Harlequin Books: In the U.S.: P.O. Box 9069, Buffalo, NY 14269-9069; In Canada, P.O. Box 637, Fort Erie, Ontario, L4A 5X3

HARLEQUIN®
Makes any time special™

HDBUG-EF